OZ

The
Complete
COLLECTION

VOLUME
5

Follow the yellow brick road to your nearest bookstore
and discover the magic of a land called

OZ

OZ, the COMPLETE COLLECTION, VOLUME 1
The WONDERFUL WIZARD of OZ
The MARVELOUS LAND of OZ
OZMA of OZ

OZ, the COMPLETE COLLECTION, VOLUME 2
DOROTHY and the WIZARD in OZ
The ROAD to OZ
The EMERALD CITY of OZ

OZ, the COMPLETE COLLECTION, VOLUME 3
The PATCHWORK GIRL of OZ
TIK-TOK of OZ
The SCARECROW of OZ

OZ, the COMPLETE COLLECTION, VOLUME 4
RINKITINK in OZ
The LOST PRINCESS of OZ
The TIN WOODMAN of OZ

OZ, the COMPLETE COLLECTION, VOLUME 5
The MAGIC of OZ
GLINDA of OZ
The ROYAL BOOK of OZ

Read them all!

Oz

The
Complete
COLLECTION
VOLUME
5

L. Frank Baum

Includes:

The MAGIC of OZ

GLINDA of OZ

The ROYAL BOOK of OZ,
by Ruth Plumly Thompson

Founded on and continuing the famous Oz series by L. Frank Baum

Aladdin

NEW YORK   LONDON   TORONTO   SYDNEY   NEW DELHI

ALADDIN

An imprint of Simon & Schuster Children's Publishing Division

1230 Avenue of the Americas, New York, NY 10020

This Aladdin edition March 2013

The Magic of Oz originally published in 1919

Glinda of Oz originally published in 1920

The Royal Book of Oz originally published in 1921

All rights reserved, including the right of reproduction in whole or in part in any form.

ALADDIN is a trademark of Simon & Schuster, Inc., and related logo is a registered trademark of Simon & Schuster, Inc.

For information about special discounts for bulk purchases, please contact Simon & Schuster Special Sales at 1-866-506-1949 or business@simonandschuster.com.

The Simon & Schuster Speakers Bureau can bring authors to your live event. For more information or to book an event contact the Simon & Schuster Speakers Bureau at 1-866-248-3049 or visit our website at www.simonspeakers.com.

Designed by Jane Archer

The text of this book was set in Baskerville.

Manufactured in the United States of America 0421 MTN

10 9 8

Library of Congress Control Number 2012950297

ISBN 978-1-4424-8894-6 (hc)

ISBN 978-1-4424-8551-8 (pbk)

ISBN 978-1-4424-8556-3 (eBook)

These books were originally published individually.

Contents

The
Magic
·····—··◄ of ►··—·····
OZ

*I dedicate this book to the children of our soldiers,
the Americans and their Allies, with unmeasured pride and affection.*

To My Readers

Curiously enough, in the events which have taken place in the last few years in our "great outside world," we may find incidents so marvelous and inspiring that I cannot hope to equal them with stories of the Land of Oz.

However, *The Magic of Oz* is really more strange and unusual than anything I have read or heard about on our side of the Great Sandy Desert which shuts us off from the Land of Oz, even during the past exciting years, so I hope it will appeal to your love of novelty.

A long and confining illness has prevented my answering all the good letters sent me—unless stamps were enclosed— but from now on I hope to be able to give prompt attention to each and every letter with which my readers favor me.

Assuring you that my love for you has never faltered and

hoping the Oz books will continue to give you pleasure as long as I am able to write them, I am

Yours affectionately,

L. Frank Baum,

"Royal Historian of Oz"

"OZCOT"

at Hollywood

in California

1919

Chapter 1

MOUNT MUNCH

On the east edge of the Land of Oz, in the Munchkin Country, is a big, tall hill called Mount Munch. One one side, the bottom of this hill just touches the Deadly Sandy Desert that separates the Fairyland of Oz from all the rest of the world, but on the other side, the hill touches the beautiful, fertile Country of the Munchkins.

The Munchkin folks, however, merely stand off and look at Mount Munch and know very little about it; for, about a third of the way up, its sides become too steep to climb, and if any people live upon the top of that great towering peak that seems to reach nearly to the skies, the Munchkins are not aware of the fact.

But people *do* live there, just the same. The top of Mount Munch is shaped like a saucer, broad and deep, and in the saucer are fields where grains and vegetables grow, and flocks are fed, and brooks flow and trees bear all sorts of things. There are houses scattered here and there, each having its family of Hyups, as the people call themselves. The Hyups seldom go down the mountain, for the same reason that the Munchkins never climb up: the sides are too steep.

In one of the houses lived a wise old Hyup named Bini Aru, who used to be a clever Sorcerer. But Ozma of Oz, who rules everyone in the Land of Oz, had made a decree that no one should practice magic in her dominions except Glinda the Good and the Wizard of Oz, and when Glinda sent this royal command to the Hyups by means of a strong-winged Eagle, old Bini Aru at once stopped performing magical arts. He destroyed many of his magic powders and tools of magic, and afterward honestly obeyed the law. He had never seen Ozma, but he knew she was his Ruler and must be obeyed.

There was only one thing that grieved him. He had discovered a new and secret method of transformations that was unknown to any other Sorcerer. Glinda the Good did not know it, nor did the little Wizard of Oz, nor Dr. Pipt nor old Mombi, nor anyone else who dealt in magic arts. It was Bini Aru's own secret. By its means, it was the simplest thing in the world to transform anyone into beast, bird or fish, or anything else, and back again, once you knew how to pronounce the mystical word: "Pyrzqxgl."

Bini Aru had used this secret many times, but not to cause evil or suffering to others. When he had wandered far from home and was hungry, he would say: "I want to become a cow—Pyrzqxgl!" In an instant he would be a cow, and then he would eat grass and satisfy his hunger. All beasts and birds can talk in the Land of Oz, so when the cow was no longer hungry, it would say: "I want to be Bini Aru again: Pyrzqxgl!" and the magic word, properly pronounced, would instantly restore him to his proper form.

Now, of course, I would not dare to write down this magic word so plainly if I thought my readers would pronounce it properly and so be able to transform themselves and others, but it is a fact that no one in all the world except Bini Aru, had ever (up to the time this story begins) been able to pronounce "Pyrzqxgl!" the right way, so I think it is safe to give it to you. It might be well, however, in reading this story aloud, to be careful not to pronounce Pyrzqxgl the proper way, and thus avoid all danger of the secret being able to work mischief.

Bini Aru, having discovered the secret of instant transformation, which required no tools or powders or other chemicals or herbs and always worked perfectly, was reluctant to have such a wonderful discovery entirely unknown or lost to all human knowledge. He decided not to use it again, since Ozma had forbidden him to do so, but he reflected that Ozma was a girl and some time might change her mind and allow her subjects to practice magic, in which case Bini Aru could again transform himself and others at will,—unless, of course, he forgot how to pronounce Pyrzqxgl in the meantime.

After giving the matter careful thought, he decided to write the word, and how it should be pronounced, in some secret place, so that he could find it after many years, but where no one else could ever find it.

That was a clever idea, but what bothered the old Sorcerer was to find a secret place. He wandered all over the Saucer at the top of Mount Munch, but found no place in which to write the secret word where others might not be likely to stumble upon it. So finally he decided it must be written somewhere in his own house.

Bini Aru had a wife named Mopsi Aru who was famous for making fine huckleberry pies, and he had a son named Kiki Aru who was not famous at all. He was noted as being cross and disagreeable because he was not happy, and he was not happy because he wanted to go down the mountain and visit the big world below and his father would not let him. No one paid any attention to Kiki Aru, because he didn't amount to anything, anyway.

Once a year there was a festival on Mount Munch which all the Hyups attended. It was held in the center of the saucer-shaped country, and the day was given over to feasting and merry-making. The young folks danced and sang songs;

the women spread the tables with good things to eat, and the men played on musical instruments and told fairy tales.

Kiki Aru usually went to these festivals with his parents, and then sat sullenly outside the circle and would not dance or sing or even talk to the other young people. So the festival did not make him any happier than other days, and this time he told Bini Aru and Mopsi Aru that he would not go. He would rather stay at home and be unhappy all by himself, he said, and so they gladly let him stay.

But after he was left alone Kiki decided to enter his father's private room, where he was forbidden to go, and see if he could find any of the magic tools Bini Aru used to work with when he practiced sorcery. As he went in Kiki stubbed his toe on one of the floor boards. He searched everywhere but found no trace of his father's magic. All had been destroyed.

Much disappointed, he started to go out again when he stubbed his toe on the same floor board. That set him thinking. Examining the board more closely, Kiki found it had been pried up and then nailed down again in such a manner that it was a little higher than the other boards. But why had his father taken up the board? Had he hidden some of his magic tools underneath the floor?

Kiki got a chisel and pried up the board, but found nothing under it. He was just about to replace the board when it slipped from his hand and turned over, and he saw something written on the underside of it. The light was rather dim, so he took the board to the window and examined it, and found that the writing described exactly how to pronounce the magic word Pyrzqxgl, which would transform anyone into anything instantly, and back again when the word was repeated.

Now, at first, Kiki Aru didn't realize what a wonderful secret he had discovered; but he thought it might be of use to him and so he took a piece of paper and made on it an exact copy of the instructions for pronouncing Pyrzqxgl. Then he folded the paper and put it in his pocket, and replaced the board in the floor so that no one would suspect it had been removed.

After this Kiki went into the garden and sitting beneath a tree made a careful study of the paper. He had always wanted to get away from Mount Munch and visit the big world—especially the Land of Oz—and the idea now came to him that if he could transform himself into a bird, he could fly to any place he wished to go and fly back again whenever he cared to. It was necessary, however, to learn by heart the way to pronounce the magic word, because a bird would have no way to carry a paper with it, and Kiki would be unable to resume his proper shape if he forgot the word or its pronunciation.

So he studied it a long time, repeating it a hundred times in his mind until he was sure he would not forget it. But to make safety doubly sure he placed the paper in a tin box in a neglected part of the garden and covered the box with small stones.

By this time it was getting late in the day and Kiki wished to attempt his first transformation before his parents returned from the festival. So he stood on the front porch of his home and said:

"I want to become a big, strong bird, like a hawk—Pyrzqxgl!" He pronounced it the right way, so in a flash he felt that he was completely changed in form. He flapped his wings, hopped to the porch railing and said: "Caw-oo! Caw-oo!"

Then he laughed and said half aloud: "I suppose that's the funny sound this sort of a bird makes. But now let me try my wings and see if I'm strong enough to fly across the desert."

For he had decided to make his first trip to the country outside the Land of Oz. He had stolen this secret of transformation and he knew he had disobeyed the law of Oz by working magic. Perhaps Glinda or the Wizard of Oz would discover him and punish him, so it would be good policy to keep away from Oz altogether.

Slowly Kiki rose into the air, and resting on his broad wings, floated in graceful circles above the saucer-shaped mountain-top. From his height, he could see, far across the burning sands of the Deadly Desert, another country that might be pleasant to explore, so he headed that way, and with strong, steady strokes of his wings, began the long flight.

Chapter 2

The HAWK

Even a hawk has to fly high in order to cross the Deadly Desert, from which poisonous fumes are constantly rising. Kiki Aru felt sick and faint by the time he reached good land again, for he could not quite escape the effects of the poisons. But the fresh air soon restored him and he alighted in a broad table-land which is called Hiland. Just beyond it is a valley known as Loland, and these two countries are ruled by the Gingerbread Man, John Dough, with Chick the Cherub as his Prime Minister. The Hawk merely stopped here long enough to rest, and then he flew north and passed over a fine country called Merryland, which is ruled by a lovely Wax Doll. Then, following the curve of the Desert, he turned north and settled on a tree-top in the Kingdom of Noland.

Kiki was tired by this time, and the sun was now setting, so he decided to remain here till morning. From his tree-top he could see a house near by, which looked very comfortable. A man was milking a cow in the yard and a pleasant-faced woman came to the door and called him to supper.

That made Kiki wonder what sort of food hawks ate. He felt hungry, but didn't know what to eat or where to get it. Also he thought a bed would be more comfortable than a tree-top for sleeping, so he hopped to the ground and said: "I want to become Kiki Aru again—Pyrzqxgl!"

Instantly he had resumed his natural shape, and going to the house, he knocked upon the door and asked for some supper.

"Who are you?" asked the man of the house.

"A stranger from the Land of Oz," replied Kiki Aru.

"Then you are welcome," said the man.

Kiki was given a good supper and a good bed, and he behaved very well, although he refused to answer all the questions the good people of Noland asked him. Having escaped from his home and found a way to see the world, the young man was no longer unhappy, and so he was no longer cross and disagreeable. The people thought him a very respectable person and gave him breakfast next morning, after which he started on his way feeling quite contented.

Having walked for an hour or two through the pretty country that is ruled by King Bud, Kiki Aru decided he could travel faster and see more as a bird, so he transformed himself into a white dove and visited the great city of Nole and saw the King's palace and gardens and many other places of interest. Then he flew westward into the Kingdom of Ix, and after a day in Queen Zixi's country went on westward into the Land of Ev. Every place he visited he thought was much more pleasant than the saucer-country of the Hyups, and he decided that when he reached the finest country of all he would settle there and enjoy his future life to the utmost.

In the land of Ev he resumed his own shape again, for the cities and villages were close together and he could easily go on foot from one to another of them.

Toward evening he came to a good inn and asked the innkeeper if he could have food and lodging.

"You can if you have the money to pay," said the man, "otherwise you must go elsewhere."

This surprised Kiki, for in the Land of Oz they do not use money at all, everyone being allowed to take what he wishes without price. He had no money, therefore, and so he turned away to seek hospitality elsewhere. Looking through an open window into one of the rooms of the inn, as he passed along, he saw an old man counting on a table a big heap of gold pieces, which Kiki thought to be money. One of these would buy him supper and a bed, he reflected, so he transformed himself into a magpie and, flying through the open window, caught up one of the gold pieces in his beak and flew out again before the old man could interfere. Indeed, the old man who was robbed was quite helpless, for he dared not leave his pile of gold to chase the magpie, and before he could place the gold in a sack and the sack in his pocket the robber bird was out of sight and to seek it would be folly.

Kiki Aru flew to a group of trees and, dropping the gold piece to the ground, resumed his proper shape, and then picked up the money and put it in his pocket.

"You'll be sorry for this!" exclaimed a small voice just over his head.

Kiki looked up and saw that a sparrow, perched upon a branch, was watching him.

"Sorry for what?" he demanded.

"Oh, I saw the whole thing," asserted the sparrow. "I saw you look in the window at the gold, and then make yourself into a magpie and rob the poor man, and then I saw you fly here and make the bird into your former shape. That's magic, and magic is wicked and unlawful; and you stole money, and that's a still greater crime. You'll be sorry, some day."

"I don't care," replied Kiki Aru, scowling.

"Aren't you afraid to be wicked?" asked the sparrow.

"No, I didn't know I was being wicked," said Kiki, "but if I was, I'm glad of it. I hate good people. I've always wanted to be wicked, but I didn't know how."

"Haw, haw, haw!" laughed someone behind him, in a big voice; "that's the proper spirit, my lad! I'm glad I've met you; shake hands."

The sparrow gave a frightened squeak and flew away.

Chapter 3

TWO BAD ONES

Kiki turned around and saw a queer old man standing near. He didn't stand straight, for he was crooked. He had a fat body and thin legs and arms. He had a big, round face with bushy, white whiskers that came to a point below his waist, and white hair that came to a point on top of his head. He wore dull-grey clothes that were tight fitting, and his pockets were all bunched out as if stuffed full of something.

"I didn't know you were here," said Kiki.

"I didn't come until after you did," said the queer old man.

"Who are you?" asked Kiki.

"My name's Ruggedo. I used to be the Nome King; but I got kicked out of my country, and now I'm a wanderer."

"What made them kick you out?" inquired the Hyup boy.

"Well, it's the fashion to kick kings nowadays. I was a pretty good King—to myself—but those dreadful Oz people wouldn't let me alone. So I had to abdicate."

"What does that mean?"

"It means to be kicked out. But let's talk about something pleasant. Who are you and where did you come from?"

"I'm called Kiki Aru. I used to live on Mount Munch in the Land of Oz, but now I'm a wanderer like yourself."

The Nome King gave him a shrewd look.

"I heard that bird say that you transformed yourself into a magpie and back again. Is that true?"

Kiki hesitated, but saw no reason to deny it. He felt that it would make him appear more important.

"Well—yes," he said.

"Then you're a wizard?"

"No; I only understand transformations," he admitted.

"Well, that's pretty good magic, anyhow," declared old Ruggedo. "I used to have some very fine magic, myself, but my enemies took it all away from me. Where are you going now?"

"I'm going into the inn, to get some supper and a bed," said Kiki.

"Have you the money to pay for it?" asked the Nome.

"I have one gold piece."

"Which you stole. Very good. And you're glad that you're wicked. Better yet. I like you, young man, and I'll go to the inn with you if you'll promise not to eat eggs for supper."

"Don't you like eggs?" asked Kiki.

"I'm afraid of 'em; they're dangerous!" said Ruggedo, with a shudder.

"All right," agreed Kiki; "I won't ask for eggs."

"Then come along," said the Nome.

When they entered the inn, the landlord scowled at Kiki and said:

"I told you I would not feed you unless you had money."

Kiki showed him the gold piece.

"And how about you?" asked the landlord, turning to Ruggedo. "Have you money?"

"I've something better," answered the old Nome, and taking a bag from one of his pockets he poured from it upon the table a mass of glittering gems—diamonds, rubies and emeralds.

The landlord was very polite to the strangers after that. He served them an excellent supper, and while they ate it, the Hyup boy asked his companion:

"Where did you get so many jewels?"

"Well, I'll tell you," answered the Nome. "When those Oz people took my kingdom away from me—just because it was my kingdom and I wanted to run it to suit myself—they said I could take as many precious stones as I could carry. So I had a lot of pockets made in my clothes and loaded them all up. Jewels are fine things to have with you when you travel; you can trade them for anything."

"Are they better than gold pieces?" asked Kiki.

"The smallest of these jewels is worth a hundred gold pieces such as you stole from the old man."

"Don't talk so loud," begged Kiki, uneasily. "Some one else might hear what you are saying."

After supper they took a walk together, and the former Nome King said:

"Do you know the Shaggy Man, and the Scarecrow, and the Tin Woodman, and Dorothy, and Ozma and all the other Oz people?"

"No," replied the boy, "I have never been away from Mount Munch until I flew over the Deadly Desert the other day in the shape of a hawk."

"Then you've never seen the Emerald City of Oz?"

"Never."

"Well," said the Nome, "I knew all the Oz people, and you can guess I do not love them. All during my wanderings I have brooded on how I can be revenged on them. Now that I've met you I can see a way to conquer the Land of Oz and be King there myself, which is better than being King of the Nomes."

"How can you do that?" inquired Kiki Aru, wonderingly.

"Never mind how. In the first place, I'll make a bargain

with you. Tell me the secret of how to perform transformations and I will give you a pocketful of jewels, the biggest and finest that I possess."

"No," said Kiki, who realized that to share his power with another would be dangerous to himself.

"I'll give you *two* pocketsful of jewels," said the Nome.

"No," answered Kiki.

"I'll give you every jewel I possess."

"No, no, no!" said Kiki, who was beginning to be frightened.

"Then," said the Nome, with a wicked look at the boy, "I'll tell the inn-keeper that you stole that gold piece and he will have you put in prison."

Kiki laughed at the threat.

"Before he can do that," said he, "I will transform myself into a lion and tear him to pieces, or into a bear and eat him up, or into a fly and fly away where he could not find me."

"Can you really do such wonderful transformations?" asked the old Nome, looking at him curiously.

"Of course," declared Kiki. "I can transform you into a stick of wood, in a flash, or into a stone, and leave you here by the roadside."

"The wicked Nome shivered a little when he heard that, but it made him long more than ever to possess the great secret. After a while he said:

"I'll tell you what I'll do. If you will help me to conquer

Oz and to transform the Oz people, who are my enemies, into sticks or stones, by telling me your secret, I'll agree to make *you* the Ruler of all Oz, and I will be your Prime Minister and see that your orders are obeyed."

"I'll help do that," said Kiki, "but I won't tell you my secret."

The Nome was so furious at this refusal that he jumped up and down with rage and spluttered and choked for a long time before he could control his passion. But the boy was not at all frightened. He laughed at the wicked old Nome, which made him more furious than ever.

"Let's give up the idea," he proposed, when Ruggedo had quieted somewhat. "I don't know the Oz people you mention and so they are not my enemies. If they've kicked you out of your kingdom, that's your affair—not mine."

"Wouldn't you like to be king of that splendid fairyland?" asked Ruggedo.

"Yes, I would," replied Kiki Aru; "but you want to be king yourself, and we would quarrel over it."

"No," said the Nome, trying to deceive him. "I don't care to be King of Oz, come to think it over. I don't even care to live in that country. What I want first is revenge. If we can conquer Oz, I'll get enough magic then to conquer my own Kingdom of the Nomes, and I'll go back and live in my underground caverns, which are more home-like than the top of the earth. So here's my proposition: Help me conquer

Oz and get revenge, and help me get the magic away from Glinda and the Wizard, and I'll let you be King of Oz forever afterward."

"I'll think it over," answered Kiki, and that is all he would say that evening.

In the night when all in the inn were asleep but himself, old Ruggedo the Nome rose softly from his couch and went into the room of Kiki Aru the Hyup, and searched everywhere for the magic tool that performed his transformations. Of course, there was no such tool, and although Ruggedo searched in all the boy's pockets, he found nothing magical whatever. So he went back to his bed and began to doubt that Kiki could perform transformations.

Next morning he said:

"Which way do you travel to-day?"

"I think I shall visit the Rose Kingdom," answered the boy.

"That is a long journey," declared the Nome.

"I shall transform myself into a bird," said Kiki, "and so fly to the Rose Kingdom in an hour."

"Then transform me, also, into a bird, and I will go with you," suggested Ruggedo. "But, in that case, let us fly together to the Land of Oz, and see what it looks like."

Kiki thought this over. Pleasant as were the countries he had visited, he heard everywhere that the Land of Oz was more beautiful and delightful. The Land of Oz was his own country, too, and if there was any possibility of his becoming its King, he must know something about it.

While Kiki the Hyup thought, Ruggedo the Nome was also thinking. This boy possessed a marvelous power, and although very simple in some ways, he was determined not to part with his secret. However, if Ruggedo could get him to transport the wily old Nome to Oz, which he could reach in no other way, he might then induce the boy to follow his advice and enter into the plot for revenge, which he had already planned in his wicked heart.

"There are wizards and magicians in Oz," remarked Kiki, after a time. "They might discover us, in spite of our transformations."

"Not if we are careful," Ruggedo assured him. "Ozma has a Magic Picture, in which she can see whatever she wishes to see; but Ozma will know nothing of our going to Oz, and so she will not command her Magic Picture to show where we are or what we are doing. Glinda the Good has a Great Book called the Book of Records, in which is magically written everything that people do in the Land of Oz, just the instant they do it."

"Then," said Kiki, "there is no use our attempting to conquer the country, for Glinda would read in her book all that we do, and as her magic is greater than mine, she would soon put a stop to our plans."

"I said 'people,' didn't I?" retorted the Nome. "The book

doesn't make a record of what birds do, or beasts. It only tells the doings of people. So, if we fly into the country as birds, Glinda won't know anything about it."

"Two birds couldn't conquer the Land of Oz," asserted the boy, scornfully.

"No; that's true," admitted Ruggedo, and then he rubbed his forehead and stroked his long pointed beard and thought some more.

"Ah, now I have the idea!" he declared. "I suppose you can transform us into beasts as well as birds?"

"Of course."

"And can you make a bird a beast, and a beast a bird again, without taking a human form in between?"

"Certainly," said Kiki. "I can transform myself or others into anything that can talk. There's a magic word that must be spoken in connection with the transformations, and as beasts and birds and dragons and fishes can talk in Oz, we may become any of these we desire to. However, if I transformed myself into a tree, I would always remain a tree, because then I could not utter the magic word to change the transformation."

"I see; I see," said Ruggedo, nodding his bushy, white head until the point of his hair waved back and forth like a pendulum. "That fits in with my idea, exactly. Now, listen, and I'll explain to you my plan. We'll fly to Oz as birds and settle in one of the thick forests in the Gillikin Country. There you will transform us into powerful beasts, and as Glinda doesn't keep any track of the doings of beasts we can act without being discovered."

"But how can two beasts raise an army to conquer the powerful people of Oz?" inquired Kiki.

"That's easy. But not an army of *people*, mind you. That would be quickly discovered. And while we are in Oz you and I will never resume our human forms until we've conquered the country and destroyed Glinda, and Ozma, and the Wizard, and Dorothy, and all the rest, and so have nothing more to fear from them."

"It is impossible to kill anyone in the Land of Oz," declared Kiki.

"It isn't necessary to kill the Oz people," rejoined Ruggedo.

"I'm afraid I don't understand you," objected the boy. "What will happen to the Oz people, and what sort of an army could we get together, except of people?"

"I'll tell you. The forests of Oz are full of beasts. Some of them, in the far-away places, are savage and cruel, and would gladly follow a leader as savage as themselves. They have never troubled the Oz people much, because they had no leader to urge them on, but we will tell them to help us conquer Oz and as a reward we will transform all the beasts into men and women, and let them live in the houses and enjoy all the good things; and we will transform all the people of Oz into beasts of various sorts, and send them to live in the forests and the jungles. That is a splendid idea, you must admit, and it's so easy that we won't have any trouble at all to carry it through to success."

"Will the beasts consent, do you think?" asked the boy.

"To be sure they will. We can get every beast in Oz on our side—except a few who live in Ozma's palace, and they won't count."

...——◂ Chapter 4 ▸...——..

CONSPIRATORS

Kiki Aru didn't know much about Oz and didn't know much about the beasts who lived there, but the old Nome's plan seemed to him to be quite reasonable. He had a faint suspicion that Ruggedo meant to get the best of him in some way, and he resolved to keep a close watch on his fellow-conspirator. As long as he kept to himself the secret word of the transformations, Ruggedo would not dare to harm him, and he promised himself that as soon as they had conquered Oz, he would transform the old Nome into a marble statue and keep him in that form forever.

Ruggedo, on his part, decided that he could, by careful

watching and listening, surprise the boy's secret, and when he had learned the magic word he would transform Kiki Aru into a bundle of faggots and burn him up and so be rid of him.

This is always the way with wicked people. They cannot be trusted even by one another. Ruggedo thought he was fooling Kiki, and Kiki thought he was fooling Ruggedo; so both were pleased.

"It's a long way across the Desert," remarked the boy, "and the sands are hot and send up poisonous vapors. Let us wait until evening and then fly across in the night when it will be cooler."

The former Nome King agreed to this, and the two spent the rest of that day in talking over their plans. When evening came they paid the inn-keeper and walked out to a little grove of trees that stood near by.

"Remain here for a few minutes and I'll soon be back," said Kiki, and walking swiftly away, he left the Nome standing in the grove. Ruggedo wondered where he had gone, but stood quietly in his place until, all of a sudden, his form changed to that of a great eagle, and he uttered a piercing cry of astonishment and flapped his wings in a sort of panic. At once his eagle cry was answered from beyond the grove, and another eagle, even larger and more powerful than the transformed Ruggedo, came sailing through the trees and alighted beside him.

"Now we are ready for the start," said the voice of Kiki, coming from the eagle.

Ruggedo realized that this time he had been outwitted. He had thought Kiki would utter the magic word in his presence, and so he would learn what it was, but the boy had been too shrewd for that.

As the two eagles mounted high into the air and began their flight across the great Desert that separates the Land of Oz from all the rest of the world, the Nome said:

"When I was King of the Nomes I had a magic way of working transformations that I thought was good, but it could not compare with your secret word. I had to have certain tools and make passes and say a lot of mystic words before I could transform anybody."

"What became of your magic tools?" inquired Kiki.

"The Oz people took them all away from me—that horrid girl, Dorothy, and that terrible fairy, Ozma, the Ruler of Oz—at the time they took away my underground kingdom and kicked me upstairs into the cold, heartless world."

"Why did you let them do that?" asked the boy.

"Well," said Ruggedo, "I couldn't help it. They rolled eggs at me—*eggs*—dreadful eggs!—and if an egg even touches a Nome, he is ruined for life."

"Is any kind of an egg dangerous to a Nome?"

"Any kind and every kind. An egg is the only thing I'm afraid of."

Chapter 5

A HAPPY CORNER of OZ

There is no other country so beautiful as the Land of Oz. There are no other people so happy and contented and prosperous as the Oz people. They have all they desire; they love and admire their beautiful girl Ruler, Ozma of Oz, and they mix work and play so justly that both are delightful and satisfying and no one has any reason to complain. Once in a while something happens in Oz to disturb the people's happiness for a brief time, for so rich and attractive a fairyland is sure to make a few selfish and greedy outsiders envious, and therefore certain evil-doers have treacherously plotted to conquer Oz and enslave its people and destroy its girl Ruler, and so gain the wealth of Oz for themselves. But up to the time when the cruel and crafty Nome, Ruggedo, conspired with Kiki Aru, the Hyup, all such attempts had failed. The Oz people suspected no danger. Life in the world's nicest fairyland was one round of joyous, happy days.

In the center of the Emerald City of Oz, the capital city of Ozma's dominions, is a vast and beautiful garden, surrounded by a wall inlaid with shining emeralds, and in the center of this garden stands Ozma's Royal Palace, the most splendid building ever constructed. From a hundred towers and domes floated the banners of Oz, which included the Ozmies, the Munchkins, the Gillikins, the Winkies and the Quadlings. The banner of the Munchkins is blue, that of the Winkies yellow; the Gillikin banner is purple, and the Quadling's banner is red. The colors of the Emerald City are of course green. Ozma's own banner has a green center, and is divided into four quarters. These quarters are colored blue, purple, yellow and red, indicating that she rules over all the countries of the Land of Oz.

This fairyland is so big, however, that all of it is not yet known to its girl Ruler, and it is said that in some far parts of the country, in forests and mountain fastnesses, in hidden valleys and thick jungles, are people and beasts that know as little about Ozma as she knows of them. Still, these unknown subjects are not nearly so numerous as the known inhabitants of Oz, who occupy all the countries near to the Emerald City.

Indeed, I'm sure it will not be long until all parts of the Fairy-land of Oz are explored and their peoples made acquainted with their Ruler, for in Ozma's palace are several of her friends who are so curious that they are constantly discovering new and extraordinary places and inhabitants.

One of the most frequent discoverers of these hidden places in Oz is a little Kansas girl named Dorothy, who is Ozma's dearest friend and lives in luxurious rooms in the Royal Palace. Dorothy is, indeed, a Princess of Oz, but she does not like to be called a princess, and because she is simple and sweet and does not pretend to be anything but an ordinary little girl, she is called just "Dorothy" by everybody and is the most popular person, next to Ozma, in all the Land of Oz.

One morning Dorothy crossed the hall of the palace and knocked on the door of another girl named Trot, also a guest and friend of Ozma. When told to enter, Dorothy found that Trot had company, an old sailor-man with one wooden leg and one meat leg, who was sitting by the open window puffing smoke from a corn-cob pipe. This sailor-man was named Cap'n Bill, and he had accompanied Trot to the Land of Oz and was her oldest and most faithful comrade and friend. Dorothy liked Cap'n Bill, too, and after she had greeted him, she said to Trot:

"You know, Ozma's birthday is next month, and I've been wondering what I can give here as a birthday present. She's so good to us all that we certainly ought to remember her birthday."

"That's true," agreed Trot. "I've been wondering, too, what I could give Ozma. It's pretty hard to decide, 'cause she's got already all she wants, and as she's a fairy and knows a lot about magic, she could satisfy any wish."

"I know," returned Dorothy, "but that isn't the point. It isn't that Ozma *needs* anything, but that it will please her to know we've remembered her birthday. But what shall we give her?"

Trot shook her head in despair.

"I've tried to think and I can't," she declared.

"It's the same way with me," said Dorothy.

"I know one thing that 'ud please her," remarked Cap'n Bill, turning his round face with its fringe of whiskers toward the two girls and staring at them with his big, light-blue eyes wide open.

"What is it, Cap'n Bill?"

"It's an Enchanted Flower," said he. "It's a pretty plant that stands in a golden flower-pot an' grows all sorts o' flowers, one after another. One minute a fine rose buds an' blooms, an' then a tulip, an' next a chrys—chrys—"

"—anthemum," said Dorothy, helping him.

"That's it; and next a dahlia, an' then a daffydil, an' on all through the range o' posies. Jus' as soon as one fades away, another comes, of a different sort, an' the perfume from 'em is mighty snifty, an' they keeps bloomin' night and day, year in an' year out."

"That's wonderful!" exclaimed Dorothy. "I think Ozma would like it."

"But where is the Magic Flower, and how can we get it?" asked Trot.

"Dun'no, zac'ly," slowly replied Cap'n Bill. "The Glass Cat tol' me about it only yesterday, an' said it was in some lonely place up at the nor'east o' here. The Glass Cat goes travelin' all around Oz, you know, an' the little critter sees a lot o' things no one else does."

"That's true," said Dorothy, thoughtfully. "Northeast of here must be in the Munchkin Country, and perhaps a good way off, so let's ask the Glass Cat to tell us how to get to the Magic Flower."

So the two girls, with Cap'n Bill stumping along on his wooden leg after them, went out into the garden, and after some time spent in searching, they found the Glass Cat curled up in the sunshine beside a bush, fast sleep.

The Glass Cat is one of the most curious creatures in all Oz. It was made by a famous magician named Dr. Pipt before Ozma had forbidden her subjects to work magic. Dr. Pipt had made the Glass Cat to catch mice, but the Cat refused to catch mice and was considered more curious than useful.

This astonishing cat was made all of glass and was so clear and transparent that you could see through it as easily as through a window. In the top of its head, however, was a mass of delicate pink balls which looked like jewels but were intended for brains. It had a heart made of blood-red ruby. The eyes were two large emeralds. But, aside from these colors, all the rest of the animal was of clear glass, and it had a spun-glass tail that was really beautiful.

"Here, wake up," said Cap'n Bill. "We want to talk to you."

Slowly the Glass Cat got upon its feet, yawned and then looked at the three who stood before it.

"How dare you disturb me?" it asked in a peevish voice. "You ought to be ashamed of yourselves."

"Never mind that," returned the Sailor. "Do you remember tellin' me yesterday 'bout a Magic Flower in a gold pot?"

"Do you think I'm a fool? Look at my brains—you can see 'em work. Of course I remember!" said the cat.

"Well, where can we find it?"

"You can't. It's none of your business, anyhow. Go away and let me sleep," advised the Glass Cat.

"Now, see here," said Dorothy; "we want the Magic Flower to give to Ozma on her birthday. You'd be glad to please Ozma, wouldn't you?"

"I'm not sure," replied the creature. "Why should I want to please anybody?"

"You've got a heart, 'cause I can see it inside of you," said Trot.

"Yes; it's a pretty heart, and I'm fond of it," said the cat, twisting around to view its own body. "But it's made from a ruby, and it's hard as nails."

"Aren't you good for *any*thing?" asked Trot.

"Yes, I'm pretty to look at, and that's more than can be said of you," retorted the creature.

Trot laughed at this, and Dorothy, who understood the Glass Cat pretty well, said soothingly:

"You are indeed beautiful, and if you can tell Cap'n Bill where to find the Magic Flower, all the people in Oz will praise your cleverness. The Flower will belong to Ozma, but everyone will know the Glass Cat discovered it."

This was the kind of praise the crystal creature liked.

"Well," it said, while the pink brains rolled around, "I found the Magic Flower way up in the north of the Munchkin Country where few people live or ever go. There's a river there that flows through a forest, and in the middle of the river in the middle of the forest there is a small island on which stands the gold pot in which grows the Magic Flower."

"How did you get to the island?" asked Dorothy. "Glass cats can't swim."

"No, but I'm not afraid of water," was the reply. "I just walked across the river on the bottom."

"Under the water?" exclaimed Trot.

The cat gave her a scornful look.

"How could I walk *over* the water on the *bottom* of the river? If you were transparent, anyone could see *your* brains were not working. But I'm sure you could never find the place alone. It has always been hidden from the Oz people."

"But you, with your fine pink brains, could find it again, I s'pose," remarked Dorothy.

"Yes; and if you want that Magic Flower for Ozma, I'll go with you and show you the way."

"That's lovely of you!" declared Dorothy. "Trot and Cap'n Bill will go with you, for this is to be their birthday present to Ozma. While you're gone I'll have to find something else to give her."

"All right. Come on, then, Cap'n," said the Glass Cat, starting to move away.

"Wait a minute," begged Trot. "How long will we be gone?"

"Oh, about a week."

"Then I'll put some things in a basket to take with us," said the girl, and ran into the palace to make her preparations for the journey.

Chapter 6

OZMA'S BIRTHDAY PRESENTS

When Cap'n Bill and Trot and the Glass Cat had started for the hidden island in the far-off river to get the Magic Flower, Dorothy wondered again what she could give Ozma on her birthday. She met the Patchwork Girl and said:

"What are you going to give Ozma for a birthday present?"

"I've written a song for her," answered the strange Patchwork Girl, who went by the name of "Scraps," and who, through stuffed with cotton, had a fair assortment of mixed brains. "It's a splendid song and the chorus runs this way:

"I am crazy;

You're a daisy,

Ozma dear;

I'm demented;

You're contented,

Ozma dear;

I am patched and gay and glary;

You're a sweet and lovely fairy;

May your birthdays all be happy,

Ozma dear!"

"How do you like it, Dorothy?" inquired the Patchwork Girl.

"Is it good poetry, Scraps?" asked Dorothy, doubtfully.

"It's as good as any ordinary song," was the reply. "I have given it a dandy title, too. I shall call the song: 'When Ozma Has a Birthday, Everybody's Sure to Be Gay, for She Cannot Help the Fact That She Was Born.'"

"That's a pretty long title, Scraps," said Dorothy.

"That makes it stylish," replied the Patchwork Girl, turning a somersault and alighting on one stuffed foot. "Now-a-days the titles are sometimes longer than the songs."

Dorothy left her and walked slowly toward the place, where she met the Tin Woodman just going up the front steps.

"What are you going to give Ozma on her birthday?" she asked.

"It's a secret, but I'll tell you," replied the Tin Woodman, who was Emperor of the Winkies. "I am having my people make Ozma a lovely girdle set with beautiful tin nuggets. Each tin nugget will be surrounded by a circle of emeralds, just to set it off to good advantage. The clasp of the girdle will be pure tin! Won't that be fine?"

"I'm sure she'll like it," said Dorothy. "Do you know what *I* can give her?"

"I haven't the slightest idea, Dorothy. It took me three months to think of my own present for Ozma."

The girl walked thoughtfully around to the back of the palace, and presently came upon the famous Scarecrow of Oz, who was having two of the palace servants stuff his legs with fresh straw.

"What are you going to give Ozma on her birthday?" asked Dorothy.

"I want to surprise her," answered the Scarecrow.

"I won't tell," promised Dorothy.

"Well, I'm having some straw slippers made for her— all straw, mind you, and braided very artistically. Ozma has always admired my straw filling, so I'm sure she'll be pleased with these lovely straw slippers."

"Ozma will be pleased with anything her loving friends give her," said the girl. "What *I'm* worried about, Scarecrow, is what to give Ozma that she hasn't got already."

"That's what worried me, until I thought of the slippers,"

said the Scarecrow. "You'll have to *think*, Dorothy; that's the only way to get a good idea. If I hadn't such wonderful brains, I'd never have thought of those straw foot-decorations."

Dorothy left him and went to her room, where she sat down and tried to think hard. A Pink Kitten was curled up on the window-sill and Dorothy asked her:

"What can I give Ozma for her birthday present?"

"Oh, give her some milk," replied the Pink Kitten; "that's the nicest thing I know of."

A fuzzy little black dog had squatted down at Dorothy's feet and now looked up at her with intelligent eyes.

"Tell me, Toto," said the girl; "what would Ozma like best for a birthday present?"

The little black dog wagged his tail.

"Your love," said he. "Ozma wants to be loved more than anything else."

"But I already love her, Toto!"

"Then tell her you love her twice as much as you ever did before."

"That wouldn't be true," objected Dorothy, "for I've always loved her as much as I could, and, really, Toto, I want to give Ozma some *present*, 'cause everyone else will give her a present."

"Let me see," said Toto. "How would it be to give her that useless Pink Kitten?"

"No, Toto; that wouldn't do."

"Then six kisses."

"No; that's no present."

"Well, I guess you'll have to figure it out for yourself, Dorothy," said the little dog. "To *my* notion you're more particular than Ozma will be."

Dorothy decided that if anyone could help her it would be Glinda the Good, the wonderful Sorceress of Oz who was Ozma's faithful subject and friend. But Glinda's castle was in the Quadling Country and quite a journey from the Emerald City.

So the little girl went to Ozma and asked permission to use the Wooden Sawhorse and the royal Red Wagon to pay a visit to Glinda, and the girl Ruler kissed Princess Dorothy and graciously granted permission.

The Wooden Sawhorse was one of the most remarkable creatures in Oz. Its body was a small log and its legs were limbs of trees stuck in the body. Its eyes were knots, its mouth was sawed in the end of the log and its ears were two chips. A small branch had been left at the rear end of the log to serve as a tail.

Ozma herself, during one of her early adventures, had brought this wooden horse to life, and so she was much attached to the queer animal and had shod the bottoms of its wooden legs with plates of gold so they would not wear out. The Sawhorse was a swift and willing traveler, and though it could talk if need arose, it seldom said anything unless spoken to. When the Sawhorse was harnessed to the Red Wagon there were no reins to guide him because all that was needed was to tell him where to go.

Dorothy now told him to go to Glinda's Castle and the Sawhorse carried her there with marvelous speed.

"Glinda," said Dorothy, when she had been greeted by the Sorceress, who was tall and stately, with handsome and dignified features and dressed in a splendid and becoming gown, "what are you going to give Ozma for a birthday present?"

The Sorceress smiled and answered:

"Come into my patio and I will show you."

So they entered a place that was surrounded by the wings of the great castle but had no roof, and was filled with flowers and fountains and exquisite statuary and many settees and chairs of polished marble or filigree gold. Here there were gathered fifty beautiful young girls, Glinda's handmaids, who had been selected from all parts of the Land of Oz on account of their wit and beauty and sweet dispositions. It was a great honor to be made one of Glinda's handmaidens.

When Dorothy followed the Sorceress into this delightful patio all the fifty girls were busily weaving, and their shuttles were filled with a sparkling green spun glass such as the little girl had never seen before.

"What is it, Glinda?" she asked.

"One of my recent discoveries," explained the Sorceress. "I have found a way to make threads from emeralds, by softening the stones and then spinning them into long, silken strands. With these emerald threads we are weaving cloth to make Ozma a splendid court gown for her birthday. You will notice that the threads have all the beautiful glitter and luster of the emeralds from which they are made, and so Ozma's new dress will be the most magnificent the world has ever seen, and quite fitting for our lovely Ruler of the Fairyland of Oz."

Dorothy's eyes were fairly dazed by the brilliance of the emerald cloth, some of which the girls had already woven.

"I've never seen *any*thing so beautiful!" she said, with a sigh. "But tell me, Glinda, what can *I* give our lovely Ozma on her birthday?"

The good Sorceress considered this question for a long time before she replied. Finally she said:

"Of course there will be a grand feast at the Royal Palace on Ozma's birthday, and all our friends will be present. So I suggest that you make a fine big birthday cake of Ozma, and surround it with candles."

"Oh, just a *cake*!" exclaimed Dorothy, in disappointment.

"Nothing is nicer for a birthday," said the Sorceress.

"How many candles should there be on the cake?" asked the girl.

"Just a row of them," replied Glinda, "for no one knows how old Ozma is, although she appears to us to be just a young girl—as fresh and fair as if she had lived but a few years."

"A cake doesn't seem like much of a present," Dorothy asserted.

"Make it a surprise cake," suggested the Sorceress. "Don't you remember the four and twenty blackbirds that were baked in a pie? Well, you need not use live blackbirds in your cake, but you could have some surprise of a different sort."

"Like what?" questioned Dorothy, eagerly.

"If I told you, it wouldn't be *your* present to Ozma, but *mine*," answered the Sorceress, with a smile. "Think it over, my dear, and I am sure you can originate a surprise that will add greatly to the joy and merriment of Ozma's birthday banquet."

Dorothy thanked her friend and entered the Red Wagon and told the Sawhorse to take her back home to the palace in the Emerald City.

On the way she thought the matter over seriously of making a surprise birthday cake and finally decided what to do.

As soon as she reached home, she went to the Wizard of Oz, who had a room fitted up in one of the high towers of the palace, where he studied magic so as to be able to perform such wizardry as Ozma commanded him to do for the welfare of her subjects.

The Wizard and Dorothy were firm friends and had enjoyed many strange adventures together. He was a little man with a bald head and sharp eyes and a round, jolly face, and because he was neither haughty nor proud he had become a great favorite with the Oz people.

"Wizard," said Dorothy, "I want you to help me fix up a present for Ozma's birthday."

"I'll be glad to do anything for you and for Ozma," he answered. "What's on your mind, Dorothy?"

"I'm going to make a great cake, with frosting and candles, and all that, you know."

"Very good," said the Wizard.

"In the center of this cake I'm going to leave a hollow place, with just a roof of the frosting over it," continued the girl.

"Very good," repeated the Wizard, nodding his bald head.

"In that hollow place," said Dorothy, "I want to hide a lot of monkeys about three inches high, and after the cake is placed on the banquet table, I want the monkeys to break through the frosting and dance around on the table-cloth. Then, I want each monkey to cut out a piece of cake and hand it to a guest."

"Mercy me!" cried the little Wizard, as he chuckled with laughter. "Is that *all* you want, Dorothy?"

"Almost," said she. "Can you think of anything more the little monkeys can do, Wizard?"

"Not just now," he replied. "But where will you get such tiny monkeys?"

"That's where you're to help me," said Dorothy. "In some of those wild forests in the Gillikin Country are lots of monkeys."

"Big ones," said the Wizard.

"Well, you and I will go there, and we'll get some of the big monkeys, and you will make them small—just three inches high—by means of your magic, and we'll put the little monkeys all in a basket and bring them home with us. Then you'll train them to dance—up here in your room, where no one can see them—and on Ozma's birthday we'll put 'em into the cake and they'll know by that time just what to do."

The Wizard looked at Dorothy with admiring approval, and chuckled again.

"That's really clever, my dear," he said, "and I see no reason why we can't do it, just the way you say, if only we can get the wild monkeys to agree to it."

"Do you think they'll object?" asked the girl.

"Yes; but perhaps we can argue them into it. Anyhow it's worth trying, and I'll help you if you'll agree to let this Surprise Cake be a present to Ozma from you and me together. I've been wondering what *I* could give Ozma, and as I've got to train the monkeys as well as make them small, I think you ought to make me your partner."

"Of course," said Dorothy; "I'll be glad to do so."

"Then, it's a bargain," declared the Wizard. "We must go to seek those monkeys at once, however, for it will take time to train them and we'll have to travel a good way to the Gillikin forests where they live."

"I'm ready to go any time," agreed Dorothy. "Shall we ask Ozma to let us take the Sawhorse?"

The Wizard did not answer that at once. He took time to think of the suggestion.

"No," he answered at length, "the Red Wagon couldn't get through the thick forests and there's some danger to us in going into the wild places to search for monkeys. So I propose we take the Cowardly Lion and the Hungry Tiger. We can ride on their backs as well as in the Red Wagon, and if there is danger to us from other beasts, these two friendly champions will protect us from all harm."

"That's a splendid idea!" exclaimed Dorothy. "Let's go now and ask the Hungry Tiger and the Cowardly Lion if they will help us. Shall we ask Ozma if we can go?"

"I think not," said the Wizard, getting his hat and his black bag of magic tools. "This is to be a surprise for her birthday, and so she mustn't know where we're going. We'll just leave word, in case Ozma inquires for us, that we'll be back in a few days."

Chapter 7

The FOREST of GUGU

In the central western part of the Gillikin Country is a great tangle of trees called Gugu Forest. It is the biggest forest in all Oz and stretches miles and miles in every direction—north, south, east and west. Adjoining it on the east side is a range of rugged mountains covered with underbrush and small twisted trees. You can find this place by looking at the Map of the Land of Oz.

Gugu Forest is the home of most of the wild beasts that inhabit Oz. These are seldom disturbed in their leafy haunts because there is no reason why Oz people should go there, except on rare occasions, and most parts of the forest have never been seen by any eyes but the eyes of the beasts who make their home there. The biggest beasts inhabit the great forest, while the smaller ones live mostly in the mountain underbrush at the east.

Now, you must know that there are laws in the forests, as well as in every other place, and these laws are made by the beasts themselves, and are necessary to keep them from fighting and tearing one another to pieces. In Gugu Forest there is a King—an enormous yellow leopard called "Gugu"—after whom the forest is named. And this King has three other beasts to advise him in keeping the laws and maintaining order—Bru the Bear, Loo the Unicorn and Rango the Gray Ape—who are known as the King's Counselors. All these are fierce and ferocious beasts, and hold their high offices because they are more intelligent and more feared then their fellows.

Since Oz became a fairyland, no man, woman or child ever dies in that land nor is anyone ever sick. Likewise the beasts of the forests never die, so that long years add to their cunning and wisdom, as well as to their size and strength. It is possible for beasts—or even people—to be destroyed, but the task is so difficult that it is seldom attempted. Because it is free from sickness and death is one reason why Oz is a fairyland, but it is doubtful whether those who come to Oz from the outside world, as Dorothy and Button-Bright and Trot and Cap'n Bill and the Wizard did, will live forever or cannot be injured. Even Ozma is not sure about this, and so the guests of Ozma from other lands are always carefully protected from any danger, so as to be on the safe side.

In spite of the laws of the forests there are often fights among the beasts; some of them have lost an eye or an ear or even had a leg torn off. The King and the King's Counselors always punish those who start a fight, but so fierce is the nature of some beasts that they will at times fight in spite of laws and punishment.

Over this vast, wild Forest of Gugu flew two eagles, one morning, and near the center of the jungle the eagles alighted on a branch of a tall tree.

"Here is the place for us to begin our work," said one, who was Ruggedo, the Nome.

"Do many beasts live here?" asked Kiki Aru, the other eagle.

"The forest is full of them," said the Nome. "There are enough beasts right here to enable us to conquer the people of Oz, if we can get them to consent to join us. To do that, we must go among them and tell them our plans, so we must now decide on what shapes we had better assume while in the forest."

"I suppose we must take the shapes of beasts?" said Kiki.

"Of course. But that requires some thought. All kinds of beasts live here, and a yellow leopard is King. If we become leopards, the King will be jealous of us. If we take the forms of some of the other beasts, we shall not command proper respect."

"I wonder if the beasts will attack us?" asked Kiki.

"I'm a Nome, and immortal, so nothing can hurt me," replied Ruggedo.

"I was born in the Land of Oz, so nothing can hurt me," said Kiki.

"But, in order to carry out our plans, we must win the favor of all the animals of the forest."

"Then what shall we do?" asked Kiki.

"Let us mix the shapes of several beasts, so we will not look like any one of them," proposed the wily old Nome. "Let us have the heads of lions, the bodies of monkeys, the wings of eagles and the tails of wild asses, with knobs of gold on the end of them instead of bunches of hair."

"Won't that make a queer combination?" inquired Kiki.

"The queerer the better," declared Ruggedo.

"All right," said Kiki. "You stay here, and I'll fly away to another tree and transform us both, and then we'll climb down our trees and meet in the forest."

"No," said the Nome, "we mustn't separate. You must transform us while we are together."

"I won't do that," asserted Kiki, firmly. "You're trying to get my secret, and I won't let you."

The eyes of the other eagle flashed angrily, but Ruggedo did not dare insist. If he offended this boy, he might have to remain an eagle always and he wouldn't like that. Some day he hoped to be able to learn the secret word of the magical transformations, but just now he must let Kiki have his own way.

"All right," he said gruffly; "do as you please."

So Kiki flew to a tree that was far enough distant so that Ruggedo could not overhear him and said: "I want Ruggedo, the Nome, and myself to have the heads of lions, the bodies of monkeys, the wings of eagles and the tails of wild asses, with knobs of gold on the ends of them instead of bunches of hair—Pyrzqxgl!"

He pronounced the magic word in the proper manner and at once his form changed to the one he had described. He spread his eagle's wings and finding they were strong enough to support his monkey body and lion head he flew swiftly to the tree where he had left Ruggedo. The Nome was also transformed and was climbing down the tree because the branches all around him were so thickly entwined that there was no room between them to fly.

Kiki quickly joined his comrade and it did not take them long to reach the ground.

···—·‹ Chapter 8 ›·····—··

The LI-MON-EAGS MAKE TROUBLE

There had been trouble in the Forest of Gugu that morning. Chipo the Wild Boar had bitten the tail off Arx the Giraffe while the latter had his head among the leaves of a tree, eating his breakfast. Arx kicked with his heels and struck Tirrip, the great Kangaroo, who had a new baby in her pouch. Tirrip knew it was the Wild Boar's fault, so she knocked him over with one powerful blow and then ran away to escape Chipo's sharp tusks. In the chase that followed a giant porcupine stuck fifty sharp quills into the Boar and a chimpanzee in a tree threw a cocoanut at the porcupine that jammed its head into its body.

All this was against the Laws of the Forest, and when the excitement was over, Gugu the Leopard King called his royal Counselors together to decide how best to punish the offenders.

The four lords of the forest were holding solemn council in a small clearing when they saw two strange beasts approaching them—beasts the like of which they had never seen before.

Not one of the four, however, relaxed his dignity or showed by a movement that he was startled. The great Leopard crouched at full length upon a fallen tree-trunk. Bru the Bear sat on his haunches before the King; Rango the Gray Ape stood with his muscular arms folded, and Loo the Unicorn reclined, much as a horse does, between his fellow-counselors. With one consent they remained silent, eyeing with steadfast looks the intruders, who were making their way into their forest domain.

"Well met, Brothers!" said one of the strange beasts, coming to a halt beside the group, while his comrade with hesitation lagged behind.

"We are not brothers," returned the Gray Ape, sternly. "Who are you, and how came you in the Forest of Gugu?"

"We are two Li-Mon-Eags," said Ruggedo, inventing the name. "Our home is in Sky Island, and we have come to earth to warn the forest beasts that the people of Oz are about to make war upon them and enslave them, so that they will become beasts of burden forever after and obey only the will of their two-legged masters."

A low roar of anger arose from the Council of Beasts.

"*Who's* going to do that?" asked Loo the Unicorn, in a high, squeaky voice, at the same time rising to his feet.

"The people of Oz," said Ruggedo.

"But what will *we* be doing?" inquired the Unicorn.

"That's what I've come to talk to you about."

"You needn't talk! We'll fight the Oz people!" screamed the Unicorn. "We'll smash 'em; we'll trample 'em; we'll gore 'em; we'll—"

"Silence!" growled Gugu the King, and Loo obeyed, although still trembling with wrath. The cold, steady gaze of the Leopard wandered over the two strange beasts. "The people of Oz," said he, "have not been our friends; they have not been our enemies. They have let us alone, and we have let them alone. There is no reason for war between us. They have no slaves. They could not use us as slaves if they should conquer us. I think you are telling us lies, you strange Li-Mon-Eag—you mixed-up beast who are neither one thing nor another."

"Oh, on my word, it's the truth!" protested the Nome in the beast's shape. "I wouldn't lie for the world; I—"

"Silence!" again growled Gugu the King; and somehow, even Ruggedo was abashed and obeyed the edict.

"What do you say, Bru?" asked the King, turning to the great Bear, who had until now said nothing.

"How does the Mixed Beast know that what he says is true?" asked the Bear.

"Why, I can fly, you know, having the wings of an Eagle," explained the Nome. "I and my comrade yonder," turning to Kiki, "flew to a grove in Oz, and there we heard the people telling how they will make many ropes to snare you beasts, and then they will surround this forest, and all other forests, and make you prisoners. So we came here to warn you, for being beasts ourselves, although we live in the sky, we are your friends."

The Leopard's lip curled and showed his enormous teeth, sharp as needles. He turned to the Gray Ape.

"What do *you* think, Rango?" he asked.

"Send these mixed beasts away, your Majesty," replied the Gray Ape. "They are mischief-makers."

"Don't do that—don't do that!" cried the Unicorn, nervously. "The stranger said he would tell us what to do. Let him tell us, then. Are we fools, not to heed a warning?"

Gugu the King turned to Ruggedo.

"Speak, Stranger," he commanded.

"Well," said the Nome, "it's this way: The Land of Oz is a fine country. The people of Oz have many good things—houses with soft beds, all sorts of nice-tasting food, pretty clothes, lovely jewels, and many other things that beasts know nothing of. Here in the dark forests the poor beasts have hard work to get enough to eat and to find a bed to rest in. But the beasts are better than the people, and why should they not have all the good things the people have? So I propose that before the Oz people have the time to make all those ropes to snare you with, that all we beasts get together and march against the Oz people and capture them. Then the beasts will become the masters and the people their slaves."

"What good would that do us?" asked Bru the Bear.

"It would save you from slavery, for one thing, and you could enjoy all the fine things the Oz people have."

"Beasts wouldn't know what to do with the things people use," said the Gray Ape.

"But this is only part of my plan," insisted the Nome. "Listen to the rest of it. We two Li-Mon-Eags are powerful magicians. When you have conquered the Oz people we will transform them all into beasts, and send them to the forests to live, and we will transform all the beasts into people, so they can enjoy all the wonderful delights of the Emerald City."

For a moment no beast spoke. Then the King said: "Prove it."

"Prove what?" asked Ruggedo.

"Prove that you can transform us. If you are a magician transform the Unicorn into a man. Then we will believe you. If you fail, we will destroy you."

"All right," said the Nome. "But I'm tired, so I'll let my comrade make the transformation."

Kiki Aru had stood back from the circle, but he had heard all that was said. He now realized that he must make good Ruggedo's boast, so he retreated to the edge of the clearing and whispered the magic word.

Instantly the Unicorn became a fat, chubby little man, dressed in the purple Gillikin costume, and it was hard to tell which was the more astonished, the King, the Bear, the Ape or the former Unicorn.

"It's true!" shouted the man-beast. "Good gracious, look what I am! It's wonderful!"

The King of Beasts now addressed Ruggedo in a more friendly tone.

"We must believe your story, since you have given us proof of your power," said he. "But why, if you are so great a magician, cannot you conquer the Oz people without our help, and so save us the trouble?"

"Alas!" replied the crafty old Nome, "no magician is able to do everything. The transformations are easy to us because we are Li-Mon-Eags, but we cannot fight, or conquer even such weak creatures as the Oz people. But we will stay with you and advise and help you, and we will transform all the Oz people into beasts, when the time comes, and all the beasts into people."

Gugu the King turned to his Counselors.

"How shall we answer this friendly stranger?" he asked.

Loo the former Unicorn was dancing around and cutting capers like a clown.

"On my word, your Majesty," he said, "this being a man is more fun than being a Unicorn."

"You look like a fool," said the Gray Ape.

"Well, I *feel* fine!" declared the man-beast.

"I think I prefer to be a Bear," said Big Bru. "I was born a Bear, and I know a Bear's ways. So I am satisfied to live as a Bear lives."

"That," said the old Nome, "is because you know nothing better. When we have conquered the Oz people, and you become a man, you'll be glad of it."

The immense Leopard rested his chin on the log and seemed thoughtful.

"The beasts of the forest must decide this matter for themselves," he said. "Go you, Rango the Gray Ape, and tell your monkey tribe to order all the forest beasts to assemble in the Great Clearing at sunrise to-morrow. When all are gathered together, this mixed-up Beast who is a magician shall talk to them and tell them what he has told us. Then, if they decide to fight the Oz people, who have declared war on us, I will lead the beasts to battle."

Rango the Gray Ape turned at once and glided swiftly through the forest on his mission. The Bear gave a grunt and walked away. Gugu the King rose and stretched himself. Then he said to Ruggedo: "Meet us at sunrise to-morrow," and with stately stride vanished among the trees.

The man-unicorn, left alone with the strangers, suddenly stopped his foolish prancing.

"You'd better make me a Unicorn again," he said. "I like being a man, but the forest beasts won't know I'm their friend, Loo, and they might tear me in pieces before morning."

So Kiki changed him back to his former shape, and the Unicorn departed to join his people.

Ruggedo the Nome was much pleased with his success.

"To-morrow," he said to Kiki Aru, "we'll win over these beasts and set them to fight and conquer the Oz people. Then I will have my revenge on Ozma and Dorothy and all the rest of my enemies."

"But I am doing all the work," said Kiki.

"Never mind; you're going to be King of Oz," promised Ruggedo.

"Will the big Leopard let me be King?" asked the boy anxiously.

The Nome came close to him and whispered:

"If Gugu the Leopard opposes us, you will transform him into a tree, and then he will be helpless."

"Of course," agreed Kiki, and he said to himself: "I shall also transform this deceitful Nome into a tree, for he lies and I cannot trust him."

Chapter 9

The ISLE of the MAGIC FLOWER

The Glass Cat was a good guide and led Trot and Cap'n Bill by straight and easy paths through all the settled part of the Munchkin Country, and then into the north section where there were few houses, and finally through a wild country where there were no houses or paths at all. But the walking was not difficult and at last they came to the edge of a forest and stopped there to make camp and sleep until morning.

From branches of trees Cap'n Bill made a tiny house that was just big enough for the little girl to crawl into and lie down. But first they ate some of the food Trot had carried in the basket.

"Don't you want some, too?" she asked the Glass Cat.

"No," answered the creature.

"I suppose you'll hunt around an' catch a mouse," remarked Cap'n Bill.

"Me? Catch a mouse! Why should I do that?" inquired the Glass Cat.

"Why, then you could eat it," said the sailor-man.

"I beg to inform you," returned the crystal tabby, "that I do not eat mice. Being transparent, so anyone can see through me, I'd look nice, wouldn't I, with a common mouse inside me? But the fact is that I haven't any stomach or other machinery that would permit me to eat things. The careless magician who made me didn't think I'd need to eat, I suppose."

"Don't you ever get hungry or thirsty?" asked Trot.

"Never. I don't complain, you know, at the way I'm made, for I've never yet seen any living thing as beautiful as I am. I have the handsomest brains in the world. They're pink, and you can see 'em work."

"I wonder," said Trot thoughtfully, as she ate her bread and jam, "if *my* brains whirl around in the same way yours do."

"No; not the same way, surely," returned the Glass Cat; "for, in that case, they'd be as good as *my* brains, except that they're hidden under a thick, boney skull."

"Brains," remarked Cap'n Bill, "is of all kinds and work different ways. But I've noticed that them as thinks that their brains is best is often mistook."

Trot was a little disturbed by sounds from the forest, that night, for many beasts seemed prowling among the trees, but she was confident Cap'n Bill would protect her from harm. And in fact, no beast ventured from the forest to attack them.

At daybreak they were up again, and after a simple breakfast Cap'n Bill said to the Glass Cat:

"Up anchor, Mate, and let's forge ahead. I don't suppose we're far from that Magic Flower, are we?"

"Not far," answered the transparent one, as it led the way into the forest, "but it may take you some time to get to it."

Before long they reached the bank of a river. It was not very wide, at this place, but as they followed the banks in a northerly direction it gradually broadened.

Suddenly the blue-green leaves of the trees changed to a purple hue, and Trot noticed this and said:

"I wonder what made the colors change like that?"

"It's because we have left the Munchkin Country and entered the Gillikin Country," explained the Glass Cat. "Also it's a sign our journey is nearly ended."

The river made a sudden turn, and after the travelers had passed around the bend, they saw that the stream had now become as broad as a small lake, and in the center of the Lake they beheld a little island, not more than fifty feet in extent, either way. Something glittered in the middle of this tiny island, and the Glass Cat paused on the bank and said:

"There is the gold flower-pot containing the Magic Flower, which is very curious and beautiful. If you can get to the island, your task is ended—except to carry the thing home with you."

Cap'n Bill looked at the broad expanse of water and began to whistle a low, quavering tune. Trot knew that the whistle meant that Cap'n Bill was thinking, and the old sailor didn't look at the island as much as he looked at the trees upon the bank where they stood. Presently he took from the big pocket of his coat an axe-blade, wound in an old cloth to keep the sharp edge from cutting his clothing. Then, with a large pocket knife, he cut a small limb from a tree and whittled it into a handle for his axe.

"Sit down, Trot," he advised the girl, as he worked. "I've got quite a job ahead of me now, for I've got to build us a raft."

"What do we need a raft for, Cap'n?"

"Why, to take us to the island. We can't walk under water, in the river bed, as the Glass Cat did, so we must float atop the water."

"Can you make a raft, Cap'n Bill?"

"O' course, Trot, if you give me time."

The little girl sat down on a log and gazed at the Island of the Magic Flower. Nothing else seemed to grow on the tiny isle. There was no tree, no shrub, no grass, even, as far as she could make out from that distance. But the gold pot glittered in the rays of the sun, and Trot could catch glimpses of glowing colors above it, as the Magic Flower changed from one sort to another.

"When I was here before," remarked the Glass Cat, lazily reclining at the girl's feet, "I saw two Kalidahs on this very bank, where they had come to drink."

"What are Kalidahs?" asked the girl.

"The most powerful and ferocious beasts in all Oz. This forest is their especial home, and so there are few other beasts to be found except monkeys. The monkeys are spry enough to keep out of the way of the fierce Kalidahs, which attack all other animals and often fight among themselves."

"Did they try to fight you when you saw 'em?" asked Trot, getting very much excited.

"Yes. They sprang upon me in an instant; but I lay flat on the ground, so I wouldn't get my legs broken by the great weight of the beasts, and when they tried to bite me I laughed at them and jeered them until they were frantic with rage, for they nearly broke their teeth on my hard glass. So, after a time, they discovered they could not hurt me, and went away. It was great fun."

"I hope they don't come here again to drink,—not while we're here, anyhow," returned the girl, "for I'm not made of glass, nor is Cap'n Bill, and if those bad beasts bit us, we'd get hurt."

Cap'n Bill was cutting from the trees some long stakes, making them sharp at one end and leaving a crotch at the other end. These were to bind the logs of his raft together. He had fashioned several and was just finishing another when the Glass Cat cried: "Look out! There's a Kalidah coming toward us."

Trot jumped up, greatly frightened, and looked at the terrible animal as if fascinated by its fierce eyes, for the Kalidah was looking at her, too, and its look wasn't at all friendly. But Cap'n Bill called to her: "Wade into the river, Trot, up to your knees—an' stay there!" and she obeyed him at once. The sailor-man hobbled forward, the stake in one hand and his axe in the other, and got between the girl and the beast, which sprang upon him with a growl of defiance.

Cap'n Bill moved pretty slowly, sometimes, but now he was quick as could be. As the Kalidah sprang toward him he stuck out his wooden leg and the point of it struck the beast between its eyes and sent it rolling upon the ground. Before it could get upon its feet again the sailor pushed the sharp stake right through its body and then with the flat side of the axe he hammered the stake as far into the ground as it would go. By this means he captured the great beast and made it harmless, for try as it would, it could not get away from the stake that held it.

Cap'n Bill knew he could not kill the Kalidah, for no living thing in Oz can be killed, so he stood back and watched the beast wriggle and growl and paw the earth with its sharp claws, and then, satisfied it could not escape, he told Trot to come out of the water again and dry her wet shoes and stockings in the sun.

"Are you sure he can't get away?" she asked.

"I'd bet a cookie on it," said Cap'n Bill, so Trot came ashore and took off her shoes and stockings and laid them on the log to dry, while the sailor-man resumed his work on the raft.

The Kalidah, realizing after many struggles that it could not escape, now became quiet, but it said in a harsh, snarling voice:

"I suppose you think you're clever, to pin me to the ground in this manner. But when my friends, the other Kalidahs, come here, they'll tear you to pieces for treating me this way."

"P'raps," remarked Cap'n Bill, coolly, as he chopped at the logs, "an' p'raps not. When are your folks comin' here?"

"I don't know," admitted the Kalidah. "But when they *do* come, you can't escape them."

"If they hold off long enough, I'll have my raft ready," said Cap'n Bill.

"What are you going to do with a raft?" inquired the beast.

"We're goin' over to that island, to get the Magic Flower."

The huge beast looked at him in surprise a moment, and then it began to laugh. The laugh was a good deal like a roar, and it had a cruel and derisive sound, but it was a laugh nevertheless.

"Good!" said the Kalidah. "Good! Very good! I'm glad

you're going to get the Magic Flower. But what will you do with it?"

"We're going to take it to Ozma, as a present on her birthday."

The Kalidah laughed again; then it became sober. "If you get to the land on your raft before my people can catch you," it said, "you will be safe from us. We can swim like ducks, so the girl couldn't have escaped me by getting into the water; but Kalidahs don't go to that island over there."

"Why not?" asked Trot.

The beast was silent.

"Tell us the reason," urged Cap'n Bill.

"Well, it's the Isle of the Magic Flower," answered the Kalidah, "and we don't care much for magic. If you hadn't had a magic leg, instead of a meat one, you couldn't have knocked me over so easily and stuck this wooden pin through me."

"I've been to the Magic Isle," said the Glass Cat, "and I've watched the Magic Flower bloom, and I'm sure it's too pretty to be left in that lonely place where only beasts prowl around it and no else sees it. So we're going to take it away to the Emerald City."

"I don't care," the beast replied in a surly tone. "We Kalidahs would be just as contented if there wasn't a flower in our forest. What good are the things anyhow?"

"Don't you like pretty things?" asked Trot.

"No."

"You ought to admire my pink brains, anyhow," declared the Glass Cat. "They're beautiful and you can see 'em work."

The beast only growled in reply, and Cap'n Bill, having now cut all his logs to a proper size, began to roll them to the water's edge and fasten them together.

....——◄ Chapter 10 ►...——..

STUCK FAST

The day was nearly gone when, at last, the raft was ready.

"It ain't so very big," said the old sailor, "but I don't weigh much, an' you, Trot, don't weigh half as much as I do, an' the glass pussy don't count."

"But it's safe, isn't it?" inquired the girl.

"Yes; it's good enough to carry us to the island an' back again, an' that's about all we can expect of it."

Saying this, Cap'n Bill pushed the raft into the water, and when it was afloat, stepped upon it and held out his hand to Trot, who quickly followed him. The Glass Cat boarded the raft last of all.

The sailor had cut a long pole, and had also whittled a flat paddle, and with these he easily propelled the raft across the river. As they approached the island, the Wonderful Flower became more plainly visible, and they quickly decided that the Glass Cat had not praised it too highly. The colors of the flowers that bloomed in quick succession were strikingly bright and beautiful, and the shapes of the blossoms were varied and curious. Indeed, they did not resemble ordinary flowers at all.

So intently did Trot and Cap'n Bill gaze upon the golden flower-pot that held the Magic Flower that they scarcely noticed the island itself until the raft beached upon its sands. But then the girl exclaimed: "How funny it is, Cap'n Bill, that nothing else grows here excep' the Magic Flower."

Then the sailor glanced at the island and saw that it was all bare ground, without a weed, a stone or a blade of grass. Trot, eager to examine the Flower closer, sprang from the raft and ran up the bank until she reached the golden flower-pot. Then she stood beside it motionless and filled with wonder. Cap'n Bill joined her, coming more leisurely, and he, too, stood in silent admiration for a time.

"Ozma will like this," remarked the Glass Cat, sitting down to watch the shifting hues of the flowers. "I'm sure she won't have as fine a birthday present from anyone else."

"Do you 'spose it's very heavy, Cap'n? And can we get it home without breaking it?" asked Trot anxiously.

"Well, I've lifted many bigger things than that," he replied; "but let's see what it weighs."

He tried to take a step forward, but could not lift his meat foot from the ground. His wooden leg seemed free enough, but the other would not budge.

"I seem stuck, Trot," he said, with a perplexed look at his foot. "It ain't mud, an' it ain't glue, but somethin's holdin' me down."

The girl attempted to lift her own feet, to go nearer to her friend, but the ground held them as fast as it held Cap'n Bill's foot. She tried to slide them, or to twist them around, but it was no use; she could not move either foot a hair's breadth.

"This is funny!" she exclaimed. "What do you 'spose has happened to us, Cap'n Bill?"

"I'm tryin' to make out," he answered. "Take off your shoes, Trot. P'raps it's the leather soles that's stuck to the ground."

She leaned down and unlaced her shoes, but found she could not pull her feet out of them. The Glass Cat, which was walking around as naturally as ever, now said:

"Your foot has got roots to it, Cap'n, and I can see the roots going into the ground, where they spread out in all directions. It's the same way with Trot. That's why you can't move. The roots hold you fast."

Cap'n Bill was rather fat and couldn't see his own feet

very well, but he squatted down and examined Trot's feet and decided that the Glass Cat was right.

"This is hard luck," he declared, in a voice that showed he was uneasy at the discovery. "We're pris'ners, Trot, on this funny island, an' I'd like to know how we're ever goin' to get loose, so's we can get home again."

"Now I know why the Kalidah laughed at us," said the girl, "and why he said none of the beasts ever came to this island. The horrid creature knew we'd be caught, and wouldn't warn us."

In the meantime, the Kalidah, although pinned fast to the earth by Cap'n Bill's stake, was facing the island, and now the ugly expression which passed over its face when it defied and sneered at Cap'n Bill and Trot, had changed to one of amusement and curiosity. When it saw the adventurers had actually reached the island and were standing beside the Magic Flower, it heaved a breath of satisfaction—a long, deep breath that swelled the deep chest until the beast could feel the stake that held him move a little, as if withdrawing itself from the ground.

"Ah ha!" murmured the Kalidah, "a little more of this will set me free and allow me to escape!"

So he began breathing as hard as he could, puffing out his chest as much as possible with each indrawing breath, and by doing this he managed to raise the stake with each powerful breath, until at last the Kalidah—using the muscles of his four legs as well as his deep breaths—found itself free of the sandy soil. The stake was sticking right through him, however, so he found a rock deeply set in the bank and pressed the sharp point of the stake upon the surface of this rock until he had driven it clear through his body. Then, by getting the stake tangled among some thorny bushes, and wiggling his body, he managed to draw it out altogether.

"There!" he exclaimed, "except for those two holes in me, I'm as good as ever; but I must admit that that old wooden-legged fellow saved both himself and the girl by making me a prisoner."

Now the Kalidahs, although the most disagreeable creatures in the Land of Oz, were nevertheless magical inhabitants of a magical Fairyland, and in their natures a certain amount of good was mingled with the evil. This one was not very revengeful, and now that his late foes were in danger of perishing, his anger against them faded away.

"Our own Kalidah King," he reflected, "has certain magical powers of his own. Perhaps he knows how to fill up these two holes in my body."

So without paying any more attention to Trot and Cap'n Bill than they were paying to him, he entered the forest and trotted along a secret path that led to the hidden lair of all the Kalidahs.

While the Kalidah was making good its escape Cap'n Bill took his pipe from his pocket and filled it with tobacco and lighted it. Then, as he puffed out the smoke, he tried to think what could be done.

"The Glass Cat seems all right," he said, "an' my wooden leg didn't take roots and grow, either. So it's only flesh that gets caught."

"It's magic that does it, Cap'n!"

"I know, Trot, and that's what sticks me. We're livin' in a magic country, but neither of us knows any magic an' so we can't help ourselves."

"Couldn't the Wizard of Oz help us—or Glinda the Good?" asked the little girl.

"Ah, now we're beginnin' to reason," he answered. "I'd probably thought o' that, myself, in a minute more. By good luck the Glass Cat is free, an' so it can run back to the Emerald City an' tell the Wizard about our fix, an' ask him to come an' help us get loose."

"Will you go?" Trot asked the cat, speaking very earnestly.

"I'm no messenger, to be sent here and there," asserted the curious animal in a sulky tone of voice.

"Well," said Cap'n Bill, "you've got to go home, anyhow, 'cause you don't want to stay here, I take it. And, when you get home, it wouldn't worry you much to tell the Wizard what's happened to us."

"That's true," said the cat, sitting on its haunches and lazily washing its face with one glass paw. "I don't mind telling the Wizard—when I get home."

"Won't you go now?" pleaded Trot. "We don't want to stay here any longer than we can help, and everybody in Oz will be interested in you, and call you a hero, and say nice things about you because you helped your friends out of trouble."

That was the best way to manage the Glass Cat, which was so vain that it loved to be praised.

"I'm going home right away," said the creature, "and I'll tell the Wizard to come and help you."

Saying this, it walked down to the water and disappeared under the surface. Not being able to manage the raft alone, the Glass Cat walked on the bottom of the river as it had done when it visited the island before, and soon they saw it appear on the farther bank and trot into the forest, where it was quickly lost to sight among the trees.

Then Trot heaved a deep sigh.

"Cap'n," said she, "we're in a bad fix. There's nothing here to eat, and we can't even lie down to sleep. Unless the Glass Cat hurries, and the Wizard hurries, I don't know what's going to become of us!"

···—·◄ Chapter 11 ►···—··

The BEASTS of the FOREST of GUGU

That was a wonderful gathering of wild animals in the Forest of Gugu next sunrise. Rango, the Gray Ape, had even called his monkey sentinels away from the forest edge, and every beast, little and big, was in the great clearing where meetings were held on occasions of great importance.

In the center of the clearing stood a great shelving rock, having a flat, inclined surface, and on this sat the stately Leopard Gugu, who was King of the Forest. On the ground beneath him squatted Bru the Bear, Loo the Unicorn, and Rango the Gray Ape, the King's three Counselors, and in front of them stood the two strange beasts who had called themselves Li-Mon-Eags, but were really the transformations of Ruggedo the Nome, and Kiki Aru the Hyup.

Then came the beasts—rows and rows and rows of them! The smallest beasts were nearest the King's rock throne; then there were wolves and foxes, lynxes and hyenas, and the like; behind them were gathered the monkey tribes, who were hard to keep in order because they teased the other animals and were full of mischievous tricks. Back of the monkeys were the pumas, jaguars, tigers and lions, and their kind; next the bears, all sizes and colors; after them bisons, wild asses, zebras and unicorns; farther on the rhinoceri and hippopotami, and at the far edge of the forest, close to the trees that shut in the clearing, was a row of thick-skinned elephants, still as statues but with eyes bright and intelligent.

Many other kinds of beasts, too numerous to mention, were there, and some were unlike any beasts we see in the menageries and zoos in our country. Some were from the mountains west of the forest, and some from the plains at the east, and some from the river; but all present acknowledged the leadership of Gugu, who for many years had ruled them wisely and forced all to obey the laws.

When the beasts had taken their places in the clearing and the rising sun was shooting its first bright rays over the treetops, King Gugu rose on his throne. The Leopard's giant form, towering above all the others, caused a sudden hush to fall on the assemblage.

"Brothers," he said in his deep voice, "a stranger has come among us, a beast of curious form who is a great magician and is able to change the shapes of men or beasts at his will. This stranger has come to us, with another of his kind, from out of the sky, to warn us of a danger which threatens us all, and to offer us a way to escape from that danger. He says he is our friend, and he has proved to me and to my Counselors his magic powers. Will you listen to what he has to say to you—to the message he has brought from the sky?"

"Let him speak!" came in a great roar from the great company of assembled beasts.

So Ruggedo the Nome sprang upon the flat rock beside Gugu the King, and another roar, gentle this time, showed how astonished the beasts were at the sight of his curious form. His lion's face was surrounded by a mane of pure white hair; his eagle's wings were attached to the shoulders of his monkey body and were so long that they nearly touched the ground; he had powerful arms and legs in addition to the wings, and at the end of his long, strong tail was a golden ball. Never had any beast beheld such a curious creature before, and so the very sight of the stranger, who was said to be a great magician, filled all present with awe and wonder.

Kiki stayed down below and, half hidden by the shelf of rock, was scarcely noticed. The boy realized that the old Nome was helpless without his magic power, but he also realized that Ruggedo was the best talker. So he was willing the Nome should take the lead.

"Beasts of the Forest of Gugu," began Ruggedo the Nome, "my comrade and I are your friends. We are magicians, and from our home in the sky we can look down into the Land of Oz and see everything that is going on. Also we can hear what the people below us are saying. That is how we heard Ozma, who rules the Land of Oz, say to her people: 'The beasts in the Forest of Gugu are lazy and are of no use to us. Let us go to their forest and make them all our prisoners. Let us tie them with ropes, and beat them with sticks, until they work for us and become our willing slaves.' And when the people heard Ozma of Oz say this, they were glad and raised a great shout and said: 'We will do it! We will make the beasts of the Forest of Gugu our slaves!'"

The wicked old Nome could say no more, just then, for such a fierce roar of anger rose from the multitude of beasts that his voice was drowned by the clamor. Finally the roar died away, like distant thunder, and Ruggedo the Nome went on with his speech.

"Having heard the Oz people plot against your liberty, we watched to see what they would do, and saw them all begin making ropes—ropes long and short—with which to snare our friends the beasts. You are angry, but we also were angry, for when the Oz people became the enemies of the beasts they also became our enemies; for we, too, are beasts, although we live in the sky. And my comrade and I said: 'We will save our friends and have revenge on the Oz people,' and so we came here to tell you of your danger and of our plan to save you."

"We can save ourselves," cried an old Elephant. "We can fight."

"The Oz people are fairies, and you can't fight against magic unless you also have magic," answered the Nome.

"Tell us your plan!" shouted the huge Tiger, and the other beasts echoed his words, crying: "Tell us your plan."

"My plan is simple," replied Ruggedo. "By our magic we will transform all you animals into men and women—like the Oz people—and we will transform all the Oz people into beasts. You can then live in the fine houses of the Land of Oz, and eat the fine food of the Oz people, and wear their fine clothes, and sing and dance and be happy. And the Oz people, having become beasts, will have to live here in the forest and hunt and fight for food, and often go hungry, as you now do, and have no place to sleep but a bed of leaves or a hole in the ground. Having become men and women, you beasts will have all the comforts you desire, and having become beasts, the Oz people will be very miserable. That is our plan, and if you agree to it, we will all march at once into the Land of Oz and quickly conquer our enemies."

When the stranger ceased speaking, a great silence fell on the assemblage, for the beasts were thinking of what he had said. Finally one of the walrus asked:

"Can you really transform beasts into men, and men into beasts?"

"He can—he can!" cried Loo the Unicorn, prancing up and down in an excited manner. "He transformed *me*, only last evening, and he can transform us all."

Gugu the King now stepped forward.

"You have heard the stranger speak," said he, "and now you must answer him. It is for you to decide. Shall we agree to this plan, or not?"

"Yes!" shouted some of the animals.

"No!" shouted others.

And some were yet silent.

Gugu looked around the great circle.

"Take more time to think," he suggested. "Your answer is very important. Up to this time we have had no trouble with the Oz people, but we are proud and free, and never will become slaves. Think carefully, and when you are ready to answer, I will hear you."

·—·« Chapter 12 »·—··

KIKI USES HIS MAGIC

Then arose a great confusion of sounds as all the animals began talking to their fellows. The monkeys chattered and the bears growled and the voices of the jaguars and lions rumbled, and the wolves yelped and the elephants had to trumpet loudly to make their voices heard. Such a hubbub had never been known in the forest before, and each beast argued with his neighbor until it seemed the noise would never cease.

Ruggedo the Nome waved his arms and fluttered his wings to try to make them listen to him again, but the beasts paid no attention. Some wanted to fight the Oz people, some wanted to be transformed, and some wanted to do nothing at all.

The growling and confusion had grown greater than ever when in a flash silence fell on all the beasts present, the arguments were hushed, and all gazed in astonishment at a strange sight.

For into the circle strode a great Lion—bigger and more powerful than any other lion there—and on his back rode a little girl who smiled fearlessly at the multitude of beasts. And behind the Lion and the little girl came another beast—a monstrous Tiger, who bore upon his back a funny little man carrying a black bag. Right past the rows of wondering beasts the strange animals walked, advancing until they stood just before the rock throne of Gugu.

Then the little girl and the funny little man dismounted, and the great Lion demanded in a loud voice:

"Who is King in this forest?"

"I am!" answered Gugu, looking steadily at the other. "I am Gugu the Leopard, and I am King of this forest."

"Then I greet your Majesty with great respect," said the Lion. "Perhaps you have heard of me, Gugu. I am called the 'Cowardly Lion,' and I am King of all Beasts, the world over."

Gugu's eyes flashed angrily.

"Yes," said he, "I have heard of you. You have long claimed to be King of Beasts, but no beast who is a coward can be King over me."

"He isn't a coward, your Majesty," asserted the little girl, "he's just cowardly, that's all."

Gugu looked at her. All the other beasts were looking at her, too.

"Who are you?" asked the King.

"Me? Oh, I'm just Dorothy," she answered.

"How dare you come here?" demanded the King.

"Why, I'm not afraid to go anywhere, if the Cowardly Lion is with me," she said. "I know him pretty well, and so I can trust him. He's always afraid, when we get into trouble, and that's why he's cowardly; but he's a terrible fighter, and that's why he isn't a coward. He doesn't like to fight, you know, but when he *has* to, there isn't any beast living that can conquer him."

Gugu the King looked at the big, powerful form of the Cowardly Lion, and knew she spoke the truth. Also the other Lions of the forest now came forward and bowed low before the strange Lion.

"We welcome your Majesty," said one. "We have known you many years ago, before you went to live at the Emerald City, and we have seen you fight the terrible Kalidahs and conquer them, so we know you are the King of all Beasts."

"It is true," replied the Cowardly Lion; "but I did not come here to rule the beasts of this forest. Gugu is King here, and I believe he is a good King and just and wise. I come, with my friends, to be the guest of Gugu, and I hope we are welcome."

That pleased the great Leopard, who said very quickly:

"Yes; you, at least, are welcome to my forest. But who are these strangers with you?"

"Dorothy has introduced herself," replied the Lion, "and you are sure to like her when you know her better. This man is the Wizard of Oz, a friend of mine who can do wonderful tricks of magic. And here is my true and tried friend, the Hungry Tiger, who lives with me in the Emerald City."

"Is he *always* hungry?" asked Loo the Unicorn.

"I am," replied the Tiger, answering the question himself. "I am always hungry for fat babies."

"Can't you find any fat babies in Oz to eat?" inquired Loo the Unicorn.

"There are plenty of them, of course," said the Tiger, "but unfortunately I have such a tender conscience that it won't allow me to eat babies. So I'm always hungry for 'em and never can eat 'em, because my conscience won't let me."

Now of all the surprised beasts in that clearing, not one was so much surprised at the sudden appearance of these four strangers as Ruggedo the Nome. He was frightened, too, for he recognized them as his most powerful enemies; but he also realized that they could not know he was the former King of the Nomes, because of the beast's form he wore, which disguised him so effectually. So he took courage and resolved that the Wizard and Dorothy should not defeat his plans.

It was hard to tell, just yet, what the vast assemblage of beasts thought of the new arrivals. Some glared angrily at them, but more of them seemed to be curious and wondering. All were interested, however, and they kept very quiet and listened carefully to all that was said.

Kiki Aru, who had remained unnoticed in the shadow of the rock, was at first more alarmed by the coming of the strangers than even Ruggedo was, and the boy told himself that unless he acted quickly and without waiting to ask the advice of the old Nome, their conspiracy was likely to be discovered and all their plans to conquer and rule Oz be defeated. Kiki didn't like the way Ruggedo acted either, for the former King of the Nomes wanted to do everything his own way, and made the boy, who alone possessed the power of transformations, obey his orders as if he were a slave.

Another thing that disturbed Kiki Aru was the fact that a real Wizard had arrived, who was said to possess many magical powers, and this Wizard carried his tools in a black bag, and was the friend of the Oz people, and so would probably try to prevent war between the beasts of the forest and the people of Oz.

All these things passed through the mind of the Hyup boy while the Cowardly Lion and Gugu the King were talking together, and that was why he now began to do several strange things.

He had found a place, near to the point where he stood, where there was a deep hollow in the rock, so he put his face into this hollow and whispered softly, so he would not be heard:

"I want the Wizard of Oz to become a fox—Pyrzqxgl!"

The Wizard, who had stood smilingly beside his friends, suddenly felt his form change to that of a fox, and his black bag fell to the ground. Kiki reached out an arm and seized the bag, and the Fox cried as loud as it could:

"Treason! There's a traitor here with magic powers!"

Everyone was startled at this cry, and Dorothy, seeing her old friend's plight, screamed and exclaimed: "Mercy me!"

But the next instant the little girl's form had changed to that of a lamb with fleecy white wool, and Dorothy was too bewildered to do anything but look around her in wonder.

The Cowardly Lion's eyes now flashed fire; he crouched low and lashed the ground with his tail and gazed around to discover who the treacherous magician might be. But Kiki, who had kept his face in the hollow rock, again whispered the magic word, and the great lion disappeared and in his place stood a little boy dressed in Munchkin costume. The little Munchkin boy was as angry as the lion had been, but he was small and helpless.

Ruggedo the Nome saw what was happening and was afraid Kiki would spoil all his plans, so he leaned over the rock and shouted: "Stop, Kiki—stop!"

Kiki would not stop, however. Instead, he transformed the Nome into a goose, to Ruggedo's horror and dismay. But the Hungry Tiger had witnessed all these transformations, and he was watching to see which of those present was to blame for them. When Ruggedo spoke to Kiki, the Hungry Tiger knew that he was the magician, so he made a sudden spring and hurled his great body full upon the form of the Li-Mon-Eag crouching against the rock. Kiki didn't see the Tiger coming because his face was still in the hollow, and the heavy body of the tiger bore him to the earth just as he said "Pyrzqxgl!" for the fifth time.

So now the tiger which was crushing him changed to a rabbit, and relieved of its weight, Kiki sprang up and, spreading his eagle's wings, flew into the branches of a tree, where no beast could easily reach him. He was not an instant too quick in doing this, for Gugu the King had crouched on the rock's edge and was about to spring on the boy.

From his tree Kiki transformed Gugu into a fat Gillikin woman, and laughed aloud to see how the woman pranced with rage, and how astonished all the beasts were at their King's new shape.

The beasts were frightened, too, fearing they would share the fate of Gugu, so a stampede began when Rango the Gray Ape sprang into the forest, and Bru the Bear and Loo the Unicorn followed as quickly as they could. The elephants backed into the forest, and all the other animals, big and little, rushed after them, scattering through the jungles until the clearing was far behind. The monkeys scrambled into the trees and swung themselves from limb to limb, to avoid being trampled upon by the bigger beasts, and they were so quick that they distanced all the rest. A panic of fear seemed to have overtaken the forest people and they got as far away from the terrible Magician as they possibly could.

But the transformed ones stayed in the clearing, being so astonished and bewildered by their new shapes that they could only look at one another in a dazed and helpless fashion, although each one was greatly annoyed at the trick that had been played on him.

"Who are you?" the Munchkin boy asked the Rabbit; and "Who are you?" the Fox asked the Lamb; and "Who are you?" the Rabbit asked the fat Gillikin woman.

"I'm Dorothy," said the woolly Lamb.

"I'm the Wizard," said the Fox.

"I'm the Cowardly Lion," said the Munchkin boy.

"I'm the Hungry Tiger," said the Rabbit.

"I'm Gugu the King," said the fat Woman.

But when they asked the Goose who he was, Ruggedo the Nome would not tell them.

"I'm just a Goose," he replied, "and what I was before, I cannot remember."

Chapter 13

The LOSS of the BLACK BAG

K iki Aru, in the form of the Li-Mon-Eag, had scrambled into the high, thick branches of the tree, so no one could see him, and there he opened the Wizard's black bag, which he had carried away in his flight. He was curious to see what the Wizard's magic tools looked like, and hoped he could use some of them and so secure more power; but after he had taken the articles, one by one, from the bag, he had to admit they were puzzles to him. For, unless he understood their uses, they were of no value whatever. Kiki Aru, the Hyup boy, was no wizard or magician at all, and could do nothing unusual except to use the Magic Word he had stolen from his father on

Mount Munch. So he hung the Wizard's black bag on a branch of the tree and then climbed down to the lower limbs that he might see what the victims of his transformations were doing.

They were all on top of the flat rock, talking together in tones so low that Kiki could not hear what they said.

"This is certainly a misfortune," remarked the Wizard in the Fox's form, "but our transformations are a sort of enchantment which is very easy to break—when you know how and have the tools to do it with. The tools are in my black bag; but where is the bag?"

No one knew that, for none had seen Kiki Aru fly away with it.

"Let's look and see if we can find it," suggested Dorothy the Lamb.

So they left the rock, and all of them searched the clearing high and low without finding the bag of magic tools. The Goose searched as earnestly as the others, for if he could discover it, he meant to hide it where the Wizard could never find it, because if the Wizard changed him back to his proper form, along with the others, he would then be recognized as Ruggedo the Nome, and they would send him out of the Land of Oz and so ruin all his hopes of conquest.

Ruggedo was not really sorry, now that he thought about it, that Kiki had transformed all these Oz folks. The forest beasts, it was true, had been so frightened that they would now never consent to be transformed into men, but Kiki could transform them against their will, and once they were all in human forms, it would not be impossible to induce them to conquer the Oz people.

So all was not lost, thought the old Nome, and the best thing for him to do was to rejoin the Hyup boy who had the secret of the transformations. So, having made sure the Wizard's black bag was not in the clearing, the Goose wandered away through the trees when the others were not looking, and when out of their hearing, he began calling, "Kiki Aru! Kiki Aru! Quack—quack! Kiki Aru!"

The Boy and the Woman, the Fox, the Lamb, and the Rabbit, not being able to find the bag, went back to the rock, all feeling exceedingly strange.

"Where's the Goose?" asked the Wizard.

"He must have run away," replied Dorothy. "I wonder who he was?"

"I think," said Gugu the King, who was the fat Woman, "that the Goose was the stranger who proposed that we make war upon the Oz people. If so, his transformation was merely a trick to deceive us, and he has now gone to join his comrade, that wicked Li-Mon-Eag who obeyed all his commands."

"What shall we do now?" asked Dorothy. "Shall we go back to the Emerald City, as we are, and then visit Glinda the Good and ask her to break the enchantments?"

"I think so," replied the Wizard Fox. "And we can take Gugu the King with us, and have Glinda restore him to his natural shape. But I hate to leave my bag of magic tools behind me, for without it I shall lose much of my power as a Wizard. Also, if I go back to the Emerald City in the shape of a Fox, the Oz people will think I'm a poor Wizard and will lose their respect for me."

"Let us make still another search for your tools," suggested the Cowardly Lion, "and then, if we fail to find the black bag anywhere in this forest, we must go back home as we are."

"Why did you come here, anyway?" inquired Gugu.

"We wanted to borrow a dozen monkeys, to use on Ozma's birthday," explained the Wizard. "We were going to make them small, and train them to do tricks, and put them inside Ozma's birthday cake."

"Well," said the Forest King, "you would have to get the consent of Rango the Gray Ape, to do that. He commands all the tribes of monkeys."

"I'm afraid it's too late, now," said Dorothy, regretfully. "It was a splendid plan, but we've got troubles of our own, and I don't like being a lamb at all."

"You're nice and fuzzy," said the Cowardly Lion.

"That's nothing," declared Dorothy. "I've never been 'specially proud of myself, but I'd rather be the way I was born than anything else in the whole world."

The Glass Cat, although it had some disagreeable ways and manners, nevertheless realized that Trot and Cap'n Bill were its friends and so was quite disturbed at the fix it had gotten them into by leading them to the Isle of the Magic Flower. The ruby heart of the Glass Cat was cold and hard, but still it was a heart, and to have a heart of any sort is to have some consideration for others. But the queer transparent creature didn't want Trot and Cap'n Bill to know it was sorry for them, and therefore it moved very slowly until it had crossed the river and was out of sight among the trees of the forest. Then it headed straight toward the Emerald City, and trotted so fast that it was like a crystal streak crossing the valleys and plains. Being glass, the cat was tireless, and with no reason to delay its journey, it reached Ozma's palace in wonderfully quick time.

"Where's the Wizard?" it asked the Pink Kitten, which was curled up in the sunshine on the lowest step of the palace entrance.

"Don't bother me," lazily answered the Pink Kitten, whose name was Eureka.

"I must find the Wizard at once!" said the Glass Cat.

"Then find him," advised Eureka, and went to sleep again.

The Glass Cat darted up the stairway and came upon Toto, Dorothy's little black dog.

"Where's the Wizard?" asked the Cat.

"Gone on a journey with Dorothy," replied Toto.

"When did they go, and where have they gone?" demanded the Cat.

"They went yesterday, and I heard them say they would

go to the Great Forest in the Munchkin Country."

"Dear me," said the Glass Cat; "that is a long journey."

"But they rode on the Hungry Tiger and the Cowardly Lion," explained Toto, "and the Wizard carried his black bag of magic tools."

The Glass Cat knew the Great Forest of Gugu well, for it had traveled through this forest many times in its journeys through the Land of Oz. And it reflected that the Forest of Gugu was nearer to the Isle of the Magic Flower than the Emerald City was, and so, if it could manage to find the Wizard, it could lead him across the Gillikin Country to where Trot and Cap'n Bill were prisoned. It was a wild country and little traveled, but the Glass Cat knew every path. So very little time need be lost, after all.

Without stopping to ask any more questions the Cat darted out of the palace and away from the Emerald City, taking the most direct route to the Forest of Gugu. Again the creature flashed through the country like a streak of light, and it would surprise you to know how quickly it reached the edge of the Great Forest.

There were no monkey guards among the trees to cry out a warning, and this was so unusual that it astonished the Glass Cat. Going farther into the forest it presently came upon a wolf, which at first bounded away in terror. But then, seeing it was only a Glass Cat, the Wolf stopped, and the Cat could see it was trembling, as if from a terrible fright.

"What's the matter?" asked the Cat.

"A dreadful Magician has come among us!" exclaimed the Wolf, "and he's changing the forms of all the beasts—quick as a wink—and making them all his slaves."

The Glass Cat smiled and said:

"Why, that's only the Wizard of Oz. He may be having some fun with you forest people, but the Wizard wouldn't hurt a beast for anything."

"I don't mean the Wizard," explained the Wolf. "And if the Wizard of Oz is that funny little man who rode a great Tiger into the clearing, he's been transformed himself by the terrible Magician."

"The Wizard transformed? Why, that's impossible," declared the Glass Cat.

"No; it isn't. I saw him with my own eyes, changed into the form of a Fox, and the girl who was with him was changed to a woolly Lamb."

The Glass Cat was indeed surprised.

"When did that happen?" it asked.

"Just a little while ago in the clearing. All the animals had met there, but they ran away when the Magician began his transformations, and I'm thankful I escaped with my natural shape. But I'm still afraid, and I'm going somewhere to hide."

With this the Wolf ran on, and the Glass Cat, which knew where the big clearing was, went toward it. But now it walked more slowly, and its pink brains rolled and tumbled around at a great rate because it was thinking over the amazing news the Wolf had told it.

When the Glass Cat reached the clearing, it saw a Fox, a Lamb, a Rabbit, a Munchkin boy and a fat Gillikin woman, all wandering around in an aimless sort of way, for they were again searching for the black bag of magic tools.

The Cat watched them a moment and then it walked slowly into the open space. At once the Lamb ran toward it, crying:

"Oh, Wizard, here's the Glass Cat!"

"Where, Dorothy?" asked the Fox.

"Here!"

The Boy and the Woman and the Rabbit now joined the Fox and the Lamb, and they all stood before the Glass Cat and speaking together, almost like a chorus, asked: "Have you seen the black bag?"

"Often," replied the Glass Cat, "but not lately."

"It's lost," said the Fox, "and we must find it."

"Are you the Wizard?" asked the Cat.

"Yes."

"And who are these others?"

"I'm Dorothy," said the Lamb.

"I'm the Cowardly Lion," said the Munchkin boy.

"I'm the Hungry Tiger," said the Rabbit.

"I'm Gugu, King of the Forest," said the fat Woman.

The Glass Cat sat on its hind legs and began to laugh.

"My, what a funny lot!" exclaimed the Creature. "Who played this joke on you?"

"It's no joke at all," declared the Wizard. "It was a cruel, wicked transformation, and the Magician that did it has the head of a lion, the body of a monkey, the wings of an eagle and a round ball on the end of his tail."

The Glass Cat laughed again. "That Magician must look funnier than you do," it said. "Where is he now?"

"Somewhere in the forest," said the Cowardly Lion. "He just jumped into that tall maple tree over there, for he can climb like a monkey and fly like an eagle, and then he disappeared in the forest."

"And there was another Magician, just like him, who was his friend," added Dorothy, "but they probably quarreled, for the wickedest one changed his friend into the form of a Goose."

"What became of the Goose?" asked the Cat, looking around.

"He must have gone away to find his friend," answered Gugu the King. "But a Goose can't travel very fast, so we could easily find him if we wanted to."

"The worst thing of all," said the Wizard, "is that my black bag is lost. It disappeared when I was transformed. If I could find it I could easily break these enchantments by means of my magic, and we would resume our own forms again. Will you help us search for the black bag, Friend Cat?"

"Of course," replied the Glass Cat. "But I expect the strange Magician carried it away with him. If he's a magician, he knows you need that bag, and perhaps he's afraid of your magic. So he's probably taken the bag with him, and you won't see it again unless you find the Magician."

"That sounds reasonable," remarked the Lamb, which was Dorothy. "Those pink brains of yours seem to be working pretty well to-day."

"If the Glass Cat is right," said the Wizard in a solemn voice, "there's more trouble ahead of us. That Magician is dangerous, and if we go near him he may transform us into shapes not as nice as these."

"I don't see how we could be any *worse* off," growled Gugu, who was indignant because he was forced to appear in the form of a fat woman.

"Anyway," said the Cowardly Lion, "our best plan is to find the Magician and try to get the black bag from him. We may manage to steal it, or perhaps we can argue him into giving it to us."

"Why not find the Goose, first?" asked Dorothy. "The Goose will be angry at the Magician, and he may be able to help us."

"That isn't a bad idea," returned the Wizard. "Come on, Friends; let's find that Goose. We will separate and search in different directions, and the first to find the Goose must bring him here, where we will all meet again in an hour."

Chapter 14

The WIZARD LEARNS the MAGIC WORD

Now, the Goose was the transformation of old Ruggedo, who was at one time King of the Nomes, and he was even more angry at Kiki Aru than were the others whose shapes had been changed. The Nome detested anything in the way of a bird, because birds lay eggs and eggs are feared by all the Nomes more than anything else in the world. A goose is a foolish bird, too, and Ruggedo was dreadfully ashamed of the shape he was forced to wear. And it would make him shudder to reflect that the Goose might lay an egg!

So the Nome was afraid of himself and afraid of every-thing around him. If an egg touched him he could then be destroyed, and almost any animal he met in the forest might easily conquer him. And that would be the end of old Ruggedo the Nome.

Aside from these fears, however, he was filled with anger against Kiki, whom he had meant to trap by cleverly stealing from him the Magic Word. The boy must have been crazy to spoil everything the way he did, but Ruggedo knew that the arrival of the Wizard had scared Kiki, and he was not sorry the boy had transformed the Wizard and Dorothy and made them helpless. It was his own transformation that annoyed him and made him indignant, so he ran about the forest hunting for Kiki, so that he might get a better shape and coax the boy to follow his plans to conquer the Land of Oz.

Kiki Aru hadn't gone very far away, for he had surprised himself as well as the others by the quick transformations and was puzzled as to what to do next. Ruggedo the Nome was overbearing and tricky, and Kiki knew he was not to be depended on; but the Nome could plan and plot, which the Hyup boy was not wise enough to do, and so, when he looked down through the branches of a tree and saw a Goose waddling along below and heard it cry out, "Kiki Aru! Quack—quack! Kiki Aru!" the boy answered in a low voice, "Here I am," and swung himself down to the lowest limb of the tree.

The Goose looked up and saw him.

"You've bungled things in a dreadful way!" exclaimed the Goose. "Why did you do it?"

"Because I wanted to," answered Kiki. "You acted as if I was your slave, and I wanted to show these forest people that I am more powerful than you."

The Goose hissed softly, but Kiki did not hear that.

Old Ruggedo quickly recovered his wits and muttered to himself: "This boy is the goose, although it is I who wear the goose's shape. I will be gentle with him now, and fierce with him when I have him in my power." Then he said aloud to Kiki:

"Well, hereafter I will be content to acknowledge you the master. You bungled things, as I said, but we can still conquer Oz."

"How?" asked the boy.

"First give me back the shape of the Li-Mon-Eag, and then we can talk together more conveniently," suggested the Nome.

"Wait a moment, then," said Kiki, and climbed higher up the tree. There he whispered the Magic Word and the Goose became a Li-Mon-Eag, as he had been before.

"Good!" said the Nome, well pleased, as Kiki joined him by dropping down from the tree. "Now let us find a quiet place where we can talk without being overheard by the beasts."

So the two started away and crossed the forest until they came to a place where the trees were not so tall nor so close together, and among these scattered trees was another clearing, not so large as the first one, where the meeting of the beasts had been held. Standing on the edge of this clearing and looking across it, they saw the trees on the farther side full of monkeys, who were chattering together at a great rate of the sights they had witnessed at the meeting.

The old Nome whispered to Kiki not to enter the clearing or allow the monkeys to see them.

"Why not?" asked the boy, drawing back.

"Because those monkeys are to be our army—the army which will conquer Oz," said the Nome. "Sit down here with me, Kiki, and keep quiet, and I will explain to you my plan."

Now, neither Kiki Aru nor Ruggedo had noticed that a sly Fox had followed them all the way from the tree where the Goose had been transformed to the Li-Mon-Eag. Indeed, this Fox, who was none other than the Wizard of Oz, had witnessed the transformation of the Goose and now decided he would keep watch of the conspirators and see what they would do next.

A Fox can move through a forest very softly, without making any noise, and so the Wizard's enemies did not suspect his presence. But when they sat down by the edge of the clearing, to talk, with their backs toward him, the Wizard did not know whether to risk being seen, by creeping closer to hear what they said, or whether it would be better for him to hide himself until they moved on again.

While he considered this question he discovered near him a great tree which had a hollow trunk, and there was a round hole in this tree, about three feet above the ground. The Wizard Fox decided it would be safer for him to hide inside the hollow tree, so he sprang into the hole and crouched down in the hollow, so that his eyes just came to the edge of the hole by which he had entered, and from here he watched the forms of the two Li-Mon-Eags.

"This is my plan," said the Nome to Kiki, speaking so low that the Wizard could only hear the rumble of his voice. "Since you can transform anything into any form you wish, we will transform these monkeys into an army, and with that army we will conquer the Oz people."

"The monkeys won't make much of an army," objected Kiki.

"We need a great army, but not a numerous one," responded the Nome. "You will transform each monkey into a giant man, dressed in a fine uniform and armed with a sharp sword. There are fifty monkeys over there and fifty giants would make as big an army as we need."

"What will they do with the swords?" asked Kiki. "Nothing can kill the Oz people."

"True," said Ruggedo. "The Oz people cannot be killed, but they can be cut into small pieces, and while every piece will still be alive, we can scatter the pieces around so that they will be quite helpless. Therefore, the Oz people will be afraid of the swords of our army, and we will conquer them with ease."

"That seems like a good idea," replied the boy, approvingly. "And in such a case, we need not bother with the other beasts of the forest."

"No; you have frightened the beasts, and they would no

longer consent to assist us in conquering Oz. But those monkeys are foolish creatures, and once they are transformed to Giants, they will do just as we say and obey our commands. Can you transform them all at once?"

"No, I must take one at a time," said Kiki. "But the fifty transformations can be made in an hour or so. Stay here, Ruggedo, and I will change the first monkey—that one at the left, on the end of the limb—into a Giant with a sword."

"Where are you going?" asked the Nome.

"I must not speak the Magic Word in the presence of another person," declared Kiki, who was determined not to allow his treacherous companion to learn his secret, "so I will go where you cannot hear me."

Ruggedo the Nome was disappointed, but he hoped still to catch the boy unawares and surprise the Magic Word. So he merely nodded his lion head, and Kiki got up and went back into the forest a short distance. Here he spied a hollow tree, and by chance it was the same hollow tree in which the Wizard of Oz, now in the form of a Fox, had hidden himself.

As Kiki ran up to the tree the Fox ducked its head, so that it was out of sight in the dark hollow beneath the hole, and then Kiki put his face into the hole and whispered: "I want that monkey on the branch at the left to become a Giant man fifty feet tall, dressed in a uniform and with a sharp sword—Pyrzqxgl!"

Then he ran back to Ruggedo, but the Wizard Fox had heard quite plainly every word that he had said.

The monkey was instantly transformed into the Giant, and the Giant was so big that as he stood on the ground his head was higher than the trees of the forest. The monkeys raised a great chatter but did not seem to understand that the Giant was one of themselves.

"Good!" cried the Nome. "Hurry, Kiki, and transform the others."

So Kiki rushed back to the tree and putting his face to the hollow, whispered:

"I want the next monkey to be just like the first—Pyrzqxgl!"

Again the Wizard Fox heard the Magic Word, and just how it was pronounced. But he sat still in the hollow and waited to hear it again, so it would be impressed on his mind and he would not forget it.

Kiki kept running to the edge of the forest and back to the hollow tree again until he had whispered the Magic Word six times and six monkeys had been changed to six great Giants. Then the Wizard decided he would make an experiment and use the Magic Word himself. So, while Kiki was running back to the Nome, the Fox stuck his head out of the hollow and said softly: "I want that creature who is running to become a hickory-nut—Pyrzqxgl!"

Instantly the Li-Mon-Eag form of Kiki Aru the Hyup disappeared and a small hickory-nut rolled upon the ground a moment and then lay still.

The Wizard was delighted, and leaped from the hollow just as Ruggedo looked around to see what had become of Kiki. The Nome saw the Fox but no Kiki, so he hastily rose to his feet. The Wizard did not know how powerful the queer beast might be, so he resolved to take no chances.

"I want this creature to become a walnut—Pyrzqxgl!" he said aloud. But he did not pronounce the Magic Word in quite the right way, and Ruggedo's form did not change. But the Nome knew at once that "Pyrzqxgl!" was the Magic Word, so he rushed at the Fox and cried:

"I want you to become a Goose—Pyrzqxgl!"

But the Nome did not pronounce the word aright, either, having never heard it spoken but once before, and then with a wrong accent. So the Fox was not transformed, but it had to run away to escape being caught by the angry Nome.

Ruggedo now began pronouncing the Magic Word in every way he could think of, hoping to hit the right one, and the Fox, hiding in a bush, was somewhat troubled by the fear that he might succeed. However, the Wizard, who was used to magic arts, remained calm and soon remembered exactly how Kiki Aru had pronounced the word. So he repeated the sentence he had before uttered and Ruggedo the Nome became an ordinary walnut.

The Wizard now crept out from the bush and said: "I want my own form again—Pyrzqxgl!"

Instantly he was the Wizard of Oz, and after picking up

the hickory-nut and the walnut, and carefully placing them in his pocket, he ran back to the big clearing.

Dorothy the Lamb uttered a bleat of delight when she saw her old friend restored to his natural shape. The others were all there, not having found the Goose. The fat Gillikin woman, the Munchkin boy, the Rabbit and the Glass Cat crowded around the Wizard and asked what had happened.

Before he explained anything of his adventure, he transformed them all—except, of course, the Glass Cat—into their natural shapes, and when their joy permitted them to quiet somewhat, he told how he had by chance surprised the Magician's secret and been able to change the two Li-Mon-Eags into shapes that could not speak, and therefore would be unable to help themselves. And the little Wizard showed his astonished friends the hickory-nut and the walnut to prove that he had spoken the truth.

"But—see here!"—exclaimed Dorothy. "What has become of those Giant Soldiers who used to be monkeys?"

"I forgot all about them!" admitted the Wizard; "but I suppose they are still standing there in the forest."

Chapter 15

The LONESOME DUCK

Trot and Cap'n Bill stood before the Magic Flower, actually rooted to the spot.

"Aren't you hungry, Cap'n?" asked the little girl, with a long sigh, for she had been standing there for hours and hours.

"Well," replied the sailor-man, "I ain't sayin' as I couldn't *eat*, Trot—if a dinner was handy—but I guess old folks don't get as hungry as young folks do."

"I'm not sure 'bout that, Cap'n Bill," she said thoughtfully. "Age *might* make a diff'rence, but seems to me *size* would make a bigger diff'rence. Seeing you're twice as big as me, you ought to be twice as hungry."

"I hope I am," he rejoined, "for I can stand it a while longer. I do hope the Glass Cat will hurry, and I hope the Wizard won't waste time a-comin' to us."

Trot sighed again and watched the wonderful Magic Flower, because there was nothing else to do. Just now a lovely group of pink peonies budded and bloomed, but soon they faded away, and a mass of deep blue lilies took their place. Then some yellow chrysanthemums blossomed on the plant, and when they had opened all their petals and reached perfection, they gave way to a lot of white floral balls spotted with crimson—a flower Trot had never seen before.

"But I get awful tired watchin' flowers an' flowers an' flowers," she said impatiently.

"They're might pretty," observed Cap'n Bill.

"I know; and if a person could come and look at the Magic Flower just when she felt like it, it would be a fine thing, but to *have to* stand and watch it, whether you want to or not, isn't so much fun. I wish, Cap'n Bill, the thing would grow fruit for a while instead of flowers."

Scarcely had she spoken when the white balls with crimson spots faded away and a lot of beautiful ripe peaches took their place. With a cry of mingled surprise and delight Trot reached out and plucked a peach from the bush and began to eat it, finding it delicious. Cap'n Bill was somewhat dazed at the girl's wish being granted so quickly, so before he could pick a peach they had faded away and bananas took their place.

"Grab one, Cap'n!" exclaimed Trot, and even while eating the peach she seized a banana with her other hand and tore it from the bush.

The old sailor was still bewildered. He put out a hand indeed, but he was too late, for now the bananas disappeared and lemons took their place.

"Pshaw!" cried Trot. "You can't eat those things; but watch out, Cap'n, for something else."

Cocoanuts next appeared, but Cap'n Bill shook his head.

"Ca'n't crack 'em," he remarked, "'cause we haven't anything handy to smash 'em with."

"Well, take one, anyhow," advised Trot; but the cocoanuts were gone now, and a deep, purple, pear-shaped fruit which was unknown to them took their place. Again Cap'n Bill hesitated, and Trot said to him:

"You ought to have captured a peach and a banana, as I did. If you're not careful, Cap'n, you'll miss all your chances. Here, I'll divide my banana with you."

Even as she spoke, the Magic Plant was covered with big red apples, growing on every branch, and Cap'n Bill hesitated no longer. He grabbed with both hands and picked two apples, while Trot had only time to secure one before they were gone.

"It's curious," remarked the sailor, munching his apple, "how these fruits keep good when you've picked 'em, but dis'pear inter thin air if they're left on the bush."

"The whole thing is curious," declared the girl, "and it couldn't exist in any country but this, where magic is so common. Those are limes. Don't pick 'em, for they'd pucker up your mouth and—Ooo! here come plums!" and she tucked her apple in her apron pocket and captured three plums—each one almost as big as an egg—before they disappeared. Cap'n Bill got some too, but both were too hungry to fast any longer, so they began eating their apples and plums and let the magic bush bear all sorts of fruits, one after another. The Cap'n stopped once to pick a fine cantaloupe, which he held under his arm, and Trot, having finished her plums, got a handful of cherries and an orange; but when almost every sort of fruit had appeared on the bush, the crop ceased and only flowers, as before, bloomed upon it.

"I wonder why it changed back," mused Trot, who was not worried because she had enough fruit to satisfy her hunger.

"Well, you only wished it would bear fruit 'for a while,'" said the sailor, "and it did. P'raps if you'd said 'forever,' Trot, it would have always been fruit."

"But why should *my* wish be obeyed?" asked the girl. "I'm not a fairy or a wizard or any kind of a magic-maker."

"I guess," replied Cap'n Bill, "that this little island is a magic island, and any folks on it can tell the bush what to produce, an' it'll produce it."

"Do you think I could wish for anything else, Cap'n, and get it?" she inquired anxiously.

"What are you thinkin' of, Trot?"

"I'm thinking of wishing that these roots on our feet would disappear, and let us free."

"Try it, Trot."

So she tried it, and the wish had no effect whatever.

"Try it yourself, Cap'n," she suggested.

Then Cap'n Bill made the wish to be free, with no better result.

"No," said he, "it's no use; the wishes only affect the Magic Plant; but I'm glad we can make it bear fruit, 'cause now we know we won't starve before the Wizard gets to us."

"But I'm gett'n' tired standing here so long," complained the girl. "If I could only lift one foot, and rest it, I'd feel better."

"Same with me, Trot. I've noticed that if you've got to do a thing, and can't help yourself, it gets to be a hardship mighty quick."

"Folks that can raise their feet don't appreciate what a blessing it is," said Trot thoughtfully. "I never knew before what fun it is to raise one foot, an' then another, any time you feel like it."

"There's lots o' things folks don't 'preciate," replied the sailor-man. "If somethin' would 'most stop your breath, you'd think breathin' easy was the finest thing in life. When a person's well, he don't realize how jolly it is, but when he gets sick he 'members the time he was well, an' wishes that time would come back. Most folks forget to thank God for givin' 'em two good legs, till they lose one o' 'em, like I did; and then it's too late, 'cept to praise God for leavin' one."

"Your wooden leg ain't so bad, Cap'n," she remarked, looking at it critically. "Anyhow, it don't take root on a Magic Island, like our meat legs do."

"I ain't complainin'," said Cap'n Bill. "What's that swimmin' towards us, Trot?" he added, looking over the Magic Flower and across the water.

The girl looked, too, and then she replied.

"It's a bird of some sort. It's like a duck, only I never saw a duck have so many colors."

The bird swam swiftly and gracefully toward the Magic Isle, and as it drew nearer its gorgeously colored plumage astonished them. The feathers were of many hues of glistening greens and blues and purples, and it had a yellow head with a red plume, and pink, white and violet in its tail. When it reached the Isle, it came ashore and approached them, waddling slowly and turning its head first to one side and then to the other, so as to see the girl and the sailor better.

"You're strangers," said the bird, coming to a halt near them, "and you've been caught by the Magic Isle and made prisoners."

"Yes," returned Trot, with a sigh; "we're rooted. But I hope we won't grow."

"You'll grow small," said the Bird. "You'll keep growing

smaller every day, until bye and bye there'll be nothing left of you. That's the usual way, on this Magic Isle."

"How do you know about it, and who are you, anyhow?" asked Cap'n Bill.

"I'm the Lonesome Duck," replied the bird. "I suppose you've heard of me?"

"No," said Trot, "I can't say I have. What makes you lonesome?"

"Why, I haven't any family or any relations," returned the Duck.

"Haven't you any friends?"

"Not a friend. And I've nothing to do. I've lived a long time, and I've got to live forever, because I belong in the Land of Oz, where no living thing dies. Think of existing year after year, with no friends, no family, and nothing to do! Can you wonder I'm lonesome?"

"Why don't you make a few friends, and find something to do?" inquired Cap'n Bill.

"I can't make friends because everyone I meet—bird, beast, or person—is disagreeable to me. In a few minutes I shall be unable to bear your society longer, and then I'll go away and leave you," said the Lonesome Duck. "And, as for doing anything, there's no use in it. All I meet are doing something, so I have decided it's common and uninteresting and I prefer to remain lonesome."

"Don't you have to hunt for your food?" asked Trot.

"No. In my diamond palace, a little way up the river, food is magically supplied me; but I seldom eat, because it is so common."

"You must be a Magician Duck," remarked Cap'n Bill.

"Why so?"

"Well, ordinary ducks don't have diamond palaces an' magic food, like you do."

"True; and that's another reason why I'm lonesome. You must remember I'm the only Duck in the Land of Oz, and I'm not like any other duck in the outside world."

"Seems to me you *like* bein' lonesome," observed Cap'n Bill.

"I can't say I like it, exactly," replied the Duck, "but since it seems to be my fate, I'm rather proud of it."

"How do you s'pose a single, solitary Duck happened to be in the Land of Oz?" asked Trot, wonderingly.

"I used to know the reason, many years ago, but I've quite forgotten it," declared the Duck. "The reason for a thing is never so important as the thing itself, so there's no use remembering anything but the fact that I'm lonesome."

"I guess you'd be happier if you tried to do something," asserted Trot. "If you can't do anything for yourself, you can do things for others, and then you'd get lots of friends and stop being lonesome."

"Now you're getting disagreeable," said the Lonesome Duck, "and I shall have to go and leave you."

"Can't you help us any," pleaded the girl. "If there's anything magic about you, you might get us out of this scrape."

"I haven't any magic strong enough to get you off the Magic Isle," replied the Lonesome Duck. "What magic I possess is very simple, but I find it enough for my own needs."

"If we could only sit down a while, we could stand it better," said Trot, "but we have nothing to sit on."

"Then you will have to stand it," said the Lonesome Duck.

"P'raps you've enough magic to give us a couple of stools," suggested Cap'n Bill.

"A duck isn't supposed to know what stools are," was the reply.

"But you're diff'rent from all other ducks."

"That is true." The strange creature seemed to reflect for a moment, looking at them sharply from its round black eyes. Then it said: "Sometimes, when the sun is hot, I grow a toadstool to shelter me from its rays. Perhaps you could sit on toadstools."

"Well, if they were strong enough, they'd do," answered Cap'n Bill.

"Then, before I go I'll give you a couple," said the Lonesome Duck, and began waddling about in a small circle. It went around the circle to the right three times, and then it went around to the left three times. Then it hopped backward three times and forward three times.

"What are you doing?" asked Trot.

"Don't interrupt. This is an incantation," replied the Lonesome Duck, but now it began making a succession of soft noises that sounded like quacks and seemed to mean nothing at all. And it kept up these sounds so long that Trot finally exclaimed:

"Can't you hurry up and finish that 'cantation? If it takes all summer to make a couple of toadstools, you're not much of a magician."

"I told you not to interrupt," said the Lonesome Duck, sternly. "If you get *too* disagreeable, you'll drive me away before I finish this incantation."

Trot kept quiet, after the rebuke, and the Duck resumed the quacky muttering. Cap'n Bill chuckled a little to himself and remarked to Trot in a whisper: "For a bird that ain't got anything to do, this Lonesome Duck is makin' consider'ble fuss. An' I ain't sure, after all, as toadstools would be worth sittin' on."

Even as he spoke, the sailor-man felt something touch him from behind and, turning his head, he found a big toadstool in just the right place and of just the right size to sit upon. There was one behind Trot, too, and with a cry of pleasure the little girl sank back upon it and found it a very comfortable seat— solid, yet almost like a cushion. Even Cap'n Bill's weight did not break his toadstool down, and when both were seated, they found that the Lonesome Duck had waddled away and was now at the water's edge.

"Thank you, ever so much!" cried Trot, and the sailor called out: "Much obliged!"

But the Lonesome Duck paid no attention. Without even looking in their direction again, the gaudy fowl entered the water and swam gracefully away.

Chapter 16

The GLASS CAT FINDS the BLACK BAG

When the six monkeys were transformed by Kiki Aru into six giant soldiers fifty feet tall, their heads came above the top of the trees, which in this part of the forest were not so high as in some other parts; and, although the trees were somewhat scattered, the bodies of the Giant Soldiers were so big that they quite filled the spaces in which they stood and the branches pressed them on every side.

Of course, Kiki was foolish to have made his soldiers so big, for now they could not get out of the forest. Indeed, they could not stir a step, but were imprisoned by the trees. Even had they been in the little clearing they could not have made their way out of it, but they were a little beyond the clearing. At first, the other monkeys who had not been enchanted were afraid of the soldiers, and hastily quitted the place; but soon finding that the great men stood stock still, although grunting indignantly at their transformation, the band of monkeys returned to the spot and looked at them curiously, not guessing that they were really monkeys and their own friends.

The soldiers couldn't see them, their heads being above the trees; they could not even raise their arms or draw their sharp swords, so closely were they held by the leafy branches. So the monkeys, finding the Giants helpless, began climbing up their bodies, and presently all the band were perched on the shoulders of the Giants and peering into their faces.

"I'm Ebu, your father," cried one soldier to a monkey who had perched upon his left ear, "but some cruel person has enchanted me."

"I'm your Uncle Peeker," said another soldier to another monkey.

So, very soon all the monkeys knew the truth and were sorry for their friends and relations and angry at the person— whoever it was—who had transformed them. There was a great chattering among the tree-tops, and the noise attracted other monkeys, so that the clearing and all the trees around were full of them.

Rango the Gray Ape, who was the Chief of all the monkey

tribes of the forest, heard the uproar and came to see what was wrong with his people. And Rango, being wiser and more experienced, at once knew that the strange magician who looked like a mixed-up beast was responsible for the transformations. He realized that the six giant soldiers were helpless prisoners, because of their size, and knew he was powerless to release them. So, although he feared to meet the terrible magician, he hurried away to the Great Clearing to tell Gugu the King what had happened and to try to find the Wizard of Oz and get him to save his six enchanted subjects.

Rango darted into the Great Clearing just as the Wizard had restored all the enchanted ones around him to their proper shapes, and the Gray Ape was glad to hear that the wicked magician-beast had been conquered.

"But now, O mighty Wizard, you must come with me to where six of my people are transformed into six great giant men," he said, "for if they are allowed to remain there, their happiness and their future lives will be ruined."

The Wizard did not reply at once, for he was thinking this a good opportunity to win Rango's consent to his taking some monkeys to the Emerald City for Ozma's birthday cake.

"It is a great thing you ask of me, O Rango the Gray Ape," said he, "for the bigger the giants are the more powerful their enchantment, and the more difficult it will be to restore them to their natural forms. However, I will think it over."

Then the Wizard went to another part of the clearing and sat on a log and appeared to be in deep thought.

The Glass Cat had been greatly interested in the Gray Ape's story and was curious to see what the giant soldiers looked like. Hearing that their heads extended above the tree-tops, the Glass Cat decided that if it climbed the tall avocado tree that stood at the side of the clearing, it might be able to see the giants' heads. So, without mentioning her errand, the crystal creature went to the tree and, by sticking her sharp glass claws in the bark, easily climbed the tree to its very top and, looking over the forest, saw the six giant heads, although they were now a long way off. It was, indeed, a remarkable sight, for the huge heads had immense soldier caps on them, with red and yellow plumes and looked very fierce and ter-rible, although the monkey hearts of the giants were at that moment filled with fear.

Having satisfied her curiosity, the Glass Cat began to climb down from the tree more slowly. Suddenly she discerned the Wizard's black bag hanging from a limb of the tree. She grasped the black bag in her glass teeth, and although it was rather heavy for so small an animal, managed to get it free and to carry it safely down to the ground. Then she looked around for the Wizard and seeing him seated upon the stump she hid the black bag among some leaves and then went over to where the Wizard sat.

"I forgot to tell you," said the Glass Cat, "that Trot and Cap'n Bill are in trouble, and I came here to hunt you up and get you to go and rescue them."

"Good gracious, Cat! Why didn't you tell me before?" exclaimed the Wizard.

"For the reason that I found so much excitement here that I forgot Trot and Cap'n Bill."

"What's wrong with them?" asked the Wizard.

Then the Glass Cat explained how they had gone to get the Magic Flower for Ozma's birthday gift and had been trapped by the magic of the queer island. The Wizard was really alarmed, but he shook his head and said sadly:

"I'm afraid I can't help my dear friends, because I've lost my black bag."

"If I find it, will you go to them?" asked the creature.

"Of course," replied the Wizard. "But I do not think that a Glass Cat with nothing but pink brains can succeed when all the rest of us have failed."

"Don't you admire my pink brains?" demanded the Cat.

"They're pretty," admitted the Wizard, "but they're not regular brains, you know, and so we don't expect them to amount to much."

"But if I find your black bag—and find it inside of five minutes—will you admit my pink brains are better than your common human brains?"

"Well, I'll admit they're better *hunters*," said the Wizard, reluctantly, "but you can't do it. We've searched everywhere, and the black bag isn't to be found."

"That shows how much you know!" retorted the Glass Cat, scornfully. "Watch my brains a minute, and see them whirl around."

The Wizard watched, for he was anxious to regain his black bag, and the pink brains really did whirl around in a remarkable manner.

"Now, come with me," commanded the Glass Cat, and led the Wizard straight to the spot where it had covered the bag with leaves. "According to my brains," said the creature, "your black bag ought to be here."

Then it scratched at the leaves and uncovered the bag, which the Wizard promptly seized with a cry of delight. Now that he had regained his magic tools, he felt confident he could rescue Trot and Cap'n Bill.

Rango the Gray Ape was getting impatient. He now approached the Wizard and said:

"Well, what do you intend to do about those poor enchanted monkeys?"

"I'll make a bargain with you, Rango," replied the little man. "If you will let me take a dozen of your monkeys to the Emerald City, and keep them until after Ozma's birthday, I'll break the enchantment of the six Giant Soldiers and return them to their natural forms."

But the Gray Ape shook his head.

"I can't do it," he declared. "The monkeys would be very lonesome and unhappy in the Emerald City and your people would tease them and throw stones at them, which would cause them to fight and bite."

"The people won't see them till Ozma's birthday dinner," promised the Wizard. "I'll make them very small—about four inches high, and I'll keep them in a pretty cage in my own room, where they will be safe from harm. I'll feed them the nicest kind of food, train them to do some clever tricks, and on Ozma's birthday I'll hide the twelve little monkeys inside a cake. When Ozma cuts the cake the monkeys will jump out on to the table and do their tricks. The next day I will bring them back to the forest and make them big as ever, and they'll have some exciting stories to tell their friends. What do you say, Rango?"

"I say no!" answered the Gray Ape. "I won't have my monkeys enchanted and made to do tricks for the Oz people."

"Very well," said the Wizard calmly; "then I'll go. Come, Dorothy," he called to the little girl, "let's start on our journey."

"Aren't you going to save those six monkeys who are giant soldiers?" asked Rango, anxiously.

"Why should I?" returned the Wizard. "If you will not do me the favor I ask, you cannot expect me to favor you."

"Wait a minute," said the Gray Ape. "I've changed my mind. If you will treat the twelve monkeys nicely and bring them safely back to the forest, I'll let you take them."

"Thank you," replied the Wizard, cheerfully. "We'll go at once and save those Giant Soldiers."

So all the party left the clearing and proceeded to the place where the giants still stood among the trees. Hundreds of monkeys, apes, baboons and orangoutangs had gathered round, and their wild chatter could be heard a mile away. But the Gray Ape soon hushed the babel of sounds, and the Wizard lost no time in breaking the enchantments. First one and then another giant soldier disappeared and became an ordinary monkey again, and the six were shortly returned to their friends in their proper forms.

This action made the Wizard very popular with the great army of monkeys, and when the Gray Ape announced that the Wizard wanted to borrow twelve monkeys to take to the Emerald City for a couple of weeks, and asked for volunteers, nearly a hundred offered to go, so great was their confidence in the little man who had saved their comrades.

The Wizard selected a dozen that seemed intelligent and good-tempered, and then he opened his black bag and took out a queerly shaped dish that was silver on the outside and gold on the inside. Into this dish he poured a powder and set fire to it. It made a thick smoke that quite enveloped the twelve monkeys, as well as the form of the Wizard, but when the smoke cleared away the dish had been changed to a golden cage with silver bars, and the twelve monkeys had become about three inches high and were all seated comfortably inside the cage.

The thousands of hairy animals who had witnessed this act of magic were much astonished and applauded the Wizard by barking aloud and shaking the limbs of the trees in which they sat. Dorothy said: "That was a fine trick, Wizard!" and the Gray Ape remarked: "You are certainly the most wonderful magician in all the Land of Oz!"

"Oh, no," modestly replied the little man. "Glinda's magic is better than mine, but mine seems good enough to use on ordinary occasions. And now, Rango, we will say good-bye, and I promise to return your monkeys as happy and safe as they are now."

The Wizard rode on the back of the Hungry Tiger and carried the cage of monkeys very carefully, so as not to joggle them. Dorothy rode on the back of the Cowardly Lion, and the Glass Cat trotted, as before, to show them the way.

Gugu the King crouched upon a log and watched them go, but as he bade them farewell, the enormous Leopard said:

"I know now that you are the friends of beasts and that the forest people may trust you. Whenever the Wizard of Oz and Princess Dorothy enter the Forest of Gugu hereafter, they will be as welcome and as safe with us as ever they are in the Emerald City."

Chapter 17

A REMARKABLE JOURNEY

You see," explained the Glass Cat, "that Magic Isle where Trot and Cap'n Bill are stuck is also in this Gillikin Country—over at the east side of it, and it's no farther to go across-lots from here than it is from here to the Emerald City. So we'll save time by cutting across the mountains."

"Are you sure you know the way?" asked Dorothy.

"I know all the Land of Oz better than any other living creature knows it," asserted the Glass Cat.

"Go ahead, then, and guide us," said the Wizard. "We've left our poor friends helpless too long already, and the sooner we rescue them the happier they'll be."

"Are you sure you can get 'em out of their fix?" the little girl inquired.

"I've no doubt of it," the Wizard assured her. "But I can't tell what sort of magic I must use until I get to the place and discover just how they are enchanted."

"I've heard of that Magic Isle where the Wonderful Flower grows," remarked the Cowardly Lion. "Long ago, when I used to live in the forests, the beasts told stories about the Isle and how the Magic Flower was placed there to entrap strangers— men or beasts."

"Is the Flower really wonderful?" questioned Dorothy.

"I have heard it is the most beautiful plant in the world," answered the Lion. "I have never seen it myself, but friendly beasts have told me that they have stood on the shore of the river and looked across at the plant in the gold flower-pot and seen hundreds of flowers, of all sorts and sizes, blossom upon it in quick succession. It is said that if one picks the flowers while they are in bloom they will remain perfect for a long time, but if they are not picked they soon disappear and are replaced by other flowers. That, in my opinion, make the Magic Plant the most wonderful in existence."

"But these are only stories," said the girl. "Has any of your friends ever picked a flower from the wonderful plant?"

"No," admitted the Cowardly Lion, "for if any living thing ventures upon the Magic Isle, where the golden flower-pot stands, that man or beast takes root in the soil and cannot get away again."

"What happens to them, then?" asked Dorothy.

"They grow smaller, hour by hour and day by day, and finally disappear entirely."

"Then," said the girl anxiously, "we must hurry up, or Cap'n Bill an' Trot will get too small to be comf'table."

They were proceeding at a rapid pace during this conversation, for the Hungry Tiger and the Cowardly Lion were obliged to move swiftly in order to keep pace with the Glass Cat. After leaving the Forest of Gugu they crossed a mountain range, and then a broad plain, after which they reached another forest, much smaller than that where Gugu ruled.

"The Magic Isle is in this forest," said the Glass Cat, "but the river is at the other side of the forest. There is no path through the trees, but if we keep going east, we will find the river, and then it will be easy to find the Magic Isle."

"Have you ever traveled this way before?" inquired the Wizard.

"Not exactly," admitted the Cat, "but I know we shall reach the river if we go east through the forest."

"Lead on, then," said the Wizard.

The Glass Cat started away, and at first it was easy to pass between the trees; but before long the underbrush and vines became thick and tangled, and after pushing their way through these obstacles for a time, our travelers came to a place where even the Glass Cat could not push through.

"We'd better go back and find a path," suggested the Hungry Tiger.

"I'm s'prised at you," said Dorothy, eyeing the Glass Cat severely.

"I'm surprised, myself," replied the Cat. "But it's a long way around the forest to where the river enters it, and I thought we could save time by going straight through."

"No one can blame you," said the Wizard, "and I think, instead of turning back, I can make a path that will allow us to proceed."

He opened his black bag and after searching among his magic tools drew out a small axe, made of some metal so highly polished that it glittered brightly even in the dark forest. The Wizard laid the little axe on the ground and said in a commanding voice:

> "Chop, Little Axe, chop clean and true;
> A path for our feet you must quickly hew.
> Chop till this tangle of jungle is passed;
> Chop to the east, Little Axe—chop fast!"

Then the little axe began to move and flashed its bright blade right and left, clearing a way through vine and brush and scattering the tangled barrier so quickly that the Lion and the Tiger, carrying Dorothy and the Wizard and the cage of monkeys on their backs, were able to stride through the forest at a fast walk. The brush seemed to melt away before them and the little axe chopped so fast that their eyes only saw a twinkling of the blade. Then, suddenly, the forest was open again, and the little axe, having obeyed its orders, lay still upon the ground.

The Wizard picked up the magic axe and after carefully wiping it with his silk handkerchief put it away in his black bag. Then they went on and in a short time reached the river.

"Let me see," said the Glass Cat, looking up and down the stream, "I think we are below the Magic Isle; so we must go up the stream until we come to it."

So up the stream they traveled, walking comfortably on the river bank, and after a while the water broadened and a sharp bend appeared in the river, hiding all below from their view. They walked briskly along, however, and had nearly reached the bend when a voice cried warningly: "Look out!"

The travelers halted abruptly and the Wizard said: "Look out for what?"

"You almost stepped on my Diamond Palace," replied the voice, and a duck with gorgeously colored feathers appeared before them. "Beasts and men are terribly clumsy," continued the Duck in an irritated tone, "and you've no business on this side of the river, anyway. What are you doing here?"

"We've come to rescue some friends of ours who are stuck fast on the Magic Isle in this river," explained Dorothy.

"I know 'em," said the Duck. "I've been to see 'em, and they're stuck fast, all right. You may as well go back home, for no power can save them."

"This is the Wonderful Wizard of Oz," said Dorothy, pointing to the little man.

"Well, I'm the Lonesome Duck," was the reply, as the fowl strutted up and down to show its feathers to best advantage. "I'm the great Forest Magician, as any beast can tell you, but even I have no power to destroy the dreadful charm of the Magic Isle."

"Are you lonesome because you're a magician?" inquired Dorothy.

"No; I'm lonesome because I have no family and no friends. But I like to be lonesome, so please don't offer to be friendly with me. Go away, and try not to step on my Diamond Palace."

"Where is it?" asked the girl.

"Behind this bush."

Dorothy hopped off the lion's back and ran around the bush to see the Diamond Palace of the Lonesome Duck, although the gaudy fowl protested in a series of low quacks. The girl found, indeed, a glistening dome formed of clearest diamonds, neatly cemented together, with a doorway at the side just big enough to admit the duck.

"Where did you find so many diamonds?" asked Dorothy, wonderingly.

"I know a place in the mountains where they are thick as pebbles," said the Lonesome Duck, "and I brought them here in my bill, one by one and put them in the river and let the water run over them until they were brightly polished. Then I built this palace, and I'm positive it's the only Diamond Palace in all the world."

"It's the only one I know of," said the little girl; "but if you live in it all alone, I don't see why it's any better than a wooden palace, or one of bricks or cobble-stones."

"You're not supposed to understand that," retorted the Lonesome Duck. "But I might tell you, as a matter of education, that a home of any sort should be beautiful to those who live in it, and should not be intended to please strangers. The Diamond Palace is my home, and I like it. So I don't care a quack whether *you* like it or not."

"Oh, but I do!" exclaimed Dorothy. "It's lovely on the outside, but—" Then she stopped speaking, for the Lonesome Duck had entered his palace through the little door without even saying good-bye. So Dorothy returned to her friends and they resumed their journey.

"Do you think, Wizard, the Duck was right in saying no magic can rescue Trot and Cap'n Bill?" asked the girl in a worried tone of voice.

"No, I don't think the Lonesome Duck was right in saying that," answered the Wizard, gravely, "but it is possible that their enchantment will be harder to overcome than I expected. I'll do my best, of course, and no one can do more than his best."

That didn't entirely relieve Dorothy's anxiety, but she said nothing more, and soon, on turning the bend in the river, they came in sight of the Magic Isle.

"There they are!" exclaimed Dorothy eagerly.

"Yes, I see them," replied the Wizard, nodding. "They are sitting on two big toadstools."

"That's queer," remarked the Glass Cat. "There were no toadstools there when I left them."

"What a lovely flower!" cried Dorothy in rapture, as her gaze fell on the Magic Plant.

"Never mind the Flower, just now," advised the Wizard. "The most important thing is to rescue our friends."

By this time they had arrived at a place just opposite the Magic Isle, and now both Trot and Cap'n Bill saw the arrival of their friends and called to them for help.

"How are you?" shouted the Wizard, putting his hands to his mouth so they could hear him better across the water.

"We're in hard luck," shouted Cap'n Bill, in reply. "We're anchored here and can't move till you find a way to cut the hawser."

"What does he mean by that?" asked Dorothy.

"We can't move our feet a bit!" called Trot, speaking as loud as she could.

"Why not?" inquired Dorothy.

"They've got roots on 'em," explained Trot.

It was hard to talk from so great a distance, so the Wizard said to the Glass Cat:

"Go to the island and tell our friends to be patient, for we have come to save them. It may take a little time to release them, for the Magic of the Isle is new to me and I shall have to experiment. But tell them I'll hurry as fast as I can."

So the Glass Cat walked across the river under the water to tell Trot and Cap'n Bill not to worry, and the Wizard at once opened his black bag and began to make his preparations.

···—·◄ Chapter 18 ►·—··

The MAGIC of the WIZARD

He first set up a small silver tripod and placed a gold basin at the top of it. Into this basin he put two powders—a pink one and a sky-blue one—and poured over them a yellow liquid from a crystal vial. Then he mumbled some magic words, and the powders began to sizzle and burn and send out a cloud of violet smoke that floated across the river and completely enveloped both Trot and Cap'n Bill, as well as the toadstools on which they sat, and even the Magic Plant in the gold flower-pot. Then, after the smoke had disappeared into air, the Wizard called out to the prisoners:

"Are you free?"

Both Trot and Cap'n Bill tried to move their feet and failed.

"No!" they shouted in answer.

The Wizard rubbed his bald head thoughtfully and then took some other magic tools from the bag.

First he placed a little black ball in a silver pistol and shot it toward the Magic Isle. The ball exploded just over the head of Trot and scattered a thousand sparks over the little girl.

"Oh!" said the Wizard, "I guess that will set her free."

But Trot's feet were still rooted in the ground of the Magic Isle, and the disappointed Wizard had to try something else.

For almost an hour he worked hard, using almost every magic tool in his black bag, and still Cap'n Bill and Trot were not rescued.

"Dear me!" exclaimed Dorothy, "I'm 'fraid we'll have to go to Glinda, after all."

That made the little Wizard blush, for it shamed him to think that his magic was not equal to that of the Magic Isle.

"I won't give up yet, Dorothy," he said, "for I know a lot of wizardry that I haven't yet tried. I don't know what magician enchanted this little island, or what his powers were, but I *do* know that I can break any enchantment known to the ordinary witches and magicians that used to inhabit the Land of Oz. It's like unlocking a door; all you need is to find the right key."

"But 'spose you haven't the right key with you," suggested Dorothy; "what then?"

"Then we'll have to make the key," he answered.

The Glass Cat now came back to their side of the river, walking under the water, and said to the Wizard: "They're getting frightened over there on the island because they're both growing smaller every minute. Just now, when I left them, both Trot and Cap'n Bill were only about half their natural sizes."

"I think," said the Wizard reflectively, "that I'd better go to the shore of the island, where I can talk to them and work to better advantage. How did Trot and Cap'n Bill get to the island?"

"On a raft," answered the Glass Cat. "It's over there now on the beach."

"I suppose you're not strong enough to bring the raft to this side, are you?"

"No; I couldn't move it an inch," said the Cat.

"I'll try to get it for you," volunteered the Cowardly Lion. "I'm dreadfully scared for fear the Magic Isle will capture me, too; but I'll try to get the raft and bring it to this side for you."

"Thank you, my friend," said the Wizard.

So the Lion plunged into the river and swam with powerful strokes across to where the raft was beached upon the island. Placing one paw on the raft, he turned and struck out with his other three legs and so strong was the great beast that he managed to drag the raft from off the beach and propel it slowly to where the Wizard stood on the river bank.

"Good!" exclaimed the little man, well pleased.

"May I go across with you?" asked Dorothy.

The Wizard hesitated.

"If you'll take care not to leave the raft or step foot on the island, you'll be quite safe," he decided. So the Wizard told the Hungry Tiger and the Cowardly Lion to guard the cage of monkeys until he returned, and then he and Dorothy got upon the raft. The paddle which Cap'n Bill had made was still there, so the little Wizard paddled the clumsy raft across the water and ran it upon the beach of the Magic Isle as close to the place where Cap'n Bill and Trot were rooted as he could.

Dorothy was shocked to see how small the prisoners had become, and Trot said to her friends: "If you can't save us soon, there'll be nothing left of us."

"Be patient, my dear," counseled the Wizard, and took the little axe from his black bag.

"What are you going to do with that?" asked Cap'n Bill.

"It's a magic axe," replied the Wizard, "and when I tell it to chop, it will chop those roots from your feet and you can run to the raft before they grow again."

"Don't!" shouted the sailor in alarm. "Don't do it! Those roots are all flesh roots, and our bodies are feeding 'em while they're growing into the ground."

"To cut off the roots," said Trot, "would be like cutting off our fingers and toes."

The Wizard put the little axe back in the black bag and took out a pair of silver pincers.

"Grow—grow—grow!" he said to the pincers, and at once they grew and extended until they reached from the raft to the prisoners.

"What are you going to do now?" demanded Cap'n Bill, fearfully eyeing the pincers.

"This magic tool will pull you up, roots and all, and land you on this raft," declared the Wizard.

"Don't do it!" pleaded the sailor, with a shudder. "It would hurt us awfully."

"It would be just like pulling teeth to pull us up by the roots," explained Trot.

"Grow small!" said the Wizard to the pincers, and at once they became small and he threw them into the black bag.

"I guess, friends, it's all up with us, this time," remarked Cap'n Bill, with a dismal sigh.

"Please tell Ozma, Dorothy," said Trot, "that we got into trouble trying to get her a nice birthday present. Then she'll forgive us. The Magic Flower is lovely and wonderful, but it's just a lure to catch folks on this dreadful island and then destroy them. You'll have a nice birthday party, without us, I'm sure; and I hope, Dorothy, that none of you in the Emerald City will forget me—or dear ol' Cap'n Bill."

Chapter 19

DOROTHY and the BUMBLEBEES

Dorothy was greatly distressed and had hard work to keep the tears from her eyes.

"Is that all you can do, Wizard?" she asked the little man.

"It's all I can think of just now," he replied sadly. "But I intend to keep on thinking as long—as long—well, as long as thinking will do any good."

They were all silent for a time, Dorothy and the Wizard sitting thoughtfully on the raft, and Trot and Cap'n Bill sitting thoughtfully on the toadstools and growing gradually smaller and smaller in size.

Suddenly Dorothy said: "Wizard, I've thought of something!"

"What have you thought of?" he asked, looking at the little girl with interest.

"Can you remember the Magic Word that transforms people?" she asked.

"Of course," said he.

"Then you can transform Trot and Cap'n Bill into birds or bumblebees, and they can fly away to the other shore. When they're there, you can transform 'em into their reg'lar shapes again!"

"Can you do that, Wizard?" asked Cap'n Bill, eagerly.

"I think so."

"Roots an' all?" inquired Trot.

"Why, the roots are now a part of you, and if you were transformed to a bumblebee the whole of you would be transformed, of course, and you'd be free of this awful island."

"All right; do it!" cried the sailor-man.

So the Wizard said slowly and distinctly:

"I want Trot and Cap'n Bill to become bumblebees— Pyrzqxgl!"

Fortunately, he pronounced the Magic Word in the right way, and instantly Trot and Cap'n Bill vanished from view, and up from the places where they had been flew two bumblebees.

"Hooray!" shouted Dorothy in delight; "they're saved!"

"I guess they are," agreed the Wizard, equally delighted.

The bees hovered over the raft an instant and then flew

across the river to where the Lion and the Tiger waited. The Wizard picked up the paddle and paddled the raft across as fast as he could. When it reached the river bank, both Dorothy and the Wizard leaped ashore and the little man asked excitedly:

"Where are the bees?"

"The bees?" inquired the Lion, who was half asleep and did not know what had happened on the Magic Isle.

"Yes; there were two of them."

"Two bees?" said the Hungry Tiger, yawning. "Why, I ate one of them and the Cowardly Lion ate the other."

"Goodness gracious!" cried Dorothy horrified.

"It was little enough for our lunch," remarked the Tiger, "but the bees were the only things we could find."

"How dreadful!" wailed Dorothy, wringing her hands in despair. "You've eaten Trot and Cap'n Bill."

But just then she heard a buzzing overhead and two bees alighted on her shoulder.

"Here we are," said a small voice in her ear. "I'm Trot, Dorothy."

"And I'm Cap'n Bill," said the other bee.

Dorothy almost fainted, with relief, and the Wizard, who was close by and had heard the tiny voices, gave a laugh and said:

"You are not the only two bees in the forest, it seems, but I advise you to keep away from the Lion and the Tiger until you regain your proper forms."

"Do it now, Wizard!" advised Dorothy. "They're so small that you never can tell what might happen to 'em."

So the Wizard gave the command and pronounced the Magic Word, and in the instant Trot and Cap'n Bill stood beside them as natural as before they had met their fearful adventure. For they were no longer small in size, because the Wizard had transformed them from bumblebees into the shapes and sizes that nature had formerly given them. The ugly roots on their feet had disappeared with the transformation.

While Dorothy was hugging Trot, and Trot was softly crying because she was so happy, the Wizard shook hands with Cap'n Bill and congratulated him on his escape. The old sailor-man was so pleased that he also shook the Lion's paw and took off his hat and bowed politely to the cage of monkeys.

Then Cap'n Bill did a curious thing. He went to a big tree and, taking out his knife, cut away a big, broad piece of thick bark. Then he sat down on the ground and after taking a roll of stout cord from his pocket—which seemed to be full of all sorts of things—he proceeded to bind the flat piece of bark to the bottom of his good foot, over the leather sole.

"What's that for?" inquired the Wizard.

"I hate to be stumped," replied the sailor-man; "so I'm goin' back to that island."

"And get enchanted again?" exclaimed Trot, with evident disapproval.

"No; this time I'll dodge the magic of the island. I noticed that my wooden leg didn't get stuck, or take root, an' neither did the glass feet of the Glass Cat. It's only a thing that's made of meat—like man an' beasts—that the magic can hold an' root to the ground. Our shoes are leather, an' leather comes from a beast's hide. Our stockin's are wool, an' wool comes from a sheep's back. So, when we walked on the Magic Isle, our feet took root there an' held us fast. But not my wooden leg. So now I'll put a wooden bottom on my other foot an' the magic can't stop me."

"But why do you wish to go back to the island?" asked Dorothy.

"Didn't you see the Magic Flower in the gold flower-pot?" returned Cap'n Bill.

"Of course I saw it, and it's lovely and wonderful."

"Well, Trot an' I set out to get the magic plant for a present to Ozma on her birthday, and I mean to get it an' take it back with us to the Emerald City."

"That would be fine," cried Trot eagerly, "if you think you can do it, and it would be safe to try!"

"I'm pretty sure it is safe, the way I've fixed my foot," said the sailor, "an' if I *should* happen to get caught, I s'pose the Wizard could save me again."

"I suppose I could," agreed the Wizard. "Anyhow, if you wish to try it, Cap'n Bill, go ahead and we'll stand by and watch what happens."

So the sailor-man got upon the raft again and paddled over to the Magic Isle, landing as close to the golden flower-pot as he could. They watched him walk across the land, put both arms around the flower-pot and lift it easily from its place. Then he carried it to the raft and set it down very gently. The removal did not seem to affect the Magic Flower in any way, for it was growing daffodils when Cap'n Bill picked it up and on the way to the raft it grew tulips and gladioli. During the time the sailor was paddling across the river to where his friends awaited him, seven different varieties of flowers bloomed in succession on the plant.

"I guess the Magician who put it on the island never thought that any one would carry it off," said Dorothy.

"He figured that only men would want the plant, and any man who went upon the island to get it would be caught by the enchantment," added the Wizard.

"After this," remarked Trot, "no one will care to go on the island, so it won't be a trap any more."

"There," exclaimed Cap'n Bill, setting down the Magic Plant in triumph upon the river bank, "if Ozma gets a better birthday present than that, I'd like to know what it can be!"

"It'll s'prise her, all right," declared Dorothy, standing in awed wonder before the gorgeous blossoms and watching them change from yellow roses to violets.

"It'll s'prise ev'rybody in the Em'rald City," Trot asserted in glee, "and it'll be Ozma's present from Cap'n Bill and me."

"I think *I* ought to have a little credit," objected the Glass Cat. "I discovered the thing, and led you to it, and brought the Wizard here to save you when you got caught."

"That's true," admitted Trot, "and I'll tell Ozma the whole story, so she'll know how good you've been."

Chapter 20

The MONKEYS HAVE TROUBLE

Now," said the Wizard, "we must start for home. But how are we going to carry that big gold flower-pot? Cap'n Bill can't lug it all the way, that's certain."

"No," acknowledged the sailor-man; "it's pretty heavy. I could carry it for a little while, but I'd have to stop to rest every few minutes."

"Couldn't we put it on your back?" Dorothy asked the Cowardly Lion, with a good-natured yawn.

"I don't object to carrying it, if you can fasten it on," answered the Lion.

"If it falls off," said Trot, "it might get smashed an' be ruined."

"I'll fix it," promised Cap'n Bill. "I'll make a flat board out of one of these tree trunks, an' tie the board on the lion's back, an' set the flower-pot on the board." He set to work at once to do this, but as he only had his big knife for a tool his progress was slow.

So the Wizard took from his black bag a tiny saw that shone like silver and said to it:

"Saw, Little Saw, come show your power;
Make us a board for the Magic Flower."

And at once the Little Saw began to move and it sawed the log so fast that those who watched it work were astonished. It seemed to understand, too, just what the board was to be used for, for when it was completed it was flat on top and hollowed beneath in such a manner that it exactly fitted the Lion's back.

"That beats whittlin'!" exclaimed Cap'n Bill, admiringly. "You don't happen to have *two* o' them saws; do you, Wizard?"

"No," replied the Wizard, wiping the Magic Saw carefully with his silk handkerchief and putting it back in the black bag. "It's the only saw of its kind in the world; and if there were more like it, it wouldn't be so wonderful."

They now tied the board on the Lion's back, flat side up, and Cap'n Bill carefully placed the Magic Flower on the board.

"For fear o' accidents," he said, "I'll walk beside the Lion and hold onto the flower-pot."

Trot and Dorothy could both ride on the back of the Hungry Tiger, and between them they carried the cage of monkeys. But this arrangement left the Wizard, as well as the sailor, to make the journey on foot, and so the procession moved slowly and the Glass Cat grumbled because it would take so long to get to the Emerald City.

The Cat was sour-tempered and grumpy, at first, but before they had journeyed far, the crystal creature had discovered a fine amusement. The long tails of the monkeys were constantly sticking through the bars of their cage, and when they did, the Glass Cat would slyly seize the tails in her paws and pull them. That made the monkeys scream, and their screams pleased the Glass Cat immensely. Trot and Dorothy tried to stop this naughty amusement, but when they were not looking the Cat would pull the tails again, and the creature was so sly and quick that the monkeys could seldom escape. They scolded the Cat angrily and shook the bars of their cage, but they could not get out and the Cat only laughed at them.

After the party had left the forest and were on the plains of the Munchkin Country, it grew dark, and they were obliged to make camp for the night, choosing a pretty place beside a brook. By means of his magic the Wizard created three tents, pitched in a row on the grass and nicely fitted with all that was needful for the comfort of his comrades. The middle tent was for Dorothy and Trot, and had in it two cosy white beds and two chairs. Another tent, also with beds and chairs, was for the Wizard and Cap'n Bill, while the third tent was for the Hungry Tiger, the Cowardly Lion, the cage of Monkeys and the Glass Cat. Outside the tents the Wizard made a fire and placed over it a magic kettle from which he presently drew all sorts of nice things for their supper, smoking hot.

After they had eaten and talked together for a while under the twinkling stars, they all went to bed and the people were soon asleep. The Lion and the Tiger had almost fallen asleep, too, when they were roused by the screams of the monkeys, for the Glass Cat was pulling their tails again. Annoyed by the uproar, the Hungry Tiger cried: "Stop that racket!" and getting sight of the Glass Cat, he raised his big paw and struck at the creature. The cat was quick enough to dodge the blow, but the claws of the Hungry Tiger scraped the monkeys' cage and bent two of the bars.

Then the Tiger lay down again to sleep, but the monkeys soon discovered that the bending of the bars would allow them to squeeze through. They did not leave the cage, however, but after whispering together they let their tails stick out and all remained quiet. Presently the Glass Cat stole near the cage again and gave a yank to one of the tails. Instantly the monkeys leaped through the bars, one after another, and although they were so small the entire dozen of them surrounded the Glass Cat and clung to her claws and tail and ears and made her a prisoner. Then they forced her out of the tent and down to the banks of the stream. The monkeys had noticed that these banks were covered with thick, slimy mud of a dark blue color, and when they had taken the Cat to the stream, they smeared this mud all over the glass body of the cat, filling the creature's ears and eyes with it, so that she could neither see nor hear. She was no longer transparent and so thick was the mud upon her that no one could see her pink brains or her ruby heart.

In this condition they led the pussy back to the tent and then got inside their cage again.

By morning the mud had dried hard on the Glass Cat and it was a dull blue color throughout. Dorothy and Trot were horrified, but the Wizard shook his head and said it served the Glass Cat right for teasing the monkeys.

Cap'n Bill, with his strong hands, soon bent the golden wires of the monkeys' cage into the proper position and then he asked the Wizard if he should wash the Glass Cat in the water of the brook.

"Not just yet," answered the Wizard. "The Cat deserves to be punished, so I think I'll leave that blue mud—which is as bad as paint—upon her body until she gets to the Emerald City. The silly creature is so vain that she will be greatly shamed when the Oz people see her in this condition, and perhaps she'll take the lesson to heart and leave the monkeys alone hereafter."

However, the Glass Cat could not see or hear, and to avoid carrying her on the journey the Wizard picked the mud out of her eyes and ears and Dorothy dampened her handkerchief and washed both the eyes and ears clean.

As soon as she could speak the Glass Cat asked indignantly: "Aren't you going to punish those monkeys for playing such a trick on me?"

"No," answered the Wizard. "You played a trick on them by pulling their tails, so this is only tit-for-tat, and I'm glad the monkeys had their revenge."

He wouldn't allow the Glass Cat to go near the water, to wash herself, but made her follow them when they resumed their journey toward the Emerald City.

"This is only part of your punishment," said the Wizard, severely. "Ozma will laugh at you, when we get to her palace, and so will the Scarecrow, and the Tin Woodman, and Tik-Tok, and the Shaggy Man, and Button-Bright, and the Patchwork Girl, and—"

"And the Pink Kitten," added Dorothy.

That suggestion hurt the Glass Cat more than anything else. The Pink Kitten always quarreled with the Glass Cat and insisted that flesh was superior to glass, while the Glass Cat would jeer at the Pink Kitten, because it had no pink brains. But the pink brains were all daubed with blue mud, just now, and if the Pink Kitten should see the Glass Cat in such a condition, it would be dreadfully humiliating.

For several hours the Glass Cat walked along very meekly, but toward noon it seized an opportunity when no one was looking and darted away through the long grass. It remembered that there was a tiny lake of pure water near by, and to this lake the Cat sped as fast as it could go.

The others never missed her until they stopped for lunch, and then it was too late to hunt for her.

"I s'pect she's gone somewhere to clean herself," said Dorothy.

"Never mind," replied the Wizard. "Perhaps this glass creature has been punished enough, and we must not forget she saved both Trot and Cap'n Bill."

"After first leading 'em onto an enchanted island," added Dorothy. "But I think, as you do, that the Glass Cat is punished enough, and p'raps she won't try to pull the monkeys' tails again."

The Glass Cat did not rejoin the party of travelers. She was still resentful, and they moved too slowly to suit her, besides. When they arrived at the Royal Palace, one of the first things they saw was the Glass Cat curled up on a bench as bright and clean and transparent as ever. But she pretended not to notice them, and they passed her by without remark.

...—...< Chapter 21 >...—...

The COLLEGE of ATHLETIC ARTS

Dorothy and her friends arrived at the Royal Palace at an opportune time, for Ozma was holding high court in her Throne Room, where Professor H. M. Wogglebug, T.E., was appealing to her to punish some of the students of the Royal Athletic College, of which he was the Principal.

This College is located in the Munchkin Country, but not far from the Emerald City. To enable the students to devote their entire time to athletic exercises, such as boating, foot-ball, and the like, Professor Wogglebug had invented an assortment of Tablets of Learning. One of these tablets, eaten by a scholar after breakfast, would instantly enable him to understand arithmetic or algebra or any other branch of mathematics. Another tablet eaten after lunch gave a student a complete knowledge of geography. Another tablet made it possible for the eater to spell the most difficult words, and still another enabled him to write a beautiful hand. There were tablets for history, mechanics, home cooking and agriculture, and it mattered not whether a boy or a girl was stupid or bright, for the tablets taught them everything in the twinkling of an eye.

This method, which is patented in the Land of Oz by Professor Wogglebug, saves paper and books, as well as the tedious hours devoted to study in some of our less favored schools, and it also allows the students to devote all their time to racing, base-ball, tennis and other manly and womanly sports, which are greatly interfered with by study in those Temples of Learning where Tablets of Learning are unknown.

But it so happened that Professor Wogglebug (who had invented so much that he had acquired the habit) carelessly invented a Square-Meal Tablet, which was no bigger than your little finger-nail but contained, in condensed form, the equal of a bowl of soup, a portion of fried fish, a roast, a salad and a dessert, all of which gave the same nourishment as a square meal.

The Professor was so proud of these Square-Meal Tablets that he began to feed them to the students at his college, instead of other food, but the boys and girls objected because they wanted food that they could enjoy the taste of. It was no fun at all to swallow a tablet, with a glass of water, and call it a dinner; so they refused to eat the Square-Meal Tablets. Professor Wogglebug insisted, and the result was that the senior class seized the learned Professor one day and threw him into the river—clothes and all. Everyone knows that a wogglebug cannot swim, and so the inventor of the wonderful Square-Meal Tablets lay helpless on the bottom of the river for three days before a fisherman caught one of his legs on a fishhook and dragged him out upon the bank.

The learned Professor was naturally indignant at such treatment, and so he brought the entire senior class to the Emerald City and appealed to Ozma of Oz to punish them for their rebellion.

I do not suppose the girl Ruler was very severe with the rebellious boys and girls, because she had herself refused to eat the Square-Meal Tablets in place of food, but while she was listening to the interesting case in her Throne Room, Cap'n Bill managed to carry the golden flower-pot containing the Magic Flower up to Trot's room without it being seen by anyone except Jellia Jamb, Ozma's chief Maid of Honor, and Jellia promised not to tell.

Also the Wizard was able to carry the cage of monkeys up to one of the top towers of the palace, where he had a room of his own, to which no one came unless invited. So Trot and Dorothy and Cap'n Bill and the Wizard were all delighted at the successful end of their adventure. The Cowardly Lion and the Hungry Tiger went to the marble stables behind the Royal Palace, where they lived while at home, and they too kept the secret, even refusing to tell the Wooden Sawhorse, and Hank the Mule, and the Yellow Hen, and the Pink Kitten where they had been.

Trot watered the Magic Flower every day and allowed no one in her room to see the beautiful blossoms except her friends, Betsy Bobbin and Dorothy. The wonderful plant did not seem to lose any of its magic by being removed from its island, and Trot was sure that Ozma would prize it as one of her most delightful treasures.

Up in his tower the little Wizard of Oz began training his twelve tiny monkeys, and the little creatures were so intelligent that they learned every trick the Wizard tried to teach them. The Wizard treated them with great kindness and gentleness and gave them the food that monkeys love best, so they promised to do their best on the great occasion of Ozma's birthday.

OZMA'S BIRTHDAY PARTY

It seems odd that a fairy should have a birthday, for fairies, they say, were born at the beginning of time and live forever. Yet, on the other hand, it would be a shame to deprive a fairy, who has so many other good things, of the delights of a birthday. So we need not wonder that the fairies keep their birthdays just as other folks do, and consider them occasions for feasting and rejoicing.

Ozma, the beautiful girl Ruler of the Fairyland of Oz, was a real fairy, and so sweet and gentle in caring for her people that she was greatly beloved by them all. She lived in the most magnificent palace in the most magnificent city in the world, but that did not prevent her from being the friend of the most humble person in her dominions. She would mount her Wooden Saw-horse, and ride out to a farm-house and sit in the kitchen to talk with the good wife of the farmer while she did her family baking; or she would play with the children and give them rides on her famous wooden steed; or she would stop in a forest to speak to a charcoal burner and ask if he was happy or desired anything to make him more content; or she would teach young girls how to sew and plan pretty dresses, or enter the shops where the jewelers and craftsmen were busy and watch them at their work, giving to each and all a cheering word or sunny smile.

And then Ozma would sit in her jeweled throne, with her chosen courtiers all about her, and listen patiently to any complaint brought to her by her subjects, striving to accord equal justice to all. Knowing she was fair in her decisions, the Oz people never murmured at her judgments, but agreed, if Ozma decided against them, she was right and they wrong.

When Dorothy and Trot and Betsy Bobbin and Ozma were together, one would think they were all about of an age, and the fairy Ruler no older and no more "grown up" than the other three. She would laugh and romp with them in regular girlish fashion, yet there was an air of quiet dignity about Ozma, even in her merriest moods, that, in a manner, distinguished her from the others. The three girls loved her devotedly, but they were never able to quite forget that Ozma was the Royal Ruler of the wonderful Fairyland of Oz, and by birth belonged to a powerful race.

Ozma's palace stood in the center of a delightful and extensive garden, where splendid trees and flowering shrubs and statuary and fountains abounded. One could walk for hours in this fascinating park and see something interesting at every step. In one place was an aquarium, where strange and beautiful fish swam; at another spot all the birds of the air gathered daily to a great feast which Ozma's servants provided for them, and were so fearless of harm that they would alight upon one's shoulders and eat from one's hand. There was also the Fountain of the Water of Oblivion, but it was dangerous to drink of this water, because it made one forget everything he had ever before known, even to his own name, and therefore Ozma had placed a sign of warning upon the fountain. But there were also fountains that were delightfully perfumed, and fountains of delicious nectar, cool and richly flavored, where all were welcome to refresh themselves.

Around the palace grounds was a great wall, thickly encrusted with glittering emeralds, but the gates stood open and no one was forbidden entrance. On holidays the people of the Emerald City often took their children to see the wonders of Ozma's gardens, and even entered the Royal Palace, if they felt so inclined, for they knew that they and their Ruler were friends, and that Ozma delighted to give them pleasure.

When all this is considered, you will not be surprised that the people throughout the Land of Oz, as well as Ozma's most intimate friends and her royal courtiers, were eager to cele-

brate her birthday, and made preparations for the festival
weeks in advance. All the brass bands practiced their nicest
tunes, for they were to march in the numerous processions
to be made in the Winkie Country, the Gillikin Country, the
Munchkin Country and the Quadling Country, as well as in
the Emerald City. Not all the people could go to congratulate
their Ruler, but all could celebrate her birthday, in one way or
another, however far distant from her palace they might be.
Every home and building throughout the Land of Oz was to
be decorated with banners and bunting, and there were to be
games, and plays, and a general good time for every one.

It was Ozma's custom on her birthday to give a grand feast
at the palace, to which all her closest friends were invited. It
was a queerly assorted company, indeed, for there are more
quaint and unusual characters in Oz than in all the rest of the
world, and Ozma was more interested in unusual people than
in ordinary ones—just as you and I are.

On this especial birthday of the lovely girl Ruler, a long
table was set in the royal Banquet Hall of the palace, at which
were place-cards for the invited guests, and at one end of the
great room was a smaller table, not so high, for Ozma's animal friends, whom she never forgot, and at the other end was
a big table where all of the birthday gifts were to be arranged.

When the guests arrived, they placed their gifts on this
table and then found their places at the banquet table. And,
after the guests were all placed, the animals entered in a

solemn procession and were placed at their table by Jellia Jamb. Then, while an orchestra hidden by a bank of roses and ferns played a march composed for the occasion, the Royal Ozma entered the Banquet Hall, attended by her Maids of Honor, and took her seat at the head of the table.

She was greeted by a cheer from all the assembled company, the animals adding their roars and growls and barks and mewing and cackling to swell the glad tumult, and then all seated themselves at their tables.

At Ozma's right sat the famous Scarecrow of Oz, whose straw-stuffed body was not beautiful, but whose happy nature and shrewd wit had made him a general favorite. On the left of the Ruler was placed the Tin Woodman, whose metal body had been brightly polished for this event. The Tin Woodman was the Emperor of the Winkie Country and one of the most important persons in Oz.

Next to the Scarecrow, Dorothy was seated, and next to her was Tik-Tok, the Clockwork Man, who had been wound up as tightly as his clockwork would permit, so he wouldn't interrupt the festivities by running down. Then came Aunt Em and Uncle Henry, Dorothy's own relations, two kindly old people who had a cozy home in the Emerald City and were very happy and contented there. Then Betsy Bobbin was seated, and next to her the droll and delightful Shaggy Man, who was a favorite wherever he went.

On the other side of the table, opposite the Tin Woodman

was placed Trot, and next to her, Cap'n Bill. Then was seated Button-Bright and Ojo the Lucky, and Dr. Pipt and his good wife Margalot, and the astonishing Frogman, who had come from the Yip country to be present at Ozma's birthday feast.

At the foot of the table, facing Ozma, was seated the queenly Glinda, the good Sorceress of Oz, for this was really the place of honor next to the head of the table where Ozma herself sat. On Glinda's right was the Little Wizard of Oz, who owed to Glinda all of the magical arts he knew. Then came Jinjur, a pretty girl farmer of whom Ozma and Dorothy were quite fond. The adjoining seat was occupied by the Tin Soldier, and next to him was Professor H. M. Wogglebug, T.E., of the Royal Athletic College.

On Glinda's left was placed the jolly Patchwork Girl, who was a little afraid of the Sorceress and so was likely to behave herself pretty well. The Shaggy Man's brother was beside the Patchwork Girl, and then came that interesting personage, Jack Pumpkinhead, who had grown a splendid big pumpkin for a new head to be worn on Ozma's birthday, and had carved a face on it that was even jollier in expression than the one he had last worn. New heads were not unusual with Jack, for the pumpkins did not keep long, and when the seeds—which served him as brains—began to get soft and mushy, he realized his head would soon spoil, and so he procured a new one from his great field of pumpkins—grown by him so that he need never lack a head.

You will have noticed that the company at Ozma's banquet table was somewhat mixed, but every one invited was a
tried and trusted friend of the girl Ruler, and their presence
made her quite happy.

No sooner had Ozma seated herself, with her back to the
birthday table, than she noticed that all present were eyeing
with curiosity and pleasure something behind her, for the gorgeous Magic Flower was blooming gloriously and the mam-
moth blossoms that quickly succeeded one another on the
plant were beautiful to view and filled the entire room with
their delicate fragrance. Ozma wanted to look, too, to see what
all were staring at, but she controlled her curiosity because it
was not proper that she should yet view her birthday gifts.

So the sweet and lovely Ruler devoted herself to her guests,
several of whom, such as the Scarecrow, the Tin Woodman,
the Patchwork Girl, Tik-Tok, Jack Pumpkinhead and the Tin
Soldier, never ate anything but sat very politely in their places
and tried to entertain those of the guests who did eat.

And, at the animal table, there was another interesting
group, consisting of the Cowardly Lion, the Hungry Tiger,
Toto—Dorothy's little shaggy black dog—Hank the Mule, the
Pink Kitten, the Wooden Sawhorse, the Yellow Hen, and the
Glass Cat. All of these had good appetites except the Sawhorse and the Glass Cat, and each was given a plentiful supply
of the food it liked best.

Finally, when the banquet was nearly over and the ice-cream was to be served, four servants entered bearing a huge cake, all frosted and decorated with candy flowers. Around the edge of the cake was a row of lighted candles, and in the center were raised candy letters that spelled the words:

OZMA'S
Birthday Cake
from
Dorothy and the Wizard

"Oh, how beautiful!" cried Ozma, greatly delighted, and Dorothy said eagerly: "Now you must cut the cake, Ozma, and each of us will eat a piece with our ice-cream."

Jellia Jamb brought a large golden knife with a jeweled handle, and Ozma stood up in her place and attempted to cut the cake. But as soon as the frosting in the center broke under the pressure of the knife there leaped from the cake a tiny monkey three inches high, and he was followed by another and another, until twelve monkeys stood on the tablecloth and bowed low to Ozma.

"Congratulations to our gracious Ruler!" they exclaimed in a chorus, and then they began a dance, so droll and amusing that all the company roared with laughter and even Ozma joined in the merriment. But after the dance the monkeys performed some wonderful acrobatic feats, and then they ran to the hollow of the cake and took out some band instruments of burnished gold—cornets, horns, drums, and the like—and forming into a procession the monkeys marched up and down the table playing a jolly tune with the ease of skilled musicians.

Dorothy was delighted with the success of her "Surprise Cake," and after the monkeys had finished their performance, the banquet came to an end.

Now was the time for Ozma to see her other presents, so Glinda the Good rose and, taking the girl Ruler by her hand, led her to the table where all her gifts were placed in magnificent array. The Magic Flower of course attracted her attention first, and Trot had to tell her the whole story of their adventures in getting it. The little girl did not forget to give due credit to the Glass Cat and the little Wizard, but it was really Cap'n Bill who had bravely carried the golden flower-pot away from the enchanted Isle.

Ozma thanked them all, and said she would place the Magic Flower in her boudoir where she might enjoy its beauty and fragrance continually. But now she discovered the marvelous gown woven by Glinda and her maidens from strands drawn from pure emeralds, and being a girl who loved pretty clothes, Ozma's ecstasy at being presented with this exquisite gown may well be imagined. She could hardly wait to put it on, but the table was loaded with other pretty gifts and the night was far spent before the happy girl Ruler had examined all her presents and thanked those who had lovingly donated them.

···—·< Chapter 23 ›··—··

The FOUNTAIN of OBLIVION

The morning after the birthday fete, as the Wizard and Dorothy were walking in the grounds of the palace, Ozma came out and joined them, saying:

"I want to hear more of your adventures in the Forest of Gugu, and how you were able to get those dear little monkeys to use in Dorothy's Surprise Cake."

So they sat down on a marble bench near to the Fountain of the Water of Oblivion, and between them Dorothy and the Wizard related their adventures.

"I was dreadfully fussy while I was a woolly lamb," said Dorothy, "for it didn't feel good, a bit. And I wasn't quite sure, you know, that I'd ever get to be a girl again."

"You might have been a woolly lamb yet, if I hadn't happened to have discovered that Magic Transformation Word," declared the Wizard.

"But what became of the walnut and the hickory-nut into which you transformed those dreadful beast magicians?" inquired Ozma.

"Why, I'd almost forgotten them," was the reply; "but I believe they are still here in my pocket."

Then he searched in his pockets and brought out the two nuts and showed them to her.

Ozma regarded them thoughtfully.

"It isn't right to leave any living creatures in such helpless forms," said she. "I think, Wizard, you ought to transform them into their natural shapes again."

"But I don't know what their natural shapes are," he objected, "for of course the forms of mixed animals which they had assumed were not natural to them. And you must not forget, Ozma, that their natures were cruel and mischievous, so if I bring them back to life they might cause us a great deal of trouble."

"Nevertheless," said the Ruler of Oz, "we must free them from their present enchantments. When you restore them to their natural forms we will discover who they really are, and surely we need not fear any two people, even though they prove to be magicians and our enemies."

"I am not so sure of that," protested the Wizard, with a shake of his bald head. "The one bit of magic I robbed them of—which was the Word of Transformation—is so simple, yet so powerful, that neither Glinda nor I can equal it. It isn't all in the word, you know, it's the way the word is pronounced. So if the two strange magicians have other magic of the same sort, they might prove very dangerous to us, if we liberated them."

"I've an idea!" exclaimed Dorothy. "I'm no wizard, and no fairy, but if you do as I say, we needn't fear these people at all."

"What is your thought, my dear?" asked Ozma.

"Well," replied the girl, "here is this Fountain of the Water of Oblivion, and that's what put the notion into my head. When the Wizard speaks that ter'ble word that will change 'em back to their real forms, he can make 'em dreadful thirsty, too, and we'll put a cup right here by the fountain, so it'll be handy. Then they'll drink the water and forget all the magic they ever knew—and everything else, too."

"That's not a bad idea," said the Wizard, looking at Dorothy approvingly.

"It's a very *good* idea," declared Ozma. "Run for a cup, Dorothy."

So Dorothy ran to get a cup, and while she was gone the Wizard said:

"I don't know whether the real forms of these magicians

are those of men or beasts. If they're beasts, they would not drink from a cup but might attack us at once and drink afterward. So it might be safer for us to have the Cowardly Lion and the Hungry Tiger here to protect us if necessary."

Ozma drew out a silver whistle which was attached to a slender gold chain and blew upon the whistle two shrill blasts. The sound, though not harsh, was very penetrating, and as soon as it reached the ears of the Cowardly Lion and the Hungry Tiger, the two huge beasts quickly came bounding toward them. Ozma explained to them what the Wizard was about to do, and told them to keep quiet unless danger threatened. So the two powerful guardians of the Ruler of Oz crouched beside the fountain and waited.

Dorothy returned and set the cup on the edge of the fountain. Then the Wizard placed the hickory-nut beside the fountain and said in a solemn voice:

"I want you to resume your natural form, and to be very thirsty—Pyrzqxgl!"

In an instant there appeared, in the place of the hickory-nut, the form of Kiki Aru, the Hyup boy. He seemed bewildered, at first, as if trying to remember what had happened to him and why he was in this strange place. But he was facing the fountain, and the bubbling water reminded him that he was thirsty. Without noticing Ozma, the Wizard and Dorothy, who were behind him, he picked up the cup, filled it with the Water of Oblivion, and drank it to the last drop.

He was now no longer thirsty, but he felt more bewildered than ever, for now he could remember nothing at all—not even his name or where he came from. He looked around the beautiful garden with a pleased expression, and then, turning, he beheld Ozma and the Wizard and Dorothy regarding him curiously and the two great beasts crouching behind them.

Kiki Aru did not know who they were, but he thought Ozma very lovely and Dorothy very pleasant. So he smiled at them—the same innocent, happy smile that a baby might have indulged in, and that pleased Dorothy, who seized his hand and led him to a seat beside her on the bench.

"Why, I thought you were a dreadful magician," she exclaimed, "and you're only a boy!"

"What is a magician?" he asked, "and what is a boy?"

"Don't you know?" inquired the girl.

Kiki shook his head. Then he laughed.

"I do not seem to know anything," he replied.

"It's very curious," remarked the Wizard. "He wears the dress of the Munchkins, so he must have lived at one time in the Munchkin Country. Of course the boy can tell us nothing of his history or his family, for he has forgotten all that he ever knew."

"He seems a nice boy, now that all the wickedness has gone from him," said Ozma. "So we will keep him here with us and teach him our ways—to be true and considerate of others."

"Why, in that case, it's lucky for him he drank the Water of Oblivion," said Dorothy.

"It is indeed," agreed the Wizard. "But the remarkable thing, to me, is how such a young boy ever learned the secret of the Magic Word of Transformation. Perhaps his companion, who is at present this walnut, was the real magician, although I seem to remember that it was this boy in the beast's form who whispered the Magic Word into the hollow tree, where I overheard it."

"Well, we will soon know who the other is," suggested Ozma. "He may prove to be another Munchkin boy."

The Wizard placed the walnut near the fountain and said, as slowly and solemnly as before:

"I want you to resume your natural form, and to be very thirsty—Pyrzqxgl!"

Then the walnut disappeared and Ruggedo the Nome stood in its place. He also was facing the fountain, and he reached for the cup, filled it, and was about to drink when Dorothy exclaimed:

"Why, it's the old Nome King!"

Ruggedo swung around and faced them, the cup still in his hand.

"Yes," he said in an angry voice, "it's the old Nome King, and I'm going to conquer all Oz and be revenged on you for kicking me out of my throne." He looked around a moment, and then continued: "There isn't an egg in sight, and I'm stronger than all of you people put together! I don't know how I came here, but I'm going to fight the fight of my life—and I'll win!"

His long white hair and beard waved in the breeze; his eyes flashed hate and vengeance, and so astonished and shocked were they by the sudden appearance of this old enemy of the Oz people that they could only stare at him in silence and shrink away from his wild glare.

Ruggedo laughed. He drank the water, threw the cup on the ground and said fiercely:

"And now—and now—and—"

His voice grew gentle. He rubbed his forehead with a puzzled air and stroked his long beard.

"What was I going to say?" he asked, pleadingly.

"Don't you remember?" said the Wizard.

"No; I've forgotten."

"Who *are* you?" asked Dorothy.

He tried to think. "I—I'm sure I don't know," he stammered.

"Don't you know who *we* are, either?" questioned the girl.

"I haven't the slightest idea," said the Nome.

"Tell us who this Munchkin boy is," suggested Ozma.

Ruggedo looked at the boy and shook his head.

"He's a stranger to me. You are all strangers. I—I'm a stranger to myself," he said.

Then he patted the Lion's head and murmured, "Good doggie!" and the Lion growled indignantly.

"What shall we do with him?" asked the Wizard, perplexed.

"Once before the wicked old Nome came here to conquer

us, and then, as now, he drank of the Water of Oblivion and became harmless. But we sent him back to the Nome Kingdom, where he soon learned the old evil ways again.

"For that reason," said Ozma, "we must find a place for him in the Land of Oz, and keep him here. For here he can learn no evil and will always be as innocent of guile as our own people."

And so the wandering ex-King of the Nomes found a new home, a peaceful and happy home, where he was quite content and passed his days in innocent enjoyment.

Glinda

of

OZ

This book is dedicated to my son Robert Stanton Baum

·····◄ Chapter 1 ►·····

The CALL to DUTY

Glinda, the good Sorceress of Oz, sat in the grand court of her palace, surrounded by her maids of honor—a hundred of the most beautiful girls of the Fairyland of Oz. The palace court was built of rare marbles, exquisitely polished. Fountains tinkled musically here and there; the vast colonnade, open to the south, allowed the maidens, as they raised their heads from their embroideries, to gaze upon a vista of rose-hued fields and groves of trees bearing fruits or laden with sweet-scented flowers. At times one of the girls would start a song, the others joining in the chorus, or one would rise and dance, gracefully swaying to the music of a harp played by a companion. And then Glinda smiled, glad to see her maids mixing play with work.

Presently among the fields an object was seen moving, threading the broad path that led to the castle gate. Some of the girls looked upon this object enviously; the Sorceress merely gave it a glance and nodded her stately head as if pleased, for it meant the coming of her friend and mistress— the only one in all the land that Glinda bowed to.

Then up the path trotted a wooden animal attached to a red wagon, and as the quaint steed halted at the gate there descended from the wagon two young girls, Ozma, Ruler of Oz, and her companion, Princess Dorothy. Both were dressed in simple white muslin gowns, and as they ran up the marble steps of the palace they laughed and chatted as gaily as if they were not the most important persons in the world's loveliest fairyland.

The maids of honor had risen and stood with bowed heads to greet the royal Ozma, while Glinda came forward with outstretched arms to greet her guests.

"We've just come on a visit, you know," said Ozma. "Both Dorothy and I were wondering how we should pass the day when we happened to think we'd not been to your Quadling Country for weeks, so we took the Sawhorse and rode straight here."

"And we came so fast," added Dorothy, "that our hair is blown all fuzzy, for the Sawhorse makes a wind of his own.

Usually it's a day's journey from the Em'rald City, but I don't s'pose we were two hours on the way."

"You are most welcome," said Glinda the Sorceress, and led them through the court to her magnificent reception hall. Ozma took the arm of her hostess, but Dorothy lagged behind, kissing some of the maids she knew best, talking with others, and making them all feel that she was their friend. When at last she joined Glinda and Ozma in the reception hall, she found them talking earnestly about the condition of the people, and how to make them more happy and contented— although they were already the happiest and most contented folks in all the world.

This interested Ozma, of course, but it didn't interest Dorothy very much, so the little girl ran over to a big table on which was lying open Glinda's Great Book of Records.

This Book is one of the greatest treasures in Oz, and the Sorceress prizes it more highly than any of her magical possessions. That is the reason it is firmly attached to the big marble table by means of golden chains, and whenever Glinda leaves home she locks the Great Book together with five jeweled padlocks, and carries the keys safely hidden in her bosom.

I do not suppose there is any magical thing in any fairyland to compare with the Record Book, on the pages of which are constantly being printed a record of every event that happens in any part of the world, at exactly the moment it happens. And the records are always truthful, although sometimes they do not give as many details as one could wish. But then, lots of things happen, and so the records have to be brief or even Glinda's Great Book could not hold them all.

Glinda looked at the records several times each day, and Dorothy, whenever she visited the Sorceress, loved to look in the Book and see what was happening everywhere. Not much was recorded about the Land of Oz, which is usually peaceful and uneventful, but today Dorothy found something which interested her. Indeed, the printed letters were appearing on the page even while she looked.

"This is funny!" she exclaimed. "Did you know, Ozma, that there were people in your Land of Oz called Skeezers?"

"Yes," replied Ozma, coming to her side, "I know that on Professor Wogglebug's Map of the Land of Oz there is a place marked 'Skeezer,' but what the Skeezers are like I do not know. No one I know has ever seen them or heard of them. The Skeezer Country is 'way at the upper edge of the Gillikin Country, with the sandy, impassable desert on one side and the mountains of Oogaboo on another side. That is a part of the Land of Oz of which I know very little."

"I guess no one else knows much about it either, unless it's the Skeezers themselves," remarked Dorothy. "But the Book says: 'The Skeezers of Oz have declared war on the Flatheads of Oz, and there is likely to be fighting and much trouble as the result.'"

"Is that all the Book says?" asked Ozma.

"Every word," said Dorothy, and Ozma and Glinda both looked at the Record and seemed surprised and perplexed.

"Tell me, Glinda," said Ozma, "who are the Flatheads?"

"I cannot, your Majesty," confessed the Sorceress. "Until now I never have heard of them, nor have I ever heard the Skeezers mentioned. In the faraway corners of Oz are hidden many curious tribes of people, and those who never leave their own countries and never are visited by those from our favored part of Oz, naturally are unknown to me. However, if you so desire, I can learn through my arts of sorcery something of the Skeezers and the Flatheads."

"I wish you would," answered Ozma seriously. "You see, Glinda, if these are Oz people they are my subjects and I cannot allow any wars or troubles in the Land I rule, if I can possibly help it."

"Very well, your Majesty," said the Sorceress, "I will try to get some information to guide you. Please excuse me for a time, while I retire to my Room of Magic and Sorcery."

"May I go with you?" asked Dorothy, eagerly.

"No, Princess," was the reply. "It would spoil the charm to have anyone present."

So Glinda locked herself in her own Room of Magic and Dorothy and Ozma waited patiently for her to come out again.

In about an hour Glinda appeared, looking grave and thoughtful.

"Your Majesty," she said to Ozma, "the Skeezers live on

a Magic Isle in a great lake. For that reason—because the Skeezers deal in magic—I can learn little about them."

"Why, I didn't know there was a lake in that part of Oz," exclaimed Ozma. "The map shows a river running through the Skeezer Country, but no lake."

"That is because the person who made the map never had visited that part of the country," explained the Sorceress. "The lake surely is there, and in the lake is an island—a Magic Isle—and on that island live the people called the Skeezers."

"What are they like?" inquired the Ruler of Oz.

"My magic cannot tell me that," confessed Glinda, "for the magic of the Skeezers prevents anyone outside of their domain knowing anything about them."

"The Flatheads must know, if they're going to fight the Skeezers," suggested Dorothy.

"Perhaps so," Glinda replied, "but I can get little information concerning the Flatheads, either. They are people who inhabit a mountain just south of the Lake of the Skeezers. The mountain has steep sides and a broad, hollow top, like a basin, and in this basin the Flatheads have their dwellings. They also are magic-workers and usually keep to themselves and allow no one from outside to visit them. I have learned that the Flatheads number about one hundred people—men, women and children—while the Skeezers number just one hundred and one."

"What did they quarrel about, and why do they wish to fight one another?" was Ozma's next question.

"I cannot tell your Majesty that," said Glinda.

"But see here!" cried Dorothy, "it's against the law for anyone but Glinda and the Wizard to work magic in the Land of Oz, so if these two strange people are magic-makers they are breaking the law and ought to be punished!"

Ozma smiled upon her little friend. "Those who do not know me or my laws," she said, "cannot be expected to obey my laws. If we know nothing of the Skeezers or the Flatheads, it is likely that they know nothing of us."

"But they ought to know, Ozma, and we ought to know. Who's going to tell them, and how are we going to make them behave?"

"That," returned Ozma, "is what I am now considering. What would you advise, Glinda?"

The Sorceress took a little time to consider this question, before she made reply. Then she said: "Had you not learned of the existence of the Flatheads and the Skeezers, through my Book of Records, you would never have worried about them or their quarrels. So, if you pay no attention to these peoples, you may never hear of them again."

"But that wouldn't be right," declared Ozma. "I am Ruler of all the Land of Oz, which includes the Gillikin Country, the Quadling Country, the Winkie Country and the Munchkin Country, as well as the Emerald City, and being the Princess of this fairyland it is my duty to make all my people—wherever they may be—happy and content and to settle their disputes and keep them from quarreling. So, while the Skeezers and Flatheads may not know me or that I am their lawful Ruler, I now know that they inhabit my kingdom and are my subjects, so I would not be doing my duty if I kept away from them and allowed them to fight."

"That's a fact, Ozma," commented Dorothy. "You've got to go up to the Gillikin Country and make these people behave themselves and make up their quarrels. But how are you going to do it?"

"That is what is puzzling me also, your Majesty," said the Sorceress. "It may be dangerous for you to go into those strange countries, where the people are possibly fierce and warlike."

"I am not afraid," said Ozma, with a smile.

"'Tisn't a question of being 'fraid," argued Dorothy. "Of course we know you're a fairy, and can't be killed or hurt, and we know you've a lot of magic of your own to help you. But, Ozma dear, in spite of all this you've been in trouble before, on account of wicked enemies, and it isn't right for the Ruler of all Oz to put herself in danger."

"Perhaps I shall be in no danger at all," returned Ozma, with a little laugh. "You mustn't imagine danger, Dorothy, for one should only imagine nice things, and we do not know that the Skeezers and Flatheads are wicked people or my enemies. Perhaps they would be good and listen to reason."

"Dorothy is right, your Majesty," asserted the Sorceress.

"It is true we know nothing of these faraway subjects, except that they intend to fight one another, and have a certain amount of magic power at their command. Such folks do not like to submit to interference and they are more likely to resent your coming among them than to receive you kindly and graciously, as is your due."

"If you had an army to take with you," added Dorothy, "it wouldn't be so bad; but there isn't such a thing as an army in all Oz."

"I have one soldier," said Ozma.

"Yes, the Soldier with the Green Whiskers; but he's dreadful 'fraid of his gun and never loads it. I'm sure he'd run rather than fight. And one soldier, even if he were brave, couldn't do much against two hundred and one Flatheads and Skeezers."

"What then, my friends, would you suggest?" inquired Ozma.

"I advise you to send the Wizard of Oz to them, and let him inform them that it is against the laws of Oz to fight, and that you command them to settle their differences and become friends," proposed Glinda. "Let the Wizard tell them they will be punished if they refuse to obey the commands of the Princess of all the Land of Oz."

Ozma shook her head, to indicate that the advice was not to her satisfaction.

"If they refuse, what then?" she asked. "I should be obliged to carry out my threat and punish them, and that would be an unpleasant and difficult thing to do. I am sure it would be better for me to go peacefully, without an army and armed only with my authority as Ruler, and plead with them to obey me. Then, if they prove obstinate I could resort to other means to win their obedience."

"It's a ticklish thing, anyhow you look at it," sighed Dorothy. "I'm sorry now that I noticed the Record in the Great Book."

"But can't you realize, my dear, that I must do my duty, now that I am aware of this trouble?" asked Ozma. "I am fully determined to go at once to the Magic Isle of the Skeezers and to the enchanted mountain of the Flatheads, and prevent war and strife between their inhabitants. The only question to decide is whether it is better for me to go alone, or to assemble a party of my friends and loyal supporters to accompany me."

"If you go I want to go, too," declared Dorothy. "Whatever happens it's going to be fun—'cause all excitement is fun—and I wouldn't miss it for the world!"

Neither Ozma nor Glinda paid any attention to this statement, for they were gravely considering the serious aspect of this proposed adventure.

"There are plenty of friends who would like to go with you," said the Sorceress, "but none of them would afford your Majesty any protection in case you were in danger. You are yourself the most powerful fairy in Oz, although both I and the Wizard have more varied arts of magic at our command.

However, you have one art that no other in all the world can equal—the art of winning hearts and making people love to bow to your gracious presence. For that reason I believe you can accomplish more good alone than with a large number of subjects in your train."

"I believe that also," agreed the Princess. "I shall be quite able to take care of myself, you know, but might not be able to protect others so well. I do not look for opposition, however. I shall speak to these people in kindly words and settle their dispute—whatever it may be—in a just manner."

"Aren't you going to take me?" pleaded Dorothy. "You'll need some companion, Ozma."

The Princess smiled upon her little friend.

"I see no reason why you should not accompany me," was her reply. "Two girls are not very warlike and they will not suspect us of being on any errand but a kindly and peaceful one. But, in order to prevent war and strife between these angry peoples, we must go to them at once. Let us return immediately to the Emerald City and prepare to start on our journey early tomorrow morning."

Glinda was not quite satisfied with this plan, but could not think of any better way to meet the problem. She knew that Ozma, with all her gentleness and sweet disposition, was accustomed to abide by any decision she had made and could not easily be turned from her purpose. Moreover she could see no great danger to the fairy Ruler of Oz in the undertaking,

even though the unknown people she was to visit proved obstinate. But Dorothy was not a fairy; she was a little girl who had
come from Kansas to live in the Land of Oz. Dorothy might
encounter dangers that to Ozma would be as nothing but to
an "Earth child" would be very serious.

The very fact that Dorothy lived in Oz, and had been
made a Princess by her friend Ozma, prevented her from
being killed or suffering any great bodily pain as long as she
lived in that fairyland. She could not grow big, either, and
would always remain the same little girl who had come to Oz,
unless in some way she left that fairyland or was spirited away
from it. But Dorothy was a mortal, nevertheless, and might
possibly be destroyed, or hidden where none of her friends
could ever find her. She could, for instance be cut into pieces,
and the pieces, while still alive and free from pain, could be
widely scattered; or she might be buried deep underground
or "destroyed" in other ways by evil magicians, were she not
properly protected. These facts Glinda was considering while
she paced with stately tread her marble hall.

Finally the good Sorceress paused and drew a ring from
her finger, handing it to Dorothy.

"Wear this ring constantly until your return," she said to
the girl. "If serious danger threatens you, turn the ring around
on your finger once to the right and another turn to the left.
That will ring the alarm bell in my palace and I will at once
come to your rescue. But do not use the ring unless you are

actually in danger of destruction. While you remain with Princess Ozma I believe she will be able to protect you from all lesser ills."

"Thank you, Glinda," responded Dorothy gratefully, as she placed the ring on her finger. "I'm going to wear my Magic Belt which I took from the Nome King, too, so I guess I'll be safe from anything the Skeezers and Flatheads try to do to me."

Ozma had many arrangements to make before she could leave her throne and her palace in the Emerald City, even for a trip of a few days, so she bade good-bye to Glinda and with Dorothy climbed into the Red Wagon. A word to the Wooden Sawhorse started that astonishing creature on the return journey, and so swiftly did he run that Dorothy was unable to talk or do anything but hold tight to her seat all the way back to the Emerald City.

Chapter 2

OZMA & DOROTHY

R esiding in Ozma's palace at this time was a live Scarecrow, a most remarkable and intelligent creature who had once ruled the Land of Oz for a brief period and was much loved and respected by all the people. Once a Munchkin farmer had stuffed an old suit of clothes with straw and put stuffed boots on the feet and used a pair of stuffed cotton gloves for hands. The head of the Scarecrow was a stuffed sack fastened to the body, with eyes, nose, mouth and ears painted on the sack. When a hat had been put on the head, the thing was a good imitation of a man. The farmer placed the Scarecrow on a pole in his cornfield and it came to life in a curious manner.

Dorothy, who was passing by the field, was hailed by the live Scarecrow and lifted him off his pole. He then went with her to the Emerald City, where the Wizard of Oz gave him some excellent brains, and the Scarecrow soon became an important personage.

Ozma considered the Scarecrow one of her best friends and most loyal subjects, so the morning after her visit to Glinda she asked him to take her place as Ruler of the Land of Oz while she was absent on a journey, and the Scarecrow at once consented without asking any questions.

Ozma had warned Dorothy to keep their journey a secret and say nothing to anyone about the Skeezers and Flatheads until their return, and Dorothy promised to obey. She longed to tell her girl friends, tiny Trot and Betsy Bobbin, of the adventure they were undertaking, but refrained from saying a word on the subject although both these girls lived with her in Ozma's palace.

Indeed, only Glinda the Sorceress knew they were going, until after they had gone, and even the Sorceress didn't know what their errand might be.

Princess Ozma took the Sawhorse and the Red Wagon, although she was not sure there was a wagon road all the way to the Lake of the Skeezers. The Land of Oz is a pretty big place, surrounded on all sides by a Deadly Desert which it is impossible to cross, and the Skeezer Country, according to the map, was in the farthest northwestern part of

Oz, bordering on the north desert. As the Emerald City was exactly in the center of Oz, it was no small journey from there to the Skeezers.

Around the Emerald City the country is thickly settled in every direction, but the farther away you get from the city the fewer people there are, until those parts that border on the desert have small populations. Also those faraway sections are little known to the Oz people, except in the south, where Glinda lives and where Dorothy has often wandered on trips of exploration.

The least known of all is the Gillikin Country, which harbors many strange bands of people among its mountains and valleys and forests and streams, and Ozma was now bound for the most distant part of the Gillikin Country.

"I am really sorry," said Ozma to Dorothy, as they rode away in the Red Wagon, "not to know more about the wonderful Land I rule. It is my duty to be acquainted with every tribe of people and every strange and hidden country in all Oz, but I am kept so busy at my palace making laws and planning for the comforts of those who live near the Emerald City, that I do not often find time to make long journeys."

"Well," replied Dorothy, "we'll prob'bly find out a lot on this trip, and we'll learn all about the Skeezers and Flatheads, anyhow. Time doesn't make much diff'rence in the Land of Oz, 'cause we don't grow up, or get old, or become sick and die, as they do other places; so, if we explore one place at a time, we'll by-an'-by know all about every nook and corner in Oz."

Dorothy wore around her waist the Nome King's Magic Belt, which protected her from harm, and the Magic Ring which Glinda had given her was on her finger. Ozma had merely slipped a small silver wand into the bosom of her gown, for fairies do not use chemicals and herbs and the tools of wizards and sorcerers to perform their magic. The Silver Wand was Ozma's one weapon of offense and defense and by its use she could accomplish many things.

They had left the Emerald City just at sunrise and the Sawhorse traveled very swiftly over the roads towards the north, but in a few hours the wooden animal had to slacken his pace because the farm-houses had become few and far between and often there were no paths at all in the direction they wished to follow. At such times they crossed the fields, avoiding groups of trees and fording the streams and rivulets whenever they came to them. But finally they reached a broad hillside closely covered with scrubby brush, through which the wagon could not pass.

"It will be difficult even for you and me to get through without tearing our dresses," said Ozma, "so we must leave the Sawhorse and the Wagon here until our return."

"That's all right," Dorothy replied, "I'm tired riding, anyhow. Do you s'pose, Ozma, we're anywhere near the Skeezer Country?"

"I cannot tell, Dorothy dear, but I know we've been going in the right direction, so we are sure to find it in time."

The scrubby brush was almost like a grove of small trees, for it reached as high as the heads of the two girls, neither of whom was very tall. They were obliged to thread their way in and out, until Dorothy was afraid they would get lost, and finally they were halted by a curious thing that barred their further progress. It was a huge web—as if woven by gigantic spiders—and the delicate, lacy film was fastened stoutly to the branches of the bushes and continued to the right and left in the form of a half circle. The threads of this web were of a brilliant purple color and woven into numerous artistic patterns, but it reached from the ground to branches above the heads of the girls and formed a sort of fence that hedged them in.

"It doesn't look very strong, though," said Dorothy. "I wonder if we couldn't break through." She tried but found the web stronger than it seemed. All her efforts could not break a single thread.

"We must go back, I think, and try to get around this peculiar web," Ozma decided.

So they turned to the right and, following the web found that it seemed to spread in a regular circle. On and on they went until finally Ozma said they had returned to the exact spot from which they had started. "Here is a handkerchief you dropped when we were here before," she said to Dorothy.

"In that case, they must have built the web behind us, after we walked into the trap," exclaimed the little girl.

"True," agreed Ozma, "an enemy has tried to imprison us."

"And they did it, too," said Dorothy. "I wonder who it was."

"It's a spider-web, I'm quite sure," returned Ozma, "but it must be the work of enormous spiders."

"Quite right!" cried a voice behind them. Turning quickly around they beheld a huge purple spider sitting not two yards away and regarding them with its small bright eyes.

Then there crawled from the bushes a dozen more great purple spiders, which saluted the first one and said:

"The web is finished, O King, and the strangers are our prisoners."

Dorothy did not like the looks of these spiders at all. They had big heads, sharp claws, small eyes and fuzzy hair all over their purple bodies.

"They look wicked," she whispered to Ozma. "What shall we do?"

Ozma gazed upon the spiders with a serious face.

"What is your object in making us prisoners?" she inquired.

"We need someone to keep house for us," answered the Spider King. "There is sweeping and dusting to be done, and polishing and washing of dishes, and that is work my people dislike to do. So we decided that if any strangers came our way we would capture them and make them our servants."

"I am Princess Ozma, Ruler of all Oz," said the girl with dignity.

"Well, I am King of all Spiders," was the reply, "and that makes me your master. Come with me to my palace and I will instruct you in your work."

"I won't," said Dorothy indignantly. "We won't have anything to do with you."

"We'll see about that," returned the Spider in a severe tone, and the next instant he made a dive straight at Dorothy, opening the claws in his legs as if to grab and pinch her with the sharp points. But the girl was wearing her Magic Belt and was not harmed. The Spider King could not even touch her. He turned swiftly and made a dash at Ozma, but she held her Magic Wand over his head and the monster recoiled as if it had been struck.

"You'd better let us go," Dorothy advised him, "for you see you can't hurt us."

"So I see," returned the Spider King angrily. "Your magic is greater than mine. But I'll not help you to escape. If you can break the magic web my people have woven you may go; if not you must stay here and starve." With that the Spider King uttered a peculiar whistle and all the spiders disappeared.

"There is more magic in my fairyland than I dreamed of," remarked the beautiful Ozma, with a sigh of regret. "It seems that my laws have not been obeyed, for even these monstrous spiders defy me by means of Magic."

"Never mind that now," said Dorothy; "let's see what we can do to get out of this trap."

They now examined the web with great care and were amazed at its strength. Although finer than the finest silken hairs, it resisted all their efforts to work through, even though both girls threw all their weight against it.

"We must find some instrument which will cut the threads of the web," said Ozma, finally. "Let us look about for such a tool."

So they wandered among the bushes and finally came to a shallow pool of water, formed by a small bubbling spring. Dorothy stooped to get a drink and discovered in the water a green crab, about as big as her hand. The crab had two big, sharp claws, and as soon as Dorothy saw them she had an idea that those claws could save them.

"Come out of the water," she called to the crab; "I want to talk to you."

Rather lazily the crab rose to the surface and caught hold of a bit of rock. With his head above the water he said in a cross voice:

"What do you want?"

"We want you to cut the web of the purple spiders with your claws, so we can get through it," answered Dorothy. "You can do that, can't you?"

"I suppose so," replied the crab. "But if I do what will you give me?"

"What do you wish?" Ozma inquired.

"I wish to be white, instead of green," said the crab. "Green crabs are very common, and white ones are rare; besides, the purple spiders, which infest this hillside, are afraid of white crabs. Could you make me white if I should agree to cut the web for you?"

"Yes," said Ozma, "I can do that easily. And, so you may know I am speaking the truth, I will change your color now."

She waved her silver wand over the pool and the crab instantly became snow-white—all except his eyes, which remained black. The creature saw his reflection in the water and was so delighted that he at once climbed out of the pool and began moving slowly toward the web, by backing away from the pool. He moved so very slowly that Dorothy cried out impatiently: "Dear me, this will never do!" Catching the crab in her hands she ran with him to the web.

She had to hold him up even then, so he could reach with his claws strand after strand of the filmy purple web, which he was able to sever with one nip.

When enough of the web had been cut to allow them to pass, Dorothy ran back to the pool and placed the white crab in the water, after which she rejoined Ozma. They were just in time to escape through the web, for several of the purple spiders now appeared, having discovered that their web had been cut, and had the girls not rushed through the opening the spiders would have quickly repaired the cuts and again imprisoned them.

Ozma and Dorothy ran as fast as they could and although the angry spiders threw a number of strands of web after them, hoping to lasso them or entangle them in the coils, they managed to escape and clamber to the top of the hill.

.. —·•◄ Ꭿhapter 3 ►•·—.·

The MIST MAIDENS

From the top of the hill Ozma and Dorothy looked down into the valley beyond and were surprised to find it filled with a floating mist that was as dense as smoke. Nothing in the valley was visible except these rolling waves of mist, but beyond, on the other side, rose a grassy hill that appeared quite beautiful.

"Well," said Dorothy, "what are we to do, Ozma? Walk down into that thick fog, an' prob'bly get lost in it, or wait till it clears away?"

"I'm not sure it will clear away, however long we wait," replied Ozma, doubtfully. "If we wish to get on, I think we must venture into the mist."

"But we can't see where we're going, or what we're stepping on," protested Dorothy. "There may be dreadful things mixed up in that fog, an' I'm scared just to think of wading into it."

Even Ozma seemed to hesitate. She was silent and thoughtful for a little while, looking at the rolling drifts that were so grey and forbidding. Finally she said:

"I believe this is a Mist Valley, where these moist clouds always remain, for even the sunshine above does not drive them away. Therefore the Mist Maids must live here, and they are fairies and should answer my call."

She placed her two hands before her mouth, forming a hollow with them, and uttered a clear, thrilling, bird-like cry. It floated far out over the mist waves and presently was answered by a similar sound, as of a far-off echo.

Dorothy was much impressed. She had seen many strange things since coming to this fairy country, but here was a new experience. At ordinary times Ozma was just like any little girl one might chance to meet—simple, merry, lovable as could be—yet with a certain reserve that lent her dignity in her most joyous moods. There were times, however, when seated on her throne and commanding her subjects, or when her fairy powers were called into use, when Dorothy and all others about her stood in awe of their lovely girl Ruler and realized her superiority.

Ozma waited. Presently out from the billows rose beautiful

forms, clothed in fleecy, trailing garments of grey that could scarcely be distinguished from the mist. Their hair was mist-color, too; only their gleaming arms and sweet, pallid faces proved they were living, intelligent creatures answering the call of a sister fairy.

Like sea nymphs they rested on the bosom of the clouds, their eyes turned questioningly upon the two girls who stood upon the bank. One came quite near and to her Ozma said:

"Will you please take us to the opposite hillside? We are afraid to venture into the mist. I am Princess Ozma of Oz, and this is my friend Dorothy, a Princess of Oz."

The Mist Maids came nearer, holding out their arms. Without hesitation Ozma advanced and allowed them to embrace her and Dorothy plucked up courage to follow. Very gently the Mist Maids held them. Dorothy thought the arms were cold and misty—they didn't seem real at all—yet they supported the two girls above the surface of the billows and floated with them so swiftly to the green hillside opposite that the girls were astonished to find themselves set upon the grass before they realized they had fairly started.

"Thank you!" said Ozma gratefully, and Dorothy also added her thanks for the service.

The Mist Maids made no answer, but they smiled and waved their hands in good-bye as again they floated out into the mist and disappeared from view.

Chapter 4

The MAGIC TENT

Well," said Dorothy with a laugh, "that was easier than I expected. It's worth while, sometimes, to be a real fairy. But I wouldn't like to be that kind, and live in a dreadful fog all the time."

They now climbed the bank and found before them a delightful plain that spread for miles in all directions. Fragrant wild flowers were scattered throughout the grass; there were bushes bearing lovely blossoms and luscious fruits; now and then a group of stately trees added to the beauty of the landscape. But there were no dwellings or signs of life.

The farther side of the plain was bordered by a row of

palms, and just in front of the palms rose a queerly shaped hill that towered above the plain like a mountain. The sides of this hill were straight up and down; it was oblong in shape and the top seemed flat and level.

"Oh, ho!" cried Dorothy; "I'll bet that's the mountain Glinda told us of, where the Flatheads live."

"If it is," replied Ozma, "the Lake of the Skeezers must be just beyond the line of palm trees. Can you walk that far, Dorothy?"

"Of course, in time," was the prompt answer. "I'm sorry we had to leave the Sawhorse and the Red Wagon behind us, for they'd come in handy just now; but with the end of our journey in sight a tramp across these pretty green fields won't tire us a bit."

It was a longer tramp than they suspected, however, and night overtook them before they could reach the flat mountain. So Ozma proposed they camp for the night and Dorothy was quite ready to approve. She didn't like to admit to her friend she was tired, but she told herself that her legs "had prickers in 'em," meaning they had begun to ache.

Usually when Dorothy started on a journey of exploration or adventure, she carried with her a basket of food, and other things that a traveler in a strange country might require, but to go away with Ozma was quite a different thing, as experience had taught her. The fairy Ruler of Oz only needed her silver wand—tipped at one end with a great sparkling emerald—to provide through its magic all that they might need. There-fore Ozma, having halted with her companion and selected a smooth, grassy spot on the plain, waved her wand in grace-ful curves and chanted some mystic words in her sweet voice, and in an instant a handsome tent appeared before them. The canvas was striped purple and white, and from the center pole fluttered the royal banner of Oz.

"Come, dear," said Ozma, taking Dorothy's hand, "I am hungry and I'm sure you must be also; so let us go in and have our feast."

On entering the tent they found a table set for two, with snowy linen, bright silver and sparkling glassware, a vase of roses in the center and many dishes of delicious food, some smoking hot, waiting to satisfy their hunger. Also, on either side of the tent were beds, with satin sheets, warm blankets and pillows filled with swansdown. There were chairs, too, and tall lamps that lighted the interior of the tent with a soft, rosy glow.

Dorothy, resting herself at her fairy friend's command, and eating her dinner with unusual enjoyment, thought of the wonders of magic. If one were a fairy and knew the secret laws of nature and the mystic words and ceremonies that com-manded those laws, then a simple wave of a silver wand would produce instantly all that men work hard and anxiously for through weary years. And Dorothy wished in her kindly, inno-cent heart, that all men and women could be fairies with silver wands, and satisfy all their needs without so much work and worry, for then, she imagined, they would have all their working hours to be happy in. But Ozma, looking into her friend's face and reading those thoughts, gave a laugh and said:

"No, no, Dorothy, that wouldn't do at all. Instead of happiness your plan would bring weariness to the world. If every one could wave a wand and have his wants fulfilled there would be little to wish for. There would be no eager striving to obtain the difficult, for nothing would then be difficult, and the pleasure of earning something longed for, and only to be secured by hard work and careful thought, would be utterly lost. There would be nothing to do you see, and no interest in life and in our fellow creatures. That is all that makes life worth our while—to do good deeds and to help those less fortunate than ourselves."

"Well, you're a fairy, Ozma. Aren't you happy?" asked Dorothy.

"Yes, dear, because I can use my fairy powers to make others happy. Had I no kingdom to rule, and no subjects to look after, I would be miserable. Also, you must realize that while I am a more powerful fairy than any other inhabitant of Oz, I am not as powerful as Glinda the Sorceress, who has studied many arts of magic that I know nothing of. Even the little Wizard of Oz can do some things I am unable to accomplish, while I can accomplish things unknown to the Wizard. This is to explain that I'm not all-powerful, by any means. My magic is simply fairy magic, and not sorcery or wizardry."

"All the same," said Dorothy, "I'm mighty glad you could make this tent appear, with our dinners and beds all ready for us."

Ozma smiled.

"Yes, it is indeed wonderful," she agreed. "Not all fairies know that sort of magic, but some fairies can do magic that fills me with astonishment. I think that is what makes us modest and unassuming—the fact that our magic arts are divided, some being given each of us. I'm glad I don't know everything, Dorothy, and that there still are things in both nature and in wit for me to marvel at."

Dorothy couldn't quite understand this, so she said nothing more on the subject and presently had a new reason to marvel. For when they had quite finished their meal, table and contents disappeared in a flash.

"No dishes to wash, Ozma!" she said with a laugh. "I guess you'd make a lot of folks happy if you could teach 'em just that one trick."

For an hour Ozma told stories, and talked with Dorothy about various people in whom they were interested. And then it was bedtime, and they undressed and crept into their soft beds and fell asleep almost as soon as their heads touched their pillows.

Chapter 5

The MAGIC STAIRWAY

The flat mountain looked much nearer in the clear light of the morning sun, but Dorothy and Ozma knew there was a long tramp before them, even yet. They finished dressing only to find a warm, delicious breakfast awaiting them, and having eaten they left the tent and started toward the mountain which was their first goal. After going a little way Dorothy looked back and found that the fairy tent had entirely disappeared. She was not surprised, for she knew this would happen.

"Can't your magic give us a horse an' wagon, or an automobile?" inquired Dorothy.

"No, dear; I'm sorry that such magic is beyond my power," confessed her fairy friend.

"Perhaps Glinda could," said Dorothy thoughtfully.

"Glinda has a stork chariot that carries her through the air," said Ozma, "but even our great Sorceress cannot conjure up other modes of travel. Don't forget what I told you last night, that no one is powerful enough to do everything."

"Well, I s'pose I ought to know that, having lived so long in the Land of Oz," replied Dorothy; "but I can't do any magic at all, an' so I can't figure out e'zactly how you an' Glinda an' the Wizard do it."

"Don't try," laughed Ozma. "But you have at least one magical art, Dorothy: you know the trick of winning all hearts."

"No, I don't," said Dorothy earnestly. "If I really can do it, Ozma, I am sure I don't know how I do it."

It took them a good two hours to reach the foot of the round, flat mountain, and then they found the sides so steep that they were like the wall of a house.

"Even my purple kitten couldn't climb 'em," remarked Dorothy, gazing upward.

"But there is some way for the Flatheads to get down and up again," declared Ozma; "otherwise they couldn't make war with the Skeezers, or even meet them and quarrel with them."

"That's so, Ozma. Let's walk around a ways; perhaps we'll find a ladder or something."

They walked quite a distance, for it was a big mountain,

and as they circled around it and came to the side that faced the palm trees, they suddenly discovered an entrance way cut out of the rock wall. This entrance was arched overhead and not very deep because it merely led to a short flight of stone stairs.

"Oh, we've found a way to the top at last," announced Ozma, and the two girls turned and walked straight toward the entrance. Suddenly they bumped against something and stood still, unable to proceed farther.

"Dear me!" exclaimed Dorothy, rubbing her nose, which had struck something hard, although she could not see what it was; "this isn't as easy as it looks. What has stopped us, Ozma? Is it magic of some sort?"

Ozma was feeling around, her hands outstretched before her.

"Yes, dear, it is magic," she replied. "The Flatheads had to have a way from their mountain top from the plain below, but to prevent enemies from rushing up the stairs to conquer them, they have built, at a small distance before the entrance a wall of solid stone, the stones being held in place by cement, and then they made the wall invisible."

"I wonder why they did that?" mused Dorothy. "A wall would keep folks out anyhow, whether it could be seen or not, so there wasn't any use making it invisible. Seems to me it would have been better to have left it solid, for then no one would have seen the entrance behind it. Now anybody can see the entrance, as we did. And prob'bly anybody that tries to go up the stairs gets bumped, as we did."

Ozma made no reply at once. Her face was grave and thoughtful.

"I think I know the reason for making the wall invisible," she said after a while. "The Flatheads use the stairs for coming down and going up. If there was a solid stone wall to keep them from reaching the plain they would themselves be imprisoned by the wall. So they had to leave some place to get around the wall, and, if the wall was visible, all strangers or enemies would find the place to go around it and then the wall would be useless. So the Flatheads cunningly made their wall invisible, believing that everyone who saw the entrance to the mountain would walk straight toward it, as we did, and find it impossible to go any farther. I suppose the wall is really high and thick, and can't be broken through, so those who find it in their way are obliged to go away again."

"Well," said Dorothy, "if there's a way around the wall, where is it?"

"We must find it," returned Ozma, and began feeling her way along the wall. Dorothy followed and began to get discouraged when Ozma had walked nearly a quarter of a mile away from the entrance. But now the invisible wall curved in toward the side of the mountain and suddenly ended, leaving just space enough between the wall and the mountain for an ordinary person to pass through.

The girls went in, single file, and Ozma explained that they were now behind the barrier and could go back to the entrance. They met no further obstructions.

"Most people, Ozma, wouldn't have figured this thing out the way you did," remarked Dorothy. "If I'd been alone the invisible wall surely would have stumped me."

Reaching the entrance they began to mount the stone stairs. They went up ten stairs and then down five stairs, following a passage cut from the rock. The stairs were just wide enough for the two girls to walk abreast, arm in arm. At the bottom of the five stairs the passage turned to the right, and they ascended ten more stairs, only to find at the top of the flight five stairs leading straight down again. Again the passage turned abruptly, this time to the left, and ten more stairs led upward.

The passage was now quite dark, for they were in the heart of the mountain and all daylight had been shut out by the turns of the passage. However, Ozma drew her silver wand from her bosom and the great jewel at its end gave out a lustrous, green-tinted light which lighted the place well enough for them to see their way plainly.

Ten steps up, five steps down, and a turn, this way or that. That was the program, and Dorothy figured that they were only gaining five stairs upward each trip that they made.

"Those Flatheads must be funny people," she said to Ozma. "They don't seem to do anything in a bold straightforward manner. In making this passage they forced everyone to walk three times as far as is necessary. And of course this trip is just as tiresome to the Flatheads as it is to other folks."

"That is true," answered Ozma; "yet it is a clever arrangement to prevent their being surprised by intruders. Every time we reach the tenth step of a flight, the pressure of our feet on the stone makes a bell ring on top of the mountain, to warn the Flatheads of our coming."

"How do you know that?" demanded Dorothy, astonished.

"I've heard the bell ever since we started," Ozma told her. "You could not hear it, I know, but when I am holding my wand in my hand I can hear sounds a great distance off."

"Do you hear anything on top of the mountain 'cept the bell?" inquired Dorothy.

"Yes. The people are calling to one another in alarm and many footsteps are approaching the place where we will reach the flat top of the mountain."

This made Dorothy feel somewhat anxious. "I'd thought we were going to visit just common, ordinary people," she remarked, "but they're pretty clever, it seems, and they know some kinds of magic, too. They may be dangerous, Ozma. P'raps we'd better stayed at home."

Finally the upstairs-and-downstairs passage seemed coming to an end, for daylight again appeared ahead of the two girls and Ozma replaced her wand in the bosom of her gown. The last ten steps brought them to the surface, where they found themselves surrounded by such a throng of queer people that for a time they halted, speechless, and stared into the faces that confronted them.

Dorothy knew at once why these mountain people were called Flatheads. Their heads were really flat on top, as if they had been cut off just above the eyes and ears. Also the heads were bald, with no hair on top at all, and the ears were big and stuck straight out, and the noses were small and stubby, while the mouths of the Flatheads were well shaped and not unusual. Their eyes were perhaps their best feature, being large and bright and a deep violet in color.

The costumes of the Flatheads were all made of metals dug from their mountain. Small gold, silver, tin and iron discs, about the size of pennies, and very thin, were cleverly wired together and made to form knee trousers and jackets for the men and skirts and waists for the women. The colored metals were skillfully mixed to form stripes and checks of various sorts, so that the costumes were quite gorgeous and reminded Dorothy of pictures she had seen of Knights of old clothed armor.

Aside from their flat heads, these people were not really bad looking. The men were armed with bows and arrows and had small axes of steel stuck in their metal belts. They wore no hats nor ornaments.

Chapter 6

FLATHEAD MOUNTAIN

When they saw that the intruders on their mountain were only two little girls, the Flatheads grunted with satisfaction and drew back, permitting them to see what the mountain top looked like. It was shaped like a saucer, so that the houses and other buildings—all made of rocks—could not be seen over the edge by anyone standing in the plain below.

But now a big fat Flathead stood before the girls and in a gruff voice demanded:

"What are you doing here? Have the Skeezers sent you to spy upon us?"

"I am Princess Ozma, Ruler of all the Land of Oz."

"Well, I've never heard of the Land of Oz, so you may be what you claim," returned the Flathead.

"This is the Land of Oz—part of it, anyway," exclaimed Dorothy. "So Princess Ozma rules you Flathead people, as well as all the other people in Oz."

The man laughed, and all the others who stood around laughed, too. Some one in the crowd called:

"She'd better not tell the Supreme Dictator about ruling the Flatheads. Eh, friends?"

"No, indeed!" they all answered in positive tones.

"Who is your Supreme Dictator?" answered Ozma.

"I think I'll let him tell you that himself," answered the man who had first spoken. "You have broken our laws by coming here; and whoever you are the Supreme Dictator must fix your punishment. Come along with me."

He started down a path and Ozma and Dorothy followed him without protest, as they wanted to see the most important person in this queer country. The houses they passed seemed pleasant enough and each had a little yard in which were flowers and vegetables. Walls of rock separated the dwellings, and all the paths were paved with smooth slabs of rock. This seemed their only building material and they utilized it cleverly for every purpose.

Directly in the center of the great saucer stood a larger building which the Flathead informed the girls was the palace of the Supreme Dictator. He led them through an entrance hall into a big reception room, where they sat upon stone benches and awaited the coming of the Dictator. Pretty soon he entered from another room—a rather lean and rather old Flathead, dressed much like the others of this strange race, and only distinguished from them by the sly and cunning expression of his face. He kept his eyes half closed and looked through the slits of them at Ozma and Dorothy, who rose to receive him.

"Are you the Supreme Dictator of the Flatheads?" inquired Ozma.

"Yes, that's me," he said, rubbing his hands slowly together. "My word is law. I'm the head of the Flatheads on this flat head-land."

"I am Princess Ozma of Oz, and I have come from the Emerald City to—"

"Stop a minute," interrupted the Dictator, and turned to the man who had brought the girls there. "Go away, Dictator Felo Flathead!" he commanded. "Return to your duty and guard the Stairway. I will look after these strangers." The man bowed and departed, and Dorothy asked wonderingly:

"Is he a Dictator, too?"

"Of course," was the answer. "Everybody here is a dictator of something or other. They're all office holders. That's what keeps them contented. But I'm the Supreme Dictator of all, and I'm elected once a year. This is a democracy, you know, where the people are allowed to vote for their Rulers. A good

many others would like to be Supreme Dictator, but as I made
a law that I am always to count the votes myself, I am always
elected."

"What is your name?" asked Ozma.

"I am called the Su-dic, which is short for Supreme Dictator.
I sent that man away because the moment you mentioned Ozma
of Oz, and the Emerald City, I knew who you are. I suppose I'm
the only Flathead that ever heard of you, but that's because I
have more brains than the rest."

Dorothy was staring hard at the Su-dic.

"I don't see how you can have any brains at all," she
remarked, "because the part of your head is gone where brains
are kept."

"I don't blame you for thinking that," he said. "Once the
Flatheads had no brains because, as you say, there is no upper
part to their heads, to hold brains. But long, long ago a band
of fairies flew over this country and made it all a fairyland,
and when they came to the Flatheads the fairies were sorry
to find them all very stupid and quite unable to think. So, as
there was no good place in their bodies in which to put brains
the Fairy Queen gave each one of us a nice can of brains to
carry in his pocket and that made us just as intelligent as
other people. See," he continued, "here is one of the cans of
brains the fairies gave us." He took from a pocket a bright tin
can having a pretty red label on it which said: "Concentrated
Brains, Extra Quality."

"And does every Flathead have the same kind of brains?" asked Dorothy.

"Yes, they're all alike. Here's another can." From another pocket he produced a second can of brains.

"Did the fairies give you a double supply?" inquired Dorothy.

"No, but one of the Flatheads thought he wanted to be the Su-dic and tried to get my people to rebel against me, so I punished him by taking away his brains. One day my wife scolded me severely, so I took away her can of brains. She didn't like that and went out and robbed several women of their brains. Then I made a law that if anyone stole another's brains, or even tried to borrow them, he would forfeit his own brains to the Su-dic. So each one is content with his own canned brains and my wife and I are the only ones on the mountain with more than one can. I have three cans and that makes me very clever—so clever that I'm a good Sorcerer, if I do say it myself. My poor wife had four cans of brains and became a remarkable witch, but alas! that was before those terrible enemies, the Skeezers, transformed her into a Golden Pig."

"Good gracious!" cried Dorothy; "is your wife really a Golden Pig?"

"She is. The Skeezers did it and so I have declared war on them. In revenge for making my wife a Pig I intend to ruin their Magic Island and make the Skeezers the slaves of the Flatheads!"

The Su-dic was very angry now; his eyes flashed and his face took on a wicked and fierce expression. But Ozma said to him, very sweetly and in a friendly voice:

"I am sorry to hear this. Will you please tell me more about your troubles with the Skeezers? Then perhaps I can help you."

She was only a girl, but there was dignity in her pose and speech which impressed the Su-dic.

"If you are really Princess Ozma of Oz," the Flathead said, "you are one of that band of fairies who, under Queen Lurline, made all Oz a Fairyland. I have heard that Lurline left one of her own fairies to rule Oz, and gave the fairy the name of Ozma."

"If you knew this why did you not come to me at the Emerald City and tender me your loyalty and obedience?" asked the Ruler of Oz.

"Well, I only learned the fact lately, and I've been too busy to leave home," he explained, looking at the floor instead of into Ozma's eyes. She knew he had spoken a falsehood, but only said:

"Why did you quarrel with the Skeezers?"

"It was this way," began the Su-dic, glad to change the subject. "We Flatheads love fish, and as we have no fish on this mountain we would sometimes go to the Lake of the Skeezers to catch fish. This made the Skeezers angry, for they declared the fish in their lake belonged to them and were under their protection and they forbade us to catch them. That was very mean and unfriendly in the Skeezers, you must admit, and when we paid no attention to their orders they set a guard on the shore of the lake to prevent our fishing.

"Now, my wife, Rora Flathead, having four cans of brains, had become a wonderful witch, and fish being brain food, she loved to eat fish better than any one of us. So she vowed she would destroy every fish in the lake, unless the Skeezers let us catch what we wanted. They defied us, so Rora prepared a kettleful of magic poison and went down to the lake one night to dump it all in the water and poison the fish. It was a clever idea, quite worthy of my dear wife, but the Skeezer Queen—a young lady named Coo-ee-oh—hid on the bank of the lake and taking Rora unawares, transformed her into a Golden Pig. The poison was spilled on the ground and wicked Queen Coo-ee-oh, not content with her cruel transformation, even took away my wife's four cans of brains, so she is now a common grunting pig without even brains enough to know her own name."

"Then," said Ozma thoughtfully, "the Queen of the Skeezers must be a Sorceress."

"Yes," said the Su-dic, "but she doesn't know much magic, after all. She is not as powerful as Rora Flathead was, nor half as powerful as I am now, as Queen Coo-ee-oh will discover when we fight our great battle and destroy her."

"The Golden Pig can't be a witch any more, of course," observed Dorothy.

"No; even had Queen Coo-ee-oh left her the four cans of brains, poor Rora, in a pig's shape, couldn't do any witchcraft. A witch has to use her fingers, and a pig has only cloven hoofs."

"It seems a sad story," was Ozma's comment, "and all the trouble arose because the Flatheads wanted fish that did not belong to them."

"As for that," said the Su-dic, again angry, "I made a law that any of my people could catch fish in the Lake of the Skeezers, whenever they wanted to. So the trouble was through the Skeezers defying my law."

"You can only make laws to govern your own people," asserted Ozma sternly. "I, alone, am empowered to make laws that must be obeyed by all the peoples of Oz."

"Pooh!" cried the Su-dic scornfully. "You can't make me obey your laws, I assure you. I know the extent of your powers, Princess Ozma of Oz, and I know that I am more powerful than you are. To prove it I shall keep you and your companion prisoners in this mountain until after we have fought and conquered the Skeezers. Then, if you promise to be good, I may let you go home again."

Dorothy was amazed by this effrontery and defiance of the beautiful girl Ruler of Oz, whom all until now had obeyed without question. But Ozma, still unruffled and dignified, looked at the Su-dic and said:

"You did not mean that. You are angry and speak unwisely, without reflection. I came here from my palace in the Emerald

City to prevent war and to make peace between you and the Skeezers. I do not approve of Queen Coo-ee-oh's action in transforming your wife Rora into a pig, nor do I approve of Rora's cruel attempt to poison the fishes in the lake. No one has the right to work magic in my dominions without my consent, so the Flatheads and the Skeezers have both broken my laws—which must be obeyed."

"If you want to make peace," said the Su-dic, "make the Skeezers restore my wife to her proper form and give back her four cans of brains. Also make them agree to allow us to catch fish in their lake."

"No," returned Ozma, "I will not do that, for it would be unjust. I will have the Golden Pig again transformed into your wife Rora, and give her one can of brains, but the other three cans must be restored to those she robbed. Neither may you catch fish in the Lake of the Skeezers, for it is their lake and the fish belong to them. This arrangement is just and honorable, and you must agree to it."

"Never!" cried the Su-dic. Just then a pig came running into the room, uttering dismal grunts. It was made of solid gold, with joints at the bends of the legs and in the neck and jaws. The Golden Pig's eyes were rubies, and its teeth were polished ivory.

"There!" said the Su-dic, "gaze on the evil work of Queen Coo-ee-oh, and then say if you can prevent my making war on the Skeezers. That grunting beast was once my wife—the most beautiful Flathead on our mountain and a skillful witch. Now look at her!"

"Fight the Skeezers, fight the Skeezers, fight the Skeezers!" grunted the Golden Pig.

"I will fight the Skeezers," exclaimed the Flathead chief, "and if a dozen Ozmas of Oz forbade me I would fight just the same."

"Not if I can prevent it!" asserted Ozma.

"You can't prevent it. But since you threaten me, I'll have you confined in the bronze prison until the war is over," said the Su-dic. He whistled and four stout Flatheads, armed with axes and spears, entered the room and saluted him. Turning to the men he said: "Take these two girls, bind them with wire ropes and cast them into the bronze prison."

The four men bowed low and one of them asked:

"Where are the two girls, most noble Su-dic?"

The Su-dic turned to where Ozma and Dorothy had stood but they had vanished!

Chapter 7

The MAGIC ISLE

O zma, seeing it was useless to argue with the Supreme Dictator of the Flatheads, had been considering how best to escape from his power. She realized that his sorcery might be difficult to overcome, and when he threatened to cast Dorothy and her into a bronze prison she slipped her hand into her bosom and grasped her silver wand. With the other hand she grasped the hand of Dorothy, but these motions were so natural that the Su-dic did not notice them. Then when he turned to meet his four soldiers, Ozma instantly rendered both herself and Dorothy invisible and swiftly led her companion around the group of Flatheads and out of the room. As they reached the entry and descended the stone steps, Ozma whispered:

"Let us run, dear! We are invisible, so no one will see us."

Dorothy understood and she was a good runner. Ozma had marked the place where the grand stairway that led to the plain was located, so they made directly for it. Some people were in the paths but these they dodged around. One or two Flatheads heard the pattering of footsteps of the girls on the stone pavement and stopped with bewildered looks to gaze around them, but no one interfered with the invisible fugitives.

The Su-dic had lost no time in starting the chase. He and his men ran so fast that they might have overtaken the girls before they reached the stairway had not the Golden Pig suddenly run across their path. The Su-dic tripped over the pig and fell flat, and his four men tripped over him and tumbled in a heap. Before they could scramble up and reach the mouth of the passage it was too late to stop the two girls.

There was a guard on each side of the stairway, but of course they did not see Ozma and Dorothy as they sped past and descended the steps. Then they had to go up five steps and down another ten, and so on, in the same manner in which they had climbed to the top of the mountain. Ozma lighted their way with her wand and they kept on without relaxing their speed until they reached the bottom. Then they ran to the right and turned the corner of the invisible wall just as the Su-dic and his followers rushed out of the arched entrance and looked around in an attempt to discover the fugitives.

Ozma now knew they were safe, so she told Dorothy to stop and both of them sat down on the grass until they could breathe freely and become rested from their mad flight.

As for the Su-dic, he realized he was foiled and soon turned and climbed his stairs again. He was very angry—angry with Ozma and angry with himself—because, now that he took time to think, he remembered that he knew very well the art of making people invisible, and visible again, and if he had only thought of it in time he could have used his magic knowledge to make the girls visible and so have captured them easily. However, it was now too late for regrets and he determined to make preparations at once to march all his forces against the Skeezers.

"What shall we do next?" asked Dorothy, when they were rested.

"Let us find the Lake of the Skeezers," replied Ozma. "From what that dreadful Su-dic said I imagine the Skeezers are good people and worthy of our friendship, and if we go to them we may help them to defeat the Flatheads."

"I s'pose we can't stop the war now," remarked Dorothy reflectively, as they walked toward the row of palm trees.

"No; the Su-dic is determined to fight the Skeezers, so all

we can do is to warn them of their danger and help them as much as possible."

"Of course you'll punish the Flatheads," said Dorothy.

"Well, I do not think the Flathead people are as much to blame as their Supreme Dictator," was the answer. "If he is removed from power and his unlawful magic taken from him, the people will probably be good and respect the laws of the Land of Oz, and live at peace with all their neighbors in the future."

"I hope so," said Dorothy with a sigh of doubt.

The palms were not far from the mountain and the girls reached them after a brisk walk. The huge trees were set close together, in three rows, and had been planted so as to keep people from passing them, but the Flatheads had cut a passage through this barrier and Ozma found the path and led Dorothy to the other side.

Beyond the palms they discovered a very beautiful scene. Bordered by a green lawn was a great lake fully a mile from shore to shore, the waters of which were exquisitely blue and sparkling, with little wavelets breaking its smooth surface where the breezes touched it. In the center of this lake appeared a lovely island, not of great extent but almost entirely covered by a huge round building with glass walls and a high glass dome which glittered brilliantly in the sunshine. Between the glass building and the edge of the island was no grass, flowers or shrubbery, but only an expanse of highly polished white marble. There were no boats on either shore and no signs of life could be seen anywhere on the island.

"Well," said Dorothy, gazing wistfully at the island, "we've found the Lake of the Skeezers and their Magic Isle. I guess the Skeezers are in that big glass palace, but we can't get at 'em."

···—◄ Chapter 8 ►···—··

QUEEN COO-EE-OH

P rincess Ozma considered the situation gravely. Then she tied her handkerchief to her wand and, standing at the water's edge, waved the handkerchief like a flag, as a signal. For a time they could observe no response.

"I don't see what good that will do," said Dorothy. "Even if the Skeezers are on that island and see us, and know we're friends, they haven't any boats to come and get us."

But the Skeezers didn't need boats, as the girls soon discovered. For on a sudden an opening appeared at the base of the palace and from the opening came a slender shaft of steel, reaching out slowly but steadily across the water in the direction of the place where they stood. To the girls this steel arrangement looked like a triangle, with the base nearest the water. It came toward them in the form of an arch, stretching out from the palace wall until its end reached the bank and rested there, while the other end still remained on the island.

Then they saw that it was a bridge, consisting of a steel footway just broad enough to walk on, and two slender guide rails, one on either side, which were connected with the footway by steel bars. The bridge looked rather frail and Dorothy feared it would not bear their weight, but Ozma at once called, "Come on!" and started to walk across, holding fast to the rail on either side. So Dorothy summoned her courage and followed after. Before Ozma had taken three steps she halted and so forced Dorothy to halt, for the bridge was again moving and returning to the island.

"We need not walk after all," said Ozma. So they stood still in their places and let the steel bridge draw them onward. Indeed, the bridge drew them well into the glass-domed building which covered the island, and soon they found themselves standing in a marble room where two handsomely dressed young men stood on a platform to receive them.

Ozma at once stepped from the end of the bridge to the marble platform, followed by Dorothy, and then the bridge disappeared with a slight clang of steel and a marble slab covered the opening from which it had emerged.

The two young men bowed profoundly to Ozma, and one of them said:

"Queen Coo-ee-oh bids you welcome, O Strangers. Her Majesty is waiting to receive you in her palace."

"Lead on," replied Ozma with dignity.

But instead of "leading on," the platform of marble began to rise, carrying them upward through a square hole above which just fitted it. A moment later they found themselves within the great glass dome that covered almost all of the island.

Within this dome was a little village, with houses, streets, gardens and parks. The houses were of colored marbles, prettily designed, with many stained-glass windows, and the streets and gardens seemed well cared for. Exactly under the center of the lofty dome was a small park filled with brilliant flowers, with an elaborate fountain, and facing this park stood a building larger and more imposing than the others. Toward this building the young men escorted Ozma and Dorothy.

On the streets and in the doorways or open windows of the houses were men, women and children, all richly dressed. These were much like other people in different parts of the Land of Oz, except that instead of seeming merry and contented they all wore expressions of much solemnity or of nervous irritation. They had beautiful homes, splendid clothes, and ample food, but Dorothy at once decided something was wrong with their lives and that they were not happy. She said nothing, however, but looked curiously at the Skeezers.

At the entrance of the palace Ozma and Dorothy were met by two other young men, in uniform and armed with queer weapons that seemed about halfway between pistols and guns, but were like neither. Their conductors bowed and left them, and the two in uniforms led the girls into the palace.

In a beautiful Throne Room, surrounded by a dozen or more young men and women, sat the Queen of the Skeezers, Coo-ee-oh. She was a girl who looked older than Ozma or Dorothy—fifteen or sixteen, at least—and although she was elaborately dressed as if she were going to a ball she was too thin and plain of feature to be pretty. But evidently Queen Coo-ee-oh did not realize this fact, for her air and manner betrayed her as proud and haughty and with a high regard for her own importance. Dorothy at once decided she was "snippy" and that she would not like Queen Coo-ee-oh as a companion.

The Queen's hair was as black as her skin was white and her eyes were black, too. The eyes, as she calmly examined Ozma and Dorothy, had a suspicious and unfriendly look in them, but she said quietly:

"I know who you are, for I have consulted my Magic Oracle, which told me that one calls herself Princess Ozma, the Ruler of all the Land of Oz, and the other is Princess Dorothy of Oz, who came from a country called Kansas. I know nothing of the Land of Oz, and I know nothing of Kansas."

"Why, this is the Land of Oz!" cried Dorothy. "It's a part of the Land of Oz, anyhow, whether you know it or not."

"Oh, in-deed!" answered Queen Coo-ee-oh, scornfully. "I suppose you will claim next that this Princess Ozma, ruling the Land of Oz, rules me!"

"Of course," returned Dorothy. "There's no doubt of it."

The Queen turned to Ozma.

"Do you dare make such a claim?" she asked.

By this time Ozma had made up her mind as to the character of this haughty and disdainful creature, whose self-pride evidently led her to believe herself superior to all others.

"I did not come here to quarrel with your Majesty," said the girl Ruler of Oz, quietly. "What and who I am is well established, and my authority comes from the Fairy Queen Lurline, of whose band I was a member when Lurline made all Oz a Fairyland. There are several countries and several different peoples in this broad land, each of which has its separate Rulers, Kings, Emperors and Queens. But all these render obedience to my laws and acknowledge me as the supreme Ruler."

"If other Kings and Queens are fools that does not interest me in the least," replied Coo-ee-oh, disdainfully. "In the Land of the Skeezers I alone am supreme. You are impudent to think I would defer to you—or to anyone else."

"Let us not speak of this now, please," answered Ozma. "Your island is in danger, for a powerful foe is preparing to destroy it."

"Pah! The Flatheads. I do not fear them."

"Their Supreme Dictator is a Sorcerer."

"My magic is greater than his. Let the Flatheads come! They will never return to their barren mountain-top. I will see to that."

Ozma did not like this attitude, for it meant that the Skeezers were eager to fight the Flatheads, and Ozma's object in coming here was to prevent fighting and induce the two quarrelsome neighbors to make peace. She was also greatly disappointed in Coo-ee-oh, for the reports of Su-dic had led her to imagine the Queen more just and honorable than were the Flatheads. Indeed Ozma reflected that the girl might be better at heart than her self-pride and overbearing manner indicated, and in any event it would be wise not to antagonize her but to try to win her friendship.

"I do not like wars, your Majesty," said Ozma. "In the Emerald City, where I rule thousands of people, and in the countries near to the Emerald City, where thousands more acknowledge my rule, there is no army at all, because there is no quarreling and no need to fight. If differences arise between my people, they come to me and I judge the cases and award justice to all. So, when I learned there might be war between two faraway people of Oz, I came here to settle the dispute and adjust the quarrel."

"No one asked you to come," declared Queen Coo-ee-oh. "It is my business to settle this dispute, not yours. You say my island is a part of the Land of Oz, which you rule, but that is all nonsense, for I've never heard of the Land of Oz, nor of you. You say you are a fairy, and that fairies gave you command over me. I don't believe it! What I do believe is that you are an impostor and have come here to stir up trouble among my people, who are already becoming difficult to manage. You two girls may even be spies of the vile Flatheads, for all I know, and may be trying to trick me. But understand this," she added, proudly rising from her jeweled throne to confront them, "I have magic powers greater than any fairy possesses, and greater than any Flathead possesses. I am a Krumbic Witch—the only Krumbic Witch in the world—and I fear the magic of no other creature that exists! You say you rule thousands. I rule one hundred and one Skeezers. But every one of them trembles at my word. Now that Ozma of Oz and Princess Dorothy are here, I shall rule one hundred and three subjects, for you also shall bow before my power. More than that, in ruling you I also rule the thousands you say you rule."

Dorothy was very indignant at this speech.

"I've got a pink kitten that sometimes talks like that," she said, "but after I give her a good whipping she doesn't think she's so high and mighty after all. If you only knew who Ozma is you'd be scared to death to talk to her like that!"

Queen Coo-ee-oh gave the girl a supercilious look. Then she turned again to Ozma.

"I happen to know," said she, "that the Flatheads intend to attack us tomorrow, but we are ready for them. Until the battle is over, I shall keep you two strangers prisoners on my island, from which there is no chance for you to escape."

She turned and looked around the band of courtiers who stood silently around her throne.

"Lady Aurex," she continued, singling out one of the young women, "take these children to your house and care for them, giving them food and lodging. You may allow them to wander anywhere under the Great Dome, for they are harmless. After I have attended to the Flatheads I will consider what next to do with these foolish girls."

She resumed her seat and the Lady Aurex bowed low and said in a humble manner:

"I obey your Majesty's commands." Then to Ozma and Dorothy she added, "Follow me," and turned to leave the Throne Room.

Dorothy looked to see what Ozma would do. To her surprise and a little to her disappointment Ozma turned and followed Lady Aurex. So Dorothy trailed after them, but not without giving a parting, haughty look toward Queen Coo-ee-oh, who had her face turned the other way and did not see the disapproving look.

Chapter 9

LADY AUREX

Lady Aurex led Ozma and Dorothy along a street to a pretty marble house near to one edge of the great glass dome that covered the village. She did not speak to the girls until she had ushered them into a pleasant room, comfortably furnished, nor did any of the solemn people they met on the street venture to speak.

When they were seated Lady Aurex asked if they were hungry, and finding they were summoned a maid and ordered food to be brought.

This Lady Aurex looked to be about twenty years old, although in the Land of Oz where people have never changed in appearance since the fairies made it a fairyland—where no one grows old or dies—it is always difficult to say how many years anyone has lived. She had a pleasant, attractive face, even though it was solemn and sad as the faces of all Skeezers seemed to be, and her costume was rich and elaborate, as became a lady in waiting upon the Queen.

Ozma had observed Lady Aurex closely and now asked her in a gentle tone:

"Do you, also, believe me to be an impostor?"

"I dare not say," replied Lady Aurex in a low tone.

"Why are you afraid to speak freely?" inquired Ozma.

"The Queen punishes us if we make remarks that she does not like."

"Are we not alone then, in this house?"

"The Queen can hear everything that is spoken on this island—even the slightest whisper," declared Lady Aurex. "She is a wonderful witch, as she has told you, and it is folly to criticise her or disobey her commands."

Ozma looked into her eyes and saw that she would like to say more if she dared. So she drew from her bosom her silver wand, and having muttered a magic phrase in a strange tongue, she left the room and walked slowly around the outside of the house, making a complete circle and waving her wand in mystic curves as she walked. Lady Aurex watched her curiously and, when Ozma had again entered the room and seated herself, she asked:

"What have you done?"

"I've enchanted this house in such a manner that Queen Coo-ee-oh, with all her witchcraft, cannot hear one word we speak within the magic circle I have made," replied Ozma. "We may now speak freely and as loudly as we wish, without fear of the Queen's anger."

Lady Aurex brightened at this.

"Can I trust you?" she asked.

"Ev'rybody trusts Ozma," exclaimed Dorothy. "She is true and honest, and your wicked Queen will be sorry she insulted the powerful Ruler of all the Land of Oz."

"The Queen does not know me yet," said Ozma, "but I want you to know me, Lady Aurex, and I want you to tell me why you, and all the Skeezers, are unhappy. Do not fear Coo-ee-oh's anger, for she cannot hear a word we say, I assure you."

Lady Aurex was thoughtful a moment; then she said: "I shall trust you, Princess Ozma, for I believe you are what you say you are—our supreme Ruler. If you knew the dreadful punishments our Queen inflicts upon us, you would not wonder we are so unhappy. The Skeezers are not bad people; they do not care to quarrel and fight, even with their enemies the Flatheads; but they are so cowed and fearful of Coo-ee-oh that they obey her slightest word, rather than suffer her anger."

"Hasn't she any heart, then?" asked Dorothy.

"She never displays mercy. She loves no one but herself," asserted Lady Aurex, but she trembled as she said it, as if afraid even yet of her terrible Queen.

"That's pretty bad," said Dorothy, shaking her head gravely. "I see you've a lot to do here, Ozma, in this forsaken corner of the Land of Oz. First place, you've got to take the magic away from Queen Coo-ee-oh, and from that awful Su-dic, too. My idea is that neither of them is fit to rule anybody, 'cause they're cruel and hateful. So you'll have to give the Skeezers and Flatheads new Rulers and teach all their people that they're part of the Land of Oz and must obey, above all, the lawful Ruler, Ozma of Oz. Then, when you've done that, we can go back home again."

Ozma smiled at her little friend's earnest counsel, but Lady Aurex said in an anxious tone:

"I am surprised that you suggest these reforms while you are yet prisoners on this island and in Coo-ee-oh's power. That these things should be done, there is no doubt, but just now a dreadful war is likely to break out, and frightful things may happen to us all. Our Queen has such conceit that she thinks she can overcome the Su-dic and his people, but it is said Su-dic's magic is very powerful, although not as great as that possessed by his wife Rora, before Coo-ee-oh transformed her into a Golden Pig."

"I don't blame her very much for doing that," remarked Dorothy, "for the Flatheads were wicked to try to catch your beautiful fish and the Witch Rora wanted to poison all the fishes in the lake."

"Do you know the reason?" asked the Lady Aurex.

"I don't s'pose there was any reason, 'cept just wickedness," replied Dorothy.

"Tell us the reason," said Ozma earnestly.

"Well, your Majesty, once—a long time ago—the Flatheads and the Skeezers were friendly. They visited our island and we visited their mountain, and everything was pleasant between the two peoples. At that time the Flatheads were ruled by three Adepts in Sorcery, beautiful girls who were not Flatheads, but had wandered to the Flat Mountain and made their home there. These three Adepts used their magic only for good, and the mountain people gladly made them their Rulers. They taught the Flatheads how to use their canned brains and how to work metals into clothing that would never wear out, and many other things that added to their happiness and content.

"Coo-ee-oh was our Queen then, as now, but she knew no magic and so had nothing to be proud of. But the three Adepts were very kind to Coo-ee-oh. They built for us this wonderful dome of glass and our houses of marble and taught us to make beautiful clothing and many other things. Coo-ee-oh pretended to be very grateful for these favors, but it seems that all the time she was jealous of the three Adepts and secretly tried to discover their arts of magic. In this she was more clever than anyone suspected. She invited the three Adepts to a banquet one day, and while they were feasting Coo-ee-oh stole their charms and magical instruments and transformed them into three fishes—a gold fish, a silver fish and a bronze fish.

While the poor fishes were gasping and flopping helplessly on the floor of the banquet room one of them said reproachfully: 'You will be punished for this, Coo-ee-oh, for if one of us dies or is destroyed, you will become shrivelled and helpless, and all your stolen magic will depart from you.' Frightened by this threat, Coo-ee-oh at once caught up the three fish and ran with them to the shore of the lake, where she cast them into the water. This revived the three Adepts and they swam away and disappeared.

"I, myself, witnessed this shocking scene," continued Lady Aurex, "and so did many other Skeezers. The news was carried to the Flatheads, who then turned from friends to enemies. The Su-dic and his wife Rora were the only ones on the mountain who were glad the three Adepts had been lost to them, and they at once became Rulers of the Flatheads and stole their canned brains from others to make themselves the more powerful. Some of the Adepts' magic tools had been left on the mountain, and these Rora seized and by the use of them she became a witch.

"The result of Coo-ee-oh's treachery was to make both the Skeezers and the Flatheads miserable instead of happy. Not only were the Su-dic and his wife cruel to their people, but our Queen at once became proud and arrogant and treated us very unkindly. All the Skeezers knew she had stolen her magic powers and so she hated us and made us humble ourselves before her and obey her slightest word. If we disobeyed, or did not please her, or if we talked about her when we were in our own homes she would have us dragged to the whipping post in her palace and lashed with knotted cords. That is why we fear her so greatly."

This story filled Ozma's heart with sorrow and Dorothy's heart with indignation.

"I now understand," said Ozma, "why the fishes in the lake have brought about war between the Skeezers and the Flatheads."

"Yes," Lady Aurex answered, "now that you know the story it is easy to understand. The Su-dic and his wife came to our lake hoping to catch the silver fish, or gold fish, or bronze fish—any one of them would do—and by destroying it deprive Coo-ee-oh of her magic. Then they could easily conquer her. Also they had another reason for wanting to catch the fish—they feared that in some way the three Adepts might regain their proper forms and then they would be sure to return to the mountain and punish Rora and the Su-dic. That was why Rora finally tried to poison all the fishes in the lake, at the time Coo-ee-oh transformed her into a Golden Pig. Of course this attempt to destroy the fishes frightened the Queen, for her safety lies in keeping the three fishes alive."

"I s'pose Coo-ee-oh will fight the Flatheads with all her might," observed Dorothy.

"And with all her magic," added Ozma, thoughtfully.

"I do not see how the Flatheads can get to this island to hurt us," said Lady Aurex.

"They have bows and arrows, and I guess they mean to shoot the arrows at your big dome, and break all the glass in it," suggested Dorothy.

But Lady Aurex shook her head with a smile.

"They cannot do that," she replied.

"Why not?"

"I dare not tell you why, but if the Flatheads come to-morrow morning you will yourselves see the reason."

"I do not think they will attempt to harm the island," Ozma declared. "I believe they will first attempt to destroy the fishes, by poison or some other means. If they succeed in that, the conquest of the island will not be difficult."

"They have no boats," said Lady Aurex, "and Coo-ee-oh, who has long expected this war, has been preparing for it in many astonishing ways. I almost wish the Flatheads would conquer us, for then we would be free from our dreadful Queen; but I do not wish to see the three transformed fishes destroyed, for in them lies our only hope of future happiness."

"Ozma will take care of you, whatever happens," Dorothy assured her. But the Lady Aurex, not knowing the extent of Ozma's power—which was, in fact, not so great as Dorothy imagined—could not take much comfort in this promise.

It was evident there would be exciting times on the morrow, if the Flatheads really attacked the Skeezers of the Magic Isle.

Chapter 10

UNDER WATER

When night fell all the interior of the Great Dome, streets and houses, became lighted with brilliant incandescent lamps, which rendered it bright as day. Dorothy thought the island must look beautiful by night from the outer shore of the lake. There was revelry and feasting in the Queen's palace, and the music of the royal band could be plainly heard in Lady Aurex's house, where Ozma and Dorothy remained with their hostess and keeper. They were prisoners, but treated with much consideration.

Lady Aurex gave them a nice supper and when they wished to retire showed them to a pretty room with comfortable beds and wished them a good night and pleasant dreams.

"What do you think of all this, Ozma?" Dorothy anxiously inquired when they were alone.

"I am glad we came," was the reply, "for although there may be mischief done to-morrow, it was necessary I should know about these people, whose leaders are wild and lawless and oppress their subjects with injustice and cruelties. My task, therefore, is to liberate the Skeezers and the Flatheads and secure for them freedom and happiness. I have no doubt I can accomplish this in time."

"Just now, though, we're in a bad fix," asserted Dorothy. "If Queen Coo-ee-oh conquers to-morrow, she won't be nice to us, and if the Su-dic conquers, he'll be worse."

"Do not worry, dear," said Ozma, "I do not think we are in danger, whatever happens, and the result of our adventure is sure to be good."

Dorothy was not worrying, especially. She had confidence in her friend, the fairy Princess of Oz, and she enjoyed the excitement of the events in which she was taking part. So she crept into bed and fell asleep as easily as if she had been in her own cosy room in Ozma's palace.

A sort of grating, grinding sound awakened her. The whole island seemed to tremble and sway, as it might do in an earthquake. Dorothy sat up in bed, rubbing her eyes to get the sleep out of them, and then found it was daybreak.

Ozma was hurriedly dressing herself.

"What is it?" asked Dorothy, jumping out of bed.

"I'm not sure," answered Ozma "but it feels as if the island is sinking."

As soon as possible they finished dressing, while the creaking and swaying continued. Then they rushed into the living room of the house and found Lady Aurex, fully dressed, awaiting them.

"Do not be alarmed," said their hostess. "Coo-ee-oh has decided to submerge the island, that is all. But it proves the Flatheads are coming to attack us."

"What do you mean by sub-sub-merging the island?" asked Dorothy.

"Come here and see," was the reply.

Lady Aurex led them to a window which faced the side of the great dome which covered all the village, and they could see that the island was indeed sinking, for the water of the lake was already half way up the side of the dome. Through the glass could be seen swimming fishes, and tall stalks of swaying seaweeds, for the water was clear as crystal and through it they could distinguish even the farther shore of the lake.

"The Flatheads are not here yet," said Lady Aurex. "They will come soon, but not until all of this dome is under the surface of the water."

"Won't the dome leak?" Dorothy inquired anxiously.

"No, indeed."

"Was the island ever sub-sub-sunk before?"

"Oh, yes; on several occasions. But Coo-ee-oh doesn't care to do that often, for it requires a lot of hard work to operate the machinery. The dome was built so that the island could disappear. I think," she continued, "that our Queen fears the Flatheads will attack the island and try to break the glass of the dome."

"Well, if we're under water, they can't fight us, and we can't fight them," asserted Dorothy.

"They could kill the fishes, however," said Ozma gravely.

"We have ways to fight, also, even though our island is under water," claimed Lady Aurex. "I cannot tell you all our secrets, but this island is full of surprises. Also our Queen's magic is astonishing."

"Did she steal it all from the three Adepts in Sorcery that are now fishes?"

"She stole the knowledge and the magic tools, but she has used them as the three Adepts never would have done."

By this time the top of the dome was quite under water and suddenly the island stopped sinking and became stationary.

"See!" cried Lady Aurex, pointing to the shore. "The Flatheads have come."

On the bank, which was now far above their heads, a crowd of dark figures could be seen.

"Now let us see what Coo-ee-oh will do to oppose them," continued Lady Aurex, in a voice that betrayed her excitement.

The Flatheads, pushing their way through the line of palm trees, had reached the shore of the lake just as the top of the island's dome disappeared beneath the surface. The water now flowed from shore to shore, but through the clear water the dome was still visible and the houses of the Skeezers could be dimly seen through the panes of glass.

"Good!" exclaimed the Su-dic, who had armed all his followers and had brought with him two copper vessels, which he carefully set down upon the ground beside him. "If Coo-ee-oh wants to hide instead of fighting our job will be easy, for in one of these copper vessels I have enough poison to kill every fish in the lake."

"Kill them, then, while we have time, and then we can go home again," advised one of the chief officers.

"Not yet," objected the Su-dic. "The Queen of the Skeezers has defied me, and I want to get her into my power, as well as to destroy her magic. She transformed my poor wife into a Golden Pig, and I must have revenge for that, whatever else we do."

"Look out!" suddenly exclaimed the officers, pointing into the lake; "something's going to happen."

From the submerged dome a door opened and something black shot swiftly out into the water. The door instantly closed behind it and the dark object cleaved its way through the water, without rising to the surface, directly toward the place where the Flatheads were standing.

"What is that?" Dorothy asked the Lady Aurex.

"That is one of the Queen's submarines," was the reply. "It is all enclosed, and can move under water. Coo-ee-oh has several of these boats which are kept in little rooms in the basement under our village. When the island is submerged, the Queen uses these boats to reach the shore, and I believe she now intends to fight the Flatheads with them."

The Su-dic and his people knew nothing of Coo-ee-oh's submarines, so they watched with surprise as the under-water boat approached them. When it was quite near the shore it rose to the surface and the top parted and fell back, disclosing a boat full of armed Skeezers. At the head was the Queen, standing up in the bow and holding in one hand a coil of magic rope that gleamed like silver.

The boat halted and Coo-ee-oh drew back her arm to throw the silver rope toward the Su-dic, who was now but a few feet from her. But the wily Flathead leader quickly realized his danger and before the Queen could throw the rope he caught up one of the copper vessels and dashed its contents full in her face!

Chapter 11

The CONQUEST of the SKEEZERS

Q ueen Coo-ee-oh dropped the rope, tottered and fell headlong into the water, sinking beneath the surface, while the Skeezers in the submarine were too surprised to assist her and only stared at the ripples in the water where she had disappeared. A moment later there arose to the surface a beautiful White Swan. This Swan was of large size, very gracefully formed, and scattered all over its white feathers were tiny diamonds, so thickly placed that as the rays of the morning sun fell upon them the entire body of the Swan glistened like one brilliant diamond. The head of the Diamond Swan had a bill of polished gold and its eyes were two sparkling amethysts.

"Hooray!" cried the Su-dic, dancing up and down with wicked glee. "My poor wife, Rora, is avenged at last. You made her a Golden Pig, Coo-ee-oh, and now I have made you a Diamond Swan. Float on your lake forever, if you like, for your web feet can do no more magic and you are as powerless as the Pig you made of my wife!

"Villain! Scoundrel!" croaked the Diamond Swan. "You will be punished for this. Oh, what a fool I was to let you enchant me!"

"A fool you were, and a fool you are!" laughed the Su-dic, dancing madly in his delight. And then he carelessly tipped over the other copper vessel with his heel and its contents spilled on the sands and were lost to the last drop.

The Su-dic stopped short and looked at the overturned vessel with a rueful countenance.

"That's too bad—too bad!" he exclaimed sorrowfully. "I've lost all the poison I had to kill the fishes with, and I can't make any more because only my wife knew the secret of it, and she is now a foolish Pig and has forgotten all her magic."

"Very well," said the Diamond Swan scornfully, as she floated upon the water and swam gracefully here and there. "I'm glad to see you are foiled. Your punishment is just beginning, for although you have enchanted me and taken away my powers of sorcery you have still the three magic fishes to deal with, and they'll destroy you in time, mark my words."

The Su-dic stared at the Swan a moment. Then he yelled to his men:

"Shoot her! Shoot the saucy bird!"

They let fly some arrows at the Diamond Swan, but she dove under the water and the missiles fell harmless. When Coo-ee-oh rose to the surface she was far from the shore and she swiftly swam across the lake to where no arrows or spears could reach her.

The Su-dic rubbed his chin and thought what to do next. Near by floated the submarine in which the Queen had come, but the Skeezers who were in it were puzzled what to do with themselves. Perhaps they were not sorry their cruel mistress had been transformed into a Diamond Swan, but the transformation had left them quite helpless. The under-water boat was not operated by machinery, but by certain mystic words uttered by Coo-ee-oh. They didn't know how to submerge it, or how to make the water-tight shield cover them again, or how to make the boat go back to the castle, or make it enter the little basement room where it was usually kept. As a matter of fact, they were now shut out of their village under the Great Dome and could not get back again. So one of the men called to the Supreme Dictator of the Flatheads, saying:

"Please make us prisoners and take us to your mountain, and feed and keep us, for we have nowhere to go."

Then the Su-dic laughed and answered:

"Not so. I can't be bothered by caring for a lot of stupid

Skeezers. Stay where you are, or go wherever you please, so long as you keep away from our mountain." He turned to his men and added: "We have conquered Queen Coo-ee-oh and made her a helpless swan. The Skeezers are under water and may stay there. So, having won the war, let us go home again and make merry and feast, having after many years proved the Flatheads to be greater and more powerful than the Skeezers."

So the Flatheads marched away and passed through the row of palms and went back to their mountain, where the Su-dic and a few of his officers feasted and all the others were forced to wait on them.

"I'm sorry we couldn't have roast pig," said the Su-dic, "but as the only pig we have is made of gold, we can't eat her. Also the Golden Pig happens to be my wife, and even were she not gold I am sure she would be too tough to eat."

Chapter 12

The DIAMOND SWAN

When the Flatheads had gone away the Diamond Swan swam back to the boat and one of the young Skeezers named Ervic said to her eagerly:

"How can we get back to the island, your Majesty?"

"Am I not beautiful?" asked Coo-ee-oh, arching her neck gracefully and spreading her diamond-sprinkled wings. "I can see my reflection in the water, and I'm sure there is no bird nor beast, nor human as magnificent as I am!"

"How shall we get back to the island, your Majesty?" pleaded Ervic.

"When my fame spreads throughout the land, people will

travel from all parts of this lake to look upon my loveliness," said Coo-ee-oh, shaking her feathers to make the diamonds glitter more brilliantly.

"But, your Majesty, we must go home and we do not know how to get there," Ervic persisted.

"My eyes," remarked the Diamond Swan, "are wonderfully blue and bright and will charm all beholders."

"Tell us how to make the boat go—how to get back into the island," begged Ervic and the others cried just as earnestly: "Tell us, Coo-ee-oh; tell us!"

"I don't know," replied the Queen in a careless tone.

"You are a magic-worker, a sorceress, a witch!"

"I was, of course, when I was a girl," she said, bending her head over the clear water to catch her reflection in it; "but now I've forgotten all such foolish things as magic. Swans are lovelier than girls, especially when they're sprinkled with diamonds. Don't you think so?" And she gracefully swam away, without seeming to care whether they answered or not.

Ervic and his companions were in despair. They saw plainly that Coo-ee-oh could not or would not help them. The former Queen had no further thought for her island, her people, or her wonderful magic; she was only intent on admiring her own beauty.

"Truly," said Ervic, in a gloomy voice, "the Flatheads have conquered us!"

Some of these events had been witnessed by Ozma and Dorothy and Lady Aurex, who had left the house and gone close to the glass of the dome, in order to see what was going on. Many of the Skeezers had also crowded against the dome, wondering what would happen next. Although their vision was to an extent blurred by the water and the necessity of looking upward at an angle, they had observed the main points of the drama enacted above. They saw Queen Coo-ee-oh's submarine come to the surface and open; they saw the Queen standing erect to throw her magic rope; they saw her sudden transformation into a Diamond Swan, and a cry of amazement went up from the Skeezers inside the dome.

"Good!" exclaimed Dorothy. "I hate that old Su-dic, but I'm glad Coo-ee-oh is punished."

"This is a dreadful misfortune!" cried Lady Aurex, pressing her hands upon her heart.

"Yes," agreed Ozma, nodding her head thoughtfully; "Coo-ee-oh's misfortune will prove a terrible blow to her people."

"What do you mean by that?" asked Dorothy in surprise. "Seems to me the Skeezers are in luck to lose their cruel Queen."

"If that were all you would be right," responded Lady Aurex; "and if the island were above water it would not be so serious. But here we all are, at the bottom of the lake, and fast prisoners in this dome."

"Can't you raise the island?" inquired Dorothy.

"No. Only Coo-ee-oh knew how to do that," was the answer.

"We can try," insisted Dorothy. "If it can be made to go down, it can be made to come up. The machinery is still here, I suppose."

"Yes; but the machinery works by magic, and Coo-ee-oh would never share her secret power with any one of us."

Dorothy's face grew grave; but she was thinking.

"Ozma knows a lot of magic," she said.

"But not that kind of magic," Ozma replied.

"Can't you learn how, by looking at the machinery?"

"I'm afraid not, my dear. It isn't fairy magic at all; it is witchcraft."

"Well," said Dorothy, turning to Lady Aurex, "you say there are other sub-sub-sinking boats. We can get in one of those, and shoot out to the top of the water, like Coo-ee-oh did, and so escape. And then we can help to rescue all the Skeezers down here."

"No one knows how to work the under-water boats but the Queen," declared Lady Aurex.

"Isn't there any door or window in this dome that we could open?"

"No; and, if there were, the water would rush in to flood the dome, and we could not get out."

"The Skeezers," said Ozma, "could not drown; they only get wet and soggy and in that condition they would be very uncomfortable and unhappy. But you are a mortal girl, Dorothy, and if your Magic Belt protected you from death you would have to lie forever at the bottom of the lake."

"No, I'd rather die quickly," asserted the little girl. "But there are doors in the basement that open—to let out the bridges and the boats—and that would not flood the dome, you know."

"Those doors open by a magic word, and only Coo-ee-oh knows the word that must be uttered," said Lady Aurex.

"Dear me!" exclaimed Dorothy, "that dreadful Queen's witchcraft upsets all my plans to escape. I guess I'll give it up, Ozma, and let you save us."

Ozma smiled, but her smile was not so cheerful as usual. The Princess of Oz found herself confronted with a serious problem, and although she had no thought of despairing she realized that the Skeezers and their island, as well as Dorothy and herself, were in grave trouble and that unless she could find a means to save them they would be lost to the Land of Oz for all future time.

"In such a dilemma," said she, musingly, "nothing is gained by haste. Careful thought may aid us, and so may the course of events. The unexpected is always likely to happen, and cheerful patience is better than reckless action."

"All right," returned Dorothy; "take your time, Ozma; there's no hurry. How about some breakfast, Lady Aurex?"

Their hostess led them back to the house, where she

ordered her trembling servants to prepare and serve break-fast. All the Skeezers were frightened and anxious over the transformation of their Queen into a swan. Coo-ee-oh was feared and hated, but they had depended on her magic to con-quer the Flatheads and she was the only one who could raise their island to the surface of the lake again.

Before breakfast was over several of the leading Skeezers came to Aurex to ask her advice and to question Princess Ozma, of whom they knew nothing except that she claimed to be a fairy and the Ruler of all the land, including the Lake of the Skeezers.

"If what you told Queen Coo-ee-oh was the truth," they said to her, "you are our lawful mistress, and we may depend on you to get us out of our difficulties."

"I will try to do that," Ozma graciously assured them, "but you must remember that the powers of fairies are granted them to bring comfort and happiness to all who appeal to them. On the contrary, such magic as Coo-ee-oh knew and practiced is unlawful witchcraft and her arts are such as no fairy would condescend to use. However, it is sometimes nec-essary to consider evil in order to accomplish good, and per-haps by studying Coo-ee-oh's tools and charms of witchcraft I may be able to save us. Do you promise to accept me as your Ruler and to obey my commands?"

They promised willingly.

"Then," continued Ozma, "I will go to Coo-ee-oh's palace

and take possession of it. Perhaps what I find there will be of use to me. In the meantime tell all the Skeezers to fear nothing, but have patience. Let them return to their homes and perform their daily tasks as usual. Coo-ee-oh's loss may not prove a misfortune, but rather a blessing."

This speech cheered the Skeezers amazingly. Really, they had no one now to depend upon but Ozma, and in spite of their dangerous position their hearts were lightened by the transformation and absence of their cruel Queen.

They got out their brass band and a grand procession escorted Ozma and Dorothy to the palace, where all of Coo-ee-oh's former servants were eager to wait upon them. Ozma invited Lady Aurex to stay at the palace also, for she knew all about the Skeezers and their island and had also been a favorite of the former Queen, so her advice and information were sure to prove valuable.

Ozma was somewhat disappointed in what she found in the palace. One room of Coo-ee-oh's private suite was entirely devoted to the practice of witchcraft, and here were countless queer instruments and jars of ointments and bottles of potions labeled with queer names, and strange machines that Ozma could not guess the use of, and pickled toads and snails and lizards, and a shelf of books that were written in blood, but in a language which the Ruler of Oz did not know.

"I do not see," said Ozma to Dorothy, who accompanied her in her search, "how Coo-ee-oh knew the use of the magic tools she stole from the three Adept Witches. Moreover, from all reports these Adepts practiced only good witchcraft, such as would be helpful to their people, while Coo-ee-oh performed only evil."

"Perhaps she turned the good things to evil uses?" suggested Dorothy.

"Yes, and with the knowledge she gained Coo-ee-oh doubtless invented many evil things quite unknown to the good Adepts, who are now fishes," added Ozma. "It is unfortunate for us that the Queen kept her secrets so closely guarded, for no one but herself could use any of these strange things gathered in this room."

"Couldn't we capture the Diamond Swan and make her tell the secrets?" asked Dorothy.

"No; even were we able to capture her, Coo-ee-oh now has forgotten all the magic she ever knew. But until we ourselves escape from this dome we could not capture the Swan, and were we to escape we would have no use for Coo-ee-oh's magic."

"That's a fact," admitted Dorothy. "But—say, Ozma, here's a good idea! Couldn't we capture the three fishes—the gold and silver and bronze ones, and couldn't you transform 'em back to their own shapes, and then couldn't the three Adepts get us out of here?"

"You are not very practical, Dorothy dear. It would be as hard for us to capture the three fishes, from among all the other fishes in the lake, as to capture the Swan."

"But if we could, it would be more help to us," persisted the little girl.

"That is true," answered Ozma, smiling at her friend's eagerness. "You find a way to catch the fish, and I'll promise when they are caught to restore them to their proper forms."

"I know you think I can't do it," replied Dorothy, "but I'm going to try."

She left the palace and went to a place where she could look through a clear pane of the glass dome into the surrounding water. Immediately she became interested in the queer sights that met her view.

The Lake of the Skeezers was inhabited by fishes of many kinds and many sizes. The water was so transparent that the girl could see for a long distance and the fishes came so close to the glass of the dome that sometimes they actually touched it. On the white sands at the bottom of the lake were star-fish, lobsters, crabs and many shell fish of strange shapes and with shells of gorgeous hues. The water foliage was of brilliant colors and to Dorothy it resembled a splendid garden.

But the fishes were the most interesting of all. Some were big and lazy, floating slowly along or lying at rest with just their fins waving. Many with big round eyes looked full at the girl as she watched them and Dorothy wondered if they could hear her through the glass if she spoke to them. In Oz, where all the animals and birds can talk, many fishes are able to talk also, but usually they are more stupid than birds and animals because they think slowly and haven't much to talk about.

In the Lake of the Skeezers the fish of smaller size were more active than the big ones and darted quickly in and out among the swaying weeds, as if they had important business and were in a hurry. It was among the smaller varieties that Dorothy hoped to spy the gold and silver and bronze fishes. She had an idea the three would keep together, being companions now as they were in their natural forms, but such a multitude of fishes constantly passed, the scene shifting every moment, that she was not sure she would notice them even if they appeared in view. Her eyes couldn't look in all directions and the fishes she sought might be on the other side of the dome, or far away in the lake.

"P'raps, because they were afraid of Coo-ee-oh, they've hid themselves somewhere, and don't know their enemy has been transformed," she reflected.

She watched the fishes for a long time, until she became hungry and went back to the palace for lunch. But she was not discouraged.

"Anything new, Ozma?" she asked.

"No, dear. Did you discover the three fishes?"

"Not yet. But there isn't anything better for me to do, Ozma, so I guess I'll go back and watch again."

Chapter 13

The ALARM BELL

Glinda the Good, in her palace in the Quadling Country, had many things to occupy her mind, for not only did she look after the weaving and embroidery of her bevy of maids, and assist all those who came to her to implore her help—beasts and birds as well as people—but she was a close student of the arts of sorcery and spent much time in her Magical Laboratory, where she strove to find a remedy for every evil and to perfect her skill in magic.

Nevertheless, she did not forget to look in the Great Book of Records each day to see if any mention was made of the visit of Ozma and Dorothy to the Enchanted Mountain of the

Flatheads and the Magic Isle of the Skeezers. The Records told her that Ozma had arrived at the mountain, that she had escaped, with her companion, and gone to the island of the Skeezers, and that Queen Coo-ee-oh had submerged the island so that it was entirely under water. Then came the statement that the Flatheads had come to the lake to poison the fishes and that their Supreme Dictator had transformed Queen Coo-ee-oh into a swan.

No other details were given in the Great Book and so Glinda did not know that since Coo-ee-oh had forgotten her magic none of the Skeezers knew how to raise the island to the surface again. So Glinda was not worried about Ozma and Dorothy until one morning, while she sat with her maids, there came a sudden clang of the great alarm bell. This was so unusual that every maid gave a start and even the Sorceress for a moment could not think what the alarm meant.

Then she remembered the ring she had given Dorothy when she left the palace to start on her venture. In giving the ring Glinda had warned the little girl not to use its magic powers unless she and Ozma were in real danger, but then she was to turn it on her finger once to the right and once to the left and Glinda's alarm bell would ring.

So the Sorceress now knew that danger threatened her beloved Ruler and Princess Dorothy, and she hurried to her magic room to seek information as to what sort of danger it was. The answer to her question was not very satisfactory, for it was only: "Ozma and Dorothy are prisoners in the great Dome of the Isle of the Skeezers, and the Dome is under the water of the lake."

"Hasn't Ozma the power to raise the island to the surface?" inquired Glinda.

"No," was the reply, and the Record refused to say more except that Queen Coo-ee-oh, who alone could command the island to rise, had been transformed by the Flathead Su-dic into a Diamond Swan.

Then Glinda consulted the past records of the Skeezers in the Great Book. After diligent search she discovered that Coo-ee-oh was a powerful sorceress who had gained most of her power by treacherously transforming the Adepts of Magic, who were visiting her, into three fishes—gold, silver and bronze—after which she had them cast into the lake.

Glinda reflected earnestly on this information and decided that someone must go to Ozma's assistance. While there was no great need of haste, because Ozma and Dorothy could live in a submerged dome a long time, it was evident they could not get out until someone was able to raise the island.

The Sorceress looked through all her recipes and books of sorcery, but could find no magic that would raise a sunken island. Such a thing had never before been required in sorcery. Then Glinda made a little island, covered by a glass dome, and sunk it in a pond near her castle, and experimented in magical ways to bring it to the surface. She made several such experiments, but all were failures. It seemed a simple thing to do, yet she could not do it.

Nevertheless, the wise Sorceress did not despair of finding a way to liberate her friends. Finally she concluded that the best thing to do was to go to the Skeezer country and examine the lake. While there she was more likely to discover a solution to the problem that bothered her, and to work out a plan for the rescue of Ozma and Dorothy.

So Glinda summoned her storks and her aerial chariot, and telling her maids she was going on a journey and might not soon return, she entered the chariot and was carried swiftly to the Emerald City.

In Princess Ozma's palace the Scarecrow was now acting as Ruler of the Land of Oz. There wasn't much for him to do, because all the affairs of state moved so smoothly, but he was there in case anything unforeseen should happen.

Glinda found the Scarecrow playing croquet with Trot and Betsy Bobbin, two little girls who lived at the palace under Ozma's protection and were great friends of Dorothy and much loved by all the Oz people.

"Something's happened!" cried Trot, as the chariot of the Sorceress descended near them. "Glinda never comes here 'cept something's gone wrong."

"I hope no harm has come to Ozma, or Dorothy," said Betsy anxiously, as the lovely Sorceress stepped down from her chariot.

Glinda approached the Scarecrow and told him of the dilemma of Ozma and Dorothy and she added: "We must save them, somehow, Scarecrow."

"Of course," replied the Scarecrow, stumbling over a wicket and falling flat on his painted face.

The girls picked him up and patted his straw stuffing into shape, and he continued, as if nothing had occurred: "But you'll have to tell me what to do, for I never have raised a sunken island in all my life."

"We must have a Council of State as soon as possible," proposed the Sorceress. "Please send messengers to summon all of Ozma's counselors to this palace. Then we can decide what is best to be done."

The Scarecrow lost no time in doing this. Fortunately most of the royal counselors were in the Emerald City or near to it, so they all met in the Throne Room of the palace that same evening.

Chapter 14

OZMA'S COUNSELORS

No Ruler ever had such a queer assortment of advisers as the Princess Ozma had gathered about her throne. Indeed, in no other country could such amazing people exist. But Ozma loved them for their peculiarities and could trust every one of them.

First there was the Tin Woodman. Every bit of him was tin, brightly polished. All his joints were kept well oiled and moved smoothly. He carried a gleaming axe to prove he was a woodman, but seldom had cause to use it because he lived in a magnificent tin castle in the Winkie Country of Oz and was the Emperor of all the Winkies. The Tin Woodman's name was Nick Chopper. He had a very good mind, but his heart was not of much account, so he was very careful to do nothing unkind or to hurt anyone's feelings.

Another counselor was Scraps, the Patchwork Girl of Oz, who was made of a gaudy patchwork quilt, cut into shape and stuffed with cotton. This Patchwork Girl was very intelligent, but so full of fun and mad pranks that a lot of more stupid folks thought she must be crazy. Scraps was jolly under all conditions, however grave they might be, but her laughter and good spirits were of value in cheering others and in her seemingly careless remarks much wisdom could often be found.

Then there was the Shaggy Man—shaggy from head to foot, hair and whiskers, clothes and shoes—but very kind and gentle and one of Ozma's most loyal supporters.

Tik-Tok was there, a copper man with machinery inside him, so cleverly constructed that he moved, spoke and thought by three separate clock-works. Tik-Tok was very reliable because he always did exactly what he was wound up to do, but his machinery was liable to run down at times and then he was quite helpless until wound up again.

A different sort of person was Jack Pumpkinhead, one of Ozma's oldest friends and her companion on many adventures. Jack's body was very crude and awkward, being formed of limbs of trees of different sizes, jointed with wooden pegs. But it was a substantial body and not likely to break or wear out, and when it was dressed the clothes covered much of its roughness. The head of Jack Pumpkinhead was, as you have guessed, a ripe pumpkin, with the eyes, nose and mouth carved upon one side. The pumpkin was stuck on Jack's wooden neck and was liable to get turned sidewise or backward and then he would have to straighten it with his wooden hands.

The worst thing about this sort of a head was that it did not keep well and was sure to spoil sooner or later. So Jack's main business was to grow a field of fine pumpkins each year, and always before his old head spoiled he would select a fresh pumpkin from the field and carve the features on it very neatly, and have it ready to replace the old head whenever it became necessary. He didn't always carve it the same way, so his friends never knew exactly what sort of an expression they would find on his face. But there was no mistaking him, because he was the only pumpkinheaded man alive in the Land of Oz.

A one-legged sailor-man was a member of Ozma's council. His name was Cap'n Bill and he had come to the Land of Oz with Trot, and had been made welcome on account of his cleverness, honesty and good nature. He wore a wooden leg to replace the one he had lost and was a great friend of all the children in Oz because he could whittle all sorts of toys out of wood with his big jack-knife.

Professor H. M. Wogglebug, T.E., was another member of the council. The "H. M." meant Highly Magnified, for the Professor was once a little bug, who became magnified to the size of a man and always remained so. The "T.E." meant that he was Thoroughly Educated. He was at the head of Princess Ozma's Royal Athletic College, and so that the students would not have to study and so lose much time that could be devoted to athletic sports, such as football, baseball and the like, Professor Wogglebug had invented the famous Educational Pills. If one of the college students took a Geography Pill after breakfast, he knew his geography lesson in an instant; if he took a Spelling Pill he at once knew his spelling lesson, and an Arithmetic Pill enabled the student to do any kind of sum without having to think about it.

These useful pills made the college very popular and taught the boys and girls of Oz their lessons in the easiest possible way. In spite of this, Professor Wogglebug was not a favorite outside his college, for he was very conceited and admired himself so much and displayed his cleverness and learning so constantly, that no one cared to associate with him. Ozma found him of value in her councils, nevertheless.

Perhaps the most splendidly dressed of all those present was a great frog as large as a man, called the Frogman, who was noted for his wise sayings. He had come to the Emerald City from the Yip Country of Oz and was a guest of honor. His long-tailed coat was of velvet, his vest of satin and his trousers of finest silk. There were diamond buckles on his shoes and he carried a gold-headed cane and a high silk hat. All of the bright colors were represented in his rich attire, so it tired one's eyes to look at him for long, until one became used to his splendor.

The best farmer in all Oz was Uncle Henry, who was Dorothy's own uncle, and who now lived near the Emerald City with his wife Aunt Em. Uncle Henry taught the Oz people how to grow the finest vegetables and fruits and grains and was of much use to Ozma in keeping the Royal Storehouses well filled. He, too, was a counselor.

The reason I mention the little Wizard of Oz last is because he was the most important man in the Land of Oz. He wasn't a big man in size but he was a man in power and intelligence and second only to Glinda the Good in all the mystic arts of magic. Glinda had taught him, and the Wizard and the Sorceress were the only ones in Oz permitted by law to practice wizardry and sorcery, which they applied only to good uses and for the benefit of the people.

The Wizard wasn't exactly handsome but he was pleasant to look at. His bald head was as shiny as if it had been varnished; there was always a merry twinkle in his eyes and he was as spry as a schoolboy. Dorothy says the reason the Wizard is not as powerful as Glinda is because Glinda didn't teach him all she knows, but what the Wizard knows he knows very well and so he performs some very remarkable magic. The ten I have mentioned assembled, with the Scarecrow and Glinda, in Ozma's Throne Room, right after dinner that evening, and the Sorceress told them all she knew of the plight of Ozma and Dorothy.

"Of course we must rescue them," she continued, "and the

sooner they are rescued the better pleased they will be; but what we must now determine is how they can be saved. That is why I have called you together in council."

"The easiest way," remarked the Shaggy Man, "is to raise the sunken island of the Skeezers to the top of the water again."

"Tell me how?" said Glinda.

"I don't know how, your Highness, for I have never raised a sunken island."

"We might all get under it and lift," suggested Professor Wogglebug.

"How can we get under it when it rests on the bottom of the lake?" asked the Sorceress.

"Couldn't we throw a rope around it and pull it ashore?" inquired Jack Pumpkinhead.

"Why not pump the water out of the lake?" suggested the Patchwork Girl with a laugh.

"Do be sensible!" pleaded Glinda. "This is a serious matter, and we must give it serious thought."

"How big is the lake and how big is the island?" was the Frogman's question.

"None of us can tell, for we have not been there."

"In that case," said the Scarecrow, "it appears to me we ought to go to the Skeezer country and examine it carefully."

"Quite right," agreed the Tin Woodman.

"We-will-have-to-go-there-any-how," remarked Tik-Tok in his jerky machine voice.

"The question is which of us shall go, and how many of us?" said the Wizard.

"I shall go of course," declared the Scarecrow.

"And I," said Scraps.

"It is my duty to Ozma to go," asserted the Tin Woodman.

"I could not stay away, knowing our loved Princess is in danger," said the Wizard.

"We all feel like that," Uncle Henry said.

Finally one and all present decided to go to the Skeezer country, with Glinda and the little Wizard to lead them. Magic must meet magic in order to conquer it, so these two skillful magic-workers were necessary to insure the success of the expedition.

They were all ready to start at a moment's notice, for none had any affairs of importance to attend to. Jack was wearing a newly made Pumpkin-head and the Scarecrow had recently been stuffed with fresh straw. Tik-Tok's machinery was in good running order and the Tin Woodman always was well oiled.

"It is quite a long journey," said Glinda, "and while I might travel quickly to the Skeezer country by means of my stork chariot the rest of you will be obliged to walk. So, as we must keep together, I will send my chariot back to my castle and we will plan to leave the Emerald City at sunrise to-morrow."

···—··· Chapter 15 ···—··

The GREAT SORCERESS

Betsy and Trot, when they heard of the rescue expedition, begged the Wizard to permit them to join it and he consented. The Glass Cat, overhearing the conversation, wanted to go also and to this the Wizard made no objection.

This Glass Cat was one of the real curiosities of Oz. It had been made and brought to life by a clever magician named Dr. Pipt, who was not now permitted to work magic and was an ordinary citizen of the Emerald City. The cat was of transparent glass, through which one could plainly see its ruby heart beating and its pink brains whirling around in the top of the head.

The Glass Cat's eyes were emeralds; its fluffy tail was of spun glass and very beautiful. The ruby heart, while pretty to look at, was hard and cold and the Glass Cat's disposition was not pleasant at all times. It scorned to catch mice, did not eat, and was extremely lazy. If you complimented the remarkable cat on her beauty, she would be very friendly, for she loved admiration above everything. The pink brains were always working and their owner was indeed more intelligent than most common cats.

Three other additions to the rescue party were made the next morning, just as they were setting out upon their journey. The first was a little boy called Button Bright, because he had no other name that anyone could remember. He was a fine, manly little fellow, well mannered and good humored, who had only one bad fault. He was continually getting lost. To be sure, Button Bright got found as often as he got lost, but when he was missing his friends could not help being anxious about him.

"Some day," predicted the Patchwork Girl, "he won't be found, and that will be the last of him." But that didn't worry Button Bright, who was so careless that he did not seem to be able to break the habit of getting lost.

The second addition to the party was a Munchkin boy of about Button Bright's age, named Ojo. He was often called "Ojo the Lucky," because good fortune followed him wherever he went. He and Button Bright were close friends, although of such different natures, and Trot and Betsy were fond of both.

The third and last to join the expedition was an enormous lion, one of Ozma's regular guardians and the most important and intelligent beast in all Oz. He called himself the Cowardly Lion, saying that every little danger scared him so badly that his heart thumped against his ribs, but all who knew him knew that the Cowardly Lion's fears were coupled with bravery and that however much he might be frightened he summoned courage to meet every danger he encountered. Often he had saved Dorothy and Ozma in times of peril, but afterward he moaned and trembled and wept because he had been so scared.

"If Ozma needs help, I'm going to help her," said the great beast. "Also, I suspect the rest of you may need me on the journey—especially Trot and Betsy—for you may pass through a dangerous part of the country. I know that wild Gillikin country pretty well. Its forests harbor many ferocious beasts."

They were glad the Cowardly Lion was to join them, and in good spirits the entire party formed a procession and marched out of the Emerald City amid the shouts of the people, who wished them success and a safe return with their beloved Ruler.

They followed a different route from that taken by Ozma and Dorothy, for they went through the Winkie Country and up north toward Oogaboo. But before they got there they swerved to the left and entered the Great Gillikin Forest, the

nearest thing to a wilderness in all Oz. Even the Cowardly Lion
had to admit that certain parts of this forest were unknown to
him, although he had often wandered among the trees, and the
Scarecrow and Tin Woodman, who were great travelers, never
had been there at all.

The forest was only reached after a tedious tramp, for
some of the Rescue Expedition were quite awkward on their
feet. The Patchwork Girl was as light as a feather and very
spry; the Tin Woodman covered the ground as easily as Uncle
Henry and the Wizard; but Tik-Tok moved slowly and the
slightest obstruction in the road would halt him until the others cleared it away. Then, too, Tik-Tok's machinery kept running down, so Betsy and Trot took turns in winding it up.

The Scarecrow was more clumsy but less bother, for
although he often stumbled and fell he could scramble up
again and a little patting of his straw-stuffed body would put
him in good shape again.

Another awkward one was Jack Pumpkinhead, for walking would jar his head around on his neck and then he would
be likely to go in the wrong direction. But the Frogman took
Jack's arm and then he followed the path more easily.

Cap'n Bill's wooden leg didn't prevent him from keeping
up with the others and the old sailor could walk as far as any
of them.

When they entered the forest the Cowardly Lion took
the lead. There was no path here for men, but many beasts

had made paths of their own which only the eyes of the Lion, practiced in woodcraft, could discern. So he stalked ahead and wound his way in and out, the others following in single file, Glinda being next to the Lion.

There are dangers in the forest, of course, but as the huge Lion headed the party he kept the wild denizens of the wilderness from bothering the travelers. Once, to be sure, an enormous leopard sprang upon the Glass Cat and caught her in his powerful jaws, but he broke several of his teeth and with howls of pain and dismay dropped his prey and vanished among the trees.

"Are you hurt?" Trot anxiously inquired of the Glass Cat.

"How silly!" exclaimed the creature in an irritated tone of voice; "nothing can hurt glass, and I'm too solid to break easily. But I'm annoyed at that leopard's impudence. He has no respect for beauty or intelligence. If he had noticed my pink brains work, I'm sure he would have realized I'm too important to be grabbed in a wild beast's jaws."

"Never mind," said Trot consolingly; "I'm sure he won't do it again."

They were almost in the center of the forest when Ojo, the Munchkin boy, suddenly said: "Why, where's Button Bright?"

They halted and looked around them. Button Bright was not with the party.

"Dear me," remarked Betsy, "I expect he's lost again!"

"When did you see him last, Ojo?" inquired Glinda.

"It was some time ago," replied Ojo. "He was trailing along at the end and throwing twigs at the squirrels in the trees. Then I went to talk to Betsy and Trot, and just now I noticed he was gone."

"This is too bad," declared the Wizard, "for it is sure to delay our journey. We must find Button Bright before we go any farther, for this forest is full of ferocious beasts that would not hesitate to tear the boy to pieces."

"But what shall we do?" asked the Scarecrow. "If any of us leaves the party to search for Button Bright he or she might fall a victim to the beasts, and if the Lion leaves us we will have no protector."

"The Glass Cat could go," suggested the Frogman. "The beasts can do her no harm, as we have discovered."

The Wizard turned to Glinda.

"Cannot your sorcery discover where Button Bright is?" he asked.

"I think so," replied the Sorceress.

She called to Uncle Henry, who had been carrying her wicker box, to bring it to her, and when he obeyed she opened it and drew out a small round mirror. On the surface of the glass she dusted a white powder and then wiped it away with her handkerchief and looked in the mirror. It reflected a part of the forest, and there, beneath a wide-spreading tree, Button Bright was lying asleep. On one side of him crouched a tiger, ready to spring; on the other side was a big grey wolf, its bared fangs glistening in a wicked way.

"Goodness me!" cried Trot, looking over Glinda's shoulder. "They'll catch and kill him sure."

Everyone crowded around for a glimpse at the magic mirror.

"Pretty bad—pretty bad!" said the Scarecrow sorrowfully.

"Comes of getting lost!" said Cap'n Bill, sighing.

"Guess he's a goner!" said the Frogman, wiping his eyes on his purple silk handkerchief.

"But where is he? Can't we save him?" asked Ojo the Lucky.

"If we knew where he is we could probably save him," replied the little Wizard, "but that tree looks so much like all the other trees, that we can't tell whether it's far away or near by."

"Look at Glinda!" exclaimed Betsy.

Glinda, having handed the mirror to the Wizard, had stepped aside and was making strange passes with her outstretched arms and reciting in low, sweet tones a mystical incantation. Most of them watched the Sorceress with anxious eyes, despair giving way to the hope that she might be able to save their friend. The Wizard, however, watched the scene in the mirror, while over his shoulders peered Trot, the Scarecrow and the Shaggy Man.

What they saw was more strange than Glinda's actions. The tiger started to spring on the sleeping boy, but suddenly lost its power to move and lay flat upon the ground. The grey wolf seemed unable to lift its feet from the ground. It pulled first at one leg and then at another, and finding itself strangely confined to the spot began to back and snarl angrily. They couldn't hear the barkings and snarls, but they could see the creature's mouth open and its thick lips move. Button Bright, however, being but a few feet away from the wolf, heard its cries of rage, which wakened him from his untroubled sleep. The boy sat up and looked first at the tiger and then at the wolf. His face showed that for a moment he was quite frightened, but he soon saw that the beasts were unable to approach him and so he got upon his feet and examined them curiously, with a mischievous smile upon his face. Then he deliberately kicked the tiger's head with his foot and catching up a fallen branch of a tree he went to the wolf and gave it a good whacking. Both the beasts were furious at such treatment but could not resent it.

Button Bright now threw down the stick and with his hands in his pockets wandered carelessly away.

"Now," said Glinda, "let the Glass Cat run and find him. He is in that direction," pointing the way, "but how far off I do not know. Make haste and lead him back to us as quickly as you can."

The Glass Cat did not obey everyone's orders, but she really feared the great Sorceress, so as soon as the words were spoken the crystal animal darted away and was quickly lost to sight.

The Wizard handed the mirror back to Glinda, for the woodland scene had now faded from the glass. Then those who cared to rest sat down to await Button Bright's coming. It was not long before he appeared through the trees and as he rejoined his friends he said in a peevish tone:

"Don't ever send that Glass Cat to find me again. She was very impolite and, if we didn't all know that she had no manners, I'd say she insulted me."

Glinda turned upon the boy sternly.

"You have caused all of us much anxiety and annoyance," said she. "Only my magic saved you from destruction. I forbid you to get lost again."

"Of course," he answered. "It won't be my fault if I get lost again; but it wasn't my fault this time."

Chapter 16

The ENCHANTED FISHES

I must now tell you what happened to Ervic and the three other Skeezers who were left floating in the iron boat after Queen Coo-ee-oh had been transformed into a Diamond Swan by the magic of the Flathead Su-dic.

The four Skeezers were all young men and their leader was Ervic. Coo-ee-oh had taken them with her in the boat to assist her if she captured the Flathead chief, as she hoped to do by means of her silver rope. They knew nothing about the witchcraft that moved the submarine and so, when left floating upon the lake, were at a loss what to do. The submarine could not be submerged by them or made to return to the sunken island. There were neither oars nor sails in the boat, which was not anchored but drifted quietly upon the surface of the lake.

The Diamond Swan had no further thought or care for her people. She had sailed over to the other side of the lake and all the calls and pleadings of Ervic and his companions were unheeded by the vain bird. As there was nothing else for them to do, they sat quietly in their boat and waited as patiently as they could for someone to come to their aid.

The Flatheads had refused to help them and had gone back to their mountain. All the Skeezers were imprisoned in the Great Dome and could not help even themselves. When evening came, they saw the Diamond Swan, still keeping to the opposite shore of the lake, walk out of the water to the sands, shake her diamond-sprinkled feathers, and then disappear among the bushes to seek a resting place for the night.

"I'm hungry," said Ervic.

"I'm cold," said another Skeezer.

"I'm tired," said a third.

"I'm afraid," said the last one of them.

But it did them no good to complain. Night fell and the moon rose and cast a silvery sheen over the surface of the water.

"Go to sleep," said Ervic to his companions. "I'll stay awake and watch, for we may be rescued in some unexpected way."

So the other three laid themselves down in the bottom of the boat and were soon fast asleep.

Ervic watched. He rested himself by leaning over the bow of the boat, his face near to the moonlit water, and thought dreamily of the day's surprising events and wondered what would happen to the prisoners in the Great Dome.

Suddenly a tiny goldfish popped its head above the surface of the lake, not more than a foot from his eyes. A silverfish then raised its head beside that of the goldfish, and a moment later a bronzefish lifted its head beside the others. The three fish, all in a row, looked earnestly with their round, bright eyes into the astonished eyes of Ervic the Skeezer.

"We are the three Adepts whom Queen Coo-ee-oh betrayed and wickedly transformed," said the goldfish, its voice low and soft but distinctly heard in the stillness of the night.

"I know of our Queen's treacherous deed," replied Ervic, "and I am sorry for your misfortune. Have you been in the lake ever since?"

"Yes," was the reply.

"I—I hope you are well—and comfortable," stammered Ervic, not knowing what else to say.

"We knew that some day Coo-ee-oh would meet with the fate she so richly deserves," declared the bronzefish. "We have waited and watched for this time. Now if you will promise to help us and will be faithful and true, you can aid us in regaining our natural forms, and save yourself and all your people from the dangers that now threaten you."

"Well," said Ervic, "you can depend on my doing the best I

can. But I'm no witch, nor magician, you must know."

"All we ask is that you obey our instructions," returned the silverfish. "We know that you are honest and that you served Coo-ee-oh only because you were obliged to in order to escape her anger. Do as we command and all will be well."

"I promise!" exclaimed the young man. "Tell me what I am to do first."

"You will find in the bottom of your boat the silver cord which dropped from Coo-ee-oh's hand when she was transformed," said the goldfish. "Tie one end of that cord to the bow of your boat and drop the other end to us in the water. Together we will pull your boat to the shore."

Ervic much doubted that the three small fishes could move so heavy a boat, but he did as he was told and the fishes all seized their end of the silver cord in their mouths and headed toward the nearest shore, which was the very place where the Flatheads had stood when they conquered Queen Coo-ee-oh.

At first the boat did not move at all, although the fishes pulled with all their strength. But presently the strain began to tell. Very slowly the boat crept toward the shore, gaining more speed at every moment. A couple of yards away from the sandy beach the fishes dropped the cord from their mouths and swam to one side, while the iron boat, being now under way, continued to move until its prow grated upon the sands.

Ervic leaned over the side and said to the fishes: "What next?"

"You will find upon the sand," said the silverfish, "a copper kettle, which the Su-dic forgot when he went away. Cleanse it thoroughly in the water of the lake, for it has had poison in it. When it is cleaned, fill it with fresh water and hold it over the side of the boat, so that we three may swim into the kettle. We will then instruct you further."

"Do you wish me to catch you, then?" asked Ervic in surprise.

"Yes," was the reply.

So Ervic jumped out of the boat and found the copper kettle. Carrying it a little way down the beach, he washed it well, scrubbing away every drop of the poison it had contained with sand from the shore.

Then he went back to the boat.

Ervic's comrades were still sound asleep and knew nothing of the three fishes or what strange happenings were taking place about them. Ervic dipped the kettle in the lake, holding fast to the handle until it was under water. The gold and silver and bronze fishes promptly swam into the kettle. The young Skeezer then lifted it, poured out a little of the water so it would not spill over the edge, and said to the fishes: "What next?"

"Carry the kettle to the shore. Take one hundred steps to the east, along the edge of the lake, and then you will see a path leading through the meadows, up hill and down dale. Follow the path until you come to a cottage which is painted a purple color with white trimmings. When you stop at the gate of this cottage we will tell you what to do next. Be careful, above all, not to stumble and spill the water from the kettle, or you would destroy us and all you have done would be in vain."

The goldfish issued these commands and Ervic promised to be careful and started to obey. He left his sleeping comrades in the boat, stepping cautiously over their bodies, and on reaching the shore took exactly one hundred steps to the east. Then he looked for the path and the moonlight was so bright that he easily discovered it, although it was hidden from view by tall weeds until one came full upon it. This path was very narrow and did not seem to be much used, but it was quite distinct and Ervic had no difficulty in following it. He walked through a broad meadow, covered with tall grass and weeds, up a hill and down into a valley and then up another hill and down again.

It seemed to Ervic that he had walked miles and miles. Indeed the moon sank low and day was beginning to dawn when finally he discovered by the roadside a pretty little cottage, painted purple with white trimmings. It was a lonely place— no other buildings were anywhere about and the ground was not tilled at all. No farmer lived here, that was certain. Who would care to dwell in such an isolated place?

But Ervic did not bother his head long with such questions. He went up to the gate that led to the cottage, set the copper kettle carefully down and bending over it asked:

"What next?"

Chapter 17

UNDER the GREAT DOME

When Glinda the Good and her followers of the Rescue Expedition came in sight of the Enchanted Mountain of the Flatheads, it was away to the left of them, for the route they had taken through the Great Forest was some distance from that followed by Ozma and Dorothy.

They halted awhile to decide whether they should call upon the Supreme Dictator first, or go on to the Lake of the Skeezers.

"If we go to the mountain," said the Wizard, "we may get into trouble with that wicked Su-dic, and then we would be delayed in rescuing Ozma and Dorothy. So I think our best plan will be to go to the Skeezer Country, raise the sunken island and save our friends and the imprisoned Skeezers. Afterward we can visit the mountain and punish the cruel magician of the Flatheads."

"That is sensible," approved the Shaggy Man. "I quite agree with you."

The others, too, seemed to think the Wizard's plan the best, and Glinda herself commended it, so on they marched toward the line of palm trees that hid the Skeezers' lake from view.

Pretty soon they came to the palms. These were set closely together, the branches, which came quite to the ground, being so tightly interlaced that even the Glass Cat could scarcely find a place to squeeze through. The path which the Flatheads used was some distance away.

"Here's a job for the Tin Woodman," said the Scarecrow.

So the Tin Woodman, who was always glad to be of use, set to work with his sharp, gleaming axe, which he always carried, and in a surprisingly short time had chopped away enough branches to permit them all to pass easily through the trees.

Now the clear waters of the beautiful lake were before them and by looking closely they could see the outlines of the Great Dome of the sunken island, far from shore and directly in the center of the lake.

Of course every eye was at first fixed upon this dome, where Ozma and Dorothy and the Skeezers were still fast prisoners. But soon their attention was caught by a more brilliant sight, for here was the Diamond Swan swimming just before them, its long neck arched proudly, the amethyst eyes gleaming and all the diamond-sprinkled feathers glistening splendidly under the rays of the sun.

"That," said Glinda, "is the transformation of Queen Coo-ee-oh, the haughty and wicked witch who betrayed the three Adepts at Magic and treated her people like slaves."

"She's wonderfully beautiful now," remarked the Frogman.

"It doesn't seem like much of a punishment," said Trot. "The Flathead Su-dic ought to have made her a toad."

"I am sure Coo-ee-oh is punished," said Glinda, "for she has lost all her magic power and her grand palace and can no longer misrule the poor Skeezers."

"Let us call to her, and hear what she has to say," proposed the Wizard.

So Glinda beckoned the Diamond Swan, which swam gracefully to a position near them. Before anyone could speak Coo-ee-oh called to them in a rasping voice—for the voice of a swan is always harsh and unpleasant—and said with much pride:

"Admire me, Strangers! Admire the lovely Coo-ee-oh, the handsomest creature in all Oz. Admire me!"

"Handsome is as handsome does," replied the Scarecrow. "Are your deeds lovely, Coo-ee-oh?"

"Deeds? What deeds can a swan do but swim around and give pleasure to all beholders?" said the sparkling bird.

"Have you forgotten your former life? Have you forgotten your magic and witchcraft?" inquired the Wizard.

"Magic—witchcraft? Pshaw, who cares for such silly things?" retorted Coo-ee-oh. "As for my past life, it seems like an unpleasant dream. I wouldn't go back to it if I could. Don't you admire my beauty, Strangers?"

"Tell us, Coo-ee-oh," said Glinda earnestly, "if you can recall enough of your witchcraft to enable us to raise the sunken island to the surface of the lake. Tell us that and I'll give you a string of pearls to wear around your neck and add to your beauty."

"Nothing can add to my beauty, for I'm the most beautiful creature anywhere in the whole world."

"But how can we raise the island?"

"I don't know and I don't care. If ever I knew I've forgotten, and I'm glad of it," was the response. "Just watch me circle around and see me glitter!"

"It's no use," said Button Bright; "the old Swan is too much in love with herself to think of anything else."

"That's a fact," agreed Betsy with a sigh; "but we've got to get Ozma and Dorothy out of that lake, somehow or other."

"And we must do it in our own way," added the Scarecrow.

"But how?" asked Uncle Henry in a grave voice, for he could not bear to think of his dear niece Dorothy being out there under water; "how shall we do it?"

"Leave that to Glinda," advised the Wizard, realizing he was helpless to do it himself.

"If it were just an ordinary sunken island," said the powerful sorceress, "there would be several ways by which I might bring it to the surface again. But this is a Magic Isle, and by some curious art of witchcraft, unknown to any but Queen Coo-ee-oh, it obeys certain commands of magic and will not respond to any other. I do not despair in the least, but it will require some deep study to solve this difficult problem. If the Swan could only remember the witchcraft that she invented and knew as a woman, I could force her to tell me the secret, but all her former knowledge is now forgotten."

"It seems to me," said the Wizard after a brief silence had followed Glinda's speech, "that there are three fishes in this lake that used to be Adepts at Magic and from whom Coo-ee-oh stole much of her knowledge. If we could find those fishes and return them to their former shapes, they could doubtless tell us what to do to bring the sunken island to the surface."

"I have thought of those fishes," replied Glinda, "but among so many fishes as this lake contains how are we to single them out?"

You will understand, of course, that had Glinda been at home in her castle, where the Great Book of Records was, she would have known that Ervic the Skeezer already had taken the gold and silver and bronze fishes from the lake. But that act had been recorded in the Book after Glinda had set out on this journey, so it was all unknown to her.

"I think I see a boat yonder on the shore," said Ojo the Munchkin boy, pointing to a place around the edge of the lake. "If we could get that boat and row all over the lake, calling to the magic fishes, we might be able to find them."

"Let us go to the boat," said the Wizard.

They walked around the lake to where the boat was stranded upon the beach, but found it empty. It was a mere shell of blackened steel, with a collapsible roof that, when in position, made the submarine watertight, but at present the roof rested in slots on either side of the magic craft. There were no oars or sails, no machinery to make the boat go, and although Glinda promptly realized it was meant to be operated by witchcraft, she was not acquainted with that sort of magic.

"However," said she, "the boat is merely a boat, and I believe I can make it obey a command of sorcery, as well as it did the command of witchcraft. After I have given a little thought to the matter, the boat will take us wherever we desire to go."

"Not all of us," returned the Wizard, "for it won't hold so many. But, most noble Sorceress, provided you can make the boat go, of what use will it be to us?"

"Can't we use it to catch the three fishes?" asked Button Bright.

"It will not be necessary to use the boat for that purpose," replied Glinda. "Wherever in the lake the enchanted fishes may be, they will answer to my call. What I am trying to discover is how the boat came to be on this shore, while the island on which it belongs is under water yonder. Did Coo-ee-oh come here in the boat to meet the Flatheads before the island was sunk, or afterward?"

No one could answer that question, of course; but while they pondered the matter three young men advanced from the line of trees, and rather timidly bowed to the strangers.

"Who are you, and where did you come from?" inquired the Wizard.

"We are Skeezers," answered one of them, "and our home is on the Magic Isle of the Lake. We ran away when we saw you coming, and hid behind the trees, but as you are Strangers and seem to be friendly we decided to meet you, for we are in great trouble and need assistance."

"If you belong on the island, why are you here?" demanded Glinda.

So they told her all the story: How the Queen had defied the Flatheads and submerged the whole island so that her enemies could not get to it or destroy it; how, when the Flatheads came to the shore, Coo-ee-oh had commanded them, together with their friend Ervic, to go with her in the submarine to conquer the Su-dic, and how the boat had shot out from the basement of the sunken isle, obeying a magic word, and risen to the surface, where it opened and floated upon the water.

Then followed the account of how the Su-dic had transformed Coo-ee-oh into a swan, after which she had forgotten all the witchcraft she ever knew. The young men told how, in the night when they were asleep, their comrade Ervic had mysteriously disappeared, while the boat in some strange manner had floated to the shore and stranded upon the beach.

That was all they knew. They had searched in vain for three days for Ervic. As their island was under water and they could not get back to it, the three Skeezers had no place to go, and so had waited patiently beside their boat for something to happen.

Being questioned by Glinda and the Wizard, they told all they knew about Ozma and Dorothy and declared the two girls were still in the village under the Great Dome. They were quite safe and would be well cared for by Lady Aurex, now that the Queen who opposed them was out of the way.

When they had gleaned all the information they could from these Skeezers, the Wizard said to Glinda:

"If you find you can make this boat obey your sorcery, you could have it return to the island, submerge itself, and enter the door in the basement from which it came. But I cannot see that our going to the sunken island would enable our friends to escape. We would only join them as prisoners."

"Not so, friend Wizard," replied Glinda. "If the boat would obey my commands to enter the basement door, it would also obey my commands to come out again, and I could bring Ozma and Dorothy back with me."

"And leave all of our people still imprisoned?" asked one of the Skeezers reproachfully.

"By making several trips in the boat, Glinda could fetch all your people to the shore," replied the Wizard.

"But what could they do then?" inquired another Skeezer. "They would have no homes and no place to go, and would be at the mercy of their enemies, the Flatheads."

"That is true," said Glinda the Good. "And as these people are Ozma's subjects, I think she would refuse to escape with Dorothy and leave the others behind, or to abandon the island which is the lawful home of the Skeezers. I believe the best plan will be to summon the three fishes and learn from them how to raise the island."

The little Wizard seemed to think that this was rather a forlorn hope.

"How will you summon them," he asked the lovely Sorceress, "and how can they hear you?"

"That is something we must consider carefully," responded stately Glinda, with a serene smile. "I think I can find a way."

All of Ozma's counselors applauded this sentiment, for they knew well the powers of the Sorceress.

"Very well," agreed the Wizard. "Summon them, most noble Glinda."

..—..◄ ₵hapter 18 ►..—..

The CLEVERNESS of ERVIC

We must now return to Ervic the Skeezer, who, when he had set down the copper kettle containing the three fishes at the gate of the lonely cottage, had asked, "What next?"

The goldfish stuck its head above the water in the kettle and said in its small but distinct voice:

"You are to lift the latch, open the door, and walk boldly into the cottage. Do not be afraid of anything you see, for however you seem to be threatened with dangers, nothing can harm you. The cottage is the home of a powerful Yookoohoo, named Reera the Red, who assumes all sorts of forms, sometimes changing her form several times in a day, according to her fancy. What her real form may be we do not know. This strange creature cannot be bribed with treasure, or coaxed through friendship, or won by pity. She has never assisted anyone, or done wrong to anyone, that we know of. All her wonderful powers are used for her own selfish amusement. She will order you out of the house but you must refuse to go. Remain and watch Reera closely and try to see what she uses to accomplish her transformations. If you can discover the secret whisper it to us and we will then tell you what to do next."

"That sounds easy," returned Ervic, who had listened carefully. "But are you sure she will not hurt me, or try to transform me?"

"She may change your form," replied the goldfish, "but do not worry if that happens, for we can break that enchantment easily. You may be sure that nothing will harm you, so you must not be frightened at anything you see or hear."

Now Ervic was as brave as any ordinary young man, and he knew the fishes who spoke to him were truthful and to be relied upon, nevertheless he experienced a strange sinking of the heart as he picked up the kettle and approached the door of the cottage. His hand trembled as he raised the latch, but he was resolved to obey his instructions. He pushed the door open, took three strides into the middle of the one room the cottage contained, and then stood still and looked around him.

The sights that met his gaze were enough to frighten

anyone who had not been properly warned. On the floor just before Ervic lay a great crocodile, its red eyes gleaming wickedly and its wide open mouth displaying rows of sharp teeth. Horned toads hopped about; each of the four upper corners of the room was festooned with a thick cobweb, in the center of which sat a spider as big around as a washbasin, and armed with pincher-like claws; a red-and-green lizard was stretched at full length on the window-sill and black rats darted in and out of the holes they had gnawed in the floor of the cottage.

But the most startling thing was a huge Gray Ape which sat upon a bench and knitted. It wore a lace cap, such as old ladies wear, and a little apron of lace, but no other clothing. Its eyes were bright and looked as if coals were burning in them. The ape moved as naturally as an ordinary person might, and on Ervic's entrance stopped knitting and raised its head to look at him.

"Get out!" cried a sharp voice, seeming to come from the ape's mouth.

Ervic saw another bench, empty, just beyond him, so he stepped over the crocodile, sat down upon the bench and carefully placed the kettle beside him.

"Get out!" again cried the voice.

Ervic shook his head.

"No," said he, "I'm going to stay."

The spiders left their four corners, dropped to the floor and made a rush toward the young Skeezer, circling around his legs with their pinchers extended. Ervic paid no attention to them. An enormous black rat ran up Ervic's body, passed around his shoulders and uttered piercing squeals in his ears, but he did not wince. The green-and-red lizard, coming from the window-sill, approached Ervic and began spitting a flaming fluid at him, but Ervic merely stared at the creature and its flame did not touch him.

The crocodile raised its tail and, swinging around, swept Ervic off the bench with a powerful blow. But the Skeezer managed to save the kettle from upsetting and he got up, shook off the horned toads that were crawling over him and resumed his seat on the bench.

All the creatures, after this first attack, remained motionless, as if awaiting orders. The old Gray Ape knitted on, not looking toward Ervic now, and the young Skeezer stolidly kept his seat. He expected something else to happen, but nothing did. A full hour passed and Ervic was growing nervous.

"What do you want?" the ape asked at last.

"Nothing," said Ervic.

"You may have that!" retorted the ape, and at this all the strange creatures in the room broke into a chorus of cackling laughter.

Another long wait.

"Do you know who I am?" questioned the ape.

"You must be Reera the Red—the Yookoohoo," Ervic answered.

"Knowing so much, you must also know that I do not like

strangers. Your presence here in my home annoys me. Do you not fear my anger?"

"No," said the young man.

"Do you intend to obey me, and leave this house?"

"No," replied Ervic, just as quietly as the Yookoohoo had spoken.

The ape knitted for a long time before resuming the conversation.

"Curiosity," it said, "has led to many a man's undoing. I suppose in some way you have learned that I do tricks of magic, and so through curiosity you have come here. You may have been told that I do not injure anyone, so you are bold enough to disobey my commands to go away. You imagine that you may witness some of the rites of witchcraft, and that they may amuse you. Have I spoken truly?"

"Well," remarked Ervic, who had been pondering on the strange circumstances of his coming here, "you are right in some ways, but not in others. I am told that you work magic only for your own amusement. That seems to me very selfish. Few people understand magic. I'm told that you are the only real Yookoohoo in all Oz. Why don't you amuse others as well as yourself?"

"What right have you to question my actions?"

"None at all."

"And you say you are not here to demand any favors of me?"

"For myself I want nothing from you."

"You are wise in that. I never grant favors."

"That doesn't worry me," declared Ervic.

"But you are curious? You hope to witness some of my magic transformations?"

"If you wish to perform any magic, go ahead," said Ervic. "It may interest me and it may not. If you'd rather go on with your knitting, it's all the same to me. I am in no hurry at all."

This may have puzzled Red Reera, but the face beneath the lace cap could show no expression, being covered with hair. Perhaps in all her career the Yookoohoo had never been visited by anyone who, like this young man, asked for nothing, expected nothing, and had no reason for coming except curiosity. This attitude practically disarmed the witch and she began to regard the Skeezer in a more friendly way. She knitted for some time, seemingly in deep thought, and then she arose and walked to a big cupboard that stood against the wall of the room. When the cupboard door was opened Ervic could see a lot of drawers inside, and into one of these drawers—the second from the bottom—Reera thrust a hairy hand.

Until now Ervic could see over the bent form of the ape, but suddenly the form, with its back to him, seemed to straighten up and blot out the cupboard of drawers. The ape had changed to the form of a woman, dressed in the pretty Gillikin costume, and when she turned around he saw that it was a young woman, whose face was quite attractive.

"Do you like me better this way?" Reera inquired with a smile.

"You look better," he said calmly, "but I'm not sure I like you any better."

She laughed, saying: "During the heat of the day I like to be an ape, for an ape doesn't wear any clothes to speak of. But if one has gentlemen callers it is proper to dress up."

Ervic noticed her right hand was closed, as if she held something in it. She shut the cupboard door, bent over the crocodile and in a moment the creature had changed to a red wolf. It was not pretty even now, and the wolf crouched beside its mistress as a dog might have done. Its teeth looked as dangerous as had those of the crocodile.

Next the Yookoohoo went about touching all the lizards and toads, and at her touch they became kittens. The rats she changed into chipmunks. Now the only horrid creatures remaining were the four great spiders, which hid themselves behind their thick webs.

"There!" Reera cried, "now my cottage presents a more comfortable appearance. I love the toads and lizards and rats, because most people hate them, but I would tire of them if they always remained the same. Sometimes I change their forms a dozen times a day."

"You are clever," said Ervic. "I did not hear you utter any incantations or magic words. All you did was to touch the creatures."

"Oh, do you think so?" she replied. "Well, touch them yourself, if you like, and see if you can change their forms."

"No," said the Skeezer, "I don't understand magic and if I did I would not try to imitate your skill. You are a wonderful Yookoohoo, while I am only a common Skeezer."

This confession seemed to please Reera, who liked to have her witchcraft appreciated.

"Will you go away now?" she asked. "I prefer to be alone."

"I prefer to stay here," said Ervic.

"In another person's home, where you are not wanted?"

"Yes."

"Is not your curiosity yet satisfied?" demanded Reera, with a smile.

"I don't know. Is there anything else you can do?"

"Many things. But why should I exhibit my powers to a stranger?"

"I can think of no reason at all," he replied.

She looked at him curiously.

"You want no power for yourself, you say, and you're too stupid to be able to steal my secrets. This isn't a pretty cottage, while outside are sunshine, broad prairies and beautiful wildflowers. Yet you insist on sitting on that bench and annoying me with your unwelcome presence. What have you in that kettle?"

"Three fishes," he answered readily.

"Where did you get them?"

"I caught them in the Lake of the Skeezers."

"What do you intend to do with the fishes?"

"I shall carry them to the home of a friend of mine who has three children. The children will love to have the fishes for pets."

She came over to the bench and looked into the kettle, where the three fishes were swimming quietly in the water.

"They're pretty," said Reera. "Let me transform them into something else."

"No," objected the Skeezer.

"I love to transform things; it's so interesting. And I've never transformed any fishes in all my life."

"Let them alone," said Ervic.

"What shapes would you prefer them to have? I can make them turtles, or cute little sea-horses; or I could make them piglets, or rabbits, or guinea-pigs; or, if you like I can make chickens of them, or eagles, or bluejays."

"Let them alone!" repeated Ervic.

"You're not a very pleasant visitor," laughed Red Reera. "People accuse me of being cross and crabby and unsociable, and they are quite right. If you had come here pleading and begging for favors, and half afraid of my Yookoohoo magic, I'd have abused you until you ran away; but you're quite different from that. You're the unsociable and crabby and disagreeable one, and so I like you, and bear with your grumpiness. It's time for my midday meal; are you hungry?"

"No," said Ervic, although he really desired food.

"Well, I am," Reera declared and clapped her hands together. Instantly a table appeared, spread with linen and bearing dishes of various foods, some smoking hot. There were two plates laid, one at each end of the table, and as soon as Reera seated herself all her creatures gathered around her, as if they were accustomed to be fed when she ate. The wolf squatted at her right hand and the kittens and chipmunks gathered at her left.

"Come, Stranger, sit down and eat," she called cheerfully, "and while we're eating let us decide into what forms we shall change your fishes."

"They're all right as they are," asserted Ervic, drawing up his bench to the table. "The fishes are beauties—one gold, one silver and one bronze. Nothing that has life is more lovely than a beautiful fish."

"What! Am I not more lovely?" Reera asked, smiling at his serious face.

"I don't object to you—for a Yookoohoo, you know," he said, helping himself to the food and eating with good appetite.

"And don't you consider a beautiful girl more lovely than a fish, however pretty the fish may be?"

"Well," replied Ervic, after a period of thought, "that might be. If you transformed my three fish into three girls—girls who would be Adepts at Magic, you know they might please me as well as the fish do. You won't do that of course, because you can't, with all your skill. And, should you be able to do so, I fear my troubles would be more than I could bear. They would not consent to be my slaves—especially if they were Adepts at Magic—and so they would command me to obey them. No, Mistress Reera, let us not transform the fishes at all."

The Skeezer had put his case with remarkable cleverness. He realized that if he appeared anxious for such a transformation the Yookoohoo would not perform it, yet he had skillfully suggested that they be made Adepts at Magic.

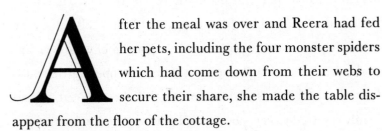

Chapter 19

RED REERA, the YOOKOOHOO

After the meal was over and Reera had fed her pets, including the four monster spiders which had come down from their webs to secure their share, she made the table disappear from the floor of the cottage.

"I wish you'd consent to my transforming your fishes," she said, as she took up her knitting again.

The Skeezer made no reply. He thought it unwise to hurry matters. All during the afternoon they sat silent. Once Reera went to her cupboard and after thrusting her hand into the same drawer as before, touched the wolf and transformed it into a bird with gorgeous colored feathers. This bird was larger than a parrot and of a somewhat different form, but Ervic had never seen one like it before.

"Sing!" said Reera to the bird, which had perched itself on a big wooden peg—as if it had been in the cottage before and knew just what to do.

And the bird sang jolly, rollicking songs with words to them—just as a person who had been carefully trained might do. The songs were entertaining and Ervic enjoyed listening to them. In an hour or so the bird stopped singing, tucked its head under its wing and went to sleep. Reera continued knitting but seemed thoughtful.

Now Ervic had marked this cupboard drawer well and had concluded that Reera took something from it which enabled her to perform her transformations. He thought that if he managed to remain in the cottage, and Reera fell asleep, he could slyly open the cupboard, take a portion of whatever was in the drawer, and by dropping it into the copper kettle transform the three fishes into their natural shapes. Indeed, he had firmly resolved to carry out this plan when the Yookoohoo put down her knitting and walked toward the door.

"I'm going out for a few minutes," said she; "do you wish to go with me, or will you remain here?"

Ervic did not answer but sat quietly on his bench. So Reera went out and closed the cottage door.

As soon as she was gone, Ervic rose and tiptoed to the cupboard.

"Take care! Take care!" cried several voices, coming from the kittens and chipmunks. "If you touch anything we'll tell the Yookoohoo!"

Ervic hesitated a moment but, remembering that he need not consider Reera's anger if he succeeded in transforming the fishes, he was about to open the cupboard when he was arrested by the voices of the fishes, which stuck their heads above the water in the kettle and called out:

"Come here, Ervic!"

So he went back to the kettle and bent over it.

"Let the cupboard alone," said the goldfish to him earnestly. "You could not succeed by getting that magic powder, for only the Yookoohoo knows how to use it. The best way is to allow her to transform us into three girls, for then we will have our natural shapes and be able to perform all the Arts of Magic we have learned and well understand. You are acting wisely and in the most effective manner. We did not know you were so intelligent, or that Reera could be so easily deceived by you. Continue as you have begun and try to persuade her to transform us. But insist that we be given the forms of girls."

The goldfish ducked its head down just as Reera re-entered the cottage. She saw Ervic bent over the kettle, so she came and joined him.

"Can your fishes talk?" she asked.

"Sometimes," he replied, "for all fishes in the Land of Oz

know how to speak. Just now they were asking me for some bread. They are hungry."

"Well, they can have some bread," said Reera. "But it is nearly supper-time, and if you would allow me to transform your fishes into girls they could join us at the table and have plenty of food much nicer than crumbs. Why not let me transform them?"

"Well," said Ervic, as if hesitating, "ask the fishes. If they consent, why—why, then, I'll think it over."

Reera bent over the kettle and asked:

"Can you hear me, little fishes?"

All three popped their heads above water.

"We can hear you," said the bronzefish.

"I want to give you other forms, such as rabbits, or turtles or girls, or something; but your master, the surly Skeezer, does not wish me to. However, he has agreed to the plan if you will consent."

"We'd like to be girls," said the silverfish.

"No, no!" exclaimed Ervic.

"If you promise to make us three beautiful girls, we will consent," said the goldfish.

"No, no!" exclaimed Ervic again.

"Also make us Adepts at Magic," added the bronzefish.

"I don't know exactly what that means," replied Reera musingly, "but as no Adept at Magic is as powerful as Yookoohoo, I'll add that to the transformation."

"We won't try to harm you, or to interfere with your magic in any way," promised the goldfish. "On the contrary, we will be your friends."

"Will you agree to go away and leave me alone in my cottage, whenever I command you to do so?" asked Reera.

"We promise that," cried the three fishes.

"Don't do it! Don't consent to the transformation," urged Ervic.

"They have already consented," said the Yookoohoo, laughing in his face, "and you have promised me to abide by their decision. So, friend Skeezer, I shall perform the transformation whether you like it or not."

Ervic seated himself on the bench again, a deep scowl on his face but joy in his heart. Reera moved over to the cupboard, took something from the drawer and returned to the copper kettle. She was clutching something tightly in her right hand, but with her left she reached within the kettle, took out the three fishes and laid them carefully on the floor, where they gasped in distress at being out of water.

Reera did not keep them in misery more than a few seconds, for she touched each one with her right hand and instantly the fishes were transformed into three tall and slender young women, with fine, intelligent faces and clothed in handsome, clinging gowns. The one who had been a goldfish had beautiful golden hair and blue eyes and was exceedingly fair of skin; the one who had been a bronzefish had dark brown

hair and clear grey eyes and her complexion matched these
lovely features. The one who had been a silverfish had snow-
white hair of the finest texture and deep brown eyes. The hair
contrasted exquisitely with her pink cheeks and ruby-red lips,
nor did it make her look a day older than her two companions.

As soon as they secured these girlish shapes, all three
bowed low to the Yookoohoo and said:

"We thank you, Reera."

Then they bowed to the Skeezer and said:

"We thank you, Ervic."

"Very good!" cried the Yookoohoo, examining her work
with critical approval. "You are much better and more interesting than fishes, and this ungracious Skeezer would scarcely
allow me to do the transformations. You surely have nothing
to thank him for. But now let us dine in honor of the occasion."

She clapped her hands together and again a table loaded
with food appeared in the cottage. It was a longer table, this
time, and places were set for the three Adepts as well as for
Reera and Ervic.

"Sit down, friends, and eat your fill," said the Yookoohoo,
but instead of seating herself at the head of the table she
went to the cupboard, saying to the Adepts: "Your beauty and
grace, my fair friends, quite outshine my own. So that I may
appear properly at the banquet table I intend, in honor of this
occasion, to take upon myself my natural shape."

Scarcely had she finished this speech when Reera transformed herself into a young woman fully as lovely as the three Adepts. She was not quite so tall as they, but her form was more rounded and more handsomely clothed, with a wonderful jeweled girdle and a necklace of shining pearls. Her hair was a bright auburn red, and her eyes large and dark.

"Do you claim this is your natural form?" asked Ervic of the Yookoohoo.

"Yes," she replied. "This is the only form I am really entitled to wear. But I seldom assume it because there is no one here to admire or appreciate it and I get tired admiring it myself."

"I see now why you are named Reera the Red," remarked Ervic.

"It is on account of my red hair," she explained smiling. "I do not care for red hair myself, which is one reason I usually wear other forms."

"It is beautiful," asserted the young man; and then remembering the other women present he added: "But, of course, all women should not have red hair, because that would make it too common. Gold and silver and brown hair are equally handsome."

The smiles that he saw interchanged between the four filled the poor Skeezer with embarrassment, so he fell silent and attended to eating his supper, leaving the others to do the talking. The three Adepts frankly told Reera who they were, how they became fishes and how they had planned secretly to induce the Yookoohoo to transform them. They admitted that they had feared, had they asked her to help, that she would have refused them.

"You were quite right," returned the Yookoohoo. "I make it my rule never to perform magic to assist others, for if I did there would always be a crowd at my cottage demanding help and I hate crowds and want to be left alone."

"However, now that you are restored to your proper shapes, I do not regret my action and I hope you will be of use in saving the Skeezer people by raising their island to the surface of the lake, where it really belongs. But you must promise me that after you go away you will never come here again, nor tell anyone what I have done for you."

The three Adepts and Ervic thanked the Yookoohoo warmly. They promised to remember her wish that they should not come to her cottage again and so, with a good-bye, took their departure.

⸱⸱⸱⸱◄ Chapter 20 ►⸱⸱⸱—⸱⸱

A PUZZLING PROBLEM

Glinda the Good, having decided to try her sorcery upon the abandoned submarine, so that it would obey her commands, asked all of her party, including the Skeezers, to withdraw from the shore of the lake to the line of palm trees. She kept with her only the little Wizard of Oz, who was her pupil and knew how to assist her in her magic rites. When they two were alone beside the stranded boat, Glinda said to the Wizard:

"I shall first try my magic recipe No. 1163, which is intended to make inanimate objects move at my command. Have you a skeropythrope with you?"

"Yes, I always carry one in my bag," replied the Wizard. He

opened his black bag of magic tools and took out a brightly polished skeropythrope, which he handed to the Sorceress. Glinda had also brought a small wicker bag, containing various requirements of sorcery, and from this she took a parcel of powder and a vial of liquid. She poured the liquid into the skeropythrope and added the powder. At once the skeropythrope began to sputter and emit sparks of a violet color, which spread in all directions. The Sorceress instantly stepped into the middle of the boat and held the instrument so that the sparks fell all around her and covered every bit of the blackened steel boat. At the same time Glinda crooned a weird incantation in the language of sorcery, her voice sounding low and musical.

After a little the violet sparks ceased, and those that had fallen upon the boat had disappeared and left no mark upon its surface. The ceremony was ended and Glinda returned the skeropythrope to the Wizard, who put it away in his black bag.

"That ought to do the business all right," he said confidently.

"Let us make a trial and see," she replied.

So they both entered the boat and seated themselves.

Speaking in a tone of command the Sorceress said to the boat: "Carry us across the lake, to the farther shore."

At once the boat backed off the sandy beach, turned its prow and moved swiftly over the water.

"Very good—very good indeed!" cried the Wizard, when the boat slowed up at the shore opposite from that whence they had departed. "Even Coo-ee-oh, with all her witchcraft, could do no better."

The Sorceress now said to the boat:

"Close up, submerge and carry us to the basement door of the sunken island—the door from which you emerged at the command of Queen Coo-ee-oh."

The boat obeyed. As it sank into the water the top sections rose from the sides and joined together over the heads of Glinda and the Wizard, who were thus enclosed in a waterproof chamber. There were four glass windows in this covering, one on each side and one on either end, so that the passengers could see exactly where they were going. Moving under water more slowly than on the surface, the submarine gradually approached the island and halted with its bow pressed against the huge marble door in the basement under the Dome. This door was tightly closed and it was evident to both Glinda and the Wizard that it would not open to admit the underwater boat unless a magic word was spoken by them or someone from within the basement of the island. But what was this magic word? Neither of them knew.

"I'm afraid," said the Wizard regretfully, "that we can't get in, after all. Unless your sorcery can discover the word to open the marble door."

"That is probably some word only known to Coo-ee-oh," replied the Sorceress. "I may be able to discover what it is, but that will require time. Let us go back again to our companions."

"It seems a shame, after we have made the boat obey us, to be balked by just a marble door," grumbled the Wizard.

At Glinda's command the boat rose until it was on a level with the glass dome that covered the Skeezer village, when the Sorceress made it slowly circle all around the Great Dome.

Many faces were pressed against the glass from the inside, eagerly watching the submarine, and in one place were Dorothy and Ozma, who quickly recognized Glinda and the Wizard through the glass windows of the boat. Glinda saw them, too, and held the boat close to the Dome while the friends exchanged greetings in pantomime. Their voices, unfortunately, could not be heard through the Dome and the water and the side of the boat. The Wizard tried to make the girls understand, through signs, that he and Glinda had come to their rescue, and Ozma and Dorothy understood this from the very fact that the Sorceress and the Wizard had appeared. The two girl prisoners were smiling and in safety, and knowing this Glinda felt she could take all the time necessary in order to effect their final rescue.

As nothing more could be done just then, Glinda ordered the boat to return to shore and it obeyed readily. First it ascended to the surface of the water, then the roof parted and fell into the slots at the side of the boat, and then the magic craft quickly made the shore and beached itself on the sands at the very spot from which it had departed at Glinda's command. All the Oz people and the Skeezers at once ran to the boat to ask if they had reached the island, and whether they had seen Ozma and Dorothy. The Wizard told them of the obstacle they had met in the way of a marble door, and how Glinda would now undertake to find a magic way to conquer the door.

Realizing that it would require several days to succeed in reaching the island, raising it and liberating their friends and the Skeezer people, Glinda now prepared a camp half way between the lake shore and the palm trees.

The Wizard's wizardry made a number of tents appear and the sorcery of the Sorceress furnished these tents all complete, with beds, chairs, tables, flags, lamps and even books with which to pass idle hours. All the tents had the Royal Banner of Oz flying from the centerpoles and one big tent, not now occupied, had Ozma's own banner moving in the breeze.

Betsy and Trot had a tent to themselves, and Button Bright and Ojo had another. The Scarecrow and the Tin Woodman paired together in one tent and so did Jack Pumpkinhead and the Shaggy Man, Cap'n Bill and Uncle Henry, Tik-Tok and Professor Wogglebug. Glinda had the most splendid tent of all, except that reserved for Ozma, while the Wizard had a little one of his own. Whenever it was meal time, tables loaded with food magically appeared in the tents of those who were in the habit of eating, and these complete arrangements made the rescue party just comfortable as they would have been in their own homes.

Far into the night Glinda sat in her tent studying a roll of mystic scrolls in search of a word that would open the basement door of the island and admit her to the Great Dome. She also made many magical experiments, hoping to discover something that would aid her. Yet the morning found the powerful Sorceress still unsuccessful.

Glinda's art could have opened any ordinary door, you may be sure, but you must realize that this marble door of the island had been commanded not to open save in obedience to one magic word, and therefore all other magic words could have no effect upon it. The magic word that guarded the door had probably been invented by Coo-ee-oh, who had now forgotten it. The only way, then, to gain entrance to the sunken island was to break the charm that held the door fast shut. If this could be done no magic would be required to open it.

The next day the Sorceress and the Wizard again entered the boat and made it submerge and go to the marble door, which they tried in various ways to open, but without success.

"We shall have to abandon this attempt, I think," said Glinda. "The easiest way to raise the island would be for us to gain admittance to the Dome and then descend to the basement and see in what manner Coo-ee-oh made the entire island sink or rise at her command. It naturally occurred to me that the easiest way to gain admittance would be by having the boat take us into the basement through the marble door from which Coo-ee-oh launched it. But there must be other ways to get inside the Dome and join Ozma and Dorothy, and such ways we must find by study and the proper use of our powers of magic."

"It won't be easy," declared the Wizard, "for we must not forget that Ozma herself understands considerable magic, and has doubtless tried to raise the island or find other means of escape from it and failed."

"That is true," returned Glinda, "but Ozma's magic is fairy magic, while you are a Wizard and I am a Sorceress. In this way the three of us have a great variety of magic to work with, and if we should all fail it will be because the island is raised and lowered by a magic power none of us is acquainted with. My idea therefore is to seek—by such magic as we possess—to accomplish our object in another way."

They made the circle of the Dome again in their boat, and once more saw Ozma and Dorothy through their windows and exchanged signals with the two imprisoned girls.

Ozma realized that her friends were doing all in their power to rescue her and smiled an encouragement to their efforts. Dorothy seemed a little anxious but was trying to be as brave as her companion.

After the boat had returned to the camp and Glinda was seated in her tent, working out various ways by which Ozma and Dorothy could be rescued, the Wizard stood on the shore dreamily eying the outlines of the Great Dome which showed beneath the clear water, when he raised his eyes and saw a group of strange people approaching from around the lake. Three were young women of stately presence, very beautifully dressed, who moved with remarkable grace. They were followed at a little distance by a good-looking young Skeezer.

The Wizard saw at a glance that these people might be very important, so he advanced to meet them. The three maidens received him graciously and the one with the golden hair said:

"I believe you are the famous Wizard of Oz, of whom I have often heard. We are seeking Glinda, the Sorceress, and perhaps you can lead us to her."

"I can, and will, right gladly," answered the Wizard. "Follow me, please."

The little Wizard was puzzled as to the identity of the three lovely visitors but he gave no sign that might embarrass them.

He understood they did not wish to be questioned, and so he made no remarks as he led the way to Glinda's tent.

With a courtly bow the Wizard ushered the three visitors into the gracious presence of Glinda the Good.

···—·◄ Chapter 21 ►···—··

The THREE ADEPTS

The Sorceress looked up from her work as the three maidens entered, and something in their appearance and manner led her to rise and bow to them in her most dignified manner. The three knelt an instant before the great Sorceress and then stood upright and waited for her to speak.

"Whoever you may be," said Glinda, "I bid you welcome."

"My name is Audah," said one.

"My name is Aurah," said another.

"My name is Aujah," said the third.

Glinda had never heard these names before, but looking closely at the three she asked:

"Are you witches or workers in magic?"

"Some of the secret arts we have gleaned from Nature," replied the brown-haired maiden modestly, "but we do not place our skill beside that of the Great Sorceress, Glinda the Good."

"I suppose you are aware it is unlawful to practice magic in the Land of Oz, without the permission of our Ruler, Princess Ozma?"

"No, we were not aware of that," was the reply. "We have heard of Ozma, who is the appointed Ruler of all this great fairyland, but her laws have not reached us, as yet."

Glinda studied the strange maidens thoughtfully; then she said to them:

"Princess Ozma is even now imprisoned in the Skeezer village, for the whole island with its Great Dome, was sunk to the bottom of the lake by the witchcraft of Coo-ee-oh, whom the Flathead Su-dic transformed into a silly swan. I am seeking some way to overcome Coo-ee-oh's magic and raise the isle to the surface again. Can you help me do this?"

The maidens exchanged glances, and the white-haired one replied:

"We do not know; but we will try to assist you."

"It seems," continued Glinda musingly, "that Coo-ee-oh derived most of her witchcraft from three Adepts at Magic, who at one time ruled the Flatheads. While the Adepts were being entertained by Coo-ee-oh at a banquet in her palace, she cruelly betrayed them and after transforming them into fishes cast them into the lake.

"If I could find these three fishes and return them to their natural shapes—they might know what magic Coo-ee-oh used to sink the island. I was about to go to the shore and call these fishes to me when you arrived. So, if you will join me, we will try to find them."

The maidens exchanged smiles now, and the golden-haired one, Audah, said to Glinda:

"It will not be necessary to go to the lake. We are the three fishes."

"Indeed!" cried Glinda. "Then you are the three Adepts at Magic, restored to your proper forms?"

"We are the three Adepts," admitted Aujah.

"Then," said Glinda, "my task is half accomplished. But who destroyed the transformation that made you fishes?"

"We have promised not to tell," answered Aurah; "but this young Skeezer was largely responsible for our release; he is brave and clever, and we owe him our gratitude."

Glinda looked at Ervic, who stood modestly behind the Adepts, hat in hand. "He shall be properly rewarded," she declared, "for in helping you he has helped us all, and perhaps saved his people from being imprisoned forever in the sunken isle."

The Sorceress now asked her guests to seat themselves and a long talk followed, in which the Wizard of Oz shared.

"We are quite certain," said Aurah, "that if we could get inside the Dome we could discover Coo-ee-oh's secrets, for in all her work, after we became fishes, she used the formulas and incantations and arts that she stole from us. She may have added to these things, but they were the foundation of all her work."

"What means do you suggest for our getting into the Dome?" inquired Glinda.

The three Adepts hesitated to reply, for they had not yet considered what could be done to reach the inside of the Great Dome. While they were in deep thought, and Glinda and the Wizard were quietly awaiting their suggestions, into the tent rushed Trot and Betsy, dragging between them the Patchwork Girl.

"Oh, Glinda," cried Trot, "Scraps has thought of a way to rescue Ozma and Dorothy and all of the Skeezers."

The three Adepts could not avoid laughing merrily, for not only were they amused by the queer form of the Patchwork Girl, but Trot's enthusiastic speech struck them as really funny. If the Great Sorceress and the famous Wizard and the three talented Adepts at Magic were unable as yet to solve the important problem of the sunken isle, there was little chance for a patched girl stuffed with cotton to succeed.

But Glinda, smiling indulgently at the earnest faces turned toward her, patted the children's heads and said:

"Scraps is very clever. Tell us what she has thought of, my dear."

"Well," said Trot, "Scraps says that if you could dry up all the water in the lake the island would be on dry land, an' everyone could come and go whenever they liked."

Glinda smiled again, but the Wizard said to the girls:

"If we should dry up the lake, what would become of all the beautiful fishes that now live in the water?"

"Dear me! That's so," admitted Betsy, crestfallen; "we never thought of that, did we Trot?"

"Couldn't you transform 'em into polliwogs?" asked Scraps, turning a somersault and then standing on one leg. "You could give them a little, teeny pond to swim in, and they'd be just as happy as they are as fishes."

"No indeed!" replied the Wizard, severely. "It is wicked to transform any living creatures without their consent, and the lake is the home of the fishes and belongs to them."

"All right," said Scraps, making a face at him; "I don't care."

"It's too bad," sighed Trot, "for I thought we'd struck a splendid idea."

"So you did," declared Glinda, her face now grave and thoughtful. "There is something in the Patchwork Girl's idea that may be of real value to us."

"I think so, too," agreed the golden-haired Adept. "The

top of the Great Dome is only a few feet below the surface of the water. If we could reduce the level of the lake until the Dome sticks a little above the water, we could remove some of the glass and let ourselves down into the village by means of ropes."

"And there would be plenty of water left for the fishes to swim in," added the white-haired maiden.

"If we succeed in raising the island we could fill up the lake again," suggested the brown-haired Adept.

"I believe," said the Wizard, rubbing his hands together in delight, "that the Patchwork Girl has shown us the way to success."

The girls were looking curiously at the three beautiful Adepts, wondering who they were, so Glinda introduced them to Trot and Betsy and Scraps, and then sent the children away while she considered how to carry the new idea into effect.

Not much could be done that night, so the Wizard prepared another tent for the Adepts, and in the evening Glinda held a reception and invited all her followers to meet the new arrivals. The Adepts were greatly astonished at the extraordinary personages presented to them, and marveled that Jack Pumpkinhead and the Scarecrow and the Tin Woodman and Tik-Tok could really live and think and talk just like other people. They were especially pleased with the lively Patchwork Girl and loved to watch her antics.

It was quite a pleasant party, for Glinda served some

dainty refreshments to those who could eat, and the Scarecrow recited some poems, and the Cowardly Lion sang a song in his deep bass voice. The only thing that marred their joy was the thought that their beloved Ozma and dear little Dorothy were yet confined in the Great Dome of the Sunken island.

The SUNKEN ISLAND

As soon as they had breakfasted the next morning, Glinda and the Wizard and the three Adepts went down to the shore of the lake and formed a line with their faces toward the submerged island. All the others came to watch them, but stood at a respectful distance in the background.

At the right of the Sorceress stood Audah and Aurah, while at the left stood the Wizard and Aujah. Together they stretched their arms over the water's edge and in unison the five chanted a rhythmic incantation.

This chant they repeated again and again, swaying their arms gently from side to side, and in a few minutes the watchers behind them noticed that the lake had begun to recede from the shore. Before long the highest point of the dome appeared above the water. Gradually the water fell, making the Dome appear to rise. When it was three or four feet above the surface Glinda gave the signal to stop, for their work had been accomplished.

The blackened submarine was now entirely out of water, but Uncle Henry and Cap'n Bill managed to push it into the lake. Glinda, the Wizard, Ervic and the Adepts got into the boat, taking with them a coil of strong rope, and at the command of the Sorceress the craft cleaved its way through the water toward the part of the Dome which was now visible.

"There's still plenty of water for the fish to swim in," observed the Wizard as they rode along. "They might like more but I'm sure they can get along until we have raised the island and can fill up the lake again."

The boat touched gently on the sloping glass of the Dome, and the Wizard took some tools from his black bag and quickly removed one large pane of glass, thus making a hole large enough for their bodies to pass through. Stout frames of steel supported the glass of the Dome, and around one of these frames the Wizard tied the end of a rope.

"I'll go down first," said he, "for while I'm not as spry as Cap'n Bill I'm sure I can manage it easily. Are you sure the rope is long enough to reach the bottom?"

"Quite sure," replied the Sorceress.

So the Wizard let down the rope and climbing through the opening lowered himself down, hand over hand, clinging to the rope with his legs and feet. Below in the streets of the village were gathered all the Skeezers, men, women and children, and you may be sure that Ozma and Dorothy, with Lady Aurex, were filled with joy that their friends were at last coming to their rescue.

The Queen's palace, now occupied by Ozma, was directly in the center of the Dome, so that when the rope was let down the end of it came just in front of the palace entrance. Several Skeezers held fast to the rope's end to steady it and the Wizard reached the ground in safety. He hugged first Ozma and then Dorothy, while all the Skeezers cheered as loud as they could.

The Wizard now discovered that the rope was long enough to reach from the top of the Dome to the ground when doubled, so he tied a chair to one end of the rope and called to Glinda to sit in the chair while he and some of the Skeezers lowered her to the pavement. In this way the Sorceress reached the ground quite comfortably and the three Adepts and Ervic soon followed her.

The Skeezers quickly recognized the three Adepts at Magic, whom they had learned to respect before their wicked Queen betrayed them, and welcomed them as friends. All the inhabitants of the village had been greatly frightened by their imprisonment under water, but now realized that an attempt was to be made to rescue them.

Glinda, the Wizard and the Adepts followed Ozma and Dorothy into the palace, and they asked Lady Aurex and Ervic to join them. After Ozma had told of her adventures in trying to prevent war between the Flatheads and the Skeezers, and Glinda had told all about the Rescue Expedition and the restoration of the three Adepts by the help of Ervic, a serious consultation was held as to how the island could be made to rise.

"I've tried every way in my power," said Ozma, "but Coo-ee-oh used a very unusual sort of magic which I do not understand. She seems to have prepared her witchcraft in such a way that a spoken word is necessary to accomplish her designs, and these spoken words are known only to herself."

"That is a method we taught her," declared Aurah the Adept.

"I can do no more, Glinda," continued Ozma, "so I wish you would try what your sorcery can accomplish."

"First, then," said Glinda, "let us visit the basement of the island, which I am told is underneath the village."

A flight of marble stairs led from one of Coo-ee-oh's private rooms down to the basement, but when the party arrived all were puzzled by what they saw. In the center of a broad, low room, stood a mass of great cog-wheels, chains and pulleys, all interlocked and seeming to form a huge machine; but there was no engine or other motive power to make the wheels turn.

"This, I suppose, is the means by which the island is lowered or raised," said Ozma, "but the magic word which is needed to move the machinery is unknown to us."

The three Adepts were carefully examining the mass of wheels, and soon the golden-haired one said:

"These wheels do not control the island at all. On the contrary, one set of them is used to open the doors of the little rooms where the submarines are kept, as may be seen from the chains and pulleys used. Each boat is kept in a little room with two doors, one to the basement room where we are now and the other letting into the lake.

"When Coo-ee-oh used the boat in which she attacked the Flatheads, she first commanded the basement door to open and with her followers she got into the boat and made the top close over them. Then the basement door being closed, the outer door was slowly opened, letting the water fill the room to float the boat, which then left the island, keeping under water."

"But how could she expect to get back again?" asked the Wizard.

"Why the boat would enter the room filled with water and after the outer door was closed a word of command started a pump which pumped all the water from the room. Then the boat would open and Coo-ee-oh could enter the basement."

"I see," said the Wizard. "It is a clever contrivance, but won't work unless one knows the magic words."

"Another part of this machinery," explained the white-haired Adept, "is used to extend the bridge from the island to the mainland. The steel bridge is in a room much like that in which the boats are kept, and at Coo-ee-oh's command it would reach out, joint by joint, until its far end touched the shore of the lake. The same magic command would make the bridge return to its former position. Of course the bridge could not be used unless the island was on the surface of the water."

"But how do you suppose Coo-ee-oh managed to sink the island, and make it rise again?" inquired Glinda.

This the Adepts could not yet explain. As nothing more could be learned from the basement they mounted the steps to the Queen's private suite again, and Ozma showed them to a special room where Coo-ee-oh kept her magical instruments and performed all her arts of witchcraft.

The MAGIC WORDS

Many interesting things were to be seen in the Room of Magic, including much that had been stolen from the Adepts when they were transformed to fishes, but they had to admit that Coo-ee-oh had a rare genius for mechanics, and had used her knowledge in inventing a lot of mechanical apparatus that ordinary witches, wizards and sorcerers could not understand.

They all carefully inspected this room, taking care to examine every article they came across.

"The island," said Glinda thoughtfully, "rests on a base of solid marble. When it is submerged, as it is now, the base of the island is upon the bottom of the lake. What puzzles me is how such a great weight can be lifted and suspended in the water, even by magic."

"I now remember," returned Aujah, "that one of the arts we taught Coo-ee-oh was the way to expand steel, and I think that explains how the island is raised and lowered. I noticed in the basement a big steel pillar that passed through the floor and extended upward to this palace. Perhaps the end of it is concealed in this very room. If the lower end of the steel pillar is firmly embedded in the bottom of the lake, Coo-ee-oh could utter a magic word that would make the pillar expand, and so lift the entire island to the level of the water."

"I've found the end of the steel pillar. It's just here," announced the Wizard, pointing to one side of the room where a great basin of polished steel seemed to have been set upon the floor.

They all gathered around, and Ozma said:

"Yes, I am quite sure that is the upper end of the pillar that supports the island. I noticed it when I first came here. It has been hollowed out, you see, and something has been burned in the basin, for the fire has left its marks. I wondered what was under the great basin and got several of the Skeezers to come up here and try to lift it for me. They were strong men, but could not move it at all."

"It seems to me," said Audah the Adept, "that we have discovered the manner in which Coo-ee-oh raised the island.

She would burn some sort of magic powder in the basin, utter the magic word, and the pillar would lengthen out and lift the island with it."

"What's this?" asked Dorothy, who had been searching around with the others, and now noticed a slight hollow in the wall, near to where the steel basin stood. As she spoke Dorothy pushed her thumb into the hollow and instantly a small drawer popped out from the wall.

The three Adepts, Glinda and the Wizard sprang forward and peered into the drawer. It was half filled with a greyish powder, the tiny grains of which constantly moved as if impelled by some living force.

"It may be some kind of radium," said the Wizard.

"No," replied Glinda, "it is more wonderful than even radium, for I recognize it as a rare mineral powder called Gaulau by the sorcerers. I wonder how Coo-ee-oh discovered it and where she obtained it."

"There is no doubt," said Aujah the Adept, "that this is the magic powder Coo-ee-oh burned in the basin. If only we knew the magic word, I am quite sure we could raise the island."

"How can we discover the magic word?" asked Ozma, turning to Glinda as she spoke.

"That we must now seriously consider," answered the Sorceress.

So all of them sat down in the Room of Magic and began to think. It was so still that after a while Dorothy grew nervous.

The little girl never could keep silent for long, and at the risk of displeasing her magic-working friends she suddenly said:

"Well, Coo-ee-oh used just three magic words, one to make the bridge work, and one to make the submarines go out of their holes, and one to raise and lower the island. Three words. And Coo-ee-oh's name is made up of just three words. One is 'Coo,' and one is 'ee,' and one is 'oh.'"

The Wizard frowned but Glinda looked wonderingly at the young girl and Ozma cried out:

"A good thought, Dorothy dear! You may have solved our problem."

"I believe it is worth a trial," agreed Glinda. "It would be quite natural for Coo-ee-oh to divide her name into three magic syllables, and Dorothy's suggestion seems like an inspiration."

The three Adepts also approved the trial but the brown-haired one said:

"We must be careful not to use the wrong word, and send the bridge out under water. The main thing, if Dorothy's idea is correct, is to hit upon the one word that moves the island."

"Let us experiment," suggested the Wizard.

In the drawer with the moving grey powder was a tiny golden cup, which they thought was used for measuring. Glinda filled this cup with the powder and carefully poured it into the shallow basin, which was the top of the great steel pillar supporting the island. Then Aurah the Adept lighted a taper and touched it to the powder, which instantly glowed fiery red and tumbled about the basin with astonishing energy. While the grains of powder still glowed red the Sorceress bent over it and said in a voice of command: "Coo!"

They waited motionless to see what would happen. There was a grating noise and a whirl of machinery, but the island did not move a particle.

Dorothy rushed to the window, which overlooked the glass side of the dome.

"The boats!" she exclaimed. "The boats are all loose an' sailing under water."

"We've made a mistake," said the Wizard gloomily.

"But it's one which shows we are on the right track," declared Aujah the Adept. "We know now that Coo-ee-oh used the syllables of her name for the magic words."

"If 'Coo' sends out the boats, it is probable that 'ee' works the bridge," suggested Ozma. "So the last part of the name may raise the island."

"Let us try that next then," proposed the Wizard.

He scraped the embers of the burned powder out of the basin and Glinda again filled the golden cup from the drawer and placed it on top the steel pillar. Aurah lighted it with her taper and Ozma bent over the basin and murmured the long drawn syllable: "Oh-h-h!"

Instantly the island trembled and with a weird groaning noise it moved upward—slowly, very slowly, but with a steady motion, while all the company stood by in awed silence. It was a wonderful thing, even to those skilled in the arts of magic, wizardry and sorcery, to realize that a single word could raise that great, heavy island, with its immense glass Dome.

"Why, we're way above the lake now!" exclaimed Dorothy from the window, when at last the island ceased to move.

"That is because we lowered the level of the water," explained Glinda.

They could hear the Skeezers cheering lustily in the streets of the village as they realized that they were saved.

"Come," said Ozma eagerly, "let us go down and join the people."

"Not just yet," returned Glinda, a happy smile upon her lovely face, for she was overjoyed at their success. "First let us extend the bridge to the mainland, where our friends from the Emerald City are waiting."

It didn't take long to put more powder in the basin, light it and utter the syllable "EE!" The result was that a door in the basement opened and the steel bridge moved out, extended itself joint by joint, and finally rested its far end on the shore of the lake just in front of the encampment.

"Now," said Glinda, "we can go up and receive the congratulations of the Skeezers and of our friends of the Rescue Expedition."

Across the water, on the shore of the lake, the Patchwork Girl was waving them a welcome.

Chapter 24

GLINDA'S TRIUMPH

Of course all those who had joined Glinda's expedition at once crossed the bridge to the island, where they were warmly welcomed by the Skeezers. Before all the concourse of people Princess Ozma made a speech from a porch of the palace and demanded that they recognize her as their lawful Ruler and promise to obey the laws of the Land of Oz. In return she agreed to protect them from all future harm and declared they would no longer be subjected to cruelty and abuse.

This pleased the Skeezers greatly, and when Ozma told them they might elect a Queen to rule over them, who in turn would be subject to Ozma of Oz, they voted for Lady Aurex, and that same day the ceremony of crowning the new Queen was held and Aurex was installed as mistress of the palace.

For her Prime Minister the Queen selected Ervic, for the three Adepts had told of his good judgment, faithfulness and cleverness, and all the Skeezers approved the appointment.

Glinda, the Wizard and the Adepts stood on the bridge and recited an incantation that quite filled the lake with water again, and the Scarecrow and the Patchwork Girl climbed to the top of the Great Dome and replaced the pane of glass that had been removed to allow Glinda and her followers to enter.

When evening came Ozma ordered a great feast prepared, to which every Skeezer was invited. The village was beautifully decorated and brilliantly lighted and there was music and dancing until a late hour to celebrate the liberation of the people. For the Skeezers had been freed, not only from the water of the lake but from the cruelty of their former Queen.

As the people from the Emerald City prepared the next morning to depart Queen Aurex said to Ozma:

"There is only one thing I now fear for my people, and that is the enmity of the terrible Su-dic of the Flatheads. He is liable to come here at any time and try to annoy us, and my Skeezers are peaceful folks and unable to fight the wild and wilful Flatheads."

"Do not worry," returned Ozma, reassuringly. "We intend to stop on our way at the Flatheads' Enchanted Mountain and punish the Su-dic for his misdeeds."

That satisfied Aurex and when Ozma and her followers trooped over the bridge to the shore, having taken leave of their friends, all the Skeezers cheered them and waved their hats and handkerchiefs, and the band played and the departure was indeed a ceremony long to be remembered.

The three Adepts at Magic, who had formerly ruled the Flatheads wisely and considerately, went with Princess Ozma and her people, for they had promised Ozma to stay on the mountain and again see that the laws were enforced.

Glinda had been told all about the curious Flatheads and she had consulted with the Wizard and formed a plan to render them more intelligent and agreeable.

When the party reached the mountain Ozma and Dorothy showed them how to pass around the invisible wall—which had been built by the Flatheads after the Adepts were transformed—and how to gain the up-and-down stairway that led to the mountain top.

The Su-dic had watched the approach of the party from the edge of the mountain and was frightened when he saw that the three Adepts had recovered their natural forms and were coming back to their former home. He realized that his power would soon be gone and yet he determined to fight to the last. He called all the Flatheads together and armed them, and told them to arrest all who came up the stairway and hurl them over the edge of the mountain to the plain below. But although they feared the Supreme Dictator, who had threatened to punish them if they did not obey his commands, as soon as they saw the three Adepts they threw down their arms and begged their former Rulers to protect them.

The three Adepts assured the excited Flatheads that they had nothing to fear.

Seeing that his people had rebelled the Su-dic ran away and tried to hide, but the Adepts found him and had him cast into a prison, all his cans of brains being taken away from him.

After this easy conquest of the Su-dic, Glinda told the Adepts of her plan, which had already been approved by Ozma of Oz, and they joyfully agreed to it. So, during the next few days, the great Sorceress transformed, in a way, every Flathead on the mountain.

Taking them one at a time, she had the can of brains that belonged to each one opened and the contents spread on the flat head, after which, by means of her arts of sorcery, she caused the head to grow over the brains—in the manner most people wear them—and they were thus rendered as intelligent and good looking as any of the other inhabitants of the Land of Oz.

When all had been treated in this manner there were no more Flatheads at all, and the Adepts decided to name their people Mountaineers. One good result of Glinda's sorcery was that no one could now be deprived of the brains that belonged to him and each person had exactly the share he was entitled to.

Even the Su-dic was given his portion of brains and his flat head made round, like the others, but he was deprived of all power to work further mischief, and with the Adepts constantly watching him he would be forced to become obedient and humble.

The Golden Pig, which ran grunting about the streets, with no brains at all, was disenchanted by Glinda, and in her woman's form was given brains and a round head. This wife of the Su-dic had once been even more wicked than her evil husband, but she had now forgotten all her wickedness and was likely to be a good woman thereafter.

These things being accomplished in a satisfactory manner, Princess Ozma and her people bade farewell to the three Adepts and departed for the Emerald City, well pleased with their interesting adventures.

They returned by the road over which Ozma and Dorothy had come, stopping to get the Sawhorse and the Red Wagon where they had left them.

"I'm very glad I went to see these peoples," said Princess Ozma, "for I not only prevented any further warfare between them, but they have been freed from the rule of the Su-dic and Coo-ee-oh and are now happy and loyal subjects of the Land of Oz. Which proves that it is always wise to do one's duty, however unpleasant that duty may seem to be."

The Royal Book of Oz

By Ruth Plumly Thompson

A Note About Ruth Plumly Thompson

Ruth Plumly Thompson was born in Philadelphia, Pennsylvania, and
began her writing career in 1914 when she took a job with the *Philadelphia
Public Ledger*. She was writing a weekly column for the newspaper and had
authored a children's book of her own when L. Frank Baum's publisher,
Reilly & Lee, approached her to continue the Oz series. L. Frank Baum
had died in 1919, but the demand for new stories was still high. Between
1921 and 1939, Thompson wrote one Oz book a year, starting with
The Royal Book of Oz, which was credited to Baum alone up until the 1980s.

···─◄ Author's Note ►···─··

Dear Children:

You will remember that, in the front part of *Glinda of Oz*, the Publishers told you that when Mr. Baum went away from this world he left behind some unfinished notes about the Princess Ozma and Dorothy and the jolly people of the Wonderful Land of Oz. The Publishers promised that they would try to put these notes together into a new Oz book for you.

Well, here it is—*The Royal Book of Oz*.

I am sure that Mr. Baum would be pleased that Ruth Plumly Thompson, who has known and loved the Oz stories ever since she was a little girl, has made this new Oz story, with all the Oz folks in it and true to life.

You see I am Mrs. Baum, the wife of the Royal Historian of Oz, and so I know how he feels about everything.

Now, about the story:

Of course, we all knew the Scarecrow was a very fine fellow, but surely we never guessed he ascended from an emperor. Most of us descend from our ancestors, but the Scarecrow really *ascended*.

The Scarecrow had a most exciting and adventurous time on the Silver Isle, and Dorothy and the Cowardly Lion just ran out of one adventure into another trying to rescue him. They made some charming new friends in their travels—Sir Hokus of Pokes, the Doubtful Dromedary, and the Comfortable Camel. You'll find them very unusual and likable. They have the same peculiar, delightful and informal natures that we love in all the queer Oz people.

This note is intended for all the children of America, who knew and loved Mr. Baum, and it goes to each of you with his love and mine.

Maud G. Baum

Ozcot

Hollywood, California

in the spring, 1921

Chapter 1

PROFESSOR WOGGLEBUG'S GREAT IDEA

The very thing!" exclaimed Professor Wogglebug, bounding into the air and upsetting his gold inkwell. "The very next idea!"

"Who, me?" A round-faced little Munchkin boy stuck his head in the door and regarded Professor Wogglebug solemnly. He was working his way through the Professor's Athletic college, and one of his duties was to wait upon this eminent educator of Oz.

"Certainly not!" snapped Professor Wogglebug. "You're a nobody or a nothing. Stop gaping and fetch me my hat. I'm off to the Emerald City. And mind the pupils take their history pills regularly while I'm gone," he added, clapping his tall hat Zif held out to him on the back of his head.

"Yes, sir!" said the little Munchkin respectfully.

"Don't hurry back, sir!" This last remark the Professor did not hear, for he was already half way down the college steps.

"Ozma will be delighted with the idea. How clever I am!" he murmured, twirling his antennae and walking rapidly down the pleasant blue lane.

The Professor, whose College of Art and Athletic Perfection is in the southwestern part of the Munchkin country, is the biggest bug in Oz, or in anyplace else, for that matter. He has made education painless by substituting school pills for books. His students take Latin, history and spelling pills; they swallow knowledge of every kind with ease and pleasure and spend the rest of their time in sport. No wonder he is so well thought of in Oz! No wonder he thinks so well of himself! Swinging his cane jauntily, the Professor hurried toward the yellow brick road that leads to the Emerald City, and by night-fall had reached the lovely capital of Oz.

Oz! That marvelous country where no one grows old, where animals and birds talk as sensibly as people, and adventures happen every day. Indeed, of all fairylands in the world, Oz is the most delightful, and of all fairy cities, the Emerald City is the most beautiful. A soft green light shone for miles about, and the gemmed turrets and spires of the palace flashed more brightly than the stars. But its loveliness was familiar to Professor Wogglebug, and without a pause he proceeded to Ozma's palace and was at once admitted to the great hall.

A roar of merriment greeted his ears. Ozma, the lovely girl Ruler of Oz, was having a party, and the room was full of most surprising people, surprising to some, that is, but old friends to most of us.

Jack, holding tightly to his pumpkin head, was running as fast as his wooden feet and wobbly legs would take him from Dorothy. A game of blind-man's-buff was in full swing, and Scraps and Tik-Tok, the Scarecrow and Nick Chopper, the Glass Cat and the Cowardly Lion, the Wizard of Oz and the Wooden Sawhorse, Cap'n Bill and Betsy Bobbin, Billina and the Hungry Tiger were tumbling over each other in an effort to keep away from the blindfolded little girl. But Dorothy was too quick for them. With a sudden whirl, she spun 'round and grasped a coatsleeve.

"The Scarecrow!" she laughed triumphantly. "I can tell by the way he skwoshes and now *he's* it!"

"I'm always *it!*" chuckled the droll person. "But hah! Behold the learned Professor standing so aloofly in our midst."

No one had noticed Professor Wogglebug, who had been quietly watching the game. "I don't like to interrupt the party," he began, approaching Ozma's throne apologetically, "but I've just had a most brilliant idea!"

"What? Another?" murmured the Scarecrow, rolling up his eyes.

"Where did you lose it?" asked Jack Pumpkinhead, edging forward anxiously.

"Lose it! Who said I'd lost it?" snapped the Professor, glaring at poor Jack.

"Well, you said you'd had it, and had is the past tense, so . . ." Jack's voice trailed off uncertainly, and Ozma, seeing he was embarrassed, begged the Professor to explain.

"Your Highness!" began Professor Wogglebug, while the company settled down in a resigned circle on the floor, "As Oz is the most interesting and delightful country on the Continent of Imagination and its people the most unusual and talented, I am about to compile a Royal Book which will give the names and history of all our people. In other words, I am to be the Great, Grand Genealogist of Oz!"

"Whatever that is," the Scarecrow whispered in Dorothy's ear.

"And," the Professor frowned severely on the Scarecrow, "with your Majesty's permission, I shall start at once!"

"Please do," said the Scarecrow with a wave toward the door, "and we will go on with the party!"

Scraps, the Patchwork Girl, who had been staring fixedly at the Professor with her silver suspender-button eyes, now sprang to her feet:

What is a genealogist?
It's something no one here has missed;

> *What puts such notions in your head?*
>
> *Turn out your toes or go to bed!"*

she shouted gaily, then, catching Ozma's disapproving glance, fell over backwards.

"I don't understand it at all," said Jack Pumpkinhead in a depressed voice. "I'm afraid my head's too ripe."

"Nor I," said Tik-Tok, the copper clockwork man. "Please wind me up a lit-tle tight-er Dor-o-thy, I want to think!"

Dorothy obligingly took a key suspended from a hook on his back and wound him up under his left arm. Everybody began to talk at once, and what with the Cowardly Lion's deep growl and Tik-Tok's squeaky voice and all the rest of the tin and meat and wooden voices, the confusion was terrible.

"Wait!" cried Ozma, clapping her hands. Immediately the room grew so still that one could hear Tik-Tok's machinery whirring 'round. "Now!" said Ozma, "One at a time, please, and let us hear from the Scarecrow first."

The Scarecrow rose. "I think, your Highness," he said modestly, "that anyone who has studied his Geozify already knows who we are and—"

"Who you are?" broke in the Wogglebug scornfully, "Of course they do. But *I* shall tell them who you *were*!"

"Who I were?" gasped the Scarecrow in a dazed voice, raising his cotton glove to his forehead. "Who I were? Well, who were I?"

"That's just the point," said Professor Wogglebug. "Who

were you? Who were your ancestors? Where is your family? Where is your family tree? From what did you descend?"

At each question, the Scarecrow looked more embarrassed. He repeated the last one several times. "From what did I descend? From what did I descend? Why, from a bean pole!" he cried.

This was perfectly true, for Dorothy, a little girl blown by a Kansas cyclone to the Kingdom of Oz, had discovered the Scarecrow in a farmer's cornfield and had lifted him down from his pole. Together they had made the journey to the Emerald City, where the Wizard of Oz had fitted him out with a fine set of brains. At one time, he had ruled Oz and was generally considered its cleverest citizen.

Before he could reply further, the Patchwork Girl, who was simply irrepressible, burst out:

"An ex-straw-ordinary man is he!
A bean pole for his family tree,
A Cornishman, upon my soul,
Descended from a tall, thin Pole!"

"Nonsense!" said Professor Wogglebug sharply, "Being stuffed with straw may make him extraordinary, but it is quite plain that the Scarecrow was nobody before he was himself. He has no ancestors, no family; only a bean pole for a family tree, and is therefore entitled to the merest mention in the Royal Book of Oz!"

"How about my brains?" asked the Scarecrow in a hurt voice. "Aren't they enough?"

"Brains have simply nothing to do with royalty!" Professor Wogglebug waved his fountain pen firmly. "Now—"

"But see here, wasn't I Ruler of Oz?" put in the Scarecrow anxiously.

"A Ruler but *never* a royalty!" snapped out the Professor. "Now, if you will all answer my questions as I call your names, I'll get the necessary data and be off." He took out a small memorandum book. "Your Highness," he bowed to Ozma, "need not bother. I have already entered your name at the head of the list. Being descended as you are from a long line of fairies, your family tree is the oldest and most illustrious in Oz. Princess Dorothy!"

At the sound of her name, the little girl stood up.

"I know you are from Kansas and were created a Princess of Oz by our gracious Ruler, but can you tell me anything of your ancestors in America?" demanded the Professor, staring over the top of his thick glasses.

"You'll have to ask Uncle Henry and Aunt Em," said Dorothy rather sulkily.

The Professor had hurt the feelings of her best friend, the Scarecrow, and ancestors did not interest her one little bit.

"Very well," said the Professor, writing industriously in his book. "I'll just enter you as 'Dorothy, Princess of Oz and sixth cousin to a President!'"

"I'm not!" Dorothy shook her head positively.

"Oh, everyone in America can claim that!" said the Professor easily. "Nick Chopper!"

Now up rose our old friend the Tin Woodman, who had also been discovered by Dorothy on her first trip to the Fairyland of Oz.

"You were a man of meat at one time and a woodman by trade?" queried Professor Wogglebug, poising his pen in the air.

"I am a Tin Woodman, and you may enter me in your book under the name of Smith, for a tin Smith made me, and as Royal Emperor of the Winkies, I do not care to go back to my meat connections," said the Tin Woodman in a dignified voice.

The company applauded, and the Cowardly Lion thumped the floor with his tail.

"Smith is a very good name. I can work up a whole chapter on that," smiled the Professor. The Tin Woodman *had* once been a regular person, but a wicked witch enchanted his ax, and first it chopped off one leg, then the other, and next both arms and his head. After each accident, Nick went to a tinsmith for repairs, and finally was entirely made of tin. Nowhere but in Oz could such a thing happen. But no one can be killed in this marvelous country, and Nick, with his tin body, went gaily on living and was considered so distinguished that the Winkies had begged him to be their Emperor.

"Scraps!" called the Professor as Nick sat stiffly down beside Dorothy.

The Patchwork Girl pirouetted madly to the front. Putting one finger in her mouth, she sang:

"I'm made of patches, as you see.
A clothes tree is my family tree
But, pshaw! It's all the same to me!"

A clothes tree? Even Professor Wogglebug grinned. Who could help laughing at Scraps? Made of odd pieces of goods and brought to life by the powder of life, the comical girl was the jolliest person imaginable.

"Put me down as a man of me-tal!" drawled Tik-Tok the copper man as the laugh following Scraps' rhyme had subsided. Tik-Tok was still another of Dorothy's discoveries, and this marvelous machine man, guaranteed to last a thousand years, could think, walk, and talk when properly wound.

The Cowardly Lion was entered as a King in his own right. One after the other, the celebrities of Oz came forward to answer Professor Wogglebug's questions. The Professor wrote rapidly in his little book. Ozma listened attentively to each one, and they all seemed interested except the Scarecrow. Slumped down beside Dorothy, he stared morosely at the ceiling, his jolly face all wrinkled down on one side.

"If I only knew who I were!" he muttered over and over. "I must think!"

"Don't you mind." Dorothy patted his shoulder kindly.

"Royalties are out of date, and I'll bet the Professor's family tree was a milkweed!"

But the Scarecrow refused to be comforted, and long after the company had retired he sat hunched sadly in his corner. "I'll do it! I'll do it!" he exclaimed at last, rising unsteadily to his feet. Jellia Jamb, Ozma's little waiting maid, returning somewhat later to fetch a handkerchief her mistress had dropped, was surprised to see him running through the long hall.

"Why, where are you going?" asked Jellia.

"To find my family tree!" said the Scarecrow darkly, and drawing himself up to his full height, he fell through the doorway.

Chapter 2

The SCARECROW'S FAMILY TREE

The moon shone brightly, but everyone in the Emerald City was fast asleep! Through the deserted streets hurried the Scarecrow. For the first time since his discovery by little Dorothy, he was really unhappy. Living as he did in a Fairyland, he had taken many things for granted and had rather prided himself on his unusual appearance. Indeed, not until Professor Wogglebug's rude remarks concerning his family had he given his past a thought.

"I am the only person in Oz without a family!" he reflected sorrowfully. "Even the Cowardly Lion has kingly parents and a palm tree! But I must keep thinking. My brains have never failed me yet. Who was I? Who were I? Who were I?"

Often he thought so hard that he forgot to look where he was going and ran headlong into fences, stumbled down gutters, and over stiles. But fortunately, the dear fellow could not hurt himself, and he would struggle up, pat his straw into shape, and walk straightway into something else. He made good time in between falls, however, and was soon well on his way down the yellow brick road that ran through the Munchkin Country. For he had determined to return to the Munchkin farm where Dorothy had first discovered him and try to find some traces of his family.

Now being stuffed with straw had many advantages, for requiring neither food nor sleep the Scarecrow could travel night and day without interruption. The stars winked out one by one, and by the time the cocks of the Munchkin farmers began to crow, he had come to the banks of a broad blue river!

The Scarecrow took off his hat and scratched his head thoughtfully. Crossing rivers is no easy matter in Oz, for there isn't a ferry in the Kingdom, and unless one is a good swimmer or equipped with some of the Wizard's magic it is mighty troublesome. Water does not agree with the Scarecrow at all, and as for swimming, he can no more swim than a bag of meal.

But he was too wise a person to give up merely because a thing appeared to be impossible. It was for just such emergencies that his excellent brains had been given to him.

"If Nick Chopper were here, he would build a raft in no

time," murmured the Scarecrow, "but as he is not, I must think of another way!"

Turning his back on the river, which distracted his mind, he began to think with all his might. Before he could collect his thoughts, there was a tremendous crash, and next minute he was lying face down in the mud. Several little crashes followed, and a shower of water. Then a wet voice called out with a cheerful chuckle:

"Come on out, my dear Rattles. Not a bad place at all, and here's breakfast already waiting!"

"Breakfast!" The Scarecrow turned over cautiously. A huge and curious creature was slashing through the grass toward him. A smaller and still more curious one followed. Both were extremely damp and had evidently just come out of the river.

"Good morning!" quavered the Scarecrow, sitting up with a jerk and at the same time reaching for a stick that lay just behind him.

"I won't eat it if it talks—so there!" The smaller creature stopped and stared fixedly at the Scarecrow.

The Scarecrow, hearing this, tried to think of something else to say, but the appearance of the two was so amazing that, as he told Dorothy afterwards, he was struck dumb. The larger was at least two hundred feet long and made entirely of blocks of wood. On each block was a letter of the alphabet. The head was a huge square block with a serpent's face and long, curling, tape-measure tongue. The little one was very much smaller and seemed to consist of hundreds of rattles, wood, celluloid, and rubber, fastened together with wires. Every time it moved, the rattles tinkled. Its face, however, was not unpleasant, so the Scarecrow took heart and made a deep bow.

"And I'm not going to eat anything that squirms." This time it was the big serpent who spoke.

"Thank you!" said the Scarecrow, bowing several times more. "You relieve my mind. I've never been a breakfast yet, and I'd rather not begin. But if I cannot be your breakfast, let me be your friend!" He extended his arms impulsively.

There was something so jolly about the Scarecrow's smile that the two creatures became friendly at once, and moreover told him the story of their lives.

"As you have doubtless noted," began the larger creature, "I am an A-B-Sea Serpent. I am employed in the nursery of the Mer children to teach them their letters. My friend, here, is a Rattlesnake, and it is his business to amuse the Mer babies while the Mermaids are mer-marketing. Once a year, we take a vacation, and proceeding from the sea depths up a strange river, we came out upon this shore. Perhaps you, Sir, will be able to tell us where we are?"

"You are in the Munchkin Country of the Land of Oz," explained the Scarecrow politely. "It is a charming place for a vacation. I would show you about myself if I were not bound on an important mission." Here the Scarecrow sighed deeply.

"Have you a family?" he asked the A-B-Sea Serpent curiously.

"Yes, indeed," replied the monster, snapping its tape-measure tongue in and out, "I have five great-grandmothers, twenty-one grandnieces, seven brothers, and six sisters-in-law!"

"Ah!" murmured the Scarecrow, clasping his hands tragically, "How I envy you. I have no one—no aunts—no ancestors—no family—no family tree but a bean pole. I am, alas, a man without a *past*!" The Scarecrow looked so dejected that the Rattlesnake thought he was going to cry.

"Oh, cheer up!" it begged in a distressed voice. "Think of your *presence*—here—I give you permission to shake me!" The Scarecrow was so affected by this kind offer that he cheered up immediately.

"No past but a presence—I'll remember that!" He swelled out his straw chest complacently, and leaning over, stroked the Rattlesnake on the head.

"Are you good at riddles?" asked the Rattlesnake timidly.

"Well," answered the Scarecrow judiciously, "I have very good brains, given me by the famous Wizard of Oz."

"Then why is the A-B-Sea Serpent like a city?" asked the Rattlesnake promptly.

The Scarecrow thought hard for several seconds.

"Because it is made up of blocks!" he roared triumphantly. "That's easy; now it's my turn. Why is the A-B-Sea Serpent such a slow talker?"

"Give it up!" said the Rattlesnake after shaking himself several times.

"Because his tongue is a tape measure, and he has to measure his words!" cried the Scarecrow, snapping his clumsy fingers. "And that's a good one, if I did make it myself. I must remember to tell it to Dorothy!"

Then he sobered quite suddenly, for the thought of Dorothy brought back the purpose of his journey. Interrupting the Rattlesnake in the midst of a new riddle, he explained how anxious he was to return to the little farm where he had been discovered and try to find some traces of his family.

"And the real riddle," he sighed with a wave of his hand, "is how to cross this river."

"That's easy and no riddle at all," rumbled the A-B-Sea Serpent, who had been listening attentively to the Scarecrow's remarks. "I'll stretch across, and you can walk over." Suiting the action to the word, he began backing very cautiously toward the river so as not to shake the Scarecrow off his feet.

"Mind your P's and Q's!" called the Rattlesnake warningly. It was well that he spoke, for the A-B-Sea Serpent had doubled the P and Q blocks under, and they were ready to snap off. Finally, however, he managed to make a bridge of himself, and the Scarecrow stepped easily over the blocks, the huge serpent holding himself rigid. Just as he reached Y, the unfortunate creature sneezed, and all the blocks rattled together. Up flew the Scarecrow and escaped falling into the stream only by the narrowest margin.

"Blockhead!" shrilled the Rattlesnake, who had taken a great fancy to the Scarecrow.

"I'm all right," cried the Scarecrow rather breathlessly. "Thank you very much!" He sprang nimbly up the bank. "Hope you have a pleasant vacation!"

"Can't, with a rattlepate like that." The A-B-Sea Serpent nodded glumly in the Rattlesnake's direction.

"Now don't quarrel," begged the Scarecrow. "You are both charming and unusual, and if you follow that Yellow Road, you will come to the Emerald City, and Ozma will be delighted to welcome you."

"The Emerald City! We must see that, my dear Rattles." Forgetting his momentary displeasure, the A-B-Sea Serpent pulled himself out of the river, and waving his X Y Z blocks in farewell to the Scarecrow, went clattering down the road, the little Rattlesnake rattling along behind him.

As for the Scarecrow, he continued his journey, and the day was so delightful and the country so pleasant that he almost forgot he had no family. He was treated everywhere with the greatest courtesy and had innumerable invitations from the hospitable Munchkins. He was anxious to reach his destination, however, so he refused them all, and traveling night and day came without further mishap or adventure late on the second evening to the little Munchkin farm where Dorothy had first discovered him. He was curious to know whether the pole on which he had been hoisted to scare away the crows still stood in the cornfield and whether the farmer who had made him could tell him anything further about his history.

"It is a shame to waken him," thought the kind Scarecrow. "I'll just take a look in the cornfield." The moon shone so brightly that he had no trouble finding his way about. With a little cry of pleasure, he pushed his way through the dry cornstalks. There in the center of the field stood a tall pole—the very identical bean pole from which he had descended.

"All the family or family tree I've got!" cried the Scarecrow, running toward it with emotion.

"What's that?" A window in the farmhouse was thrown up, and a sleepy Munchkin thrust out his head. "What are you doing?" he called crossly.

"Thinking!" said the Scarecrow, leaning heavily against the bean pole.

"Well, don't do it out loud," snapped the farmer. Then, catching a better view of the Scarecrow, he cried in surprise: "Why, it's you!—Come right in, my dear fellow, and give us the latest news from the Emerald City. I'll fetch a candle!"

The farmer was very proud of the Scarecrow. He had made him long ago by stuffing one of his old suits with straw, painting a jolly face on a sack, stuffing that, and fastening the two together. Red boots, a hat, and yellow gloves had finished his man—and nothing could have been jollier than the result.

Later on, when the Scarecrow had run off with Dorothy and got his brains from the Wizard of Oz and become Ruler of the Emerald City, the little farmer had felt highly gratified.

The Scarecrow, however, was not in a humor for conversation. He wanted to think in peace. "Don't bother!" he called up. "I'm going to spend the night here. I'll see you in the morning."

"All right! Take care of yourself," yawned the farmer, and drew in his head.

For a long time the Scarecrow stood perfectly still beside the bean pole—thinking. Then he got a spade from the shed and began clearing away the cornstalks and dried leaves from around the base of the pole. It was slow work, for his fingers were clumsy, but he persevered. Then a wonderful idea came to him.

"Perhaps if I dig down a bit, I may discover—" He got no further, for at the word "discover," he pushed the spade down with all his might. There was a loud crash. The bottom dropped out of things, and the Scarecrow fell through.

"Gr-eat cornstalks!" cried the Scarecrow, throwing up his arms. To his surprise, they came in contact with a stout pole, which he embraced. It was a lifesaver, for he was shooting down into the darkness at a great rate.

"Why!" he gasped as soon as he regained his breath, for he was falling at a terrific rate of speed, "Why, I believe I'm sliding down the *bean pole*!"

⸺∙⋟◁ Chapter 3 ▷∙⸺∙∙

DOWN the MAGIC BEAN POLE

Hugging the bean pole for dear life, the Scarecrow slid rapidly downward, Everything was dark, but at times a confused roaring sounded in his ears.

"Father, I hear something falling past!" shouted a gruff voice all at once.

"Then reach out and pull it in," growled a still deeper voice. There was a flash of light, a door opened suddenly, and a giant hand snatched the air just above the Scarecrow's head.

"It's a good thing I haven't a heart to fail me," murmured the Scarecrow, glancing up fearfully and clinging more tightly to the pole. "Though I fall, I shall not falter. But where under the earth am I falling to?" At that minute, a door opened far below, and someone called up:

"Who are you? Have out your toll and be ready to salute the Royal Ruler of the Middlings!"

The Scarecrow had learned in the course of his many and strange adventures that it was best to accede to every request that was reasonable or possible. Realizing that unless he answered at once he would fall past his strange questioners, he shouted amiably:

"I am the Scarecrow of Oz, sliding down my family tree!" The words echoed oddly in the narrow passageway, and by the time he reached the word "tree" the Scarecrow could make out two large brown men leaning from a door somewhere below. Next minute he came to a sharp stop. A board had shot out and closed off the passageway. So sudden was the stop that the Scarecrow was tossed violently upward. While he endeavored to regain his balance, the two Middlings eyed him curiously.

"So this is the kind of thing they grow on top," said one, holding a lantern close to the Scarecrow's head.

"Toll, Toll!" droned the other, holding out a horribly twisted hand.

"One moment, your Royal Middleness!" cried the Scarecrow, backing as far away from the lantern as he could, for with a straw stuffing one cannot be too careful of fire. He felt in his pocket for an emerald he had picked up in the Emerald City a few days before and handed it gingerly to the Muddy monarch.

"Why do you call me Middleness?" the King demanded angrily, taking the emerald.

"Is your kingdom not in the middle of the earth, and are you not royalty? What could be more proper than Royal Middleness?" asked the Scarecrow, flecking the dust from his hat.

Now that he had a better view, he saw that the two were entirely men of mud, and very roughly put together. Dried grass hair stood erect upon each head, and their faces were large and lumpy and had a disconcerting way of changing shape. Indeed, when the King leaned over to examine the Scarecrow, his features were so soft they seemed to run into his cheek, which hung down alarmingly, while his nose turned sideways and lengthened at least an inch!

Muddle pushed the King's nose back and began spreading his cheek into place. Instead of hands and feet, the Middlings had gnarled and twisted roots which curled up in a perfectly terrifying manner. Their teeth were gold, and their eyes shone like small electric lights. They wore stiff coats of dried mud, buttoned clumsily with lumps of coal, and the King had a tall mud crown. Altogether, the Scarecrow thought he had never seen more disagreeable looking creatures.

"What he needs," spluttered the King, fingering the jewel greedily, "is a coat of mud! Shall we pull him in, Muddle?"

"He's very poorly made, your Mudjesty. Can you work, Carescrow?" asked Muddle, thumping him rudely in the chest.

"Scarecrow, if you please!" The Scarecrow drew himself up

and spoke with great difficulty. "I can work with my head!" he
added proudly.

"Your head!" roared the King. "Did you hear that, Muddle?
He works with his head. What's the matter with your hands?"
Again the King lunged forward, and this time his face fell on
the other side and had bulged enormously before Muddle could
pat it into shape. They began whispering excitedly together,
but the Scarecrow made no reply, for looking over their shoulder he glimpsed a dark, forbidding cavern lighted only by the
flashing red eyes of thousands of Middlings. They appeared to
be digging, and above the rattle of the shovels and picks came
the hoarse voice of one of them singing the Middling National
Air. Or so the Scarecrow gathered from the words:

> "Oh, chop the brown clods as they fall with a thud!
> Three croaks for the Middlings, who stick in the Mud.
> Oh, mud, rich and wormy! Oh, mud, sweet and squirmy!
> Oh what is so lovely as Mud! Oh what is so lovely as Mud!
> Three croaks for the Middlings, who delve all the day
> In their beautiful Kingdom of soft mud and clay!"

The croaks that came at the end of the song were so terrifying that the Scarecrow shivered in spite of himself.

"Ugh! Hardly a place for a pleasant visit!" he gasped, flat-
tening himself against the wall of the passage. Feeling that
matters had gone far enough, he repeated in a loud voice:

"I am the Scarecrow of Oz and desire to continue my fall. I have paid my toll and unless your Royal Middleness release me—"

"Might as well drop him—a useless creature!" whispered Muddle, and before the King had time to object, he jerked the board back. "Fall on!" he screeched maliciously, and the Scarecrow shot down into the darkness, the hoarse screams of the two Middlings echoing after him through the gloom.

No use trying to think! The poor Scarecrow bumped and banged from side to side of the passage. It was all he could do to keep hold of the bean pole, so swiftly was he falling.

"A good thing I'm not made of meat like little Dorothy," he wheezed breathlessly. His gloves were getting worn through from friction with the pole, and the rush of air past his ears was so confusing that he gave up all idea of thinking. Even magic brains refuse to work under such conditions. Down—down—down he plunged till he lost all count of time. Down—down—down—hours and hours! Would he never stop? Then suddenly it grew quite light, and he flashed through what appeared to be a hole in the roof of a huge silver palace, whirled down several stories and landed in a heap on the floor of a great hall. In one hand he clutched a small fan, and in the other a parasol that had snapped off the beanstalk just before he reached the palace roof.

Shaken and bent over double though he was, the Scarecrow could see that he had fallen into a company of great magnificence. He had a confused glimpse of silken clad courtiers, embroidered screens, inlaid floors, and flashing silver lanterns, when there was a thundering bang that hurled him halfway to the roof again. Falling to a sitting position and still clinging to the bean pole, he saw two giant kettle drums nearby, still vibrating from the terrible blows they had received.

The company were staring at him solemnly, and as he attempted to rise, they fell prostrate on their faces. Up flew the poor flimsy Scarecrow again, such was the draught, and this time landed on his face. He was beginning to feel terribly annoyed, but before he could open his mouth or stand up, a deep voice boomed:

"He has come!"

"He has come!" shrilled the rest of the company, thumping their heads on the stone floor. The language seemed strange to the Scarecrow, but oddly enough, he could understand it perfectly. Keeping a tight grasp on the bean pole, he gazed at the prostrate assemblage, too astonished to speak. They looked exactly like the pictures of some Chinamen he had seen in one of Dorothy's picture books back in Oz, but instead of being yellow, their skin was a curious grey, and the hair of old and young alike was silver and worn in long, stiff queues. Before he had time to observe any more, an old, old courtier hobbled forward and beckoned imperiously to a page at the door. The page immediately unfurled a huge silk umbrella and, running forward, held it over the Scarecrow's head.

"Welcome home, sublime and noble Ancestor! Welcome, honorable and exalted Sir." The old gentleman made several deep salaams.

"Welcome, immortal and illustrious Ancestor! Welcome, ancient and serene Father!" cried the others, banging their heads hard on the floor—so hard that their queues flew into the air.

"Ancestor! Father!" mumbled the Scarecrow in a puzzled voice. Then, collecting himself somewhat, he made a deep bow, and sweeping off his hat with a truly royal gesture began: "I am indeed honored—" But he got no farther. The silken clad courtiers sprang to their feet in a frenzy of joy. A dozen seized him bodily and carried him to a great silver Throne Room.

"The same beautiful voice!" cried the ancient gentleman, clasping his hands in an ecstasy of feeling.

"It is he! The Emperor! The Emperor has returned! Long live the Emperor!" shouted everyone at once. The confusion grew worse and worse.

"Ancestor! Father! Emperor!" The Scarecrow could scarcely believe his ears. "For a fallen man, I am rising like yeast!" he murmured to himself. Half a dozen courtiers had run outdoors to spread the wonderful news, and soon silver gongs and bells began ringing all over the kingdom, and cries of "The Emperor! The Emperor!" added to the general excitement. Holding fast to the sides of the throne and still grasping the little fan and parasol, the Scarecrow sat blinking with embarrassment.

"If they would just stop emperoring, I could ask them who I am," thought the poor Scarecrow. As if in answer to his thoughts, the tottery old nobleman raised his long arm, and at once the hall became absolutely silent.

"Now!" sighed the Scarecrow, leaning forward. "Now I shall hear something of interest."

Chapter 4

DOROTHY'S LONELY BREAKFAST

orothy, who occupied one of the coziest apartments in Ozma's palace, wakened the morning after the party with a feeling of great uneasiness. At breakfast, the Scarecrow was missing. Although he, the Tin Woodman and Scraps did not require food, they always livened up the table with their conversation. Ordinarily Dorothy would have thought nothing of the Scarecrow's absence, but she could not forget his distressed expression when Professor Wogglebug had so rudely remarked on his family tree. The Professor himself had left before breakfast, and everybody but Dorothy had forgotten all about the Royal Book of Oz.

Already many of Ozma's guests who did not live in the palace were preparing to depart, but Dorothy could not get over her feeling of uneasiness. The Scarecrow was her very best friend, and it was not like him to go without saying good-bye. So she hunted through the gardens and in every room of the palace and questioned all the servants. Unfortunately, Jellia Jamb, who was the only one who had seen the Scarecrow go, was with her mistress. Ozma always breakfasted alone and spent the morning over state matters. Knowing how busy she was, Dorothy did not like to disturb her. Betsy Bobbin and Trot, real little girls like Dorothy, also lived in the Fairy palace, and Ozma was a great chum for them. But the Kingdom of Oz had to be governed in between times, and they all knew that unless Ozma had the mornings to herself, she could not play with them in the afternoons. So Dorothy searched by herself.

"Perhaps I didn't look hard enough," thought the little girl, and searched the palace all over again.

"Don't worry," advised the Tin Woodman, who was playing checkers with Scraps. "He's probably gone home."

> "He is a man of brains; why worry
> Because he's left us in a hurry?"

chuckled Scraps with a careless wave of her hand, and Dorothy, laughing in spite of herself, ran out to have another look in the garden.

"That is just what he has done, and if I hurry, I may overtake him. Anyway, I believe I'll go and pay him a visit," thought Dorothy.

Trot and Betsy Bobbin were swinging in one of the royal hammocks, and when Dorothy invited them to go along, they explained that they were going on a picnic with the Tin Woodman. So without waiting to ask anyone else or even whistling for Toto, her little dog, Dorothy skipped out of the garden.

The Cowardly Lion, half asleep under a rose bush, caught a glimpse of her blue dress flashing by, and bounding to his feet thudded after her.

"Where are you going?" he asked, stifling a giant yawn.

"To visit the Scarecrow," explained Dorothy. "He looked so unhappy last night. I am afraid he is worrying about his family tree, and I thought p'raps I could cheer him up."

The Cowardly Lion stretched luxuriously. "I'll go too," he rumbled, giving himself a shake. "But it's the first time I ever heard of the Scarecrow worrying."

"But you see," Dorothy said gently, "Professor Wogglebug told him he had no family."

"Family! Family fiddlesticks! Hasn't he got us?" The Cowardly Lion stopped and waved his tail indignantly.

"Why, you dear old thing!" Dorothy threw her arms around his neck. "You've given me a lovely idea!" The Cowardly Lion tried not to look pleased.

"Well, as long as I've given it to you, you might tell me what it is," he suggested mildly.

"Why," said Dorothy, skipping along happily, "we'll let him adopt us and be his really relations. I'll be his sister, and you'll be—"

"His cousin—that is, if you think he wouldn't mind having a great coward like me for a cousin," finished the Cowardly Lion in an anxious voice.

"Do you still feel as cowardly as ever?" asked Dorothy sympathetically.

"More so!" sighed the great beast, glancing apprehensively over his shoulder. This made Dorothy laugh, for although the lion trembled like a cup custard at the approach of danger, he always managed to fight with great valor, and the little girl felt safer with him than with the whole army of Oz, who never were frightened but who always ran away.

Now anyone who is at all familiar with his geozify knows that the Fairyland of Oz is divided into four parts, exactly like a parchesi board, with the Emerald City in the very center, the purple Gillikin Country to the north, the red Quadling Country to the south, the blue Munchkin Country to the east, and the yellow Country of the Winkies to the west. It was toward the west that Dorothy and the Cowardly Lion turned their steps, for it was in the Winkie Country that the Scarecrow had built his gorgeous golden tower in exactly the shape of a huge ear of corn.

Dorothy ran along beside the Cowardly Lion, chatting over their many adventures in Oz, and stopping now and then to pick buttercups and daisies that dotted the roadside. She tied a big bunch to the tip of her friend's tail and twined some more in his mane, so that he presented a very festive appearance indeed. Then, when she grew tired, she climbed on his big back, and swiftly they jogged through the pleasant land of the Winkies. The people waved to them from windows and fields, for everyone loved little Dorothy and the big lion, and as they passed a neat yellow cottage, a little Winkie Lady came running down the path with a cup of tea in one hand and a bucket in the other.

"I saw you coming and thought you might be thirsty," she called hospitably. Dorothy drank her cup without alighting.

"We're in an awful hurry; we're visiting the Scarecrow," she exclaimed apologetically. The lion drank his bucket of tea at one gulp. It was so hot that it made his eyes water.

"How I loathe tea! If I hadn't been such a coward, I'd have upset the bucket," groaned the lion as the little Winkie Lady went back into her house. "But no, I was afraid of hurting her feelings. Ugh, what a terrible thing it is to be a coward!"

"Nonsense!" said Dorothy, wiping her eyes with her handkerchief. "You're not a coward, you're just polite. But let's run very fast so we can reach the Scarecrow's in time for lunch."

So like the wind away raced the Cowardly Lion, Dorothy holding fast to his mane, with her curls blowing straight out behind, and in exactly two Oz hours and seventeen Winkie minutes they came to the dazzling corn-ear residence of their old friend. Hurrying through the cornfields that surrounded his singular mansion, Dorothy and the Cowardly Lion rushed through the open door.

"We've come for lunch," announced Dorothy.

"And I'm hungry enough to eat crow," rumbled the lion. Then both stopped in dismay, for the big reception room was empty. From a room above came a shuffling of feet, and Blink, the Scarecrow's gentlemanly housekeeper, came running down the stairs.

"Where's the Scarecrow?" asked Dorothy anxiously. "Isn't he here?"

"Here! Isn't he there? Isn't he in the Emerald City?" gasped the little Winkie, putting his specs on upside down.

"No—at least, I don't think so. Oh, dear, I just felt that something had happened to him!" wailed Dorothy, sinking into an ebony armchair and fanning herself with a silk sofa cushion.

"Now don't be alarmed." The Cowardly Lion rushed to Dorothy's side and knocked three vases and a clock off a little table, just to show how calm he was. "Think of his brains! The Scarecrow has never come to harm yet, and all we have to do is to return to the Emerald City and look in Ozma's Magic Picture. Then, when we know where he is, we can go and find him and tell him about our little adoption plan," he added, looking hopefully at Dorothy.

"The Scarecrow himself couldn't have spoken more

sensibly," observed Blink with a great sigh of relief, and even Dorothy felt better.

In Ozma's palace, as many of you know, there is a Magic Picture, and when Ozma or Dorothy want to see any of their friends, they have merely to wish to see them, and instantly the picture shows the person wished for and exactly what he is doing at that certain time.

"Of course!" sighed Dorothy. "Why didn't I think of it myself?"

"Better have some lunch before you start back," suggested Blink, and bustling about had soon set out an appetizing repast. Dorothy was too busy worrying about the Scarecrow to have much appetite, but the Cowardly Lion swallowed seventeen roasts and a bucket of corn syrup.

"To give me courage!" he explained to Dorothy, licking his chops. "There's nothing that makes me so cowardly as an empty stomach!"

It was quite late in the afternoon before they could get away. Blink insisted on putting up a lunch, and it took some time to make enough sandwiches for the Cowardly Lion. But at last it was ready and packed into an old hat box belonging to Mops, the Scarecrow's cook. Then Dorothy, balancing the box carefully on her lap, climbed on the Cowardly Lion's back, and assuring Blink that they would return in a few days with his master, they bade him farewell. Blink almost spoiled things by bursting into tears, but he managed to restrain himself long enough to say good-bye, and Dorothy and the Cowardly Lion, feeling a little solemn themselves, started toward the Emerald City.

"My, but it's growing dark," said Dorothy after they had gone several miles. "I believe it's going to storm."

Scarcely had she finished speaking before there was a terrific crash of thunder. The Cowardly Lion promptly sat down. Off of his back bounced the sandwich box and into the sandwich box rolled Dorothy, head first.

"How terribly upsetting," coughed the Cowardly Lion.

"I should say it was!" Dorothy crawled indignantly out of the hat box and began wiping the butter from her nose. "You've simply ruined the supper!"

"It was my heart," explained the Cowardly Lion sorrowfully. "It jumped so hard that it upset me, but climb on my back again, and I'll run very fast to some place of shelter."

"But where are you?" Dorothy asked in real alarm, for it had grown absolutely dark.

"Here," quavered the Cowardly Lion, and guided by his voice, Dorothy stumbled over to him and climbed again on his back. One crash of thunder followed another, and at each crash the Cowardly Lion leapt forward a bit faster until they fairly flew through the dark.

"It won't take us long to reach the Emerald City at this rate!" called Dorothy, but the wind tossed the words far behind her, and seeing that conversation was impossible, she clung fast to the lion's mane and began thinking about the Scarecrow. The thunder continued at frequent intervals, but there was no rain, and after they had been running for what seemed to Dorothy hours and hours, a sudden terrific bump sent her flying over the lion's head into a bush. Too breathless to speak, she felt herself carefully all over. Then, finding that she was still in one piece, she called to the Cowardly Lion. She could hear him moaning and muttering about his heart.

"Any bones broken?" she asked anxiously.

"Only my head," groaned the lion dismally. Just then the darkness lifted as suddenly as it had fallen, and Dorothy saw him leaning against a tree with his eyes closed. There was a big bump on his head. With a little cry of sympathy, Dorothy hurried toward him, when all at once something strange about their surroundings struck her.

"Why, where are we?" cried the little girl, stopping short. The lion's eyes flew open, and forgetting all about his bump, he looked around in dismay. No sign of the Emerald City anywhere. Indeed, they were in a great, dim forest, and considering the number of trees, it is a wonder that they had not run into one long ago.

"I must have run the wrong way," faltered the Cowardly Lion in a distressed voice.

"You couldn't help that; anyone would lose his way in the dark," said Dorothy generously. "But I wish we hadn't fallen in the sandwiches. I'm hungry!"

"So am I. Do you think anyone lives in this forest, Dorothy?"

Dorothy did not answer, for just then she caught sight of a big sign nailed to one of the trees.

"Turn to the right," directed the sign.

"Oh, come on!" cried Dorothy, cheering up immediately. "I believe we're going to have another adventure."

"I'd rather have some supper," sighed the Cowardly Lion wistfully, "but unless we want to spend the night here, we might as well move along. I'm to be fed up on adventure, I suppose."

"Turn to the left," advised the next sign, and the two turned obediently and hurried on, trying to keep a straight course through the trees. In a Fairyland like Oz, where there are no trains or trolleys or even horses for traveling ('cepting Ozma's Sawhorse), there are bound to be unexplored portions. And though Dorothy had been at one time or another in almost every part of Oz, the country through which they were now passing was totally unfamiliar to her. Night was coming on, and it was growing so dark that she could hardly read the third sign when they presently came upon it.

"Don't sing," directed the sign sternly.

"Sing!" snapped Dorothy indignantly, "Who wants to sing?"

"We might as well keep to the left," said the Cowardly Lion in a resigned voice, and they walked along for some time in silence. The trees were thinning out, and as they came to the edge of the forest, another sign confronted them.

"Slow down," read Dorothy with great difficulty. "What

nonsense! If we slow down, how shall we ever get anywhere?"

"Wait a minute," mused the Cowardly Lion, half closing his eyes. "Aren't there two roads just ahead, one going up and one going down? We're to take the down road, I suppose. 'Slow down,' isn't that what it says?"

Slow down it surely was, for the road was so steep and full of stones that Dorothy and the Cowardly Lion had to pick their way with utmost care. But even bad roads must end somewhere, and coming suddenly to the edge of the woods, they saw a great city lying just below. A dim light burned over the main gate, and toward this the Cowardly Lion and Dorothy hurried as fast as they could. This was not very fast, for an unaccountable drowsiness was stealing over them.

Slowly and more slowly, the tired little girl and her great four-footed companion advanced toward the dimly lighted gate. They were so drowsy that they had ceased to talk. But they dragged on.

"Hah, hoh, hum!" yawned the Cowardly Lion. "What makes my feet so heavy?"

He stopped short and examined each of his four feet sleepily.

Dorothy swallowed a yawn and tried to run, but a walk was all she could manage.

"Hah, hoh, hum!" she gaped, stumbling along with her eyes closed.

By the time they had reached the gate, they were yawning so hard that the Cowardly Lion had nearly dislocated his jaw, and Dorothy was perfectly breathless. Holding to the lion's mane to steady herself, Dorothy blinked up uncertainly at the sign over the gate.

"Hah—here we are—Hoh!" She held her hand wearily before her mouth.

Then, with a great effort, she read the words of the sign.

"Um—Great—Grand and Mighty Slow Kingdom of Pokes! Uh-hah—Pokes! Do you hear? Hah, hoh, hu, uum!"

Dorothy looked about in alarm, despite her sleepiness.

"Do you hear?" she repeated anxiously as no answer came through the gloom.

The Cowardly Lion did not hear. He had fallen down and was fast asleep, and so in another minute was Dorothy, her head pillowed against his kind, comfortable, cowardly heart. Fast asleep at the gates of a strange grey city!

Chapter 5

SIR HOKUS of POKES

It was long past sunup before Dorothy awoke. She rubbed her eyes, yawned once or twice, and then shook the Cowardly Lion. The gates of the city were open, and although it looked even greyer in the daytime than it looked at night, the travelers were too hungry to be particular. A large placard was posted just inside:

THIS IS POKES!
DON'T RUN!
DON'T SING!
TALK SLOWLY!
DON'T WHISTLE!
Order of the Chief Poker.

read Dorothy. "How cheerful! Hah, hoh, hum-mm!"

"Don't!" begged the Cowardly Lion with tears in his eyes. "If I yawn again, I'll swallow my tail, and if I don't have something to eat soon, I'll do it anyway. Let's hurry! There's something queer about this place, Dorothy! Ah, hah, hoh, hum-mm!"

Stifling their yawns, the two started down the long, narrow street. The houses were of grey stone, tall and stiff with tiny barred windows. It was absolutely quiet, and not a person was in sight. But when they turned the corner, they saw a crowd of queer-looking people creeping toward them. These singular individuals stopped between each step and stood perfectly still, and Dorothy was so surprised at their unusual appearance that she laughed right in the middle of a yawn.

In the first place, they never lifted their feet, but pushed them along like skates. The women were dressed in grey polka-dot dresses with huge poke bonnets that almost hid their fat, sleepy, wide-mouthed faces. Most of them had pet snails on strings, and so slowly did they move that it looked as though the snails were tugging them along.

The men were dressed like a party of congressmen, but instead of high hats wore large red nightcaps, and they were all as solemn as owls. It seemed impossible for them to keep both eyes open at the same time, and at first Dorothy thought they were winking at her. But as the whole company continued to stare fixedly with one open eye, she burst out laughing. At the unexpected sound (for no one had ever laughed in Pokes before), the women picked up their snails in a great fright, and the men clapped their fingers to their ears or to the places where their ears were under the red nightcaps.

"These must be the Slow Pokes," giggled Dorothy, nudging the Cowardly Lion. "Let's go to meet them, for they'll never reach us at the rate they are coming!"

"There's something wrong with my feet," rumbled the Cowardly Lion without looking up. "Hah, hoh, hum! What's the use of hurrying?" The fact of the matter was that they couldn't hurry if they tried. Indeed, they could hardly lift their feet at all.

"I wish the Scarecrow were with us," sighed the Cowardly Lion, shuffling along unhappily. "He never grows sleepy, and he always knows what to do."

"No use wishing," yawned Dorothy. "I only hope he's not as lost as we are."

By struggling hard, they just managed to keep moving, and by the time they came up with the Slow Pokes, they were completely worn out. A cross-looking Poke held up his arm threateningly, and Dorothy and the Cowardly Lion stopped.

"You—" said the Poke; then closed his mouth and stood staring vacantly for a whole minute.

"Are—" He brought out the word with a perfectly enormous yawn, and Dorothy began fanning the Cowardly Lion with her hat, for he showed signs of falling asleep again.

"What?" she asked crossly.

"Under—" sighed the Poke after a long pause, and Dorothy, seeing that there was no hurrying him, began counting to herself. Just as she reached sixty, the Poke pushed back his red nightcap and shouted:

"Arrest!"

"Arrest!" shouted all the other Pokes so loud that the Cowardly Lion roused himself with a start, and the pet snails stuck out their heads. "A rest? A rest is not what we want! We want breakfast!" growled the lion irritably and started to roar, but a yawn spoiled it. (One simply cannot look fierce by yawning.)

"You—" began the Poke. But Dorothy could not stand hearing the same slow speech again. Putting her fingers in her ears, she shouted back:

"What for?"

The Pokes regarded her sternly. Some even opened both eyes. Then the one who had first addressed them, covering a terrific gape with one hand, pointed with the other to a sign on a large post at the corner of the street.

"Speed limit 1/4 mile an hour" said the sign.

"We're arrested for speeding!" shouted Dorothy in the Cowardly Lion's ear.

"Did you say feeding?" asked the poor lion, waking up with a start. "If I go to sleep again before I'm fed, I'll starve to death!"

"Then keep awake," yawned Dorothy. By this time, the Pokes had surrounded them and were waving them imperiously ahead. They looked so threatening that Dorothy and the Cowardly Lion began to creep in the direction of a gloomy, grey castle. Of the journey neither of them remembered a thing, for with the gaping and yawning Pokes it was almost impossible to keep awake. But they must have walked in their sleep, for the next thing Dorothy knew, a harsh voice called slowly:

"Poke—him!"

Greatly alarmed, Dorothy opened her eyes. They were in a huge stone hall hung all over with rusty armor, and seated on a great stone chair, snoring so loudly that all the steel helmets rattled, was a Knight. The tallest and crossest of the Pokes rushed at him with a long poker, giving him such a shove that he sprawled to the floor.

"So—" yawned the Cowardly Lion, awakened by the clatter, "Knight has fallen!"

"Prisoners—Sir Hokus!" shouted the Chief Poker, lifting the Knight's plume and speaking into the helmet as if he were telephoning.

The Knight arose with great dignity, and after straightening his armor, let down his visor, and Dorothy saw a kind, timid face with melancholy blue eyes—not at all Pokish, as she explained to Ozma later.

"What means this unwonted clamor?" asked Sir Hokus, peering curiously at the prisoners.

"We're sorry to waken you," said Dorothy politely, "but could you please give us some breakfast?"

"A lot!" added the Cowardly Lion, licking his chops.

"It's safer for me to sing," said the Knight mournfully, and throwing back his head, he roared in a high, hoarse voice:

"Don't yawn! Don't yawn!
We're out of breath—
Begone—BEGONE
Or die the death!"

The Cowardly Lion growled threateningly and began lashing his tail.

"If he weren't in a can, I'd eat him," he rumbled, "but I never could abide tinned meat."

"He's not in a can, he's in armor," explained Dorothy, too interested to pay much attention to the Cowardly Lion, for at the first note of the Knight's song, the Pokes began scowling horribly, and by the time he had finished they were backing out of the room faster than Dorothy ever imagined they could go.

"So that's why the sign said don't sing," thought Dorothy to herself. The air seemed clearer somehow, and she no longer felt sleepy.

When the last Poke had disappeared, the Knight sighed and climbed gravely back on his stone chair.

"My singing makes them very wroth. In faith, they cannot endure music; it wakens them," explained Sir Hokus. "But hold, 'twas food you asked of me. Breakfast, I believe you called it." With an uneasy glance at the Cowardly Lion, who was sniffing the air hungrily, the Knight banged on his steel armor with his sword, and a fat, lazy Poke shuffled slowly into the hall.

"Pid, bring the stew," roared Sir Hokus as the Poke stood blinking at them dully.

"Stew, Pid!" he repeated loudly, and began to hum under his breath, at which Pid fairly ran out of the room, returning in a few minutes with a large yellow bowl. This he handed ungraciously to Dorothy. Then he brought a great copper tub of the stuff for the Cowardly Lion and retired sulkily.

Dorothy thought she had never tasted anything more delicious. The Cowardly Lion was gulping down his share with closed eyes, and both, I am very sorry to say, forgot even to thank Sir Hokus.

"Are you perchance a damsel in distress?"

Quite startled, Dorothy looked up from her bowl and saw the Knight regarding her wistfully.

"She's in Pokes, and that's the same thing," said the Cowardly Lion without opening his eyes.

"We're lost," began the little girl, "but—"

There was something so quaint and gentle about the Knight, that she soon found herself talking to him like an old friend. She told him all of their adventures since leaving the Emerald City and even told about the disappearance of the Scarecrow.

"Passing strange, yet how refreshing," murmured Sir Hokus. "And if I seem a little behind times, you must not blame me. For centuries, I have dozed in this grey castle, and it cometh over me that things have greatly changed. This beast now, he talks quite manfully, and this Kingdom that you mention, this Oz? Never heard of it!"

"Never heard of Oz?" gasped the little girl. "Why, you're a subject of Oz, and Pokes is in Oz, though I don't know just where."

Here Dorothy gave him a short history of the Fairy country, and of the many adventures she had had since she had come there. Sir Hokus listened with growing melancholy.

"To think," he sighed mournfully, "that I was prisoner here while all that was happening!"

"Are *you* a prisoner?" asked Dorothy in surprise. "I thought you were King of the Pokes!"

"Uds daggers!" thundered Sir Hokus so suddenly that Dorothy jumped. "I am a *knight*!"

Seeing her startled expression, he controlled himself. "I was a knight," he continued brokenly. "Long centuries ago, mounted on my goodly steed, I fared from my father's castle to offer my sword to a mighty king. His name?" Sir Hokus tapped his forehead uncertainly. "Go to, I have forgot."

"Could it have been King Arthur?" exclaimed Dorothy, wide-eyed with interest. "Why, just think of your being still alive!"

"That's just the point," choked the Knight. "I've been alive—still, so still that I've forgotten everything. Why, I can't even remember how I used to talk," he confessed miserably.

"But how did you get here?" rumbled the Cowardly Lion, who did not like being left out of the conversation.

"I had barely left my father's castle before I met a stranger," said Sir Hokus, sitting up very straight, "who challenged me to battle. I spurred my horse forward, our lances met, and the stranger was unseated. But by my faith, 'twas no mortal Knight." Sir Hokus sighed deeply and lapsed into silence.

"What happened?" asked Dorothy curiously, for Sir Hokus seemed to have forgotten them.

"The Knight," said he with another mighty sigh, "struck the ground with his lance and cried, 'Live Wretch, for centuries in the stupidest country out of the world,' and disappeared. And here—here I am!" With a despairing gesture, Sir Hokus arose, big tears splashing down his armor.

"I feel that I am brave, very brave, but how am I to know until I have encountered danger? Ah, friends, behold in me a Knight who has never had a real adventure, never killed a dragon, nor championed a Lady, nor gone on a Quest!"

Dropping on his knees before the little girl, Sir Hokus took her hand. "Let me go with you on this Quest for the valiant Scarecrow. Let me be your good Night!" he begged eagerly.

"Good night," coughed the Cowardly Lion, who, to tell the truth, was feeling a bit jealous. But Dorothy was thrilled, and as Sir Hokus continued to look at her pleadingly, she took off her hair ribbon and bound it 'round his arm.

"You shall be my own true Knight, and I your Lady Fair!" she announced solemnly, and exactly as she had read in books.

At this interesting juncture the Cowardly Lion gave a tremendous yawn, and Sir Hokus with an exclamation of alarm jumped to his feet. The Pokes had returned to the hall, and Dorothy felt herself falling asleep again.

> *"Up, up, my lieges and away!*
> *We take the field again—*
> *For Ladies fair we fight today*
> *And KING! Up, up, my merry men!"*

shrilled the Knight as if he were leading an army to battle. The Pokes opened both eyes, but did not immediately retire. Sir Hokus bravely swallowed a yawn and hastily clearing his throat shouted another song, which he evidently made up on the spur of the moment:

> *"Avaunt! Be off! Be gone—Methinks*
> *We'll be asleep in forty winks!"*

This time the Pokes left sullenly, but the effect of their presence had thrown Dorothy, the Cowardly Lion, and the Knight into a violent fit of the gapes.

"If I fall asleep, nothing can save you," said Sir Hokus in an agitated voice. "Hah, hoh, hum! Hah—!"

The Knight's eyes closed.

"Don't do it, don't do it!" begged Dorothy, shaking him violently. "Can't we run away?"

"I've been trying for five centuries," wailed the Knight in a discouraged voice, "but I always fall asleep before I reach the gate, and they bring me back here. They're rather fond of me in their slow way," he added apologetically.

"Couldn't you keep singing?" asked the Cowardly Lion anxiously, for the prospect of a five-century stay in Pokes was more than he could bear.

"Couldn't we *all* sing?" suggested Dorothy. "Surely all three of us won't fall asleep at once."

"I'm not much of a singer," groaned the Cowardly Lion, beginning to tremble, "but I'm willing to do my share!"

"I like you," said Sir Hokus, going over and thumping the Cowardly Lion approvingly on the back. "You ought to be knighted!"

The lion blinked his eyes, for Sir Hokus' iron fist bruised him severely, but knowing it was kindly meant, he bore it bravely.

"I am henceforth a beknighted lion," he whispered to

Dorothy while Sir Hokus was straightening his armor. Next the Knight took down an iron poker, which he handed to Dorothy.

"To wake us up with," he explained. "And now, Lady Dorothy, if you are ready, we will start on the Quest for the honorable Scarecrow, and remember, everybody sing—*Sing for your life!*"

Chapter 6

SINGING THEIR WAY out of POKES

Taking a deep breath, Sir Hokus, the Cowardly Lion and Dorothy burst out of the hall singing at the top of their voices.

"Three blind mice—!" sang Dorothy.

"Across the plain!" shouted Sir Hokus.

"I am the Cowardly Lion of Oz!" roared the lion.

The Pokes were so taken aback at the horrid sounds that they ran scurrying right and left. In another minute the three were out of the castle and singing their way through the gloomy garden. Dorothy stuck to the "Three Blind Mice." Sir Hokus sang verse after verse of an old English ballad, and the Cowardly Lion roared and gurgled a song of his own

making, which, considering it was a first attempt, was not
so bad:

"I am the Cowardly Lion of Oz!
Be good! Begone! Beware! Becoz
When I am scared full fierce I be;
Br—rah—grr—ruff, look out for me!"

The Pokes stumbled this way and that, and all went well
until they rushed into a company of Pokes who were playing
croquet. The slowness with which they raised their mallets
fascinated Dorothy, and she stopped to watch them in spite
of herself.

"Don't stop! Sing!" growled the Cowardly Lion in the
middle of a line. To make up for lost time, Dorothy closed her
eyes and sang harder than ever, but alas! next instant she fell
over a wicket, which so deprived her of breath that she could
barely scramble up, let alone sing. As soon as she stopped singing, the Pokes paused in their flight, and as soon as they paused
Dorothy began to gape. Singing for dear life, Sir Hokus jerked
Dorothy by the arm, and the Cowardly Lion roared so loud that
the Pokes covered their ears and began backing away.

"There was a Knight! Come on, come on!" sang Sir Hokus,
and Dorothy came, and in a few minutes was able to take up
the "Three Blind Mice" again. But running and singing at the
same time is not an easy task. And running through Pokes is

like trying to run through water. (You know how hard that is?)

"Three Blind Mice—uh—hah—Three Blind—Mice—uh-hah—I can't sing another note! Thu—ree—!" gasped poor Dorothy, stumbling along, while the Cowardly Lion was puffing like an engine. The Pokes in the garden had recovered from their first alarm and were following at a safe distance. The gates of the city were only a short distance off, but it seemed to Dorothy that she could not go another step.

A large group of Pokes had gathered at the gates, and unless they could sing their way through, they would fall asleep and be carried ignominiously back to the castle.

"Now!" wheezed Sir Hokus, "Remember, it is for the Scarecrow!" All of them swallowed, took a deep breath, and put their last remaining strength into their voices. But a wily Poke who had stuffed some cotton in his ears now approached pushing a little cart.

"Take—!" he drawled, and before Dorothy realized what she was doing, she had accepted a cone from the Poke.

"Hah, hoh, hum! Why, it's hokey pokey!" spluttered Dorothy, and with a deep sigh of delight she took a large bite of the pink ice cream. How cool it felt on her dry throat! She opened her mouth for a second taste, yawned terrifically, and fell with a thud to the stone pavement.

"Dorothy!" wailed Sir Hokus, stopping short in his song and bending over the little girl. The poor Cowardly Lion gave a gulp of despair and began running around the two, roaring and singing in a choked voice. The Pokes nodded to each other in a pleased fashion, and the Chief Poker started cautiously toward them with a long, thick rope. The Cowardly Lion redoubled his efforts. Then, seeing Sir Hokus about to fall, he jumped on the Knight with all his strength. Down crashed Sir Hokus, his armor clanging against the stones that paved the gateway.

"Sing!" roared the Cowardly Lion, glaring at him fiercely. The fall wakened the poor Knight, but he had not the strength to rise. Sitting on the hard stones and looking reproachfully at the Cowardly Lion, he began his ballad in a half-hearted fashion. The Cowardly Lion's heart was like to burst between lack of breath and fear, but making one last tremendous effort and still roaring his song, he bounded at the Chief Poker, seized the rope, and was back before the stupid creature had time to yawn.

"Tie it around your waist; take Dorothy in your arms!" gasped the Cowardly Lion out of the corner of his mouth. Sir Hokus, though completely dazed, had just enough presence of mind to obey, and the next minute the Cowardly Lion, growling between his teeth like a good fellow, was dashing through the group of Pokes, the other end of the rope in his mouth.

Bumpety bump—bump—bump! Bangety-bang-bang! went Sir Hokus over the cobbles, holding his helmet with one hand and Dorothy fast in the other arm. The Pokes fell this way and that, and such was the determination of the Cowardly

Lion that he never stopped till he was out of the gate and half-way up the rough road they had so recently traveled. Then with a mighty sigh, he dropped the rope, rolled over and over down the hill, and lay panting with exhaustion at the bottom.

The bumping over the cobbles had wakened Sir Hokus thoroughly. Indeed, the poor Knight was black and blue, and his armor dented and scraped frightfully in important places.

Dorothy, considerably shaken, opened her eyes and began feebly singing "Three Blind Mice."

"No need," puffed Sir Hokus, lifting her off his lap and rising stiffly.

"Yon noble beast has rescued us."

"Won't the Pokes come up here?" asked Dorothy, staring around a bit dizzily.

"They cannot live out of the kingdom," said the Knight, and Dorothy drew a big sigh of relief. Sir Hokus, however, was looking very grave.

"I have failed on my first adventure. Had it not been for the Cowardly Lion, we would now be prisoners in Pokes," he murmured sadly. Then he unfastened the plume from his helmet. "It beseemeth me not to wear it," sighed the Knight mournfully, and though Dorothy tried her best to comfort him, he refused to put it back. Finally, she fastened the plume to her dress, and they went down to the Cowardly Lion.

There was a little spring nearby, and after they had poured six helmets of water over his head, the lion opened his eyes.

"Been in a good many fights," gasped the lion, "but I never fought one like this. Singing, bah!"

"Noble Sir, how can I ever repay you?" faltered the Knight. "Alas, that I have failed in the hour of trial!"

"Why, it wasn't a question of courage at all," rumbled the Cowardly Lion, greatly embarrassed. "I had the loudest voice and the most breath, that's all! You got the rough end of it." Sir Hokus looked ruefully at his armor. The back was entirely squashed.

"Never mind!" said the Knight bravely. "It is the front one presents to the foe."

"Now you're talking like a real Knight," said Dorothy. "A while ago you said, 'Yon' and 'beseemeth,' and first thing you know the talk will all come back to you." Sir Hokus' honest face shone with pleasure.

"Odds bludgeons and truncheons! The little maid is right!" he exclaimed, striking an attitude. "And once it does, the rest will be easy."

"Don't say rest to me," begged the Cowardly Lion, getting slowly to his feet. "Hah, hoh, hum! Just to think of it makes me yawn. Now don't you think we had better start off?"

"If you're rested," began Dorothy. The Cowardly Lion put his paw over his ear and looked so comical that both Dorothy and Sir Hokus laughed heartily.

"If you're ready," amended Dorothy, and the three adventurers started up the steep road. "The first thing to do," said the little girl, "is to get back to the Emerald City as quickly as we can."

At this very minute Glinda, the Good Sorceress of Oz, in her palace in the Quadling Country, was puzzling over an entry in the Magic Record Book. This book tells everything that is happening in the world and out, and while it does not give details, it is a very useful possession.

"The Emperor of the Silver Islands," read Glinda, "has returned to his people."

"Now who is the Emperor of the Silver Islands?" she asked herself. She puzzled about it for a long while, and then, deciding that it had nothing to do with the Fairy Kingdom of Oz, she closed the book and went for a walk in the palace garden.

Dorothy and Sir Hokus and the Cowardly Lion had meanwhile reached the first sign in the dim forest, the sign directing travelers to Pokes. Two roads branched out through the forest, and after much debating they took the wider.

"Do you 'spose this leads to the Emerald City?" asked Cowardly Lion dubiously.

"Time will tell, time will tell," said Sir Hokus cheerfully.

"Yes," murmured the Cowardly Lion, "time will tell. But what?"

⋯─⋯◂ ℂhapter 7 ▸⋯─⋯

The SCARECROW IS HAILED as EMPEROR!

Leaning forward on the great throne, the Scarecrow waited impatiently for the ancient gentleman to speak. The grey-skinned courtiers were eyeing him expectantly, and just as the suspense became almost unendurable, the old man threw up his arms and cried sharply:

"The prophecy of the magic beanstalk has been fulfilled. In this radiant and sublime Scarecrowcus, the spirit of Chang Wang Woe, the mighty, has returned. And I, the Grand Chew Chew of the realm, prostrate myself before this wonderful Scarecrowcus, Emperor of the Silver Islands." So, likewise, did all the company present, and the Scarecrow, taken unawares, flew up several feet and landed in a heap on the steps leading to the throne. He climbed back hurriedly, picking up the fan and parasol that he had plucked from the beanstalk.

"I wish Professor Wogglebug could hear this," said the Scarecrow, settling himself complacently. "But I must watch out, and remember to hold on."

The Grand Chew Chew was the first to rise, and folding his arms, he asked solemnly:

"What are your commands, Ancient and Honorable Scarecrowcus?"

"If you'd just omit the Cus," begged the Scarecrow in an embarrassed voice, "I believe I could think better. Am I in China, or where? Are you Chinamen, or what?"

"We are Silvermen," said the Grand Chew Chew impressively, "and a much older race than our Chinese cousins. They are people of the sun. We are people of the stars. Has your Highness so soon forgotten?"

"I am afraid," said the Scarecrow, rubbing his chin reflectively, "that I have." He gazed slowly around the great Throne Room. Ozma's palace itself was not more dazzling. The floor of dull silver blocks was covered with rich blue rugs. Furniture, chairs, screens and everything were made of silver inlaid with precious stones. Filigreed silver lanterns hung from the high ceilings, and tall silver vases filled with pink and blue blossoms filled the rooms with their perfume. Blue flags embroidered with silver stars fluttered from the walls and the tips of the pikebearers' spears, and silver seemed to be so plentiful that even shoes were fashioned of it. Faintly through the windows came the sweet tones of a hundred silver chimes, and altogether the Scarecrow was quite dazed by his apparent good fortune. Surely they had called him Emperor, but how could that be? He turned to address the Grand Chew Chew; then as he saw out of the corner of his eye that the assemblage were making ready to fall upon their faces, he exclaimed in a hoarse whisper:

"May I speak to you alone?" The Grand Chew Chew waved his hand imperiously, and the courtiers with a great crackling of silver brocade backed from the hall.

"Very kind of them to bow, but I wish they wouldn't," sighed the Scarecrow, sinking back on the great throne. "It blows one about so. I declare, if another person falls at my feet, I'll have nervous prostration."

Again he took a long survey of the hall, then turned to the Grand Chew Chew. "Would you mind," he asked simply, "telling me again who I am and how?"

"Who and how? Who—You are, illustrious Sir, the Emperor Chang Wang Woe, or to be more exact, his spirit!"

"I have always been a spirited person," observed the Scarecrow dubiously, "but never a spirit without a person. I must insist on being a person."

"How?" the Grand Chew Chew proceeded without noticing the Scarecrow's remarks. "Fifty years ago—after your

Extreme Highness had defeated in battle the King of the Golden Islands—a magician entered the realm. This magician, in the employ of this wicked king, entered a room in the palace where your Highness lay sleeping and by an act of necromancy changed you to a crocus!"

"Ouch!" exclaimed the Scarecrow, shuddering involuntarily.

"And had it not been for the Empress, your faithful wife, you would have been lost forever to the Empire."

"Wife?" gasped the Scarecrow faintly. "Have I a wife?"

"If your Highness will permit me to finish," begged the Grand Chew Chew with great dignity. The Scarecrow nodded. "Your wife, Tsing Tsing, the beautiful, took the crocus, which was fading rapidly, and planted it in a silver bowl in the center of this very hall and for three days kept it fresh with her tears. Waking on the third morning, the Empress was amazed to see in place of the crocus a giant bean pole that extended to the roof of the palace and disappeared among the clouds."

"Ah!" murmured the Scarecrow, looking up, "My family tree!"

"Beside the bean pole lay a crumpled parchment." The Grand Chew Chew felt in the sleeve of his kimono and brought out a bit of crumpled silver paper, and adjusting his horn spectacles, read slowly.

"Into the first being who touches this magic pole—on the other side of the world—the spirit of Emperor Chang Wang Woe will enter. And fifty years from this day, he will return—to save his people."

The Grand Chew Chew took off his specs and folded up the paper. "The day has come! You have come down the bean pole, and are undoubtedly that being who has gone from Emperor to crocus to Scarecrowcus. I have ruled the Islands these fifty years; have seen to the education of your sons and grandsons. And now, gracious and exalted Master, as I am an old man I ask you to relieve me from the cares of state."

"Sons! Grandsons!" choked the Scarecrow, beginning to feel very much alarmed indeed. "How old am I?"

"Your Highness," said the Grand Chew Chew with a deep salaam, "is as old as I. In other words, you are in the ripe and glorious eighty-fifth year of your Majesty's illustrious and useful age."

"Eighty five!" gasped the Scarecrow, staring in dismay at the grey, wrinkled face of the old Silverman. "Now see here, Chew Chew, are you sure of that?"

"Quite sure, Immortal and Honored Master!"

The Scarecrow could not help but be convinced of the truth of the Grand Chew Chew's story. The pole in the Munchkin farmer's cornfield was none other than the magic beanstalk, and he, thrust on the pole by the farmer to scare away the crows, had received the spirit of the Emperor Chang Wang Woe. "Which accounts for my cleverness," he thought gloomily. Now, surely he should have been pleased, for he had come in search of a family, but the acquisition of an empire, sons and grandsons, and old age, all in a trice, fairly took his breath away.

"Does the prophecy say anything about restoring my imperial person?" he asked anxiously, for the thought of looking like Chew Chew was not a cheerful one.

"Alas, no!" sighed the Grand Chew Chew sorrowfully. "But we have very clever wizards on the Island, and I shall set them at work on the problem at once."

"Now don't be in such a rush," begged the Scarecrow, secretly determined to lock up the wizards at the first opportunity. "I'm rather fond of this shape. You see, it requires no food and never grows tired—or old!"

"The royal robes will in a measure conceal it," murmured the Grand Chew Chew politely, and clapped his hands. A little servitor bounced into the hall.

"A royal robe, Quick Silver, for his Radiant Highness," snapped the Grand Chew Chew. In a moment Quick Silver had returned with a magnificent purple satin robe embroidered in silver threads and heavy with jewels, and a hat of silver cloth with upturned brim. The Scarecrow wrapped himself in the purple robe, took off his old Munchkin hat, and substituted the Imperial headpiece.

"How do I look, Chew?" he asked anxiously.

"Quite like your old Imperial Self, except—" The old Prime Minister ran unsteadily out of the room. There was a muffled scream from the hall, and the next instant he returned with a long, shiny, silver queue which he had evidently clipped from the head of one of the servants. Removing the Scarecrow's hat, he pinned the queue to the back, set it on the Scarecrow's head, and stood regarding him with great satisfaction. "Ah, if the Empress could only see you!" he murmured rapturously.

"Where—where is she?" asked the Scarecrow, looking around nervously. His long, care-free life in Oz had somewhat unfitted him, he reflected, for family life.

"Alas!" sighed the Grand Chew Chew, wiping his eyes on the sleeve of his kimono, "She has returned to her silver ancestors."

"Then show me her picture," commanded the Scarecrow, visibly affected. The Grand Chew Chew stepped to a side wall, and pulling on a silken cord, disclosed the picture of a large, grey lady with curiously small eyes and a curiously large nose.

"Is she not beautiful?" asked the Grand Chew Chew, bowing his head.

"Beautiful—er—er, beautiful!" gulped the Scarecrow. He thought of lovely little Ozma and dear little Dorothy, and all at once felt terribly upset and homesick. He had no recollection of the Silver Islands or his life here whatever. Who was he, anyway—the Scarecrow of Oz or Emperor Chang Wang Woe? He couldn't be both.

"Ah!" whispered the Grand Chew Chew, seeing his agitation. "You remember her?" The Scarecrow shook his head, with an inward shudder.

"Now show me myself, Chew," he asked curiously. Pulling the cord of a portrait beside the Empress, Chew Chew revealed the picture of Chang Wang Woe as he had been fifty years ago. His face was bland and jolly, and to be perfectly truthful, quite like the Scarecrow's in shape and expression. "I am beside myself," murmured the Scarecrow dazedly—which in truth he was.

"You were—er—are a very royal and handsome person," stammered the Grand Chew Chew.

The Scarecrow, stepping off the throne to examine himself more closely, dropped the little fan and parasol. He had really not had time to examine them since they snapped off the beanstalk, and now, looking at them carefully, he found them extremely pretty.

"Dorothy will like these," thought the Scarecrow, slipping them into a large inside pocket of his robe. Already, in the back of his head, was a queer notion that he would at some time or other return to Oz. He started to give the Grand Chew Chew a spirited description of that wonderful country, but the ancient gentleman yawned and, waving his hands toward the door, interrupted him with:

"Would not your Supreme Highness care to inspect your present dominions?"

"I suppose I may as well!" With a deep sigh, the Scarecrow took the Grand Chew Chew's arm and, holding up his royal kimono (which was rather long) with the other hand, walked unsteadily down the great salon. They were about to pass into the garden when a little fat Silverman slid around the door, a huge silver drumstick upraised in his right hand and a great drum hung about his neck.

The drummer beamed on the Scarecrow.

"Chang Wang Woe, the Beautiful,
The Beautiful has come!
Sublime and silver Scarecrow,
Let sound the royal drum!"

chanted the little man in a high, thin voice, and started to bring the drumstick down upon the huge head of his noisy instrument.

"No you don't!" cried the Scarecrow, leaping forward and catching his arm.

"I positively forbid it!"

"Then I shall have no work!" screamed the drummer, falling on his face. "Ah, Gracious Master, don't you remember me?"

"Yes," said the Scarecrow kindly, "who are you?"

"Oh, don't you remember little Happy Toko?" wheezed the little man, the tears rolling down his cheeks. "I was only a boy, but you used to be fond of me."

"Why, of course, my dear Tappy," said the Scarecrow, not liking to hurt the little fellow's feelings. "But why do you beat the drum?"

"It is customary to sound the drum at the approach of your Royal Highness," put in the Grand Chew Chew importantly.

"Was customary," said the Scarecrow firmly. "My dear Tappy Oko, never sound it in my presence again; it is too upsetting." Which was true enough, for one blow of the drum sent the flimsy Scarecrow flying into the air.

"You're dismissed, Happy," snapped the Grand Chew Chew. At this, the little Silver Islander began weeping and roaring with distress.

"Stop! What else can you do besides beat a drum?" asked the Scarecrow kindly.

"I can sing, stand on my head, and tell jokes," sniffed Happy Toko, shuffling from one foot to the other.

"Very good," said the Scarecrow. "You are henceforth Imperial Punster to my Person. Come along, we're going to look over the Island."

The Grand Chew Chew frowned so terribly that Happy Toko's knees shook with terror.

"It is not fitting for a slave to accompany the Grand Chew Chew and the Emperor," he hissed angrily.

The Scarecrow looked surprised, for the Kingdom of Oz is quite democratic, and no one is considered better than another. But seeing this was not the time to argue, he winked broadly behind the Grand Chew Chew's back.

"I'll see you again, Tappy my boy," he called genially, and passed out into the garden, where a magnificent silver palanquin, surrounded by pikemen and shieldbearers, awaited him.

···—··◄ Chapter 8 ►··—··

The SCARECROW STUDIES the SILVER ISLANDS

Two days had passed since the Scarecrow had fallen into his Kingdom. He was not finding his royal duties as pleasant as he had anticipated. The country was beautiful enough, but being Emperor of the Silver Islands was not the simple affair that ruling Oz had been. The pigtail on the back of his hat was terribly distracting, and he was always tripping over his kimono, to which he could not seem to accustom himself. His subjects were extremely quarrelsome, always pulling one another's queues or stealing fruit, umbrellas, and silver polish. His ministers, the Grand Chew Chew, the Chief Chow Chow, and General Mugwump, were no better, and keeping peace in the palace took all the Scarecrow's cleverness.

In the daytime he tried culprits in the royal court, interviewed his seventeen secretaries, rode out in the royal palanquin, and made speeches to visiting princes. At night he sat in the great silver salon and by the light of the lanterns studied the Book of Ceremonies. His etiquette, the Grand Chew Chew informed him, was shocking. He was always doing something wrong, dodging the Imperial Umbrella, speaking kindly to a palace servant, or walking unattended in the gardens.

The royal palace itself was richly furnished, and the Scarecrow had more than five hundred robes of state. The gardens, with their sparkling waterfalls, glowing orange trees, silver temples, towers and bridges, were too lovely for words. Poppies, roses, lotus and other lilies perfumed the air, and at night a thousand silver lanterns turned them to a veritable fairyland.

The grass and trees were green as in other lands, but the sky as always full of tiny silver clouds, the waters surrounding the island were of a lovely liquid silver, and as all the houses and towers were of this gleaming metal, the effect was bewildering and beautiful.

But the Silver Islanders themselves were too stupid to appreciate this beauty. "And what use is it all when I have no one to enjoy it with me," sighed the Scarecrow. "And no time to *play!*"

In Oz no one thought it queer if Ozma, the little Queen,

jumped rope with Dorothy or Betsy Bobbin, or had a quiet game of croquet with the palace cook. But here, alas, everything was different. If the Scarecrow so much as ventured a game of ball with the gardener's boy, the whole court was thrown into an uproar. At first, the Scarecrow tried to please everybody, but finding that nothing pleased the people in the palace, he decided to please himself.

"I don't care a kinkajou if I am the Emperor, I'm going to talk to whom I please!" he exclaimed on the second night, and shaking his glove at a bronze statue, he threw the Book of Ceremonies into the fountain. The next morning, therefore, he ascended the throne with great firmness. Immediately, the courtiers prostrated themselves, and the Scarecrow's arms and legs blew about wildly.

"Stand up at once," puffed the Scarecrow when he had regained his balance.

"You are giving me nervous prostration. Chew, kindly issue an edict forbidding prostrations. Anyone caught bowing in my presence again shall lose—" the courtiers looked alarmed "—his pigtail!" finished the Scarecrow.

"And now, Chew, you will take my place, please. I am going for a walk with Tappy Oko."

The Grand Chew Chew's mouth fell open with surprise, but seeing the Scarecrow's determined expression, he dared not disobey, and he immediately began making strange marks on a long, red parchment. Happy Toko trembled as the Scarecrow

Emperor took his arm, and the courtiers stared at one another in dismay as the two walked quietly out into the garden.

Nothing happened, however, and Tappy, regaining his composure, took out a little silver flute and started a lively tune.

"I had to take matters into my own hands, Tappy," said the Scarecrow, listening to the music with a pleased expression. "Are there any words to that song?"

"Yes, illustrious and Supreme Sir!"

"Two spoons went down a Por-ce-Lane,
To meet a China saucer,
A 'talking China in a way
To break a white man's jaw, Sir!"

sang Happy, and finished by standing gravely on his head.

"Your Majesty used to be very fond of this song," spluttered Happy. (It is difficult to speak while upside down, and if you don't think so, try it!)

"Ah!" said the Scarecrow, beginning to feel more cheerful, "Tell me something about myself and my family, Tappy Oko."

"Happy Toko, if it pleases your Supreme Amiability," corrected the little silver man, somersaulting to a standstill beside the Scarecrow.

"It does and it doesn't," murmured the Scarecrow. "There is something about you that reminds me of a pudding, and you tapped the drum, didn't you? I believe I shall call you Tappy Oko, if you don't mind!"

The Scarecrow seated himself on a silver bench and motioned for the Imperial Punster to sit down beside him. Tappy Oko sat down fearfully, first making sure that he was not observed.

"Saving your Imperial Presence, this is not permitted," said Tappy uneasily.

"Never mind about my Imperial Presence," chuckled the Scarecrow. "Tell me about my Imperial Past."

"Ah!" said Tappy Oko, rolling up his eyes, "You were one of the most magnificent and magnanimous of monarchs."

"Was I?" asked the Scarecrow in a pleased voice.

"You distributed rice among the poor, and advice among the rich, and fought many glorious battles," continued the little man. "I composed a little song about you. Perhaps you would like to hear it?"

The Scarecrow nodded, and Tappy, throwing back his head, chanted with a will:

> *"Chang Wang Woe did draw the bow—*
> *And twist the queues of a thousand foe!"*

"In Oz," murmured the Scarecrow reflectively as Tappy finished, "I twisted the necks of a flock of wild crows—that was before I had my excellent brains, too. Oh, I'm a fighting

man, there's no doubt about it. But tell me, Tappy, where did
I meet my wife?"

"In the water!" chuckled Tappy Oko, screwing up his eyes.

"Never!" The Scarecrow looked out over the harbor and
then down at his lumpy figure.

"Your Majesty forgets you were then a man like me—er—
not stuffed with straw, I mean," exclaimed Happy, looking
embarrassed. "She was fishing," continued the little Punster,
"when a huge silver fish became entangled in her line. She
stood up, the fish gave a mighty leap and pulled her out of
the boat. Your Majesty, having seen the whole affair from the
bank, plunged bravely into the water and, swimming out, rescued her, freed the fish, and in due time made her your bride.
I've made a song about that, also."

"Let's hear it," said the Scarecrow. And this is what Happy
sung:

> "Tsing Tsing, a Silver Fisher's daughter,
> Was fishing in the silver water.
> The moon shone on her silver hair
> And there were fishes everywhere!

> "Then came a mighty silver fish,
> It seized her line and with a swish
> Of silver fins upset her boat.
> Tsing Tsing could neither swim nor float.

"She raised her silver voice in fear
And who her call of help should hear
But Chang Wang Woe, the Emperor,
Who saved and married her, what's more!"

"Did I really?" asked the Scarecrow, feeling quite flattered by Happy's song.

"Yes," said Happy positively, "and invited me to the wedding, though I was only a small boy."

"Was Chew Chew there?" The Scarecrow couldn't help wondering how the old Nobleman had taken his marriage with a poor fisherman's daughter.

Happy chuckled at the memory. "He had a Princess all picked out for you," he confided merrily:

"And there he stood in awful pride
And scorned the father of the bride!"

"Hoh!" roared the Scarecrow, falling off the bench. "That's the Ozziest thing I've heard since I landed in the Silver Islands. Tappy, my boy, I believe we are going to be friends! But let's forget the past and think of the present!"

The Scarecrow embraced his Imperial Punster on the spot. "Let's find something jolly to do," he suggested.

"Would your Extreme Highness care for kites?" asked Happy. "'Tis a favorite sport here!"

"Would I! But wait, I will disguise myself." Hiding his royal hat under the bench, he put on Happy Toko's broad-rimmed peasant hat. It turned down all 'round and almost hid his face. Then he turned his robe inside out and declared himself ready.

They passed through a small silver town before they reached the field where the kites were to be flown, and the Scarecrow was delighted with its picturesque and quaint appearance. The streets were narrow and full of queer shops. Silver lanterns and little pennants hung from each door, the merchants and maidens in their gay sedans and the people afoot made a bright and lively picture.

"If I could just live here instead of in the palace," mused the Scarecrow, pausing before a modest rice shop. It is dangerous to stop in the narrow streets, and Happy jerked his master aside just in time to prevent his being trodden on by a huge camel. It sniffed at the Scarecrow suspiciously, and they were forced to flatten themselves against a wall to let it pass. Happy anxiously hurried the Emperor through the town, and they soon arrived at the kite flying field. A great throng had gathered to watch the exhibition, and there were more kites than one would see in a lifetime here. Huge fish, silver paper dragons, birds—every sort and shape of kite was tugging at its string, and hundreds of Silver Islanders—boys, girls and grown-ups—were looking on.

"How interesting," said the Scarecrow, fascinated by a

huge dragon that floated just over his head. "I wish Dorothy could see this, I do indeed!"

But the dragon kite seemed almost alive, and horrors! Just as it swooped down, a hook in the tail caught in the Scarecrow's collar, and before Happy Toko could even wink, the Emperor of the Silver Islands was sailing towards the clouds. The Scarecrow, as you must know, weighs almost nothing, and the people shouted with glee, for they thought him a dummy man and part of the performance. But Happy Toko ran after the kite as fast as his fat little legs would carry him.

"Alas, alas, I shall lose my position!" wailed Happy Toko, quite convinced that the Scarecrow would be dashed to pieces on the rocks. "Oh, putty head that I am to set myself against the Grand Chew Chew!"

The Scarecrow, however, after recovering from the first shock, began to enjoy himself. Holding fast to the dragon's tail, he looked down with great interest upon his dominions. Rocks, mountains, tall silver pagodas, drooping willow trees, flashed beneath him. Truly a beautiful island! His gaze strayed over the silver waters surrounding the island, and he was astonished to see a great fleet sailing into the harbor—a great fleet of singular vessels with silken sails.

"What's this?" thought the Scarecrow. But just then the dragon kite became suddenly possessed. It jerked him up, it jerked him down, and shook him this way and that. His hat flew off, his arms and legs whirled wildly, and pieces of straw began to float downward. Then the hook ripped and tore through his coat and, making a terrible slit in his back, came out. Down, down, down flashed the Scarecrow and landed in a heap on the rocks. Poor Happy Toko rushed toward him with streaming eyes.

"Oh radiant and immortal Scarecrowcus, what have they done to you?" he moaned, dropping on his knees beside the flimsy shape of the Emperor.

"Merely knocked out my honorable stuffing," mumbled the Scarecrow. "Now Tappy, my dear fellow, will you just turn me over? There's a rock in my eye that keeps me from thinking."

Happy Toko, at the sound of a voice from the rumpled heap of clothing, gave a great leap.

"Is there any straw about?" asked the Scarecrow anxiously. "Why don't you turn me over?"

"It's his ghost," moaned Happy Toko, and because he dared not disobey a royal ghost, he turned the Scarecrow over with trembling hands.

"Don't be alarmed," said the Scarecrow, smiling reassuringly. "I'm not breakable like you meat people. A little straw will make me good as new. A little straw—straw, do you hear?" For Happy's pigtail was still on end, and he was shaking so that his silver shoes clattered on the rocks.

"I command you to fetch straw!" cried the Scarecrow at last, in an angry voice. Happy dashed away.

When he returned with an arm full of straw, the Scarecrow managed to convince him that he was quite alive. "It is impossible to kill a person from Oz," he explained proudly, "and that is why my present figure is so much more satisfactory than yours. I do not have to eat or sleep and can always be repaired. Have you some safety pins?" Happy produced several and under the Scarecrow's direction stuffed out his chest and pinned up his rents.

"Let us return," said the Scarecrow. "I've had enough pleasure for one day, and can't you sing something, Tappy?" Running and fright had somewhat affected Happy's voice, but he squeaked out a funny little song, and the two, keeping time to the tune, came without further mishap to the Imperial gardens. Happy had just set the royal hat upon the Scarecrow's head and brushed off his robes when a company of courtiers dashed out of the palace door and came running toward them.

"Great Cornstarch!" exclaimed the Scarecrow, sitting heavily down on the silver bench. "What's the matter now? Here are all the Pig-heads on the Island, and look how old Chew Chew is puffing!"

"One would expect a Chew Chew to puff," observed Happy slyly. "One would—" But he got no further, for the whole company was upon them.

"Save us! Save us!" wailed the courtiers, forgetting the royal edict and falling on their faces.

"What from?" asked the Scarecrow, holding fast to the silver bench.

"The King—the King of the Golden Islands!" shrieked the Grand Chew Chew.

"Ah yes!" murmured the Scarecrow, frowning thoughtfully. "Was that his fleet coming into the harbor?"

The Grand Chew Chew jumped up in astonishment. "How could your Highness see the fleet from here?" he stuttered.

"Not from here—there," said the Scarecrow, pointing upward and winking at Happy Toko. "My Highness goes very high, you see!"

"Your Majesty does not seem to realize the seriousness of the matter," choked the Grand Chew Chew. "He will set fire to the island and make us all slaves." At this, the courtiers began banging their heads distractedly on the grass.

"Set fire to the island!" exclaimed the Scarecrow, jumping to his feet. "Then peace to *my* ashes! Tappy, will you see that they are sent back to Oz?"

"Save us! Save us!" screamed the frightened Silvermen.

"The prophecy of the beanstalk has promised that you would save us. You are the Emperor Chang Wang Woe," persisted the Grand Chew Chew, waving his long arms.

"Woe is me," murmured the Scarecrow, clasping his yellow gloves. "But let me think."

Chapter 9

"SAVE US with YOUR MAGIC, EXALTED ONE!"

For several minutes, the Scarecrow sat perfectly still while the company stood shaking in their shoes. Then he asked loudly, "Where is the Imperial Army?"

"It has retired to the caves at the end of the Island," quavered the Grand Chew Chew.

"I thought as much," said the Scarecrow. "But never mind, there are quite a lot of us."

"Us!" spluttered a tall Silverman indignantly. "We are not common soldiers."

"No, very uncommon ones, but you have hard heads and

long nails, and I dare say will manage somehow. Come on, let's go. Chew, you may take the lead."

"Go!" shrieked the Grand Chew Chew. "Us?" The courtiers began backing away in alarm. "Where—er—what—are your Highness' plans?"

"Why, just to conquer the King of the Golden Islands and send him back home," said the Scarecrow, smiling engagingly. "That's what you wanted, isn't it?"

"But it is not honorable for noblemen to fight. It—"

"Oh, of course, if you prefer burning—" The Scarecrow rose unsteadily and started for the garden gates. Not a person stirred. The Scarecrow looked back, and his reproachful face was too much for Happy Toko.

"I'll come, exalted and radiant Scarecrowcus! Wait, honorable and valiant Sir!"

"Bring a watering can, if you love me," called the Scarecrow over his shoulder, and Happy, snatching one from a frightened gardener, dashed after his Master.

"If things get too hot, I'd like to know that you can put me out," said the Scarecrow, his voice quivering with emotion. "You shall be rewarded for this, my brave Tappy."

Happy did not answer, for his teeth were chattering so he could not speak.

The harbor lay just below the Imperial Palace, and the Scarecrow and Happy hurried on through the crowds of fleeing

Silvermen, their household goods packed upon their heads. Some cheered faintly for Chang Wang Woe, but none offered to follow, save the faithful Happy.

"Is this king old?" asked the Scarecrow, looking anxiously at the small boats full of warriors that were putting out from the fleet.

"He is the son of the King whom your Majesty conquered fifty years ago," gulped Happy. "Ha—has your Imperial Highness any—plan?"

"Not yet," said the Scarecrow cheerfully, "but I'm thinking very hard."

"Then, good-bye to Silver Islands!" choked Happy Toko, dropping the watering can with a crash.

"Never mind," said the Scarecrow kindly. "If they shoot me and I catch fire, I'll jump in the water and you must fish me out, Tappy. Now please don't talk any more. I must think!"

Poor Happy Toko had nothing else to say, for he considered his day finished. The first of the invaders were already landing on the beach, and standing up in a small boat, encased in glittering gold armor, was the King of the Golden Islands, himself. The sun was quite hot, and there was a smell of gunpowder in the air.

Now the Scarecrow had encountered many dangers in Oz and had usually thought his way out of them, but as they came nearer and nearer to the shore and no idea presented itself, he began to feel extremely nervous. A bullet fired from the king's boat tore through his hat, and the smoke made him more anxious than ever about his straw stuffing. He felt hurriedly in his pocket, and his clumsy fingers closed over the little fan he had plucked from the bean pole.

Partly from agitation and partly because he did not know what else to do, the Scarecrow flipped the fan open. At that minute, a mighty roar went up from the enemy, for at the first motion of the fan they had been jerked fifty feet into the air, and there they hung suspended over their ships, kicking and squealing for dear life. The Scarecrow was as surprised as they, and as for Happy Toko, he fell straightway on his nose!

"Magic!" exclaimed the Scarecrow. "Someone is helping us," and he began fanning himself gently with the little fan, waiting to see what would happen next. At each wave of the fan, the King of the Golden Islands and his men flew higher until at last not one of them could be seen from the shore.

"The fan. The magic is in the fan!" gasped Happy Toko, jumping up and embracing the Scarecrow.

"Why, what do you mean?" asked the Scarecrow, closing the fan with a snap. Happy's answer was drowned in a huge splash. As soon as the fan was closed, down whirled the king's army into the sea, and each man struck the water with such force that the spray rose high as a skyscraper. And not till then did the Scarecrow realize the power of the little fan he had been saving for Dorothy.

"Saved!" screamed Happy Toko, dancing up and down. "Hurrah for the Emperor!"

"The Emperor, without a plan,
Has won the victory with a fan."

The Silver Islanders had paused in their flight at the queer noises coming from the harbor, and now all of them, hearing Happy Toko's cries, came crowding down to the shore and were soon cheering themselves hoarse. No wonder! The drenched soldiers of the king were climbing swiftly back into their boats, and when they were all aboard, the Scarecrow waved his fan sidewise (he did not want to blow them up again), and the ships swept out of the harbor so fast that the water churned to silver suds behind them, and they soon were out of sight.

"Ah!" cried the Grand Chew Chew, arriving breathlessly at this point, "We have won the day!"

"So we have!" chuckled the Scarecrow, putting his arm around Happy Toko. "Call the brave army and decorate the generals!"

"It shall be done," said the Grand Chew Chew, frowning at Happy. "There shall be a great celebration, a feast, and fireworks."

"Fireworks," quavered the Scarecrow, clutching his Imperial Punster. By this time, the Silver Islanders were crowding around the Emperor, shouting and squealing for joy, and before he could prevent it, they had placed him on their shoulders and carried him in triumph to the palace. He managed to signal Happy, and Happy nodded reassuringly and ran off as fast as his fat little legs could patter. He arrived at the palace almost as soon as the Scarecrow, lugging a giant silver watering can, and, sitting calmly on the steps of the throne, fanned himself with his hat. The Scarecrow eyed the watering can with satisfaction.

"Now let them have their old fireworks," he muttered under his breath, and settled himself comfortably. The Grand Chew Chew was hopping about like a ditched kite, arranging for the celebration. The courtiers were shaking hands with themselves and forming in a long line. A great table was being set in the hall.

"What a fuss they are making over nothing," said the Scarecrow to Happy Toko. "Now in Oz when we win a victory, we all play some jolly game and sit down to dinner with Ozma. Why, they haven't even set a place for you, Happy!"

"I'd rather sit here, amiable Master," sighed Happy Toko happily. "Is the little fan safely closed?"

The Scarecrow felt in his pocket to make sure, then leaned forward in surprise. The Royal Silver Army were marching stiffly into the hall, and the courtiers were bobbing and bowing and cheering like mad.

The General came straight to the great silver throne, clicked his silver heels, bowed, and stood at attention.

"Well," said the Scarecrow, surveying this splendid person curiously, "what is it?"

"They have come for their decorations," announced the Grand Chew Chew, stepping up with a large silver platter full of medals.

"But I thought Tappy Oko and I saved the Island," chuckled the Scarecrow, nudging the Imperial Punster.

"Had the Imperial Army not retired and left the field to you, there would have been no victory," faltered the General in a timid voice. "Therefore, in a way we are responsible for the victory. A great general always knows when to retire."

"There's something in that," admitted the Scarecrow, scratching his head thoughtfully. "Go ahead and decorate 'em, Chew Chew!"

This the Grand Chew Chew proceeded to do, making such a long speech to each soldier that half of the Court fell asleep and the Scarecrow fidgeted uncomfortably.

"They remind me of the Army of Oz," he confided to Happy Toko, "but we never have long speeches in Oz. I declare, I wish I could go to sleep, too, and that's something I have never seen any use in before."

"They've just begun," yawned Happy Toko, nearly rolling down the steps of the throne, and Happy was not far wrong, for all afternoon one after the other of the courtiers arose and droned about the great victory, and as they all addressed themselves to the Scarecrow, he was forced to listen politely. When the speeches were over, there was still the grand banquet to be got through, and as the Silver Islanders ate much the same fare as their Chinese cousins, you can imagine the poor Scarecrow's feelings.

"Ugh!" shivered the Scarecrow as the strange dishes appeared, "I'm glad none of my friends are here. How fortunate that I'm stuffed with straw!" The broiled mice, the stewed shark fins and the bird nest soup made him stare. He had ordered Happy Toko to be placed at his side, and to watch him happily at work with his silver chopsticks and porcelain spoon was the only satisfaction he got out of the feast.

"And what is that?" he asked, pointing to a steaming bowl that had just been placed before Happy.

"Minced cat, your Highness," replied Happy, sprinkling it generously with silver polish.

"Cat?" shrieked the Scarecrow, pouncing to his feet in horror. "Do you mean to tell me you are eating a poor, innocent, little cat?"

"Not a poor one at all. A very rich one, I should say," replied Happy Toko with his mouth full. "Ah, had your Highness only your old body, how you would enjoy this!"

"Never!" shouted the Scarecrow so loudly that all of the courtiers looked up in surprise. "How dare you eat innocent cats?" Indignantly he thought of Dorothy's pet kitten back in Oz. Oz—why had he ever left that wonderful country?

"Your Highness has eaten hundreds," announced the Grand Chew Chew calmly. "Hundreds!"

The Scarecrow dropped back into his chair, too shocked

for speech. He, the Scarecrow of Oz, had eaten hundreds of cats! What would Dorothy say to that? Ugh! This was his first experience with Silver Islands fare. He had always spent the dinner hours in the garden. He sighed, and looked wistfully at the bean pole in the center of the hall. Every minute he was feeling less and less like the Emperor of the Silver Islands and more and more like the plain Scarecrow of Oz.

"Your Majesty seems out of spirits," said Happy Toko as he placed himself and the huge watering can beside the Emperor's bench in the garden later in the evening.

"I wish I were," said the Scarecrow. "To have an Emperor's spirit wished on you is no joke, my dear Tappy. It's a blinking bore!" At that moment, the fireworks commenced. The garden, ablaze with many shaped silver lanterns, looked more like Fairyland than ever. But each rocket made the Scarecrow wince. Showers of stars and butterflies fell 'round his head, fiery dragons leaped over the trees, and in all the Fourth of July celebrations you could imagine there were never such marvelous fireworks as these. No wonder Happy Toko, gazing in delight, forgot his promises to his Royal Master.

Soon the Scarecrow's fears were realized, and his straw stuffing began to smoke.

"Put me out! Put me out!" cried the Scarecrow, as a shower of sparks settled in his lap. The royal band made such a din and the courtiers such a clatter that Happy did not hear.

All of the Silver Islanders were intent on the display, and they forgot all about their unhappy and smoking Emperor.

"Help! Water! Water! Fire!" screamed the Scarecrow, jumping off his throne and knocking Happy head over heels. Thus brought to his senses, Happy hurriedly seized the watering can and sprinkled its contents on the smoking Emperor.

"Am I out?" gasped the Emperor anxiously. "A fine way to celebrate a victory, lighting me up like a Roman candle!"

"Yes, dear Master," said the repentant Happy, helping the dripping Scarecrow to his feet, "it only scorched your royal robe. And it's all over, anyway. Let us go in."

The dripping Emperor was quite ready to follow his Imperial Punster's advice.

"Now that I am put out, let us by all means go in," said the Scarecrow gloomily, and the two slipped off without anyone noticing their departure.

"I'm afraid I'll have to have some new stuffing tomorrow," observed the Scarecrow, sinking dejectedly on his throne. "Tappy, my dear boy, after this never leave me alone, do you hear?" Happy Toko made no reply. He had fallen asleep beside the Imperial Throne.

The Scarecrow might have called his court, but he was in no mood for more of the Silver Islanders' idea of a good time. He longed for the dear friends of his loved Land of Oz.

One by one the lights winked out in the gardens, and the noisy company dispersed, and soon no one in the palace was awake but the Scarecrow. His straw was wet and soggy, and even his excellent brains felt damp and dull.

"If it weren't for Tappy Oko, how lonely I should be." He stared through the long, dim, empty hall with its shimmering silver screens and vases. "I wonder what little Dorothy is doing," sighed the Scarecrow wistfully.

Chapter 10

PRINCESS OZMA and BETSY BOBBIN TALK IT OVER

Dorothy must be having a lovely time at the Scarecrow's," remarked Betsy Bobbin to Ozma one afternoon as they sat reading in the Royal Gardens several days after Dorothy's departure from the Emerald City of Oz.

"One always has a jolly time at the Scarecrow's," laughed the little Queen of Oz. "I must look in my Magic Picture and see what they are doing. Too bad she missed the A-B-Sea Serpent and Rattlesnakes. Weren't they the funniest creatures?"

Both the little girls (for Ozma is really just a little girl) went off into a gale of laughter. The two queer creatures had followed the Scarecrow's advice and had spent their vacation in the Emerald City, and partly because they were so dazzled by their surroundings and partly because they have no sort of memories whatever, they never mentioned the Scarecrow himself or said anything about his plan to hunt his family tree. They talked incessantly of the Mer City and told innumerable A-B-Sea stories to Scraps and the Tin Woodman and the children of the Emerald City. When they were ready to go, the A-B-Sea Serpent snapped off its X block for Ozma. X, he said, meant almost everything, and pretty well expressed his gratitude to the lovely little Ruler of Oz. Ozma in turn gave each of the visitors an emerald collar, and that very morning they had started back to the Munchkin River, and all the celebrities of Oz had gotten up to see them off.

"Maybe they'll come again some time," said Betsy Bobbin, swinging her feet. "But look, Ozma, here comes a messenger." A messenger it surely was, dressed in the quaint red costume of the Quadlings. It was from Glinda, the Good Sorceress, and caused the Princess to sigh with vexation.

"Tell Jack Pumpkinhead to harness the Sawhorse to the Red Wagon," said Ozma after glancing hastily at the little note. "The Horners and Hoppers are at war again. And tell the Wizard to make ready for a journey."

"May I come, too?" asked Betsy. Ozma nodded with a troubled little frown, and Betsy bustled off importantly. Not many little girls are called upon to help settle wars and rule a country as wonderful as Oz.

The Horners and Hoppers are a quarrelsome and curious folk living in the Quadling mountains, and soon Ozma, Jack Pumpkinhead, Betsy and the Wizard of Oz were rattling off at the best speed the Sawhorse could manage. This was pretty fast, for the little horse, being made of wood and magically brought to life, never tires and could outrun anything on legs in the fairy Kingdom of Oz.

But the fact that interests us is that Ozma did not look in the Magic Picture or see what exciting adventures the Scarecrow and Dorothy really were having!

As for Professor Wogglebug, who had caused all the trouble, he was busily at work on the twelfth chapter of the Royal Book of Oz, which he had modestly headed:

H. M. WOGGLEBUG, T.E., PRINCE OF BUGS,
Cultured and Eminent Educator
and also
Great Grand and General Genealogist of Oz.

Chapter 11

SIR HOKUS OVERCOMETH the GIANT

I don't believe we'll ever find the way out of this forest."

Dorothy stopped with a discouraged little sigh and leaned against a tree. They had followed the road for several hours. First it had been fine and wide, but it had gradually dwindled to a crooked little path that wound crazily in and out through the trees. Although it was almost noonday, not a ray of sun penetrated through the dim green depths.

"Methinks," said Sir Hokus, peering into the gloom ahead, "that a great adventure is at hand."

The Cowardly Lion put back his ears. "What makes you methink so?" he rumbled anxiously.

"Hark thee!" said Sir Hokus, holding up his finger warningly. From a great way off sounded a curious thumping. It was coming nearer and nearer.

"Good gracious!" cried Dorothy, catching hold of the Cowardly Lion's mane.

"This is worse than Pokes!"

"Perchance it is a dragon," exulted the Knight, drawing his short sword. "Ah, how it would refresh me to slay a dragon!"

"I don't relish dragons myself. Scorched my tongue on one once," said the Cowardly Lion huskily. "But I'll fight with you, brother Hokus. Stand back, Dorothy dear."

As the thuds grew louder, the Knight fairly danced up and down with excitement. "Approach, villain!" he roared lustily.

"Approach till I impale thee on my lance. Ah, had I but a horse!"

"I'd let you ride on my back if it weren't for that hard tin suit," said the Cowardly Lion. "But cheer up, my dear Hokus, your voice is a little hoarse." Dorothy giggled nervously, then seized hold of a small tree, for the whole forest was rocking.

"How now!" gasped the Knight. There was a terrific quake that threw Sir Hokus on his face and sent every hair in the lion's mane on end, and then a great foot came crashing down through the treetops not three paces from the little party. Before they could even swallow, a giant hand flashed downward, jerked up a handful of trees by the roots, and disappeared, while a voice from somewhere way above shouted:

"What are little humans for?
To feed the giant Bangladore.
Broiled or toasted, baked or roasted,
I smell three or maybe four!"

"You hear that?" quavered the Cowardly Lion. Sir Hokus did not answer. His helmet had been jammed down by his fall, and he was tugging it upward with both hands. Frightened though Dorothy was, she ran to the Knight's assistance.

"Have at you!" cried Sir Hokus as soon as the opening in his helmet was opposite his eyes. "Forward!"

"My heart is beating a retreat," gulped the Cowardly Lion, but he bounded boldly after Sir Hokus.

"Varlet!" hissed the Knight, and raising his sword gave a mighty slash at the giant's ankle, which was broad as three tree trunks, while the Cowardly Lion gave a great spring and sank his teeth in the giant's huge leg.

"Ouch!" roared the giant in a voice that shook every leaf in the forest. "You stop, or I'll tell my father!" With that, he gave a hop that sent Sir Hokus flying into the treetops, stumbling over a huge rock, and came crashing to the earth, smashing trees like grass blades. At the giant's first scream, Dorothy shut her eyes and, putting her hands over her ears, had run as far and as fast as she could. At the awful crash, she stopped short, opened her eyes, and stared 'round giddily.

The giant was flat on his back, but as he was stretched

as far as four city blocks, only half of him was visible. The Cowardly Lion still clung to his leg, and he was gurgling and struggling in a way Dorothy could not understand.

She looked around in a panic for the Knight. Just then, Sir Hokus dropped from the branch of a tree.

"Uds daggers!" he puffed, looking ruefully at his sword, which had snapped off at the handle, "'Tis a pretty rogue!"

"Don't you think we'd better run?" shivered Dorothy, thinking of the giant's song.

"Not while I wear these colors!" exclaimed Sir Hokus, proudly touching Dorothy's hair ribbon, which still adorned his arm. "Come, my good Lion, let us dispatch this braggart and saucy monster."

"Father!" screamed the giant, making no attempt to move.

"He seems to be frightened, himself," whispered Dorothy to the Knight. "But whatever is the matter with the Cowardly Lion?"

At that minute, the Cowardly Lion gave a great jerk and began backing with his four feet braced. The piece of giant leg that he had hold of stretched and stretched, and while Sir Hokus and Dorothy stared in amazement, it snapped off and the Cowardly Lion rolled head over paws.

"Taffy!" roared the Cowardly Lion, sitting up and trying to open his jaws, which were firmly stuck together.

"Taffy!" At this, Sir Hokus sprang nimbly on the giant's

leg, ran up his chest, and perched bravely on his peppermint collar.

"Surrender, Knave!" he demanded threateningly. Dorothy, seeing she could do nothing to help the Cowardly Lion, followed. On her way up, she broke off a tiny piece of his coat and found it most delicious chocolate.

"Why, he's all made of candy!" she cried excitedly.

"Oh, hush!" sobbed the giant, rolling his great sourball eyes. "I'd be eaten in a minute if it were known."

"You were mighty anxious to eat us a while ago," said Dorothy, looking longingly at the giant's coat buttons. They seemed to be large marshmallows.

"Go away!" screamed the giant, shaking so that Dorothy slid into his vest pocket. "No one under forty feet is allowed in this forest!"

Dorothy climbed crossly out of the giant's pocket. "We didn't come because we wanted to," she assured him, wiping the chocolate off her nose.

"Odds bodikins! I cannot fight a great baby like this," sighed Sir Hokus, dodging just in time a great, sugary tear that had rolled down the giant's nose. "He's got to apologize for that song, though."

"Wait!" cried Dorothy suddenly. "I have an idea. If you set us down on the edge of the forest and give us all your vest buttons for lunch, we won't tell anyone you're made of candy. We'll let you go," she called loudly, for the giant had begun to sob again.

"Won't you? Will you?" sniffed the foolish giant.

"Never sing that song again!" commanded the Knight sternly.

"No, Sir," answered the giant meekly. "Did your dog chew much of my leg, Sir?" Then, before Dorothy or Sir Hokus had time to say a word, they were snatched up in sticky fingers and next minute were dropped with a thump in a large field of daisies.

"Oh!" spluttered Dorothy as the giant made off on his taffy legs. "Oh, we've forgotten the Cowardly Lion!" But at that minute, the giant reappeared, and the lion was dropped beside them.

"What's this? What's this?" growled the Cowardly Lion, looking around wildly.

"We got him to lift us out of the forest," explained Dorothy. "Have you swallowed the taffy?" The lion was still dizzy from his ride and only shook his head feebly.

Sir Hokus sighed and sat heavily down on a large rock. "There is no sort of honor, methinks, in overcoming a candy giant," he observed, looking wistfully at the plume still pinned to Dorothy's dress. "Ah, had it but been a proper fight!"

"You didn't know he was candy. I think you were just splendid." Jumping up, Dorothy fastened the plume in the Knight's helmet. "And you're talking just beautifully, more like a Knight every minute," she added with conviction. Sir Hokus tried not to look pleased.

"Give me a meat enemy! My teeth ache yet! First singing, then candy-leg pulling! Gr-ugh! What next?" growled the Cowardly Lion.

"Why, lunch, if you feel like eating," said Dorothy, beginning to give out the vest buttons which the giant had obediently ripped off and left for them. They *were* marshmallows, the size of pie plates, and Dorothy and Sir Hokus found them quite delicious. The Cowardly Lion, however, after a doubtful sniff and sneeze from the powdered sugar, declined and went off to find something more to his taste.

"We had better take some of these along," said Dorothy when she and Sir Hokus had eaten several. "We may need them later."

"Everything is yellow, so we must be in the Winkie Country," announced the Cowardly Lion, who had just returned from his lunch. "There's a road, too."

"Mayhap it will take us to the jeweled city of your gracious Queen." Sir Hokus shaded his eyes and stared curiously at the long lane stretching invitingly ahead of them.

"Well, anyway, we're out of the forest and Pokes, and maybe we'll meet someone who will tell us about the Scarecrow. Come on!" cried Dorothy gaily. "I think we're on the right track this time."

DOROTHY and SIR HOKUS
COME to FIX CITY

The afternoon went pleasantly for the three travelers. The road was wide and shady and really seemed a bit familiar. Dorothy rode comfortably on the Cowardly Lion's back and to pass the time told Sir Hokus all about Oz. He was particularly interested in the Scarecrow.

"Grammercy! He should be knighted!" he exclaimed, slapping his knee, as Dorothy told how the clever straw man had helped outwit the Nome King when that wicked little rascal had tried to keep them prisoners in his underground kingdom.

"But, go to! Where is the gallant man now?" The Knight

sobered quickly. "Mayhap in need of a strong arm! Mayhap at the mercy of some terrible monster!"

"Oh, I hope not!" cried Dorothy, dismayed at so dark a picture. "Why, oh why, did he bother about his family tree?"

"Trust the Scarecrow to take care of himself," said the Cowardly Lion in a gruff voice. Nevertheless, he quickened his steps. "The sooner we reach the Emerald City, the sooner we'll know where he is!"

The country through which they were passing was beautiful, but quite deserted. About five o'clock, they came to a clear little stream, and after Dorothy and Sir Hokus had washed their faces and the Cowardly Lion had taken a little plunge, they all felt refreshed. Later they came to a fine pear orchard, and as no one was about they helped themselves generously.

The more Dorothy and the Cowardly Lion saw of Sir Hokus, the fonder of him they grew. He was so kind-hearted and so polite.

"He'll be great company for us back in the Emerald City," whispered the Cowardly Lion as the Knight went off to get Dorothy a drink from a little spring. "That is, if he forgets this grammercy, bludgeon stuff."

"I think it sounds lovely," said Dorothy, "and he's remembering more of it all the time. But I wonder why there are no people here. I do hope we meet some before night." But no person did they meet. As it grew darker, Sir Hokus' armor began to creak in a quite frightful manner. Armor is not meant for walking, and the poor Knight was stiff and tired, but he made no complaint.

"Need oiling, don't you?" asked the Cowardly Lion, peering anxiously at him through the gloom.

"Joints in my armor a bit rusty," puffed Sir Hokus, easing one foot and then the other. "Ah, had I my good horse!" He expressively waved a piece of the giant's button at which he had been nibbling.

"Better climb up behind Dorothy," advised the Cowardly Lion, but Sir Hokus shook his head, for he knew the lion was tired, too.

"I'll manage famously. This very night I may find me a steed!"

"How?" asked the lion with a yawn.

"If I sleep beneath these trees, I may have a Knight mare," chuckled Sir Hokus triumphantly.

"Br-rrr!" roared the Cowardly Lion while Dorothy clapped her hands. But they were not to sleep beneath the trees after all, for a sudden turn in the road brought them right to the gates of another city. They knew it must be a city because a huge, lighted sign hung over the gate.

"Fix City," read Dorothy. "What a funny name!"

"Maybe they can fix us up," rumbled the lion, winking at Sir Hokus.

"Perchance we shall hear news of the valiant Scarecrow!" cried the Knight, and limping forward he thumped on the gate with his mailed fist. Dorothy and the Cowardly Lion pressed close behind him and waited impatiently for someone to open the gate.

A bell rang loud back in the town. The next instant, the gates flew open so suddenly that the three adventurers were flung violently on their faces.

"Out upon them!" blustered Sir Hokus, getting up stiffly and running to help Dorothy. "What way is this to welcome strangers?" He pulled the little girl hastily to her feet, then they all ran forward, for the gates were swinging shut again.

It was almost as light as day, for lanterns were everywhere, but strangely enough they seemed to dart about like huge fire-flies, and Dorothy ducked involuntarily as a red one bobbed down almost in her face. Then she gasped in real earnest and caught hold of Sir Hokus.

"Uds daggers!" wheezed the Knight. Two large bushes were running down the path, and right in front of Dorothy the larger caught the smaller and began pulling out its leaves.

"Leave off! Leave off!" screamed the little bush.

"That's what I'm doing," said the big bush savagely. "There won't be a leaf on when I get through with you."

"Unhand him, villain!" cried Sir Hokus, waving his sword at the large bush. The two bushes looked up in surprise, and when they saw Dorothy, the Cowardly Lion and Sir Hokus, they fell into each other's branches and burst into the most uproarious laughter.

"My dear Magnolia, this is rich! Oh, dear fellow, wait till Sit sees this; he will be convulsed!" Quite forgetting their furious quarrel, the two went rollicking down the path together, stopping every few minutes to look back and laugh at the three strangers.

"Is this usual?" asked Sir Hokus, looking quite dazed.

"I never heard of bushes talking or running around, but I confess I'm a few centuries behind times!"

"Neither did I!" exclaimed Dorothy. "But then—almost anything's likely to happen in Oz."

"If these lanterns don't look out something will happen. I'll break 'em to bits," growled the Cowardly Lion, who had been dodging half a dozen at once.

"How would we look—out?" sniffed one, flying at Dorothy.

"You could light out—or go out," giggled the little girl.

"We never go out unless we're put out," cried another, but as the Cowardly Lion made a few springs, they flew high into the air and began talking indignantly among themselves. By this time, the three had become accustomed to the changing lights.

"I wonder where the people are," said Dorothy, peering down a wide avenue. "There don't seem to be any houses. Oh, look!"

Three tables set for dinner with the most appetizing viands were walking jauntily down the street, talking fluent china.

"There must be people!" cried Dorothy.

"One dinner for each of us," rumbled the Cowardly Lion, licking his chops. "Come on!"

"Perchance they will invite us. If we follow the dinners, we'll come to the diners," said Sir Hokus mildly.

"Right—as usual." The Cowardly Lion looked embarrassed, for he had intended pouncing on the tables without further ceremony.

"Hush! Let's go quietly. If they hear us, they may run and upset the dishes," warned Dorothy. So the three walked softly after the dinner tables, their curiosity about the people of Fix growing keener at every step. Several chairs, a sofa and a clothes tree rushed past them, but as Dorothy said later to Ozma, after talking bushes, nothing surprised them. The tables turned the corner at the end of the avenue three abreast, and the sight that greeted Dorothy and her comrades was strange indeed. Down each side of a long street as far as they could see stood rows and rows of people. Each one was in the exact center of a chalked circle, and they were so still that Dorothy thought they must be statues.

But no sooner had the three tables made their appearance than bells began ringing furiously all up and down the street, and dinner tables and chairs came running from every direction. All the inhabitants of Fix City looked alike. They had large, round heads, broad placid faces, double chins, and no waists whatever. Their feet were flat and about three times as long as the longest you have ever seen. The women wore plain

Mother Hubbard dresses and straw sailor hats, and the men gingham suits.

While the three friends were observing all this, the tables had been taking their places. One stopped before each Fix, and the chairs, after much bumping and quarreling, placed themselves properly. At a signal from the Fix in the center, the whole company sat down without so much as moving their feet. Dorothy, Sir Hokus and the Cowardly Lion had been too interested to speak, but at this minute a whole flock of the mischievous lanterns clustered over their heads, and at the sudden blare of light the whole street stopped eating and stared.

"Oh!" cried the Fix nearest them, pointing with his fork, "Look at the runabouts!"

"This way, please! This way, please! Don't bark your shins. Don't take any more steps than you can help!" boomed an important voice from the middle of the street. So down the center marched the three, feeling—as the Cowardly Lion put it—exactly like a circus.

"Stop! Names, please!" The Fix next to the center put up his knife commandingly. Sir Hokus stepped forward with a bow:

"Princess Dorothy of Oz, the Cowardly Lion of Oz."

"And Sir Hokus of Pokes," roared the Lion as the Knight modestly stepped back without announcing himself.

"Sir Pokus of Hoax, Howardly Kion of Boz, and Little Girl Beginning with D," bellowed the Fix, "meet His Royal Highness, King Fix Sit, and the noble Fixitives."

"Little Girl Beginning with D! That's too long," complained the King, who, with the exception of his crown, looked like all the rest of them, "I'll leave out the middle. What do you want, Little With D?"

"My name is Dorothy, and if your Highness could give us some dinner and tell us something about the Scarecrow and—"

"One thing at a time, please," said the King reprovingly. "What does Poker want, and Boz? Have they anything to spend?"

"Only the night, an' it please your Gracious Highness," said Sir Hokus with his best bow.

"It doesn't please me especially," said the King, taking a sip of water. "And there! You've brought up another question. How do you want to spend it?"

He folded his hands helplessly on the table and looked appealingly at the Fix next to him. "How am I to settle all these questions, Sticken? First they come running around like crazy chairs, and—"

"You might ring for a settle," suggested Sticken, looking curiously at Sir Hokus. The King leaned back with a sigh of relief, then touched a bell. There were at least twenty bells set on a high post at his right hand, and all of the Fixes seemed to have similar bell posts.

"He's talking perfect nonsense," said Dorothy angrily. The Cowardly Lion began to roll his eyes ominously.

"Let me handle this, my dear. I'm used to Kings," whispered Sir Hokus. "Most of 'em talk nonsense. But if he grows wroth, we'll have all the furniture in the place around our ears. Now just—"

Bump! Sir Hokus and Dorothy sat down quite suddenly. The settle had arrived and hit them smartly behind the knees. The Cowardly Lion dodged just in time and lay down with a growl beside it.

"Now that you're settled," began the King in a resigned voice, "we might try again. What is your motto?"

This took even Sir Hokus by surprise, but before he could answer, the King snapped out:

"Come late and stay early! How's that?"

"Very good," said Sir Hokus with a wink at Dorothy.

"Next time, don't come at all," mumbled Sticken Plaster, his mouth full of biscuit.

"And you wanted?" the King asked uneasily.

"Dinner for three," said the Knight promptly and with another bow.

"Now that's talking." The King looked admiringly at Sir Hokus. "This Little With D had matters all tangled up. One time at a thing! That's my motto!"

Leaning over, the King pressed another button. By this time, the Fixes had lost interest in the visitors and went calmly on with their dinners. Three tables came pattering up, and the settle drew itself up of its own accord. Dorothy placed the

Cowardly Lion's dinner on the ground, and then she and Sir Hokus enjoyed the first good meal they had had since they left Pokes. They were gradually becoming used to their strange surroundings.

"You ask him about the Scarecrow," begged Dorothy. Everybody had finished, and the tables were withdrawing in orderly groups. The King was leaning sleepily back in his chair.

"Ahem," began the Knight, rising stiffly, "has your Majesty seen aught of a noble Scarecrow? And could your Supreme Fixity tell us aught—"

The King's eyes opened. "You're out of turn," he interrupted crossly. "We're only to the second question. How will you spend the night?"

"In sleep," answered Sir Hokus promptly, "if your Majesty permits."

"I do," said the King solemnly. "That gets me out of entertaining. Early to bed and late to rise, that's my motto. Next! It's your turn," he added irritably as Sir Hokus did not immediately answer.

"Have you seen aught of the noble Scarecrow?" asked Sir Hokus, and all of them waited anxiously for the King's reply.

"I don't know about *the* Scarecrow. I've seen *a* Scarecrow, and a sensible chap he was, hanging still like a reasonable person and letting chairs and tables chase themselves 'round."

"Where was he?" asked Sir Hokus in great agitation.

"In a picture," said the King. "Wait, I'll ring for it."

"No use," said the Knight in a disappointed voice. "We're looking for a man."

"Would you mind telling me why you are all so still, and why all your furniture runs around?" asked Dorothy, who was growing a little restless.

"You forget where you are, and you're out of turn. But I'll overlook it this once," said the King. "Have you ever noticed, Little With D, that furniture lasts longer than people?"

"Why, yes," admitted Dorothy.

"Well, there you are!" King Fix Sit folded his hands and regarded her complacently. "Here we manage things better. We stand still and let the furniture run around and wear itself out. How does it strike you?"

"It seem sensible," acknowledged Dorothy. "But don't you ever grow tired of standing still?"

"I've heard of growing hair and flowers and corn, but never of growing tired. What is it?" asked Sticken Plaster, leaning toward Dorothy.

"I think she's talked enough," said the King, closing his eyes.

Sir Hokus had been staring anxiously at the King for some time. Now he came close to the monarch's side, and standing on tiptoe whispered hoarsely: "Hast any dragons here?"

"Did you say wagons?" asked the King, opening his eyes with a terrible yawn.

"Dragons!" hissed the Knight.

"Never heard of 'em," said the King. The Cowardly Lion chuckled behind his whiskers, and Sir Hokus in great confusion stepped back.

"What time is it?" demanded the King suddenly. He touched a bell, and next minute a whole company of clocks came running down the street. The big ones pushed the little ones, and a grandfather clock ran so fast that it tripped over a cobblestone and fell on its face, which cracked all the way across.

"You've plenty of time; why don't you take it?" called the King angrily, while two clothes trees helped the clock to its feet.

"They're all different," giggled Dorothy, nudging the Cowardly Lion. Some pointed to eight o'clock, some to nine, and others to half past ten.

"Why shouldn't they be different?" asked Sticken haughtily. "Some run faster than others!"

"Pass the time, please," said the King, looking hard at Dorothy.

"The lazy lump!" growled the Cowardly Lion. But Dorothy picked up the nearest little clock and handed it to King Fix Sit.

"I thought so," yawned the King, pointing at the clock. At this, everybody began ringing bells till Dorothy was obliged to cover her ears. In an instant, the whole street was filled with beds, "rolling up just as if they were taxis," laughed Dorothy to Sir Hokus. The Knight smiled faintly, but as he had never seen a taxi, he could not appreciate Dorothy's remark.

"Here come your beds," said the King shortly. "Tell them to take you around the corner. I can't abide snoring."

"I don't snore, thank you," said Dorothy angrily, but the King had stepped into his bed and drawn the curtains tight.

"We might as well go to bed, I 'spose," said the little girl. "I'm so tired!"

The three beds were swaying restlessly in the middle of the street. They were tall, four-post affairs with heavy chintz hangings. Dorothy chose the blue one, and Sir Hokus lifted her up carefully and then went off to catch his bed, which had gotten into an argument with a lamppost. When he spoke to it sharply, it left off and came trotting over to him. The Cowardly Lion, contrary to his usual custom, leaped into his bed, and soon the three four-posters were walking quietly down the street, evidently following the King's instructions.

Dorothy slipped off her shoes and dress and nestled comfortably down among the soft covers. "Just like sleeping in a train," she thought drowsily. "What a lot I shall have to tell the Scarecrow and Ozma when I get home."

"Good night!" said the bed politely.

"Good night!" said Dorothy, too nearly asleep to even think it strange for a bed to talk. "Good night!"

Chapter 13

DANCING BEDS and the ROADS THAT UNROLLED

It must be a shipwreck," thought Dorothy, sitting up in alarm. She seemed to be tossing about wildly.

"Time for little girls to get up," grumbled a harsh voice that seemed to come from the pillows.

Dorothy rubbed her eyes. One of the bedposts was addressing her, and the big four-poster itself was dancing a regular jig.

"Oh, stop!" cried Dorothy, holding on to the post to keep from bouncing out. "Can't you see I'm awake?"

"Well, I go off duty now, and you'll have to hurry," said the bed sulkily. "I'm due at the lecture at nine."

"Lecture?" gasped Dorothy.

"What's so queer about that?" demanded the bed coldly.

"I've got to keep well posted, haven't I? I belong to a polished set, I do. Hurry up, little girl, or I'll throw you out."

"I'm glad my bed doesn't talk to me in this impertinent fashion," thought Dorothy, slipping into her dress and combing her hair with her side comb. "Imagine being ordered about by a bed! I wonder if Sir Hokus is up." Parting the curtains, she jumped down, and the bed, without even saying good-bye, took itself off.

Sir Hokus was sitting on a stile, polishing his armor with a pillowslip he had taken from his bed, and the Cowardly Lion was lying beside him lazily thumping his tail and making fun of the passing furniture.

"Have you had breakfast?" asked Dorothy, joining her friends.

"We were waiting for your Ladyship," chuckled the Cowardly Lion. "Would you mind ordering two for me, Hokus? I find one quite insufficient."

Sir Hokus threw away the pillowslip, and talking cheerfully they walked toward King Fix Sit's circle. The beds had been replaced by breakfast tables, and the whole street was eating busily.

"Good morning, King," said Sir Hokus. "Four breakfasts, please."

The King rang a bell four times without looking up from his oatmeal. Seeing that he did not wish to be disturbed, the three waited quietly for their tables.

"In some ways," said Dorothy, contentedly munching a hot roll, "in some ways this is a very comfortable place."

"In sooth 'tis that," mumbled Sir Hokus, his mouth full of baked apple. As for the Cowardly Lion, he finished his two breakfasts in no time. "And now," said Sir Hokus as the tables walked off, "let us continue our quest. Could'st tell us the way to the Emerald City, my good King Fix?"

"If you go, go away. And if you stay, stay away. That's my motto," answered King Fix shortly. "I can't have people running around here like common furniture," he added in a grieved voice. All the Fixes nodded vigorously.

"Let them take their stand or their departure," said Sticken Plaster firmly.

The King felt in his pocket and brought out three pieces of chalk. "Go to the end of the street. Choose a place and draw your circle. In five minutes you will find it impossible to move out of the circle, and you will be saved all this unnecessary motion."

"But we don't want to come to a standstill," objected Dorothy.

"No, by my good sword!" spluttered the Knight, glaring around nervously. Then, seeing the King looked displeased, he made a low bow. "If your Highness could graciously direct us out of the city—"

"Buy a piece of road and go where it takes you," snapped the King.

Seeing no more was to be got out of him, they started down the long street.

"I wonder what they do when it rains?" said Dorothy, looking curiously at the solemn rows of people.

"Call for roofs, silly!" snapped a Fix, staring at her rudely. "If you would spend your time thinking instead of walking, you'd know more."

"Go to, and swallow a gooseberry!" roared the Knight, waving his sword at the Fix, and Dorothy, fearing an encounter, begged him to come on, which he did—though with many backward glances.

Fix City seemed to consist of one long street, and they had soon come to the very end.

"Uds daggers!" gasped Sir Hokus.

"Great palm trees," roared the Cowardly Lion.

As for Dorothy, she could do nothing but stare. The street ended surely enough, and beyond there was nothing at all. That is, nothing but air.

"Well," said the Cowardly Lion, backing a few paces, "this is a pretty fix."

"Glad you like it," said a wheezy voice. The three travelers turned in surprise. A huge Fix was regarding them with interest. His circle, which was the last in the row, was about twenty times as large as the other circles, and on the edge stood a big sign:

ROAD SHOP

"Don't you remember, the King said something about buying a road," said Dorothy in an excited undertone to the Knight.

"Can'st direct us to a road, my good man?" asked Sir Hokus with a bow. The Fix jerked his thumb back at the sign. "What kind of a road to you want?" he asked hoarsely.

"A road that will take us back to the Emerald City, please," said Dorothy.

"I can't guarantee anything like that," declared the Fix, shaking his head.

"Our roads go where they please, and you'll have to go where they take you. Do you want to go on or off?"

"On," shivered the Cowardly Lion, looking with a shudder over the precipice at the end of the street.

"What kind of a road will you have? Make up your minds, please. I am busy."

"What kind of roads have you?" asked Dorothy timidly. It was her first experience at buying roads, and she felt a bit perplexed.

"Sunny, shady, straight, crooked, and cross-roads," snapped the Fix.

"We wouldn't want a cross one," said Dorothy positively. "Have you any with trees at both sides and water at the end?"

"How many yards?" asked the Fix, taking a pair of shears as large as himself off a long counter beside him.

"Five miles," said Sir Hokus as Dorothy looked confused. "That ought to take us somewhere!"

The Fix rang one of the bells in the counter. The next minute, a big trap door in the ground opened, and a perfectly huge roll bounced out at his feet.

"Get on," commanded the Fix in such a sharp tone that the three jumped to obey. Holding fast to Sir Hokus, Dorothy stepped on the piece of road that had already unrolled. The Cowardly Lion, looking very anxious, followed. No sooner had they done so than the road gave a terrific leap forward that stretched the three flat upon their backs and started unwinding from its spool at a terrifying speed. As it unrolled, tall trees snapped erect on each side and began laughing derisively at the three travelers huddled together in the middle.

"G-g-glad we only took five miles," stuttered Dorothy to the Knight, whose armor was rattling like a Ford.

The Cowardly Lion had wound his tail around a tree and dug his claws into the road, for he had no intention of falling off into nothingness. As for the road, it snapped along at about a mile a minute, and before they had time to grow accustomed to this singular mode of travel, it gave a final jump that sent them circling into the air, and began rapidly winding itself up.

Down, down, down whirled Dorothy, falling with a resounding splash into a broad stream of water. Then down, down, down again, almost to the bottom.

"Help!" screamed Dorothy as her head rose above water,

and she began striking out feebly. But the fall through the air had taken all her breath.

"What do you want?" A thin, neat little man was watching her anxiously from the bank, making careful notes in a book that he held in one hand.

"Help! Save me!" choked Dorothy, feeling herself going down in the muddy stream again.

"Wait! I'll look it up under the 'H's," called the little man, making a trumpet of his hands. "Are you an island? An island is a body of land entirely surrounded by water, but this seems to be a some-body," Dorothy heard him mutter as he whipped over several pages of his book. "Sorry," he called back, shaking his head slowly, "but this is the wrong day. I only save lives on Monday."

"Stand aside, Mem, you villain!" A second little man exactly like the first except that he was exceedingly untidy plunged into the stream.

"It's no use," thought Dorothy, closing her eyes, for he had jumped in far below the spot where she had fallen and was making no progress whatever. The waters rushed over her head the second time. Then she felt herself being dragged upward.

When she opened her eyes, the Cowardly Lion was standing over her. "Are you all right?" he rumbled anxiously. "I came as soon as I could. Fell in way upstream. Seen Hokus?"

"Oh, he'll drown," cried Dorothy, forgetting her own

narrow escape. "He can't swim in that heavy armor!"

"Never fear, I'll get him," puffed the Cowardly Lion, and without waiting to catch his breath he plunged back into the stream. The little man who only saved lives on Monday now approached timidly. "I'd like to get a statement from you, if you don't mind. It might help me in the future."

"You might have helped me in the present," said Dorothy, wringing out her dress. "You ought to be ashamed of yourself."

"I'll make a note of that," said the little man earnestly. "But how did you feel when you went down?" He waited, his pencil poised over the little book.

"Go away," cried Dorothy in disgust.

"But my dear young lady—"

"I'm not your dear young lady. Oh, dear, why doesn't the Cowardly Lion come back?"

"Go away, Mem." The second little man, dripping wet, came up hurriedly.

"I was only trying to get a little information," grumbled Mem sulkily.

"I'm sorry I couldn't swim faster," said the wet little man, approaching Dorothy apologetically.

"Well, thank you for trying," said Dorothy. "Is he your brother? And could you tell me where you are? You're dressed in yellow, so I 'spose it must be somewhere in the Winkie Country."

"Right in both cases," chuckled the little fellow. "My name

is Ran and his name is Memo." He jerked his thumb at the retiring twin. "Randum and Memo—see?"

"I think I do," said Dorothy, half closing her eyes. "Is that why he's always taking notes?"

"Exactly," said Ran. "I do everything at Random, and he does everything at memorandum."

"It must be rather confusing," said Dorothy. Then as she caught sight of the Cowardly Lion dragging Sir Hokus, she jumped up excitedly. Ran, however, took one look at the huge beast and then fled, calling for Mem at the top of his voice. And that is the last Dorothy saw of these singular twins.

The Lion dropped Sir Hokus in a limp heap. When Dorothy unfastened his armor, gallons of water rushed out.

"Sho good of—of—you," choked the poor Knight, trying to straighten up.

"Save your breath, old fellow," said the Cowardly Lion, regarding him affectionately.

"Oh, why did I ask for water on the end of the road?" sighed Dorothy. "But, anyway, we're in some part of the Winkie Country."

Sir Hokus, though still spluttering, was beginning to revive. "Yon noble bheast shall be knighted. Uds daggers! That's the shecond time he's shaved my life!" Rising unsteadily, he tottered over to the Lion and struck him a sharp blow on the shoulder. "Rishe, Shir Cowardly Lion," he cried hoarsely, and fell headlong, and before Dorothy or the lion had recovered from their surprise he was fast asleep, mumbling happily of dragons and bludgeons.

"We'll have to wait till he gets rested," said Dorothy. "And until I get dry." She began running up and down, then stopped suddenly before the Lion.

"And there's something else for Professor Wogglebug to put in his book, Sir Cowardly Lion."

"Oh, that!" mumbled the Cowardly Lion, looking terribly embarrassed. "Whoever heard of a Cowardly Knight? Nonsense!"

"No, it isn't nonsense," said Dorothy stoutly. "You're a knight from now on. Won't the Scarecrow be pleased?"

"If we ever find him," sighed the Lion, settling himself beside Sir Hokus.

"We will," said Dorothy gaily. "I just feel it."

...—... ⓒhapter 14 ...—...

SONS and GRANDSONS GREET the SCARECROW

Although the Scarecrow had been on Silver Islands only a few days, he had already instituted many reforms, and thanks to his cleverness the people were more prosperous than ever before. Cheers greeted him wherever he went, and even old Chew Chew was more agreeable and no longer made bitter remarks to Happy Toko. The Scarecrow himself, however, had four new wrinkles and was exceedingly melancholy. He missed the carefree life in Oz, and every minute that he was not ruling the island he was thinking about his old home and dear, jolly comrades in the Emerald City.

"I almost hope they will look in the Magic Picture and wish

me back again," he mused pensively. "But it is my duty to stay here. I have a family to support." So he resolved to put the best face he could on the matter, and Happy Toko did his utmost to cheer up his royal master. The second morning after the great victory, he came running into the silver Throne Room in a great state of excitement.

"The honorable Offspring have arriven!" announced Happy, turning a somersault. "Come, ancient and amiable Sir, and gaze upon your sons and grandsons!" The Scarecrow sprang joyously from his silver throne, upsetting a bowl of silver fish and three silver vases. At last a real family! Ever since his arrival, the three Princes and their fifteen little sons had been cruising on the royal pleasure barge, so that the Scarecrow had not caught a glimpse of them.

"This is the happiest moment of my life!" he exclaimed, clasping his yellow gloves and watching the door intently. Happy looked a little uneasy, for he knew the three Princes to be exceedingly haughty and overbearing, but he said nothing, and next minute the Scarecrow's family stepped solemnly into the royal presence.

"Children!" cried the Scarecrow, and with his usual impetuousness rushed forward and flung his arms around the first richly clad Prince.

"Take care! Take care, ancient and honorable papa!" cried the young Silverman, backing away. "Such excitement is not good for one of your advanced years." He drew himself away firmly and, adjusting a huge pair of silver spectacles, regarded the Scarecrow attentively. "Ah, how you have changed!"

"He looks very feeble, Too Fang, but may he live long to rule this flowery island and our humble selves!" said the second Prince, bowing stiffly.

"Do you not find the affairs of state fatiguing, darling papa?" inquired the third Prince, fingering a jeweled chain that hung around his neck.

"I, as your eldest son, shall be delighted to relieve you should you wish to retire. Get back ten paces, you!" he roared at Happy Toko.

The poor Scarecrow had been so taken aback by this cool reception that he just stared in disbelief.

"If the three honorable Princes will retire themselves, I will speak with my grandsons," he said dryly, bowing in his most royal manner. The three Princes exchanged startled glances. Then, with three low salaams, they retired backward from the hall.

"And now, my dears—!" The Scarecrow looked wistfully at his fifteen silken-clad little grandsons. Their silver hair, plaited tightly into little queues, stood out stiffly on each side of their heads and gave them a very curious appearance. At his first word, the fifteen fell dutifully on their noses. As soon as they were right side up, the Scarecrow, beginning at the end of the row, addressed a joking question to each in his most approved Oz style. But over they went again, and answered merely:

"Yes, gracious Grandpapapapah!" or "No honorable

Grandpapapapah!" And the constant bobbing up and down and papahing so confused the poor Scarecrow that he nearly gave up the conversation.

"It's no use trying to talk to these children," he wailed in disgust, "they're so solemn. Don't you ever laugh?" he cried in exasperation, for he had told them stories that would have sent the Oz youngsters into hysterics.

"It is not permissible for a Prince to laugh at the remarks of his honorable grandparent," whispered Happy Toko, while the fifteen little Princes banged their heads solemnly on the floor.

"Honorable fiddlesticks!" exclaimed the Scarecrow, slumping back on his throne. "Bring cushions." Happy Toko ran off nimbly, and soon the fifteen little Princes were seated in a circle at the Scarecrow's feet. "To prevent prostrations," said the Scarecrow.

"Yes, old Grandpapapapah!" chorused the Princes, bending over as far as they could.

"Wait!" said the Scarecrow hastily, "I'll tell you a story. Once upon a time, to a beautiful country called Oz, which is surrounded on all sides by a deadly desert, there came a little girl named Dorothy. A terrible gale—Well, what's the matter now?" The Scarecrow stopped short, for the oldest Prince had jerked a book out of his sleeve and was flipping over the pages industriously.

"It is not on the map, great Grandpapapapah," he announced solemnly, and all of the other little Princes shook their heads and said dully, "Not on the map."

"Not on the map—Oz? Of course it's not. Do you suppose we want all the humans in creation coming there?" Calming down, the Scarecrow tried to continue his story, but every time he mentioned Oz, the little Princes shook their heads stubbornly and whispered, "Not on the map," till the usually good-tempered Scarecrow flew into perfect passion.

"Not on the map, you little villains!" he screamed, forgetting they were his grandsons. "What difference does that make? Are your heads solid silver?"

"We do not believe in Oz," announced the oldest Prince serenely. "There is no such place."

"No such place as Oz—Happy, do you hear that?" The Scarecrow's voice fairly crackled with indignation. "Why, I thought everybody believed in Oz!"

"Perhaps your Highness can convince them later," suggested the Imperial Punster. "This way, Offspring." His Master, he felt, had had enough family for one day. So the fifteen little Princes, with fifteen stiff little bows, took themselves back to the royal nursery. As for the Scarecrow, he paced disconsolately up and down his magnificent Throne Room, tripping over his kimono at every other step.

"You're a good boy, Tappy," said the Scarecrow as Happy returned, "but I tell you being a grandparent is not what I thought it would be. Did you hear them tell me right to my face they did not believe in Oz? And my sons—ugh!"

"Fault of their bringing up," said Happy Toko comfortingly. "If your serene Highness would just tell me more of that illustrious country!" Happy knew that nothing cheered the Scarecrow like talking of Oz, and to tell the truth Happy himself never tired of the Scarecrow's marvelous stories. So the two slipped quietly into the palace gardens, and the Scarecrow related for the fourteenth time the story of his discovery by Dorothy and the story of Ozma, and almost forgot that he was an Emperor.

"Your Highness knows the history of Oz by heart," said Happy admiringly as the Scarecrow paused.

"I couldn't do that," said the Scarecrow gently, "for you see, Happy, I have no heart."

"Then I wish we all had none!" exclaimed Happy Toko, rolling up his eyes. The Scarecrow looked embarrassed, so the little Punster threw back his head and sang a song he had been making up while the Scarecrow had been telling his stories:

"The Scarecrow was standing alone in a field,
Inviting the crows to keep off,
When the straw in his chest began tickling his vest
And he couldn't resist a loud cough.

"The noise that was heard so surprised ev'ry bird,
That the flock flew away in a fright,
But the Scarecrow looked pleased, and he said "If I'd sneezed
It wouldn't have been so polite."

"Ho!" roared the Scarecrow, "You're almost as good at making verses as Scraps, Write that down for me, Tappy. I'd like to show it to her."

"Hush!" whispered Happy, holding up his finger warningly. The Scarecrow turned so suddenly that the silver pigtail pinned to the back of his hat wound itself tightly around his neck. No wonder! On the other side of the hedge the three Princes were walking up and down, conversing in indignant whispers.

"What a horrible shape our honorable Papa has reappeared in. I hear that it never wears out," muttered one. "He may continue just as he is for years and years. How am I ever to succeed him, I'd like to know. Why, he may outlive us all!"

"We might throw him into the silver river," said the second hopefully.

"No use," choked the third. "I was just talking to the Imperial Soothsayer, and he tells me that no one from this miserable Kingdom of Oz can be destroyed. But I have a plan. Incline your Royal ears—listen." The voices dropped to such a low whisper that neither Happy nor the Scarecrow could hear one word.

"Treason!" spluttered Happy, making ready to spring through the hedge, but the Scarecrow seized him by the arm and drew him away.

"I don't believe they like their poor papa," exclaimed the Scarecrow when they were safely back in the Throne Room. "I'm feeling older than a Kinkajou. Ah, Happy Oko, why did I ever slide down my family tree? It has brought me nothing but unhappiness."

Chapter 15

The THREE PRINCES PLOT to UNDO the EMPEROR

Let me help your Imperial Serenity!"

"Bring a cane!"

"Carefully, now!"

The three royal Princes, with every show of affection, were supporting the Scarecrow to the silver bench in the garden where he usually sat during luncheon.

"Are you quite comfortable?" asked the elder. "Here, Happy, you rogue, fetch a scarf for his Imperial Highness. You must be careful, dear Papa Scarecrow. At your age, drafts are dangerous." The rascally Prince wound the scarf about the Scarecrow's neck.

"What do you suppose they are up to?" asked the Scarecrow,

staring after the three suspiciously. "Why this sudden devotion? It upsets my Imperial Serenity a lot."

"Trying to make you feel old," grumbled Happy. Several hours had passed since they had overheard the conversation in the garden. The Scarecrow had decided to watch his sons closely and fall in with any plan they suggested so they would suspect nothing. Then, when the time came, he would act. Just what he would do he did not know, but his excellent brains would not, he felt sure, desert him. Happy Toko sat as close to the Scarecrow as he could and scowled terribly whenever the Princes approached, which was every minute or so during the afternoon.

"How is the Scarecrow's celestial old head?"

"Does he suffer from honorable gout?"

"Should they fetch the Imperial Doctor?"

The Scarecrow, who had never thought of age in his whole straw life, became extremely nervous.

Was he really old? Did his head ache? When no one was looking, he felt himself carefully all over. Then something of his old time Oz spirit returned. Seizing the cushion that his eldest son was placing at his back, he hurled it over his head. Leaping from his throne, he began turning handsprings in a careless and sprightly manner.

"Don't you worry about your honorable old papa," chuckled the Scarecrow, winking at Happy Toko. "He's good for a couple of centuries!"

The three Princes stared sourly at this exhibition of youth.

"But your heart," objected the eldest Prince.

"Have none," laughed the Scarecrow. Snatching off the silver cord from around his waist, he began skipping rope up and down the hall. The Princes, tapping their foreheads significantly, retired, and the Scarecrow, throwing his arm around Happy Toko, began whispering in his ear. He had a plan himself. They would see!

Meanwhile, off in his dark cave in one of the silver mountains, the Grand Gheewizard of the Silver Islands was stirring a huge kettle of magic. Every few moments he paused to read out of a great yellow book that he had propped up on the mantle. The fire in the huge grate leaped fiercely under the big, black pot, and the sputtering candles on each side of the book sent creepy shadows into the dark cave. Dark chests, books, bundles of herbs, and heaps of gold and silver were everywhere. Whenever the Gheewizard turned his back, a rheumatic silver-scaled old dragon would crawl toward the fire and swallow a mouthful of coals, until the old Gheewizard caught him in the act and chained him to a ring in the corner of the cave.

"Be patient, little joy of my heart! Our fortune is about to be made," hissed the wizened little man, waving a long iron spoon at the dragon. "You shall have a bucket of red-hot coals every hour and I a silver cap with a tassel. Have not the Royal Princes promised it?" The dragon shuffled about and finally went to sleep, smoking sulkily.

"Is it finished, son of a yellow dog?" Through the narrow opening of the cave, the youngest Prince stuck his head.

"I am working as fast as I can, Honorable Prince, but the elixir must boil yet one more night. Tomorrow, when the sun shines on the first bar of your celestial window, come, and all will be ready."

"Are you sure you have found it?" asked the Prince, withdrawing his head, for the smoking dragon and steam from the kettle made him cough.

"Quite sure," wheezed the Grand Gheewizard, and fell to stirring the kettle with all his might.

The Scarecrow, although busy with trials in the great courtroom of the palace, felt that something unusual was in the air. The Princes kept nodding to one another, and the Grand Chew Chew and General Mugwump had their heads together at every opportunity.

"Something's going to happen, Tappy. I feel it in my straw," whispered the Scarecrow as he finished trying the last case. At that very minute, the Grand Chew Chew arose and held up his hand for silence. Everybody paused in their way to the exits and looked with surprise at the old Silverman.

"I have to announce," said the Grand Chew Chew in a solemn voice, "that the Great and Imperial Chang Wang Woe will tomorrow be restored to his own rightful shape. The Grand

Gheewizard of the realm has discovered a magic formula to break the enchantment and free him from this distressing Scarecrow body. Behold for the last the Scarecrow of Oz. Tomorrow he will be our old and glorious Emperor!"

"Old and glorious?" gasped the Scarecrow, nearly falling from his throne.

"Tappy! I forgot to lock up the wizards. Great Cornstarch! Tomorrow I will be eighty-five years old."

Such cheers greeted the Grand Chew Chew's announcement that no one even noticed the Scarecrow's distress.

"I, also, have an announcement!" cried the eldest Prince, standing up proudly. "To make the celebration of my royal Papa's restoration complete, we have chosen the lovely and charming Orange Blossom for his bride."

"Bride!" gulped the Scarecrow. "But I do not approve of second marriages. I refuse to—"

No one paid the slightest attention to the Scarecrow's remarks.

"Hold my hand, Tappy," sighed the Scarecrow weakly. "It may be your last chance." Then he sat up and stared in good earnest, for the Prince was leading forward a tall, richly clad lady.

"Orange Blossom!" muttered the Scarecrow under his breath. "He means Lemon Peel! Silver grandmother, Tappy!" Orange Blossom was a cross-looking Princess of seventy-five, at least.

"She is a sister of the King of the Golden Islands," whispered General Mugwump. "Of a richness surpassing your own. Let me felicitate your Highness."

"Fan me, Tappy! Fan me!" gasped the Scarecrow. Then he straightened himself suddenly. The time had come for action. He would say nothing to anyone, but that night he would escape and try to find his way back to Oz, family or no family! He bowed graciously to Princess Orange Blossom, to the Grand Chew Chew, and to his sons.

"Let everything be made ready for the ceremony, and may tomorrow indeed bring me to myself," he repeated solemnly. Nothing was talked of that evening but the Emperor's impending marriage and the Grand Gheewizard's discovery. The Scarecrow seemed the least excited person in the palace. Sitting on his throne, he pretended to read the Royal Silver Journal, but he was really waiting impatiently for the courtiers to retire. Finally, when the last one had bowed himself out and only Happy Toko remained in the Throne Room, the Scarecrow began making his plans.

"It's no use, Tappy," said he, tying up a few little trinkets for Dorothy in a silk handkerchief, "I'd rather be straw than meat. I'd rather be a plain Scarecrow in Oz than Emperor of the Earth! They may be my sons, but all they want is my death. I'm going back to my old friends. I'd rather—" He got no farther. A huge slave seized him suddenly from behind, while another caught Happy Toko around his fat little waist.

"Tie them fast," said the eldest Prince, smiling wickedly at the Scarecrow. "Here, tie him to the beanstalk. Merely a part of the Grand Gheewizard's formula," he exclaimed maliciously as the struggling Scarecrow was bound securely to his family tree. "Good night, dear papa Scarecrow. Tomorrow you will be your old self again, and in a few short years *I* will be Emperor of the Silver Islands!"

"This rather upsets our plans, eh Tappy?" wheezed the Scarecrow after a struggle with his bonds.

"Pigs! Weasels!" choked Happy. "What are we to do?"

"Alas!" groaned the Scarecrow. "Tomorrow there will be no Scarecrow in Oz. What will Dorothy and Ozma think? And once I am changed into my old Imperial self, I can never make the journey to the Emerald City. Eighty-six is too old for traveling."

"Has your Majesty forgotten the wonderful brains given to you by the Wizard of Oz?"

"I had—for a moment," confessed the Scarecrow. "Be quiet, Tappy, while I think." Pressing his head against the magic beanpole, the Scarecrow thought and thought, harder than he had ever done in the course of his adventurous life, and in the great, silent hall Happy Toko struggled to set himself free.

Chapter 16

DOROTHY and HER GUARDIANS MEET NEW FRIENDS

While all these exciting things were happening to the poor Scarecrow, Dorothy, Sir Hokus and the Cowardly Lion had been having adventures of their own. For three days, they had wandered through a deserted part of the Winkie Country, subsisting largely on berries, sleeping under trees, and looking in vain for a road to lead them back to the Emerald City. On the second day, they had encountered an ancient woodsman, too old and deaf to give them any information. He did, however, invite them into his hut and give them a good dinner and a dozen sandwiches to carry away with them.

"But, oh, for a good old pasty!" sighed Sir Hokus late on

the third afternoon as they finished the last of the crumbly sandwiches.

"Do you know," said Dorothy, looking through the straggly fields and woods ahead, "I believe we've been going in the wrong direction again."

"Again!" choked the Cowardly Lion. "You mean still. I've been in a good many parts of Oz, but this—this is the worst."

"Not even one little dragon!" Sir Hokus shook his head mournfully. Then, seeing that Dorothy was tired and discouraged, he pretended to strum on a guitar and sang in his high-pitched voice:

> "A rusty Knight in steel bedite
> And Lady Dot, so fair,
> Sir Lion bold, with mane of gold
> And might besides to spa-ha-hare!
> And might beside to spare!
> The dauntless three, a company
> Of wit and bravery are,
> Who seek the valiant Scarecrow man,
> Who seek him near and fa-har-har,
> Who seek him near and fa-har!"

"Oh, I like that!" cried Dorothy, jumping up and giving Sir Hokus a little squeeze. "Only you should have said trusty Knight."

The Cowardly Lion shook his golden mane. "Let's do a little reconnoitering, Hokus," he said carelessly. He felt he must live up to the song somehow. "Perhaps we'll find a sign."

"I don't believe in signs anymore," laughed Dorothy, "but I'm coming too." Sir Hokus' song had cheered them all, and it wasn't the first time the Knight had helped make the best of a tiresome journey.

"The air seemeth to grow very hot," observed Sir Hokus after they had walked along silently for a time. "Hast noticed it, Sir Cowardly?"

"No, but I've swallowed some of it," coughed the Cowardly Lion, looking suspiciously through the trees.

"I'll just step forward and see what it is," said the Knight. As he disappeared, the truth dawned on Dorothy.

"Wait! Wait! Don't go! Please, please, Sir Hokus, come back, come back!" cried the little girl, running after him as fast as she could.

"What's the matter?" rumbled the Cowardly Lion, thudding behind her. Then both, coming suddenly out of the woods, gave a terrible scream, which so startled Sir Hokus that he fell over backwards. Just in time, too, for another step would have taken him straight on to the Deadly Desert, which destroys every living thing and keeps all intruders away from Oz.

"What befell?" puffed Sir Hokus, getting to his feet. Naturally, he knew nothing of the poisonous sands.

"You did," wheezed the Cowardly Lion in an agitated voice.

"Was it a dragon?" asked the Knight, limping toward them hopefully.

"Sit down!" The Cowardly Lion mopped his brow with his tail. "One step on that desert and it would have been one long goodnight."

"I should say it would!" shuddered Dorothy, and explained to Sir Hokus the deadly nature of the sands. "And do you know what this means?" Dorothy was nearer to tears than even I like to think about. "It means we've come in exactly the wrong direction and are farther away from the Emerald City than we were when we started."

"And seek him near and fa—hah—har," mumbled Sir Hokus with a very troubled light in his kindly blue eyes.

"And seek him near and far."

"Fah-har-har! I should say it was," said the Cowardly Lion bitterly. "But you needn't sing it."

"No, I s'pose not. Uds helmets and hauberks! I s'pose not!" The Knight lapsed into a discouraged silence, and all three sat and stared drearily at the stretch of desert before them and thought gloomily of the rough country behind.

"It's a caravan," wheezed a hoarse voice.

"I doubt that, Camy, I doubt it very much." The shrill nasal voices so startled the three travelers that they swung about in astonishment.

"Great dates and deserts!" burst out the Cowardly Lion, jumping up. And on the whole, this exclamation was entirely suitable, for ambling toward them were a long-legged camel and a wobbly-necked dromedary.

"At last! A steed!" cried the Knight, bounding to his feet.

"I doubt that." The Dromedary stopped and looked at him coldly.

"Try me," said the Camel amiably. "I'm more comfortable."

"I doubt that, too."

> *"The doubtful dromedary wept,*
> *As o'er the desert sands he stept,*
> *Association with the sphinx*
> *Has made him doubtful, so he thinks!"*

chortled the Knight with his head on one side.

"How did you know?" asked the Dromedary, opening his eyes wide.

"It just occurred to me," admitted Sir Hokus, clearing his throat modestly.

"I doubt that. Somebody told you," said the Doubtful Dromedary bitterly.

"Pon my honor," said Sir Hokus.

"I doubt it, I doubt it very much," persisted the Dromedary, wagging his head sorrowfully.

"You seem to doubt everything!" Dorothy laughed in spite of herself, and the Dromedary regarded her sulkily.

"He does," said the Camel. "It makes him very doubtful company. Now, I like to be comfortable and happy, and you can't be if you're always doubting things and people and places. Eh, my dear?"

"Where did you comfortable and doubtful parties come from?" asked the Cowardly Lion. "Strangers here?"

"Well, yes," admitted the Camel, nibbling the branch of a tree. "There was a terrific sandstorm, and after blowing and blowing and blowing, we found ourselves in this little wood. The odd part of it is that you talk in our language. Never knew a two-leg to understand a word of Camelia before."

"You're not talking Camelia, you're talking Ozish," laughed Dorothy. "All animals can talk here."

"Well, now, that's very comfortable, I must say," sighed the Camel, "and if you'd just tell me where to go, it would be more comfortable still."

"I doubt that," snapped the Dromedary. "They're no caravan."

"Where do you want to go?" asked the Cowardly Lion, ignoring the Doubtful Dromedary.

"Anywhere, just so we keep moving. We're used to being told when to start and stop, and life is mighty lonely without our Karwan Bashi," sighed the Comfortable Camel.

"Why, I didn't know you smoked!" exclaimed Dorothy in

surprise. She thought the Camel was referring to a brand of tobacco.

"He means his camel driver," whispered Sir Hokus, eyeing the soft, pillowed seat on the Camel's back longingly. Besides the seat, great sacks and bales of goods hung from its sides. The Doubtful Dromedary was similarly loaded.

"Goodness!" exclaimed Dorothy. A sudden idea had struck her. "You haven't anything to eat in those sacks, have you?"

"Plenty, my child—plenty!" answered the Camel calmly.

"Three cheers for the Comfortable Camel!" roared the Cowardly Lion, while Sir Hokus, following the Camel's directions, carefully unfastened a large, woven basket from one of the sacks on its side.

"You may be my Karwan Bashi," announced the Comfortable Camel judiciously as Sir Hokus paused for breath.

"Hear that, Lady Dot?" Sir Hokus swept the Camel a bow and fairly beamed with pleasure. Dorothy, meanwhile, had set out an appetizing repast on a small, rocky ledge—a regular feast, it appeared to the hungry travelers. There were loaves of black bread, figs, dates, cheese, and a curious sort of dried meat which the Cowardly Lion swallowed in great quantities.

"Isn't this cozy?" said Dorothy, forgetting the long, weary way ahead. "My, I'm glad we met you!"

"Very comforting to us, too, my dear," said the Camel, swaying complacently. "Isn't it, Doubty?"

"There are some silk cushions in my right-hand saddle sack,

but I doubt very much whether you'll like 'em," mumbled the Dromedary gruffly.

"Out with them!" cried Sir Hokus, pouncing on the Doubtful Dromedary, and in a minute each of the party had a cushion and was as snug as possible.

"Could anything have been more fortunate?" exulted the Knight. "We can now resume our journey properly mounted."

"I think I'll ride the Cowardly Lion," said Dorothy, looking uneasily at the high seat on the Camel's back. "Let's start before it grows any darker."

They had eaten to heart's content, and now, packing up the remainder of the feast, the little party made ready to start.

Sir Hokus, using the Cowardly Lion as a footstool, mounted the Camel, and then Dorothy climbed on her old friend's back, and the little caravan moved slowly through the forest.

"There's a tent in my left-hand saddle sack, but I doubt very much whether you can put it up," said the Doubtful Dromedary, falling in behind the Comfortable Camel. "I doubt it very much indeed."

"How now, what means this doubting?" called Sir Hokus from his perilous seat. "I'll pitch it when the time comes."

"Mind you don't pitch out when the Camel goes!" called the Cowardly Lion, who would have his little joke. Sir Hokus, to tell the truth, was feeling tossed about and dizzy, but he was too polite to mention the fact. As they proceeded, Dorothy told the Comfortable Camel all about the Scarecrow and Oz.

An occasional word jolted down from above told her that the Knight was singing. They had gone possibly a mile when Dorothy pointed in excitement to a road just ahead.

"We must have missed it before! Wait, I'll see what it's like." Jumping down from the Cowardly Lion's back, she peered curiously at the narrow, tree-lined path. "Why, here's a sign!"

"What of?" asked the Comfortable Camel, lurching forward eagerly and nearly unseating the Knight.

WISH WAY

read Dorothy in a puzzled voice.

"Looks like a pretty good road," said the Comfortable Camel, squinting up its eyes.

"I doubt it, Camy, I doubt it very much," said the Doubtful Dromedary tremulously.

"What does my dear Karwan Bashi think?" asked the Comfortable Camel, looking adoringly back at the Knight.

"It is unwise to go back when the journey lieth forward," said the Knight, and immediately returned to his song. So, single file, the little company turned in at the narrow path, the Comfortable Camel advancing with timid steps and the Doubtful Dromedary bobbing his head dubiously.

Chapter 17

DOUBTY and CAMY VANISH
into SPACE

For a short time, everything went well. Then Dorothy, turning to see how Sir Hokus was getting along, discovered that the Doubtful Dromedary had disappeared.

"Why, where in the world?" exclaimed Dorothy. The Comfortable Camel craned his wobbly neck and, when he saw that his friend was gone, burst into tears. His sobs heaved Sir Hokus clear out of his seat and flung him, helmet first, into the dust.

"Go to!" exploded the Knight, sitting up. "If I were a bird, riding in yon nest would be easier." The last of his sentence ended in a hoarse croak. Sir Hokus vanished, and a great raven flopped down in the center of the road.

"Oh, where is my dear Karwan Bashi? Oh, where is Doubty?" screamed the Comfortable Camel, running around in frenzied circles. "I wish I'd never come on this path!"

"Magic!" gasped Dorothy, clutching the Cowardly Lion's mane. The Comfortable Camel had melted into air before their very eyes.

"I doubt it, I doubt it very much!" coughed a faint voice close to her ear. Dorothy ducked her head involuntarily as a big yellow butterfly settled on the Cowardly Lion's ear.

"Our doubtful friend," whispered the lion weakly. "Oh, be careful, Dorothy dear. We may turn into frogs or something worse any minute."

Dorothy and the Cowardly Lion had had experiences with magic transformations, and the little girl, pressing her fingers to her eyes, tried to think of something to do. The raven was making awkward attempts to fly and cawing "Go to, now!" every other second.

"Oh, I wish dear Sir Hokus were himself again," wailed Dorothy after trying in vain to recall some magic sentences. Presto! The Knight stood before them, a bit breathless from flying, but hearty as ever.

"I see! I see!" said the Cowardly Lion with a little prance. "Every wish you make on this road comes true. Remember the sign: 'Wish Way.' I wish the Comfortable Camel were back. I wish the Doubtful Dromedary were himself again," muttered the Cowardly Lion rapidly, and in an instant the two creatures were standing in the path.

"Uds bodikins! So I did wish myself a bird!" gasped the Knight, rubbing his gauntlets together excitedly.

"There you are! There you are!" cried the Comfortable Camel, stumbling toward him and resting his foolish head on his shoulder. "Dear, dear Karwan Bashi! And Doubty, old fellow, there you are too! Ah, how comfortable this all is."

"Not two—one," wheezed the Doubtful Dromedary. "And Camy, I doubt very much whether I'd care for butterflying. I just happened to wish myself one!"

"Don't make any more wishes," said the Cowardly Lion sternly.

"Methinks a proper wish might serve us well," observed Sir Hokus. He had been pacing up and down in great excitement. "Why not wish—"

"Oh, stop!" begged Dorothy. "Wait till we've thought it all out. Wishing's awfully particular work!"

"One person better speak for the party," said the Cowardly Lion. "Now, I suggest—"

"Oh, be careful!" screamed Dorothy again. "I wish you would all stop wishing!" Sir Hokus looked at her reproachfully. No wonder. At Dorothy's words, they all found themselves unable to speak. The Doubtful Dromedary's eyes grew rounder and rounder. For the first time in its life, it was unable to doubt anything.

"Now I'll have to do it all," thought Dorothy, and closing her eyes she tried to think of the very best wish for everybody concerned. It was night and growing darker. The Cowardly Lion, the Camel and Dromedary and Sir Hokus peered anxiously at the little girl, wondering what in the world was going to happen. Being wished around is no joke. For five minutes Dorothy thought and thought. Then, standing in the middle of the road, she made her wish in a clear, distinct voice. It was not a very long wish. To be exact, it had only eight words. Eight—short—little words! But stars! No sooner were they out of Dorothy's mouth than the earth opened with a splintering crash and swallowed up the whole company!

Chapter 18

DOROTHY FINDS the SCARECROW!

The next thing Dorothy knew, she was sitting on the hard floor of a great, dark hall. One lantern burned feebly, and in the dim, silvery light she could just make out the Comfortable Camel scrambling awkwardly to his feet.

"I smell straw," sniffed the Camel softly.

"I doubt very much whether I am going to like this place." The voice of the Doubtful Dromedary came hesitatingly through the gloom.

"By sword and scepter!" gasped the Knight, "Are you there, Sir Cowardly?"

"Thank goodness, they are!" said Dorothy. Wishing other

people about is a risky and responsible business. "They're all here, but I wonder where here is." She jumped up, but at a shuffle of feet drew back.

"Pigs! Weasels!" shrilled an angry voice, and a fat little man hurled himself at Sir Hokus, who happened to have fallen in the lead.

"Uds trudgeons and bludgeons and maugre thy head!" roared the Knight, shaking him off like a fly.

"Tappy, Tappy, my dear boy. Caution! What's all this?" At the sound of that dear, familiar voice Dorothy's heart gave a skip of joy, and without stopping to explain she rushed forward.

"Dorothy!" cried the Scarecrow, stepping on his kimono and falling off his silvery throne. "Lights, Tappy! More lights, at once!" But Tappy was too busy backing away from Sir Hokus of Pokes.

"Approach, vassal!" thundered the Knight, who understood not a word of Tappy's speech. "Approach! I think I've been insulted!" He drew his sword and glared angrily through the darkness, and Tappy, having backed as far as possible, fell heels over pigtail into the silver fountain. At the loud splash, Dorothy hastened to the rescue.

"They're friends, and we've found the Scarecrow, we've found the Scarecrow!" She seized Sir Hokus and shook him till his armor rattled.

"Tappy! Tappy!" called the Scarecrow. "Where in the world

did he pagota?" That's exactly what he said, but to Dorothy it sounded like no language at all.

"Why," she cried in dismay, "it's the Scarecrow, but I can't understand a word he's saying!"

"I think he must be talking Turkey," droned the Comfortable Camel, "or donkey! I knew a donkey once, a very uncomfortable party, I—"

"I doubt it's donkey," put in the Dromedary importantly, but no one paid any attention to the two beasts. For Happy Toko had at last dragged himself out of the fountain and set fifteen lanterns glowing.

"Oh!" gasped Dorothy as the magnificent silver Throne Room was flooded with light, "Where are we?"

The Scarecrow had picked himself up, and with outstretched arms came running toward her talking a perfect Niagara of Silver Islandish.

"Have you forgotten your Ozish so soon?" rumbled the Cowardly Lion reproachfully as Dorothy flung her arms around the Scarecrow. The Scarecrow, seeing the Cowardly Lion for the first time, fairly fell upon his neck. Then he brushed his clumsy hand across his forehead.

"Wasn't I talking Ozish?" he asked in a puzzled voice.

"Oh, now you are!" exclaimed Dorothy. And sure enough, the Scarecrow was talking plain Ozish again. (Which I don't mind telling you is also plain English.)

The Knight had been watching this little reunion with

hardly repressed emotion. Advancing hastily, he dropped on one knee.

"My good sword and lance are ever at thy service, my Lord Scarecrow!" he exclaimed feelingly.

"Who is this impulsive person?" gulped the Scarecrow, staring in undisguised astonishment at the kneeling figure of the Sir Hokus of Pokes.

"He's my Knight Errant, and he's taken such good care of me," explained Dorothy eagerly.

"Splendid fellow," hissed the Cowardly Lion in the Scarecrow's other painted ear, "if he does talk odds and ends."

"Any friend of little Dorothy's is my friend," said the Scarecrow, shaking hands with Sir Hokus warmly. "But what I want to know is how you all got here."

"First tell us where we are," begged the little girl, for the Scarecrow's silver hat and queue filled her with alarm.

"You are on the Silver Islands," said the Scarecrow slowly. "And I am the Emperor—or his good-for-nothing spirit—and tomorrow," the Scarecrow glared around wildly, "tomorrow I'll be eighty-five going on eighty-six." His voice broke and ended in a barely controlled sob.

"Doubt that," drawled the Doubtful Dromedary sleepily.

"Eighty-five years old!" gasped Dorothy. "Why, no one in Oz grows any older!"

"We are no longer in Oz." The Scarecrow shook his

head sadly. Then, fixing the group with a puzzled stare, he exclaimed, "But how did you get here?"

"On a *wish*," said the Knight in a hollow voice.

"Yes," said Dorothy, "we've been hunting you all over Oz, and at last we came to Wish Way, and I said 'I wish we were all with the Scarecrow,' just like that—and next minute—"

"We fell and fell—and fell—and fell," wheezed the Comfortable Camel.

"And fell—and fell—and fell—and fell," droned the Dromedary, "And—"

"Here you are," finished the Scarecrow hastily, for the Dromedary showed signs of going on forever.

"Now tell us every single thing that has happened to you," demanded Dorothy eagerly.

Happy Toko had recognized Dorothy and the Cowardly Lion from the Scarecrow's description, and he now approached with an arm full of cushions. These he set in a circle on the floor, with one for the Scarecrow in the center, and with a warning finger on his lips placed himself behind his Master.

"Tappy is right!" exclaimed the Scarecrow. "We must be as quiet as possible, for a great danger hangs over me."

Without more ado, he told them of his amazing fall down the beanstalk; of his adventures on Silver Islands; of his sons and grandsons and the Gheewizard's elixir which would turn him from a lively Scarecrow into an old, old Emperor. All that I have told you, he told Dorothy, up to the very point where his eldest son had bound him to the bean pole and tied up poor, faithful Happy Toko. Happy, it seems, had at last managed to free himself, and they were about to make their escape when Dorothy and her party had fallen into the Throne Room. The Comfortable Camel and Doubtful Dromedary listened politely at first, but worn out by their exciting adventures, fell asleep in the middle of the story.

Nothing could have exceeded Dorothy's dismay to learn that the jolly Scarecrow of Oz, whom she had discovered herself, was in reality Chang Wang Woe, Emperor of Silver Islands.

"Oh, this spoils everything!" wailed the little girl. (The thought of Oz without the Scarecrow was unthinkable.) "It spoils everything! We were going to adopt you and be your truly family. Weren't we?"

The Cowardly Lion nodded. "I was going to be your cousin," he mumbled in a choked voice, "but now that you have a family of your own—" The lion miserably slunk down beside Dorothy.

Sir Hokus looked fierce and rattled his sword, but he could think of nothing that would help them out of their trouble.

"To-morrow there won't be any Scarecrow in Oz!" wailed Dorothy. "Oh, dear! Oh, dear!" And the little girl began to cry as if her heart would break.

"Stop! Stop!" begged the Scarecrow, while Sir Hokus awkwardly patted Dorothy on the back. "I'd rather have you for my family any day. I don't care a Kinkajou for being Emperor, and as for my sons, they are unnatural villains who make my life miserable by telling me how old I am!"

"Just like a poem I once read," said Dorothy, brightening up:

> *"You are old, Father William," the young man said,*
> *"And your hair has become very white,*
> *And yet you incessantly stand on your head!*
> *Do you think, at your age, it is right?"*

"That's it, that's it exactly!" exclaimed the Scarecrow as Dorothy finished repeating the verse. "'You are old, Father Scarecrow!' That's all I hear. I did stand on my head, too. And Dorothy, I can't seem to get used to being a grandparent," added the Scarecrow in a melancholy voice. "It's turning my straws grey." He plucked several from his chest and held them out to her. "Why, those little villains don't even believe in Oz! 'It's not on the map, old Grandpapapapah!'" he mumbled, imitating the tones of his little grandsons so cleverly that Dorothy laughed in spite of herself.

"This is what becomes of pride!" The Scarecrow extended his hands expressively. "Most people who hunt up their family trees are in for a fall, and I've had mine."

"But who do you want to be?" asked the Knight gravely. "A Scarecrow in Oz— or the—er—Emperor that you were?"

"I don't care who I were!" In his excitement, the Scarecrow

lost his grammar completely. "I want to be who I am. I want to be myself."

"But which one?" asked the Cowardly Lion, who was still a bit confused.

"Why, my best self, of course," said the Scarecrow with a bright smile. The sight of his old friends had quite restored his cheerfulness. "I've been here long enough to know that I am a better Scarecrow than an Emperor."

"Why, how simple it is!" sighed Dorothy contentedly. "Professor Wogglebug was all wrong. It's not what you were, but what you are—it's being yourself that counts."

"By my Halidom, the little maid is right!" said Sir Hokus, slapping his knee in delight. "Let your Gheewizard but try his transformations! Out on him! But what says yon honest henchman?" Happy Toko, although he understood no word of the conversation, had been watching the discussion with great interest. He had been trying to attract the Scarecrow's attention for some time, but the Knight was the only one who had noticed him.

"What is it, Tappy?" asked the Scarecrow, dropping easily back into Silver Islandish.

"Honored Master, the dawn approaches and with it the Royal Princes and the Grand Gheewizard—and your bride!" Happy paused significantly. The Scarecrow shuddered.

"Let's go back to Oz!" said the Cowardly Lion uneasily.

The Scarecrow was feeling in the pocket of his old Munchkin suit which he always wore under his robes of state. "Here!"

said he, giving a little pill to Happy Toko. "It's one of Professor Wogglebug's language pills," he exclaimed to Dorothy, "and will enable him to speak and understand Ozish." Happy swallowed the pill gravely.

"Greetings, honorable Ozites!" he said politely as soon as the pill was down. Dorothy clapped her hands in delight, for it was so comfortable to have him speak their own language.

"I could never have stood it here without Tappy Oko!" The Scarecrow looked fondly at his Imperial Punster.

"Queer name he has," rumbled the Cowardly Lion, looking at Happy Toko as if he had thoughts of eating him.

"Methinks he should be knighted," rumbled Sir Hokus, beaming on the little Silverman. "Rise, Sir Pudding!"

"The sun will do that in a minute or more, and then, then we shall all be thrown into prison!" wailed Happy Toko dismally.

"We were going to escape in a small boat," explained the Scarecrow, "but—" It was not necessary for him to finish. A boat large enough to hold Dorothy, the Cowardly Lion, the Scarecrow, Happy Toko, the Camel and the Dromedary could not very well be launched in secret.

"Oh, dear!" sighed Dorothy, "If I'd only wished you and all of us back in the Emerald City!"

"You wished very well, Lady Dot," said the Knight. "When I think of what I was going to wish for—"

"What were you going to wish, Hokus?" asked the Cowardly Lion curiously.

"For a dragon!" faltered the Knight, looking terribly ashamed.

"A dragon!" gasped Dorothy. "Why, what good would that have done us?"

"Wait!" interrupted the Scarecrow. "I have thought of something! Why not climb my family tree? It is a long, long way, but at the top lies Oz!"

"Grammercy, a pretty plan!" exclaimed Sir Hokus, peering up at the bean pole.

"Wouldn't that be social climbing?" chuckled Happy Toko, recovering his spirits with a bound. The Cowardly Lion said nothing, but heaved a mighty sigh which no one heard, for they were all running toward the bean pole. It was a good family tree to climb, sure enough, for there were handy little notches in the stalk.

"You go first!" Sir Hokus helped Dorothy up. When she had gone a few steps, the Scarecrow, holding his robes carefully, followed, then honest Happy Toko.

"I'll go last," said Sir Hokus bravely, and had just set his foot on the first notch when a hoarse scream rang through the hall.

Chapter 19

PLANNING to FLY from the SILVER ISLANDS

It was the Comfortable Camel. Waking suddenly, he found himself deserted. "Oh, where is my dear Karwan Bashi?" he roared dismally. "Come back! Come back!"

"Hush up, can't you?" rumbled the Cowardly Lion. "Do you want Dorothy and everybody to be thrown into prison on our account? We can't climb the bean pole and will have to wait here and face it out."

"But how uncomfortable," wailed the Camel. He began to sob heavily. Dorothy, although highest up the bean pole, heard all of this distinctly. "Oh," she cried remorsefully, "we can't desert the Cowardly Lion like this. I never thought about him."

"Spoken like the dear little Maid you are," said the Knight. "The good beast never reminded us of it, either. There's bravery for you!"

"Let us descend at once, I'll not move a step without the Cowardly Lion!" In his agitation, the Scarecrow lost his balance and fell headlong to the ground, knocking Sir Hokus's helmet terribly askew as he passed. The others made haste to follow him and were soon gathered gravely at the foot of the beanstalk.

"I'll have to think of some other plan," said the Scarecrow, looking nervously at the sky, which showed, through the long windows, the first streaks of dawn. The Comfortable Camel controlled its sobs with difficulty and pressed as close to Sir Hokus as it could. The Doubtful Dromedary was still asleep.

"It would have been a terrible climb," mused the Scarecrow, thinking of his long, long fall down the pole. "Ah, I have it!"

"What?" asked Dorothy anxiously.

"I wonder I did not think of it before. Ah, my brains are working better! I will abdicate," exclaimed the Scarecrow triumphantly. "I will abdicate, make a farewell speech, and return with you to Oz!"

"What if they refuse to let your radiant Highness go?" put in Happy Toko tremulously. "What if the Gheewizard should work his magic before you finished your speech?"

"Then we'll make a dash for it!" said Sir Hokus, twirling his sword recklessly.

"I'm with you," said the Cowardly Lion huskily, "but you needn't have come back for me."

"All right!" said the Scarecrow cheerfully. "And now that everything's settled so nicely, we might as well enjoy the little time left. Put out the lights, Tappy. Dorothy and I will sit on the throne, and the rest of you come as close as possible."

Sir Hokus wakened the Doubtful Dromedary and pulled and tugged it across the hall, where it immediately fell down asleep again. The Comfortable Camel ambled about eating the flowers out of the vases. The Cowardly Lion had placed himself at Dorothy's feet, and Sir Hokus and Happy Toko seated themselves upon the first step of the gorgeous silver throne.

Then, while they waited for morning, Dorothy told the Scarecrow all about the Pokes and Fix City, and the Scarecrow told once again of his victory over the King of the Golden Islands.

"Where is the magic fan now?" asked Dorothy at the end of the story.

The Scarecrow smiled broadly, and feeling in a deep pocket brought out the little fan and also the parasol he had plucked from the beanstalk. "Do you know," he said smiling, "so much has happened I haven't thought of them since the battle. I was saving them for you, Dorothy."

"For me!" exclaimed the little girl in delight. "Let me see them!" The Scarecrow handed them over obligingly, but Happy Toko trembled so violently he rolled down the steps of the throne.

"I beg of you!" He scrambled to his feet and held up his

hands in terror. "I beg of you, don't open that fan!"

"She's used to magic, Tappy. You needn't worry," said the Scarecrow easily.

"Of course I am," said Dorothy with great dignity. "But this'll be mighty useful if anyone tries to conquer Oz again. We can just fan 'em away."

Dorothy pulled a hair from the Cowardly Lion's mane, and winding it around the little fan, put it carefully in the pocket of her dress. The parasol she hung by its ribbon to her arm.

"Perhaps Ozma will look in the Magic Picture and wish us all back again," said the girl after they had sat for a time in silence.

"I doubt it." The Dromedary stirred and mumbled in its sleep.

"Singular beast, that!" ejaculated the Knight. "Doubting never gets one anywhere."

"Hush!" warned the Scarecrow. "I hear footsteps!"

"Come here." Sir Hokus called hoarsely to the Camel, who was eating a paper lantern at the other end of the room. The beast ran awkwardly over to the throne, and swallowing the lantern with a convulsive gulp, settled down beside the Dromedary.

"Whatever happens, we must stick together," said the Knight emphatically. "Ah—!"

Dorothy held fast to the Scarecrow with one hand and to the throne with the other. The sun had risen at last. There was a loud crash of drums and trumpets, a rush of feet, and into the hall marched the most splendid company Dorothy had seen in her whole life of adventures.

Chapter 20

DOROTHY UPSETS the CEREMONY of the ISLAND

A caravan!" whistled the Comfortable Camel, lurching to his feet. "How nice!"

"I doubt that!" The Dromedary's eyes flew open, and he stared sleepily at the magnificent procession of Silver Islanders.

First came the musicians, playing their shining silver trumpets and flutes. The Grand Chew Chew and General Mugwump followed, attired in brilliant silk robes of state. Then came the three Princes, glittering with jeweled chains and medals, and the fifteen little Princes, like so many silver butterflies in their satin kimonos. Next appeared a palanquin bearing the veiled Princess Orange Blossom, followed by a whole company of splendid courtiers and after them as many of the everyday Silver Islanders as the hall would hold. There was a moment of silence. Then the whole assemblage, contrary to the Scarecrow's edict, fell upon their faces.

"My!" exclaimed Dorothy, impressed in spite of herself. "Are you sure you want to give up all this?"

"Great Emperor, beautiful as the sun, wise as the stars, and radiant as the clouds, the Ceremony of Restoration is about to begin!" quavered the Grand Chew Chew, rising slowly. Then he paused, for he was suddenly confused by the strange company around the Scarecrow's throne.

"Treachery!" hissed the eldest Prince to the others. "We left him tied to the bean pole. Ancient Papa Scarecrow needs watching! Who are these curious objects he has gathered about him, pray?"

Now by some magic which even I cannot explain, the people from Oz found they could understand all that was being said. When Dorothy heard herself called an object and saw the wicked faces of the three Princes and the stupid little grandsons, she no longer wondered at the Scarecrow's decision.

The Scarecrow himself bowed calmly. "First," said he cheerfully, "let me introduce my friends and visitors from Oz."

The Silver Islanders, who really loved the Scarecrow, bowed politely as he called out the names of Dorothy and the others. But the three Silver Princes scowled and whispered indignantly among themselves.

"I am growing very wroth!" choked Sir Hokus to the Cowardly Lion.

"Let the ceremony proceed!" called the eldest Prince harshly, before the Scarecrow had finished his introductions. "Let the proper body of his Serene Highness be immediately restored. Way for the Grand Gheewizard! Way for the Grand Gheewizard!"

"One moment," put in the Scarecrow in a dignified voice. "I have something to say." The Silver Islanders clapped loudly at this, and Dorothy felt a bit reassured. Perhaps they would listen to reason after all and let the Scarecrow depart peacefully. How they were ever to escape if they didn't, the little girl could not see.

"My dear children," began the Scarecrow in his jolly voice, "nothing could have been more wonderful than my return to this lovely island, but in the years I have been away from you I have changed very much, and I find I no longer care for being Emperor. So with your kind permission, I will keep the excellent body I now have and will abdicate in favor of my eldest son and return with my friends to Oz. For in Oz I really belong."

A dead silence followed the Scarecrow's speech—then perfect pandemonium.

"No! No! You are a good Emperor! We will not let you go!" shrieked the people. "You are our honorable little Father. The Prince shall be Emperor after you have peacefully returned to your ancestors, but not now. No! No! We will not have it!"

"I feared this!" quavered Happy Toko.

"It is not the Emperor, but the Scarecrow who speaks!" shrilled the Grand Chew Chew craftily. "He knows not what he says. But after the transformation—Ah, you shall see!"

The company calmed down at this. "Let the ceremony proceed! Way for the Grand Gheewizard!" they cried exultantly.

"Chew Chew," wailed the Scarecrow, "you're off the track!" But it was too late. No one would listen.

"I'll have to think of something else," muttered the Scarecrow, sinking dejectedly back on his throne.

"Oh!" shuddered Dorothy, clutching the Scarecrow, "Here he comes!"

"Way for the Grand Gheewizard! Way for the Grand Gheewizard!"

The crowd parted. Hobbling toward the throne came the ugly little Gheewizard of the Silver Islands holding a large silver vase high above his head, and after him—!

When Sir Hokus caught a glimpse of what came after, he leaped clean over the Comfortable Camel.

"Uds daggers!" roared the Knight. *"At last!"* He rushed forward violently. There was a sharp thrust of his good sword, then an explosion like twenty giant firecrackers in one, and the room became quite black with smoke. Before anyone realized what had happened, Sir Hokus was back, dragging something after him and shouting exuberantly, "A dragon! I have slain a dragon! What happiness!"

Everyone was coughing and spluttering from the smoke, but as it cleared Dorothy saw that it was indeed a dragon Sir Hokus had slain, the rheumatic dragon of the old Gheewizard himself.

"Why didn't you get the wizard?" rumbled the Cowardly Lion angrily.

"Must have exploded," said the Comfortable Camel, sniffing the skin daintily.

"Treason!" yelled the three Princes, while the Grand Gheewizard flung himself on the stone floor and began tearing strand after strand from his silver pigtail.

"He has killed the little joy of my hearth!" screeched the old man. "I will turn him to a cat, a miserable yellow cat, and roast him for dinner!"

"Oh!" cried Dorothy, looking at Sir Hokus sorrowfully. "How could you?"

The slaying of the dragon had thrown the whole hall into utmost confusion. Sir Hokus turned a little pale under his armor, but faced the angry mob without flinching.

"Oh, my dear Karwan Bashi, this is so uncomfortable!" wheezed the Camel, glancing back of him with frightened eyes.

"There's a shiny dagger in my left-hand saddlesack. I doubt very much whether they would like it," coughed the Doubtful Dromedary, pressing close to the Knight.

"On with the ceremony!" cried the eldest Prince, seeing that the excitement was giving the Scarecrow's friends too much time to think. "The son of an iron pot shall be punished later!"

"That's right!" cried a voice from the crowd. "Let the Emperor be restored!"

"I guess it's all over," gulped the Scarecrow. "Give my love to Ozma and tell her I tried to come back."

In helpless terror, the little company watched the Ghee-wizard approach. One could fight real enemies, but *magic*! Even Sir Hokus, brave as he was, felt that nothing could be done.

"One move and you shall be so many prunes," shrilled the angry old man, fixing the people from Oz with his wicked little eyes. The great room was so still you could have heard a pin drop. Even the Doubtful Dromedary had not the heart to doubt the wizard's power, but stood rigid as a statue.

The wizard advanced slowly, holding the sealed vase carefully over his head. The poor Scarecrow regarded it with gloomy fascination. One more moment and he would be an old, old Silverman. Better to be lost forever! He held convulsively to Dorothy.

As for Dorothy herself, she was trembling with fright and grief. When the Grand Gheewizard raised the vase higher and higher and made ready to hurl it at the Scarecrow, disregarding his dire threat she gave a shrill scream and threw up both hands.

"Great grandmothers!" gasped the Scarecrow, jumping to

his feet. As Dorothy had thrown up her arms, the little parasol swinging at her wrist had jerked open. Up, up, up, and
out through the broken skylight in the roof sailed the little
Princess of Oz!

The Grand Gheewizard, startled as anyone, failed to
throw the vase. Every neck was craned upward, and everyone
was gasping with astonishment.

The oldest Prince, as usual, was the first to recover. "Don't
stand staring like an idiot! Now's your chance!" he hissed
angrily in the Gheewizard's ear.

"I didn't come here to be harried and hurried by foreign-
ers," sobbed the little man. "How is one to work magic when
interrupted every other minute? I want my little dragon."

"Oh, come on now, just throw it. I'll get you another
dragon," begged the Prince, his hands trembling with excitement.

In the face of this new disaster, the Scarecrow had forgotten all about the Gheewizard. He and the Cowardly Lion and
Sir Hokus were running distractedly around the great throne
trying to think up a way to rescue Dorothy. As for the Doubtful
Dromedary, he was doubting everything in a loud, bitter voice,
while the Comfortable Camel fairly snorted with sorrow.

"There! Now's your chance," whispered the Prince. The
Scarecrow, with his back to the crowd, was gesturing franti-
cally.

Taking a firm hold on the neck of the vase and with a long

incantation which there is no use at all in repeating, the Ghee-wizard flung the bottle straight at the Scarecrow's head. But scarcely had it left his hand before there was a flash and a flutter and down came Dorothy and the magic parasol right on top of the vase.

Zip! The vase flew in quite another direction, and next minute had burst over the luckless heads of the three plotting Princes, while Dorothy floated gently to earth.

Sir Hokus embraced the Scarecrow, and the Scarecrow hugged the Cowardly Lion, and I don't wonder at all. For no sooner had the magic elixir touched the Princes, than two of them became silver pigs and the eldest a weasel. They had been turned to their true shapes instead of the Scarecrow. And while the company hopped about in alarm, they ran squealing from the hall and disappeared in the gardens.

"Seize the Gheewizard and take him to his cave," ordered the Scarecrow, asserting his authority for the first time since the proceedings has started. He had noticed the old man making queer signs and passes toward Sir Hokus. A dozen took hold of the struggling Gheewizard and hurried him out of the hall.

Sir Hokus, at the request of the Scarecrow, clapped his iron gauntlets for silence.

"You will agree with me, I'm sure," said the Scarecrow in a slightly unsteady voice, "that magic is a serious matter to meddle with. If you will all return quietly to your homes, I will try to find a way out of our difficulties."

The Silver Islanders listened respectfully and after a little arguing among themselves backed out of the Throne Room. To tell the truth, they were anxious to spread abroad the tale of the morning's happenings.

Princess Orange Blossom, however, refused to depart. Magic or no magic, she had come to marry the Emperor, and she would not leave till the ceremony had been performed.

"But my dear old Lady, would you wish to marry a Scarecrow?" coaxed the Emperor.

"All men are Scarecrows," snapped the Princess sourly.

"Then why marry at all?" rumbled the Cowardly Lion, making a playful leap at her palanquin. This was too much. The Princess swooned on the spot, and the Scarecrow, taking advantage of her unconscious condition, ordered her chair bearers to carry her away as far and as fast as they could run.

"Now," said the Scarecrow when the last of the company had disappeared, "let us talk this over."

<small>...—·◄</small> Chapter 21 <small>►···—··</small>

The ESCAPE from the
SILVER ISLANDS

W ell!" gasped Dorothy, fanning herself
with her hat, "I never was so s'prised in
my life!"

"Nor I," exclaimed the Scarecrow. "The
Grand Gheewizard will be suing you for parassault and bat-
tery. But how did it happen?"

"Well," began Dorothy, "as soon as the parasol opened, I
flew up so fast that I could hardly breathe. Then, after I'd gone
ever so far, it came to me that if the parasol went up when it
was up, it would come down when it was down. I couldn't leave
you all in such a fix—so I closed it, and—"

"Came down!" finished the Scarecrow with a wave of his

hand. "You always do the right thing in the right place, my dear."

"It was lucky I hit the vase, wasn't it?" sighed Dorothy. "But I'm rather sorry about the Princes."

"Served 'em right," growled the Cowardly Lion. "They'll make very good pigs!"

"But who's to rule the island?" demanded Sir Hokus, turning his gaze reluctantly from the smoking dragonskin.

"This will require thought," said the Scarecrow pensively. "Let us all think."

"I doubt that I can ever think again." The Doubtful Dromedary wagged his head from side to side in a dazed fashion.

"Just leave it to our dear Karwan Bashi." The Comfortable Camel nodded complacently at the Knight and began plucking sly wisps from the Scarecrow's boot top. For a short time there was absolute silence.

Then Sir Hokus, who had been thinking tremendously with his elbows on his knees, burst out, "Why not Sir Pudding, here? Why not this honest Punster? Who but Happy Toko deserves the throne?"

"The very person!" cried the Scarecrow, clasping his yellow gloves, and taking off his silver hat, he set it impulsively upon the head of the fat little Silver Islander.

"He'll make a lovely Emperor," said Dorothy. "He's so kind-hearted and jolly. And now the Scarecrow can abdicate and come home to Oz."

They all looked triumphantly at the Imperial Punster, but Happy Toko, snatching off the royal hat, burst into tears.

"Don't leave me behind, amiable Master!" he sobbed disconsolately. "Oh, how I shall miss you!"

"But don't you see," coaxed Dorothy, "the Scarecrow needs you here more than anyplace, and think of all the fine clothes you will have and how rich you will be!"

"And Tappy, my dear boy," said the Scarecrow, putting his arm around Happy Toko, "you might not like Oz any more than I like Silver Islands. Then think—if everything goes well, you can visit me—just as one Emperor visits another!"

"And you won't forget me?" sniffed Happy, beginning to like the idea of being Emperor.

"Never!" cried the Scarecrow with an impressive wave.

"And if anything goes wrong, will you help me out?" questioned Happy uncertainly.

"We'll look in the Magic Picture of Oz every month," declared Dorothy, "and if you need us we'll surely find some way to help you."

"An' you ever require a trusty sword, Odds Bodikins!" exclaimed Sir Hokus, pressing Tappy's hand, "I'm your man!"

"All right, dear Master!" Happy slowly picked up the Imperial hat and set it sideways on his head. "I'll do my best."

"I don't doubt it at all," said the Doubtful Dromedary to everyone's surprise.

"Three cheers for the Emperor! Long live the Emperor of

the Silver Islands," rumbled the Cowardly Lion, and everybody from Oz, even the Camel and Dromedary, fell upon their knees before Happy Toko.

"You may have my bride, too, Tappy," chuckled the Scarecrow with a wink at Dorothy. "And Tappy," he asked, sobering suddenly, "will you have my grandsons brought up like real children? Just as soon as I return, I shall send them all the Books of Oz."

Happy bowed, too confused and excited for speech.

"Now," said the Scarecrow, seizing Dorothy's hand, "I can return to Oz with an easy mind."

"Doubt that," said the Doubtful Dromedary.

"You needn't!" announced Dorothy. "I've thought it all out." In a few short sentences she outlined her plan.

"Bravo!" roared the Cowardly Lion, and now the little party began in real earnest the preparation for the journey back to Oz.

First, Happy brought them a delicious luncheon, with plenty of twigs and hay for the Camel and Dromedary and meat for the Cowardly Lion. The Scarecrow packed into the Camel's sacks a few little souvenirs for the people of Oz. Then they dressed Happy Toko in the Scarecrow's most splendid robe and ordered him to sit upon the throne. Next, the Scarecrow rang for one of the palace servants and ordered the people of the Silver Islands to assemble in the hall.

Presently the Silvermen began to come trooping in,

packing the great Throne Room until it could hold no more. Everyone was chattering excitedly.

It was quite a different company that greeted them. The Scarecrow, cheerful and witty in his old Munchkin suit, Dorothy and Sir Hokus smiling happily, and the three animal members of the party fairly blinking with contentment.

"This," said the Scarecrow pleasantly when everyone was quiet, "is your new Emperor, to whom I ask you to pledge allegiance." He waved proudly in the direction of Happy Toko, who, to tell the truth, presented a truly royal appearance. "It is not possible for me to remain with you, but I shall always watch over this delightful island and with the magic fan vanquish all its enemies and punish all offenders."

Happy Toko bowed to his subjects.

The Silver Islanders exchanged startled glances, then, as the Scarecrow carelessly lifted the fan, they fell prostrate to the earth.

"Ah!" said the Scarecrow with a broad wink at Happy. "This is delightful. You agree with me, I see. Now then, three cheers for Tappy Oko, Imperial Emperor of the Silver Islands."

The cheers were given with a will, and Happy in acknowledgement made a speech that has since been written into the Royal Book of state as a masterpiece of eloquence.

Having arranged affairs so satisfactorily, the Scarecrow embraced Happy Toko with deep emotion. Dorothy and Sir Hokus shook hands with him and wished him every success and happiness. Then the little party from Oz walked deliberately to the bean pole in the center of the hall.

The Silver Islanders were still a bit dazed by the turn affairs had taken and stared in astonishment as the Scarecrow and Sir Hokus fastened thick ropes around the Cowardly Lion, the Doubtful Dromedary and the Comfortable Camel. Similar ropes they tied around their own waists and Dorothy's, and the ends of all were fastened securely to the handle of the magic parasol, which Dorothy held carefully.

"Good-bye, everybody!" called the little girl, suddenly opening the parasol.

"Good-bye!" cried the genial Scarecrow, waving his hand.

Too stupefied for speech, the assemblage gaped with amazement as the party floated gently upward. Up—up—and out of sight whirled the entire party.

....•◄ Chapter 22 ►...—..

The FLIGHT of the PARASOL

Holding the handle of the parasol, Dorothy steered it with all the skill of an aviator, and in several minutes after their start the party had entered the deep, black passage down which the Scarecrow had fallen. Each one of the adventurers was fastened to the parasol with ropes of different length so that none of them bumped together, but even with all the care in the world it was not possible to keep them from bumping the sides of the tube. The Comfortable Camel grunted plaintively from time to time, and Dorothy could hear the Doubtful Dromedary complaining bitterly in the darkness. It was pitch dark, but by keeping one hand in touch with the bean pole, Dorothy managed to hold the parasol in the center.

"How long will it take?" she called breathlessly to the Scarecrow, who was dangling just below.

"Hours!" wheezed the Scarecrow, holding fast to his hat. "I hope none of the parties on this line hear us," he added nervously, thinking of the Middlings.

"What recks it?" blustered Sir Hokus. "Hast forgotten my trusty sword?" But his words were completely drowned in the rattle of his armor.

"Hush!" warned the Scarecrow, "Or we'll be pulled in." So for almost an hour, they flew up the dark, chimney-like tube with only an occasional groan as one or another scraped against the rough sides of the passage. Then, before they knew what was happening, the parasol crashed into something, half closed, and the whole party started to fall head over heels over helmets.

"O!" gasped Dorothy, turning a complete somersault, "catch hold of the bean pole, somebody!"

"Put up the parasol!" shrieked the Scarecrow. Just then Dorothy, finding herself right side up, grasped the pole herself and snapped the parasol wide open. Up, up, up they soared again, faster than ever!

"We're flying up much faster than I fell down. We must be at the top!" called the Scarecrow hoarsely, "and somebody has closed the opening!"

Chapter 23

SAFE at LAST in the LAND of OZ

Must we keep bumping until we bump through?" panted Dorothy anxiously.

"No, by my hilts!" roared Sir Hokus, and setting his foot in a notch of the beanstalk, he cut with his sword the rope that bound him to the parasol. "Put the parasol down half way, and I'll climb ahead and cut an opening."

With great difficulty Dorothy partially lowered the parasol, and instantly their speed diminished. Indeed, they barely moved at all, and the Knight had soon passed them on his climb to the top.

"Are you there?" rumbled the Cowardly Lion anxiously.

A great clod of earth landed on his head, filling his eyes and mouth with mud.

"Ugh!" roared the lion.

"It's getting light! It's getting light!" screamed Dorothy, and in her excitement snapped the parasol up.

Sir Hokus, having cut with his sword a large circular hole in the thin crust of earth covering the tube, was about to step out when the parasol, hurling up from below, caught him neatly on its top, and out burst the whole party and sailed up almost to the clouds!

"Welcome to Oz!" cried Dorothy, looking down happily on the dear familiar Munchkin landscape.

"Home at last!" exulted the Scarecrow, wafting a kiss downward.

"Let's get down to earth before we knock the sun into a cocked hat," gasped the Cowardly Lion, for Dorothy, in her excitement, had forgotten to lower the parasol.

Now the little girl lowered the parasol carefully at first, then faster and faster and finally shut it altogether.

Sir Hokus took a high dive from the top. Down tumbled the others, over and over. But fortunately for all, there was a great haystack below, and upon this they landed in a jumbled heap close to the magic bean pole. As it happened, there was no one in sight. Up they jumped in a trice, and while the Comfortable Camel and Doubtful Dromedary munched contentedly at the hay, Sir Hokus and the Scarecrow placed some loose boards over the opening around the bean pole and covered them with dirt and cornstalks.

"I will get Ozma to close it properly with the Magic Belt," said the Scarecrow gravely. "It wouldn't do to have people sliding down my family tree and scaring poor Tappy. As for me, I shall never leave Oz again!"

"I hope not," growled the Cowardly Lion, tenderly examining his scratched hide.

"But if you hadn't, I'd never have had such lovely adventures or found Sir Hokus and the Comfortable Camel and Doubtful Dromedary," said Dorothy. "And what a lot I have to tell Ozma! Let's go straight to the Emerald City."

"It's quite a journey," explained the Scarecrow to Sir Hokus, who was cleaning off his armor with a handful of straw.

"I go where Lady Dot goes," replied the Knight, smiling affectionately at the little girl and straightening the ragged hair ribbon which he still wore on his arm.

"Don't forget me, dear Karwan Bashi," wheezed the Comfortable Camel, putting his head on the Knight's shoulder.

"You're a sentimental dunce, Camy. I doubt whether they'll take us at all!" The Doubtful Dromedary looked wistfully at Dorothy.

"Go to, now!" cried Sir Hokus, putting an arm around each neck. "You're just like two of the family!"

"It will be very comfortable to go to now," sighed the Camel.

"We're all a big, jolly family here," said the Scarecrow, smiling brightly, "and Oz is the friendliest country in the world."

"Right," said the Cowardly Lion, "but let's get started!" He stretched his tired muscles and began limping stiffly toward the yellow brick road.

"Wait," cried Dorothy, "have you forgotten the parasol?"

"I wish I could," groaned the Cowardly Lion, rolling his eyes.

Sir Hokus, with folded arms, was gazing regretfully at the bean pole. "It has been a brave quest," he sighed, "but now, I take it, our adventures are over!" Absently, the Knight felt in his boot-top and drawing out a small red bean popped it into his mouth. Just before reaching the top of the tube, he had pulled a handful of them from the beanstalk, but the others had fallen out when he dove into the hay.

"Shall we use the parasol again, Lady Dot?" he asked, still staring pensively at the bean pole. "Shall—?"

He got no farther, nor did Dorothy answer his question. Instead, she gave a loud scream and clutched the Scarecrow's arm. The Scarecrow, taken by surprise, fell over backward, and the Comfortable Camel, raising his head inquiringly, gave a bellow of terror. From the Knight's shoulders a green branch had sprung, and while the company gazed in round-eyed amazement it stretched toward the bean pole, attached itself firmly, and then shot straight up into the air, the Knight kicking and struggling on the end. In another second, he was out of sight.

"Come back! Come back!" screamed the Comfortable Camel, running around distractedly.

"I doubt we'll ever see him again!" groaned the Doubtful Dromedary, craning his neck upward.

"Do something! Do something!" begged Dorothy. At which the Scarecrow jumped up and dashed toward the little farmhouse.

"I'll get an ax," he called over his shoulder, "and chop down the bean pole."

"No, don't do that!" roared the Cowardly Lion, starting after him. "Do you want to break him to pieces?"

"Oh! Oh! Can't you think of something else?" cried Dorothy. "And hurry, or he'll be up to the moon!"

The Scarecrow put both hands to his head and stared around wildly. Then, with a triumphant wave of his hat, declared himself ready to act.

"The parasol!" cried the late Emperor of Silver Islands. "Quick, Dorothy, put up the parasol!"

Snatching the parasol, which lay at the foot of the bean pole, Dorothy snapped it open, and the Scarecrow just had time to make a flying leap and seize the handle before it soared upward, and in a trice they, too, had disappeared.

"Doubty! Doubty!" wailed the Comfortable Camel, crowding up to his humpbacked friend, "we're having a pack of trouble. My knees are all a-tremble!"

"Now don't you worry," advised the Cowardly Lion, sitting down resignedly. "I'm frightened myself, but that's because I'm so cowardly. Queer things happen in Oz, but they usually turn out all right. Why, Hokus is just growing up with the country, that's all, just growing up with the country."

"Doubt that," sniffed the Doubtful Dromedary faintly. "He was grown up in the beginning."

"But think of the Scarecrow's brains. You leave things to the Scarecrow." But it was no use. Both beasts began to roar dismally.

"I don't want a plant. I want my Karwan Bashi," sobbed the Comfortable Camel broken-heartedly.

"Well, don't drown me," begged the Cowardly Lion, moving out of the way of the Camel's tears. "Say, what's that draft?"

What indeed? In the trees overhead, a very cyclone whistled, and before the three had even time to catch their breath, they were blown high into the air and the next instant were hurtling toward the Emerald City like three furry cannon-balls, faster and faster.

Chapter 24

HOMEWARD BOUND to the EMERALD CITY

Dorothy and the Scarecrow, clinging fast to the magic parasol, had followed the Knight almost to the clouds. At first, it looked as if they would never catch up with him, so swiftly was the branch growing, but it was not long before the little umbrella began to gain, and in several minutes more they were beside Sir Hokus himself.

"Beshrew me, now!" gasped the Knight, stretching out his hand toward Dorothy. "Can'st stop this reckless plant?"

"Give me your sword," commanded the Scarecrow, "and I'll cut you off."

Dorothy, with great difficulty, kept the parasol close to

the Knight while the Scarecrow reached for the sword. But Sir Hokus backed away in alarm.

"'Tis part of me, an' you cut it off, I will be cut off, too. 'Tis rooted in my back," he puffed.

"What shall we do?" cried Dorothy in distress. "Maybe if we take hold of his hands we can keep him from going any higher."

The Scarecrow, jamming down his hat so it wouldn't blow off, nodded approvingly, and each holding the parasol with one hand gave the other to the Knight. And when Dorothy pointed the parasol down, to her great delight Sir Hokus came also, the thin green branch growing just about as fast as they moved.

Just then the little fan, which had been rolling around merrily in Dorothy's pocket, slipped out and fell straight down toward the three unsuspecting beasts below. Draft! No wonder!

But Dorothy never missed it, and quite unconscious of such a calamity anxiously talked over the Knight's predicament with the Scarecrow. They both decided that the best plan was to fly straight to the Emerald City and have Ozma release the Knight from the enchanted beanstalk.

"I'm sorry you got tangled up in my family tree, old fellow," said the Scarecrow after they had flown some time in silence, "but this makes us relations, doesn't it?" He winked broadly at the Knight.

"So it does," said Sir Hokus jovially. "I'm a branch of your family now. Yet methinks I should not have swallowed that bean."

"Bean?" questioned Dorothy. "What bean?" The Knight carefully explained how he had plucked a handful of red beans from the beanstalk just before reaching the top of the tube and how he had eaten one.

"So that's what started you growing!" exclaimed Dorothy in surprise.

"Alas, yes!" admitted the Knight. "I've never felt more grown-up in my life," he finished solemnly. "An adventurous country, this Oz!"

"I should say it was," chuckled the Scarecrow. "But isn't it almost time we were reaching the Emerald City, Dorothy?"

"I think I'm going in the right direction," answered the little girl, "but I'll fly a little lower to be sure."

"Not too fast! Not too fast!" warned Sir Hokus, looking nervously over his shoulder at his long, wriggling stem.

"There's Ozma's palace!" cried the Scarecrow all at once.

"And there's Ozma!" screamed Dorothy, peering down delightedly. "And Scraps and Tik-Tok and everybody!"

She pointed the parasol straight down, when a sharp tug from Sir Hokus jerked them all back. They were going faster than the poor Knight was growing, so Dorothy lowered the parasol half way, and slowly they floated toward the earth, landing gently in one of the flower beds of Ozma's lovely garden.

"Come along and meet the folks," said the Scarecrow as Dorothy closed the parasol. But Sir Hokus clutched him in alarm.

"Hold! Hold!" gasped the Knight. "I've stopped growing, but if you leave me I'll shoot up into the air again."

The Scarecrow and Dorothy looked at each other in dismay. Sure enough, the Knight had stopped growing, and it was all they could do to hold him down to earth, for the stubborn branch of beanstalk was trying to straighten up. They had fallen quite a distance from the palace itself, and all the people of Oz had their backs turned, so had not seen their singular arrival.

"Hello!" called the Scarecrow loudly. Then "Help! Help!" as the Knight jerked him twice into the air. But Ozma, Trot, Jack Pumpkinhead and all the rest were staring upward and talking so busily among themselves that they did not hear either Dorothy's or the Scarecrow's cries. First one, then the other was snatched off his feet, and although Sir Hokus, with tears in his eyes, begged them to leave him to his fate, they held on with all their might. Just as it looked as if they all three would fly into the air again, the little Wizard of Oz happened to turn around.

"Look! Look!" he cried, tugging Ozma's sleeve.

"Why, it's Dorothy!" gasped Ozma, rubbing her eyes. "It's Dorothy and—"

"Help! Help!" screamed the Scarecrow, waving one arm wildly. Without waiting another second, all the celebrities of Oz came running toward the three adventurers.

"Somebody heavy come take hold!" puffed Dorothy, out of breath with her efforts to keep Sir Hokus on the ground.

The Ozites, seeing that help was needed at once, suppressed their curiosity.

"I'm heavy," said Tik-Tok solemnly, clasping the Knight's arm. The Tin Woodman seized his other hand, and Dorothy sank down exhausted on the grass.

Princess Ozma pressed forward.

"What does it all mean? Where did you come from?" asked the little Ruler of Oz, staring in amazement at the strange spectacle before her.

"And who is this medieval person?" asked Professor Wogglebug, pushing forward importantly. (He had returned to the palace to collect more data for the Royal Book of Oz.)

"He doesn't look evil to me," giggled Scraps, dancing up to Sir Hokus, her suspender button eyes snapping with fun.

"He isn't," said Dorothy indignantly, for Sir Hokus was too shaken about to answer. "He's my Knight Errant."

"Ah, I see," replied Professor Wogglebug. "A case of 'When Knighthood was in flower.'" And would you believe it—the beanstalk at that minute burst into a perfect shower of red blossoms that came tumbling down over everyone. Before they had recovered from their surprise, the branch snapped off close to the Knight's armor, and Tik-Tok, the Tin Woodman and Sir Hokus rolled over in a heap. The branch itself whistled through the air and disappeared.

"Oh," cried Dorothy, hugging the Knight impulsively, "I'm so glad."

"Are you all right?" asked the Scarecrow anxiously.

"Good as ever!" announced Sir Hokus, and indeed all traces of the magic stalk had disappeared from his shoulders.

"Dorothy!" cried Ozma again. "What does it all mean?"

"Merely that I slid down my family tree and that Dorothy and this Knight rescued me," said the Scarecrow calmly.

"And he's a real Royalty—so there!" cried Dorothy with a wave at the Scarecrow and making a little face at Professor Wogglebug. "Meet his Supreme Highness, Chang Wang Woe of Silver Islands, who had abdicated his throne and returned to be a plain Scarecrow in Oz!"

Then, as the eminent Educator of Oz stood gaping at the Scarecrow, "Oh, Ozma, I've so much to tell you!"

"Begin! Begin!" cried the little Wizard. "For everything's mighty mysterious. First, the Cowardly Lion and two unknown beasts shoot through the air and stop just outside the third-story windows, and there they hang although I've tried all my magic to get them down. Then you and the Scarecrow drop in with a strange Knight!"

"Oh, the poor Cowardly Lion!" gasped Dorothy as the Wizard finished speaking. "The magic fan!" She felt hurriedly in her pocket. "It's gone!"

"It must have slipped out of your pocket and blown them here, and they'll never come down till that fan is closed," cried the Scarecrow in an agitated voice.

All of this was Greek to Ozma and the others, but when

Dorothy begged the little Ruler to send for her Magic Belt, she did it without question. This belt Dorothy had captured from the Nome King, and it enabled the wearer to wish people and objects wherever one wanted them.

"I wish the magic fan to close and to come safely back to me," said Dorothy as soon as she had clasped the belt around her waist. No sooner were the words out before there was a loud crash and a series of roars and groans. Everybody started on a run for the palace, Sir Hokus ahead of all the rest. The fan had mysteriously returned to Dorothy's pocket.

The three animals had fallen into a huge cluster of rose bushes and, though badly scratched and frightened, were really unhurt.

"I doubt that I'll like Oz," quavered the Doubtful Dromedary, lurching toward Sir Hokus.

"You might have been more careful of that fan," growled the Cowardly Lion reproachfully, plucking thorns from his hide. The Comfortable Camel was so overjoyed to see the Knight that he rested his head on Sir Hokus's shoulder and began weeping down his armor.

And now that their adventures seemed really over, what explanations were to be made! Sitting on the top step of the palace with all of them around her, Dorothy told the whole wonderful story of the Scarecrow's family tree. When her breath gave out, the Scarecrow took up the tale himself, and as they all realized how nearly they had lost their jolly comrade, many of the party shed real tears. Indeed, Nick Chopper hugged the Scarecrow till there was not a whole straw in his body.

"Never leave us again," begged Ozma, and the Scarecrow, crossing Nick Chopper's heart (he had none of his own), promised that he never would.

And what a welcome they gave Sir Hokus, the Doubtful Dromedary and the Comfortable Camel! Only Professor Wogglebug seemed disturbed. During the strange recital, he had grown quieter and quieter and finally, with an embarrassed cough, had excused himself and hurried into the palace.

He went directly to the study, and seating himself at a desk opened a large book, none other than *The Royal Book of Oz*. Dipping an emerald pen in the ink, he began a new chapter headed thus:

HIS IMPERIAL MAJESTY, THE SCARECROW
Late Emperor and Imperial Sovereign of
Silver Islands

Then, flipping over several pages to a chapter headed "Princess Dorothy!", he wrote carefully at the end, "Dorothy, Princess and Royal Discoverer of Oz."

Meanwhile, below stairs, the Scarecrow was distributing his gifts. There were silver chains for everyone in the palace and shining silver slippers for Ozma, Betsy Bobbin, Trot and

Dorothy, and a bottle of silver polish for Nick Chopper.

Dorothy presented Ozma with the magic fan and parasol, and they were safely put away by Jellia Jamb with the other magic treasures of Oz.

Next, because they were all curious to see the Scarecrow's wonderful Kingdom, they hurried upstairs to look in the Magic Picture.

"Show us the Emperor of Silver Islands," commanded Ozma. Immediately the beautiful silver Throne Room appeared. Happy Toko had removed his imperial hat and was standing on his head to the great delight of the whole court, and a host of little Silver Islander boys were peeking in at the windows.

"Now doesn't that look cheerful?" asked the Scarecrow delightedly. "I knew he'd make a good Emperor."

"I wish we would hear what he's saying," said Dorothy. "Oh, do look at Chew Chew!" The Grand Chew Chew was standing beside the throne scowling horribly.

"I think I can arrange for you to hear," muttered the Wizard of Oz, and taking a queer magic instrument from his pocket, he whispered "Aohbeeobbuy."

Instantly they heard the jolly voice of Happy Toko singing:

> *"Oh shine his shoes of silver,*
> *And brush his silver queue,*
> *For I am but an Emperor*
> *And he's the Grand Chew Chew!"*

Ozma laughed heartily as the picture faded away, and so did the others. Indeed, there was so much to ask and wonder about that it seemed as if they never would finish talking.

"Let's have a party—an old-fashioned Oz party," proposed Ozma when the excitement had calmed down a bit. And an old-fashioned party it was, with places for everybody and a special table for the Cowardly Lion, the Hungry Tiger, Toto, the Glass Cat, the Comfortable Camel, the Doubtful Dromedary and all the other dear creatures of that amazing Kingdom.

Sir Hokus insisted upon stirring up a huge pasty for the occasion, and there were songs, speeches and cheers for everyone, not forgetting the Doubtful Dromedary.

At the cheering he rose with an embarrassed jerk of his long neck. "In my left-hand saddle-sack," he said gruffly, "there is a quantity of silken shawls and jewels. I doubt whether they are good enough, but I would like Dorothy and Princess Ozma to have them."

"Hear! Hear!" cried the Scarecrow, pounding on the table with his knife. Then everything grew quiet as Ozma told how she, with the help of Glinda, the Good Sorceress, had stopped the war between the Horners and Hoppers.

When she had finished, Sir Hokus sprang up impulsively. "I prithee, lovely Lady, never trouble your royal head about wars again. From now on, I will do battle for you and little Dorothy and Oz, and *I* will be your good Knight every day." At this, the applause was tremendous.

"Ye good Knight of Oz, full of courage and vim,
Will do battle for us, and we'll take care of him!"

shouted Scraps, who was becoming more excited every minute.

"I'll lend you some of my polish for your armor, old fellow," said Nick Chopper as the Knight sat down, beaming with pleasure.

"Well," said Ozma with a smile when everyone had feasted and talked to heart's content, "is everybody happy?"

"I am!" cried the Comfortable Camel. "For here I am perfectly comfortable."

"I am!" cried Dorothy, putting her arm around the Scarecrow, who sat next to her. "For I have found my old friend and made some new ones."

"I'm happy!" cried the Scarecrow, waving his glass, "because there is no age in Oz, and I am still my old Ozish self."

"As for me," said the Knight, "I am happy, for I have served a Lady, gone on a Quest, and Slain a Dragon! Ozma, and Oz forever!"